"Take me," Riley wanted to plead but bit her lip to stop herself. The last thing she wanted was to admit to Lynchburg that he could conquer her this way. He was still her enemy.

He teased her. And just when she felt she would go mad with desire, he filled her sweetly, hungrily.

"Am I your master?" he grinned down at her.

"You are my captor," she breathed. "I am your prisoner."

"Am I your master?" he asked again, and withdrew.

"Aye," she panted. "You are my master."

The grin faded from his face, and he entered her fully, bringing a cry of passion from her. She clung to him, her breath hissing between clenched teeth.

He could feel the wild pulse in her heart. "Am I your master?" he whispered in her ear.

"Aye," she said, dazed. "And I am yours."

"Aye," he agreed.

Heart of a Warrior

Betty Davidson

JOVE BOOKS, NEW YORK

HEART OF A WARRIOR

A Jove Book / published by arrangement with
the author

PRINTING HISTORY
Jove edition / July 2001

The Penguin Putnam Inc. World Wide Web site address is
www.penguinputnam.com

ISBN: 0-515-13101-6

A JOVE BOOK®
Jove Books are published by The Berkley Publishing Group,
a division of Penguin Putnam Inc.,
375 Hudson Street, New York, New York 10014.
JOVE and the "J" design
are trademarks belonging to Penguin Putnam Inc.

PRINTED IN THE UNITED STATES OF AMERICA

10 9 8 7 6 5 4 3 2 1

Chapter One

December 31, 1460
Wakefield, England

The Earl of Lynchburg strode across the field in his armor of Dutch plate like a great black beast emerging from the shadows of twilight. The land was filled with the moans of wounded soldiers and the sound of the wind mourning. Pulling off his helmet, he felt the breeze blow harshly against his cheeks. His brown hair caught in the wind and whipped about his face as his eyes scanned the landscape. Although the battle had ended hours ago, he was unable to throw off the rigor of the fight. His arm muscles still twitched, and his heart pounded as if it would break free.

At his side hung the sword that had been his father's, and he protectively placed his hand against its hilt. It was all he had left of his father, Charles D'Aubere. On the forte was the unicorn, the D'Aubere insignia inlaid in gold, and on the tip of the hilt was a cluster of rubies. As he began to walk toward the queen's camp, his scabbard clinked against his armor.

The dusk was fading into darkness, the last day of 1460. A mile away lay the battleground of Wakefield, strewn with the corpses of two thousand rebels, many of whom were of noble birth.

And yet I must shed more blood this night, he thought, *and that of a prince.*

As he reached the campfire, he felt the first licks of its warmth and breathed deeply, strengthening his resolve for the task ahead. The night air was bitter cold and filled his lungs with smoke and the stench of blood.

"God in heaven forgive me," he murmured in prayer. "But I must do this deed else my queen think me as impotent a fool as her husband."

"Bring me the prisoner!" he bellowed, his voice echoing across the field.

A circle of knights parted, and Richard, Duke of York, stumbled forward peppered by the punches and kicks of his gaolers. He was naked but for a linen cloth that girded his loins and a paper crown that had been pushed down over his head. In an act to further humiliate him, a knight had placed a chain around his neck like a halter. The great Richard of York was being led to his doom by a squire as if he were a cow being taken to market.

Although he was a man of middle years, the duke was as fierce-looking as a young lion, with golden hair cropped close and the finely muscled arms of a warrior.

As the two men came face to face, their eyes caught the glow of firelight. The earl handed his helmet to the youth. "Be gone," he barked, and the squire fled, leaving the shackled duke alone with his captor. "It pains me to raise my sword against another Englishman."

"Ye be no Englishman," the duke reviled him. The battle had been long, and he'd fought well against King Henry's forces. He was exhausted from the fight and angry, for on this night he was about to lose far more than just a battle. "Ye be French," he spat out the word as if it burned his tongue.

"And ye be a traitor to England," Lynchburg retorted.

Only a few fathoms away was the queen's tent of yellow canvas, still visible in the final rays of sunset. Her chamberlain, muffled in a fur-lined cloak, emerged and strolled toward the two men.

"Tell the queen that I await her orders," Lynchburg growled at him, causing the man to stumble to a halt. Although the earl was a member of the lesser nobility, his commands did not go unheeded. His father had been one of England's wealthiest magnates, but the nobility respected Lynchburg more for his power on the battlefield than for his father's station. The queen would not fight without him. The chamberlain nodded respectfully and strode back toward the queen's tent.

Only a year ago, Lynchburg had inherited an impoverished earldom. The incompetence of Henry VI had cost England all of its territory in France except for Calais. The D'Aubere estates were gone and with them the Crown's wine revenues that had enriched the family. It still stung his noble pride to think that he had been forced to sell his remaining estates in Salisbury and Essex and go into service to the Crown, the very Crown whose incompetence had cost him his fortune. Now he must gain the favor of Queen Margaret, through whose grace he might regain some wealth.

The duke opened his mouth to speak, and Lynchburg stiffened, wondering what last words he might wish to convey. A plea for mercy? A request for a pardon?

"What say you, Richard of York?" he demanded. "What plea is poised on your tongue?"

The duke stood firm, displaying his unbending pride. For the first time, Lynchburg noticed that his golden hair was streaked with mud, and his face was splattered with the blood of his fallen men. Even in defeat, there was a sureness in his stance that made his captor feel a bit vulnerable in his presence.

"I will die by your hand today, Lynchburg," he said, straining against his bonds. "But I will die knowing that my death gains you nothing. You think to present my head to your bitch queen and curry her favor."

"Do not profane her name," he shouted, "or I shall smite you now for the traitor that you are. You will die tonight by my hand, for I am a true servant of Henry VI."

"Are you?" he seethed through teeth gritted in anger. "Or do you serve the French bitch? Henry has traded in his crown for a woman's wimple. Does not the queen wield the king's power?"

A retort froze on his tongue, for he knew the duke was right. "I serve the lawful regent of England," he replied.

Richard laughed, and the sound was as brittle as the rattling of tree limbs in a winter's breeze. "I have more right to the throne than Henry. God's blood, man, my head will gain you nothing." His eyes simmered with passion, even as he was facing death. "Your queen has no reward to give you. She has given away all of her wealth to assemble her troops. She has nothing left but the very crown on her own head. Smite her, and I will be King of England. And my rewards will be far greater than ever were those of the Lancastrians."

The young earl stared at him blandly, his grip tightening around the hilt of his sword. "There are many who have tried to claim the throne, Richard. The soil runs rich with their blood."

"If you murder me, then you shed the blood of England's rightful king. And God's judgment will rain down upon you."

"Silence!" he ordered, his heart pounding. He knew the magnitude of what he was doing. By shedding the blood of a prince he was testing the wrath of God. Turning his face into the wind, he watched for the queen, his eyes as cold as blue ice. "Only the queen can decide your fate."

Queen Margaret emerged from her tent and walked slowly toward the fire escorted by her secretary on one side and her chamberlain on the other. Her gown was a rich blue velvet shrouded in an ermine-trimmed cloak that trailed behind her. On her head was an embroidered headdress that completely covered her hair. A short veil flowed down around her face outlining her features in soft gauze. At thirty-one, she was a beautiful woman with auburn eyes that snapped with intelligence.

"Kneel before your queen," Lynchburg commanded, but the duke stood stubbornly.

The queen stepped into the circle of firelight and looked to her young warrior for a response to this treason. She had not long to wait, for it was swift in coming. Lynchburg drew his sword and struck it across the backs of Richard's knees. The mighty Duke of York crumpled to the ground, a grimace creasing his bloodied features.

The chamberlain brought a stool for the queen to sit upon, and she sank slowly, her ermine cloak falling in folds around her ankles. A breeze blew across the camp, lifting the paper crown from Richard's head and sending it tumbling to her feet. She raised her heel and brought it down on the crown, crushing it.

"So will all traitors to the king be crushed," she stated calmly.

The earl touched the back of the duke's neck with the tip of his sword. "Richard, Duke of York, you are guilty of high treason," he proclaimed. "What say you?" A drop of blood trickled from the pricked skin and rolled down his neck.

Richard lifted his head and gazed into the eyes of the queen. "I am guilty of nothing but love for my country. I am guilty of nothing but preserving and protecting England. Someone must rule this land else all will be lost."

The queen eyed him coolly.

"Margaret of Anjou, where is your husband?" he rasped. "Is he not imprisoned in the Tower of London? Is that not a fitting place for so wretched a king? How much longer will England suffer under the rule of that bloodless fool!"

Lynchburg raised his sword and felt the weight of it straining deep into his muscles. "I await your pleasure, Your Grace."

She regarded the prisoner for a moment, her face dark and stern. The fire crackled as it reflected across the duke's naked back.

With a small shrug, she gave her command. "Execute him."

Lynchburg brought his sword down, ending the duke quickly. His squire rushed forward to take the sword and clean it, tugging it from Lynchburg's stiff fingers. The deed was done; his enemy was dead. "Long live King Henry," he prayed as he stood in a welling pool of blood.

"I want his head placed on a pike over the gates of York," the queen ordered.

"Yes, Your Grace," he said. The duke's warning burned deep within his heart. Would she indeed give him nothing?

He stared at his queen, and their eyes met in mutual distrust. As she watched him, a knowing smile played at her lips.

"You have served me well, Lynchburg. I shall send my chamberlain to summon Lord Philip De Proileau, the Earl of Cornwich."

Cornwich, he thought, with a sense of dread descending over him. *What is she about? Cornwich is one of the richest magnates in England. Does she mean to confiscate a portion of his lands and give them to me? Such a move would be unwise. She needs to maintain Cornwich's trust.*

The chamberlain paled at her orders, and his eyes widened. "But Your Majesty, the Earl of Cornwich is on the field. His son, Alfred, lies slain by the River Calder."

"We have business to attend to," she snapped, jolting him with her sharp tone. "There is time enough for grief. Bring him to me now."

The chamberlain bowed profusely as he backed away, vanishing into the darkness. She clapped her hands together, and two knights rushed forward to serve her. "Take this thing and burn it," she commanded, pointing to the body of Richard. "'Tis the only way to destroy such a perverse beast."

They knelt and grasped the body, dragging it away into the night as the fire snapped and popped, sending motes of ash up into the black heavens.

The queen huddled deeper into her cloak and turned her

attention back to Lynchburg. "You are handsome, Lynchburg," she mused, her eyes sliding along his features. Her face was shaded by night fall, but her eyes flickered through the shadows as a warm fantasy rose in her mind. The naked, muscular warmth of him was a pleasing thought indeed. And she had been without a man for such a very long time. Perhaps someday she would share with him the exquisite pleasure he would never find through the prize she was about to confer on him.

"You are the handsomest of all my servants," she continued. "You should be a magnate yourself. You have the strength, the breeding. You lack only the power."

"The power is yours, Majesty, and I am content to be your servant," he lied, feeling a seizure of excitement. What was she about to bestow on him?

Her gaze turned sullen as she ran her hands idly along the ermine trim of her cloak. "As you know, I have no land to give you. No wealth. Not even a ruby."

His excitement began to cool.

"However," she added. "I can give you an heiress."

"An heiress, Your Grace?" he asked in mild surprise. Yes, she would give him heiress, he thought. What else could she do? An heiress was exactly what he needed, preferably an orphaned one. He did not wish to be in service to a father-in-law. It might be years before he could control the estates and obtain the power and influence he craved.

The Earl of Cornwich rode in from the darkened field looking old and tired. His hair was starkly white against the night sky, and his cheeks were red with cold. His missodor snorted and tossed its head, still nervous from the battle and the smell of blood. As the earl dismounted, he handed the reins to his squire and wearily approached his queen.

Sinking to one knee, he greeted her. "You summoned me, Your Majesty?"

Lynchburg noticed the dazed look in his eyes and felt

the weight of his loss. He had known death, too, and could
well understand the earl's heavy air of bewilderment.

"Rise, dear Cornwich," she implored him. "I am sorry
for your loss. How unfortunate for all of England. Never
can so great a warrior as your dear son be replaced." She
touched her breast. "'Tis a Yorkist lance through my
heart."

He rose to stand before her, his head bowed in grief.
"'Tis a lance through my own heart, Your Majesty."

"I will personally handle his interment," she offered. "I
will have his body removed to York. When I regain London, I will see that he is laid to rest at St. George's Chapel
at Windsor." She spoke as if she were promising sweets to
a distraught child. "Would you like that?"

Cornwich nodded, unhearing.

Her eyes shifted to Lynchburg, melding for a moment
into his expectant gaze, then she turned back to Cornwich's hollow expression. "I wish to ease your suffering,
dear Cornwich. I have good news for you on this night.
News that will comfort you though your loss be great."
She gave him a brief smile. "I am prepared to give you a
new son."

The old earl looked at her blankly.

She lifted her hand, indicating Lynchburg. "I have decided to give your daughter in marriage to the Earl of
Lynchburg, who has served me so faithfully." Cornwich
lowered his eyes to the blood-soaked ground, saying nothing. "You have no more sons and no grandsons. But now
you will have a son-in-law. Through this marriage the future of your estates and title will be secured." She leaned
forward, clasping her hands in her lap. "Does this not
please you?"

The earl gazed past her head into the darkness beyond,
wishing he could walk away from this scene. He looked
ghostly pale, as if all the blood had drained from his face,
his lifeforce having fled.

"Queen Margaret," he said deadly. "You are . . . generous . . . to wish to protect the future of my family. But my

daughter has spent her life in a convent. She cannot be married."

The queen's brows lifted in amused shock. "Come now, Cornwich. She has not taken any religious vows. I daresay 'tis time for her to marry. She is what—eighteen now?"

He closed his eyes, shuttering his thoughts, his memories. "I suppose. I . . . I don't know."

"She should have been wedded years ago. Most girls of her station are betrothed by the age of ten." Taking a deep breath, she glanced encouragingly at Lynchburg. "This young earl needs a dowried wife so that he will have lands again. And you need a son and heirs. You will both have what you need on this night."

He stood silently, his shoulders stooped like a man who is but half-alive. A cold wind wrapped around them, seeping through the chinks of Lynchburg's armor.

"Your Grace," he said at last, "to fulfill your wish would be my greatest pleasure. But . . . But my daughter, the Lady Jeanette, cannot be married."

The queen's eyes flared in warning. "She will be married because I have decreed it!" she shouted, then quickly composed herself. Spreading her hands out across her lap, she stared sternly at the aged earl. "Her dowry must be Glenwood Castle in the county of Northampton. I need Lynchburg there to fortify the south against the Yorkists."

Lynchburg felt his heart swell with excitement. Glenwood Castle was a greater prize than he had dared hope for.

"T'is my greatest holding," the earl said, astonished.

"Then you should want Lynchburg to have it," she chirped. "He will protect it from the Yorkists and preserve it for your future heirs, your grandchildren." She emphasized this last word.

Cornwich rubbed his head as if his temples were beginning to throb. "As you wish," he murmured.

"I have acted as marriage broker, wouldn't you say?" she asked with an air of victory.

Lynchburg flinched as he realized her true intent. She

was planning to extort money from Cornwich. They had both become her pawns.

"A marriage broker is entitled to a percentage of the dowry," she reminded him.

"Yes, Your Grace." Cornwich sighed, his arms falling limply to his sides. "I have estates in twenty counties. I shall be pleased to convey lands to you as a portion of my daughter's dowry."

She watched him austerely, the coolness like a white light emitting from her eyes. Arched brows lifted slightly as she studied him the way a cat might stare into the grass, sensing prey. "I would like as payment your entire estate to the north of Carlisle."

Cornwich's eyes jumped at the request. Surely not, he seemed to bellow silently. The young earl recognized her ploy immediately. The estate was in the county of Cumberland at the northernmost tip of England. It joined the Scottish border. For months he had suspected that she was secretly dealing with the Scots. They had lent her their troops, and now she must pay off her debt to them for their allegiance. She was planning to give them the earl's territory in Cumberland, he thought sickly. She would give them all of northern England to keep the crown on Henry's head, the bitch.

"What think you of the Scots, Cornwich?" she asked, her voice hearty with triumph.

"I think they are self-righteous barbarians."

"Self-righteous barbarians." She smiled thoughtfully. "Why, there is no better soldier than a self-righteous barbarian. Wouldn't you agree, Lynchburg?"

"Yes, Your Grace," he agreed. They had lost everything in France but Calais, and now she was slicing off the tip of England and handing it to the Scots.

"Majesty." Cornwich gazed at her, his eyes pleading. "Perhaps you would find another of my estates more to your liking. I prefer Cumberland."

Her eyes glazed over frostily as she peered at him. "As you've said, you have estates in twenty counties. Many of them comparable to your lands in Cumberland, even Northampton." Her voice turned harsh and cold. "If you wish to hold on to your remaining lands and your title, then you had best do whatever necessary to win this war. Else you will lose everything that you own. For if Henry falls, so will his nobles." She leaned forward slightly and narrowed her eyes at him. "Do we understand each other, Philip?"

"Yes, Majesty," he whispered like a chastised child.

She turned to her chamberlain. "Fetch the chaplain. I wish for Lynchburg to be married tonight."

"Tonight?" they both sputtered.

"But my daughter is not here," Cornwich blurted.

"No, but I am. And I will serve as proxy. David D'Aubere, Earl of Lynchburg, will be married on this night to Jeanette De Proileau. The contract will be valid." Her eyes slid to Lynchburg, checking his response.

"As you wish, Your Majesty." He acquiesced with a bow.

When the chamberlain returned with the chaplain in tow, the ceremony commenced. By the leaping flames the marriage vows were spoken as smoke wafted upward, dissipating into the darkness. The moon rose and shadows shifted eerily across the ground.

No doubt the queen will gain the most from this union, Lynchburg thought as he glimpsed her standing beside him, her head barely reaching his shoulder. To his right, Cornwich stood, stiff and numb with grief.

Lynchburg did not trust his new father-in-law any more than he trusted his queen. The man was a widower and could remarry, especially now that Alfred was dead. There might be more heirs, direct heirs, to challenge his claim to the estate. No, this arrangement did not suit him at all. And his bride, what did he know of her? Only that she was eighteen years old and shut away in a convent, that she knew nothing of her brother's death or of her own marriage. It would be startling to her when she found out. Jesu, it had been startling to him. When the day had begun, he had thought he might be dead by dusk, or wounded, but not married.

"Married you are," the queen announced and held out her hand to be kissed.

Lynchburg bowed and brushed his lips across the cool leather of her glove. Yes, he was married, and he would accept this "reward" from his queen, but by God, he swore inwardly, he would not be betrayed by her or by Cornwich.

At sunrise he would order his knights to mount York's head on a pike on Micklegate Bar then pack his camp. Messengers would be sent out, and the girl would be brought immediately to Glenwood Castle. With the Earl of Cornwich and his mesnie of a thousand men, he would prepare to head south to meet his bride. As soon as she arrived at Glenwood Castle, he would consummate this marriage and plant a babe in her belly. There would be no delay.

Chapter Two

Lynchburg left the north country as snow fell in a torrent of white flakes. His horse plodded across the open fields, its breath flowing out in white streams. Thankfully, the sound of its hooves was muffled by the two inches of powder that covered the ground. Even with a thousand men at his back, the earl was concerned for their safety. He wanted to pass through the midlands with as little fanfare as possible. Nothing was beyond the Yorkists, certainly not ambush.

He wore fur-lined boots up to his knees with a woolen cloak covering his houppelande and a beaver hat pulled down around his face. With the weather turning colder, he'd grown his beard three days to protect his face from frost. The wind was biting and ceaseless as the mesnie moved through Nottingham to the River Trent and crossed into the southern realm of England.

Throughout the journey the Earl of Cornwich had remained strangely quiet, but Lynchburg understood his need for distance. He had suffered much from the loss of his son. It was as if it pained him to look upon his son-in-law, the man who would now take Alfred's place. Lynchburg wondered if it was more than grief that affected his father-in-law. If it was the execution of Richard that troubled him. Perhaps he feared that the young earl, having slain a prince, would bring the wrath of God down upon his house.

Whatever the matter, Cornwich remained silent on it. As they crossed the open land through the diocese of Lincoln, the old earl sent a messenger ahead to Glenwood Castle to herald their arrival.

They trodded onward, and Lynchburg watched with growing satisfaction as the castle's four towers rose on the horizon. Built on a manmade hill, the castle looked like a majestic crown on a white and aging head. Soon it would be his crown, he thought with a smile. Kicking his horse to a gallop, he caught up to Cornwich and rode beside him. They would enter the gates together at the head of the mesnie, and all who saw him would recognize his place of authority.

"'Tis a fine estate," he said, his words coming out in puffs of frosty mist.

"It needs protection," the earl remarked. "'Tis an island in a sea of Yorkist rebellion."

Indeed he was right, Lynchburg realized. The south of England was strongly Yorkist while the north favored the Lancastrian dynasty.

"I will protect the estate," he promised. "On my honor and with my life."

The old earl looked at him almost fondly. There was compassion in his eyes, regret. "You will do well, my son," he said. "But be warned. My enemies will stop at nothing to destroy me. You must be ever watchful of the Snowden family."

"The Snowdens?" He was surprised to hear a name that had been extinct at court for many years. "I thought them all dead."

Cornwich shook his head in wistful longing. "I wish they were, but alas 'tis not true. I killed Snowden at the Battle of St. Albans five years ago. That same year his son, William, avenged his father's death. He murdered my youngest son, Terrence, in an ambush on the road to London." Lifting his face to the clouds, he felt the sleet sting his cheeks and relished the anger that momentarily assuaged his grief. "I had the Snowdens attainted by Parliament, their name legally annihilated, their lands confiscated by the Crown. Like rats, they fled into France."

Lynchburg steadied his mount as he tramped through the freezing crust along the edge of a pond. "And yet they live?"

"Only one is left alive. Riley Snowden, old Snowden's last heir. A youngster. But one who is growing up to be a formidable enemy."

Lynchburg looked up to see the gray light of day glowing across the stone exterior of the towers. He inhaled deeply, trying with difficulty to contain his mounting excitement. This was his home now. This was his land.

"An attack must be financed, and Snowden has nothing. Why do you fear the cur?"

"The cur has a thirst for vengeance," Cornwich replied. "And vengeance needs no money or title. Vengeance needs only a brain, crafty and quick, and an unquenchable ambition. Young Snowden has these characteristics that turn mere mortals into Satan's angels."

Lynchburg smiled at the thought of taking on an opponent, a young warrior, in a legal battle. Perhaps he would ask Queen Margaret to allow him to challenge the youthful upstart and finish the feud.

First he must take care of the matter at hand. He must consummate his marriage and quickly. The legality of a marriage by proxy was too questionable.

"When will I meet my wife?" he asked as they rode into the shadow of the castle. The walls towered above them and men moved about high up on the toothlike ramparts, calling orders. The drawbridge creaked as it was lowered across a dry moat, and he caught his first glimpse into the inner bailey. The earl's administrators were assembling to greet them.

"You will meet her this night," the earl replied heavily.

What was her name? he wondered. He had forgotten.

"The master is home," Gertie panted as she rushed into the kitchen. A basket of fresh eggs swayed on her arm, and her cheeks were flushed with excitement.

Although she was a serving woman, almost fifty years of age, her gait was as spry as a young girl's. Her eyes gleamed hungrily and a merry cackle sprang from her lips.

"Why so gleeful, Gertie?" the rotisser asked as he sat by the hearth, roasting swan and peacock over the fire. "He's your master, not your suitor. When he's home, there's only more work for all of us."

The patisser was pressing pastry dough into molds of Saint Katherine while a cook was kneeling at a second fireplace, boiling powdered rice in almond milk. The pantler stood at the table carving trenchers from loaves of bread, and the Chief Cook stood against the far wall surveying the chaotic scene.

"Why should I not be gleeful that my master is safely returned?" she cried. "As for work, I'm no stranger to it when 'tis an honorable task." Cutting her eyes toward the far hearth, she focused her gaze on a young kitchen maid. "Unlike Rose," she scowled. "She wouldn't recognize an honest day's work if it bore the face of Christ."

The young maid had been sitting quietly by the fire, stirring a sauce of sweet milk and broth. At Gertie's harsh words, she glanced up nervously, her eyes wide. A strand of reddish hair fell across her face, and she combed it back with her fingers. With her soft beauty and quiet sense of pride, she had often fallen victim to their mockery. They were gazing on her now, their jealousy unmasked, and she knew that their verbal barbs were about to be launched against her. Like worms they fed their need for self-importance through hurtful jests and taunts.

"I bet she come from London where she was whore to some merchant," Gertie goaded her as she set her basket on the table. "When he was done with her, he sold her into servitude. If he got a farthing for her, 'twas a farthing too much."

"That's not what I heard," the rotisser joined in on the sport. "I heard she was raised as gentry. But her father died, and the sheriff demanded her hand in marriage. When she refused him, he took her land for taxes. So she was reduced to servitude." He gave her a slow, toothless smile. "Is that so, Rose?"

Rose glanced at him in boredom, her eyes as deep green as an Irish mead, then she turned away, refusing to answer.

"Aye," Cook agreed, "she's got a queenly air about her. Vain as Jezebel, she is. I've seen her rubbing green hazel on her teeth to keep them white. But she can't seem to rub salt on a fish. I don't know where she came from, but 'twas more a throne than a kitchen. She's got no knowledge of work."

The door opened, groaning on its iron hinges and diverting their attention from the girl. As they turned to see who entered, the groom, Daggot, stomped into the chamber. The winter wind swept in around him, causing the servants to draw closer to the hearths. Stamping the ice from his boots, he slammed the door shut against the cold and held up a russet sack filled with eels. Barely out of his teens, his body was still lanky from adolescence, and his eyes were bright with youth. His black hair crowned his head like a shaggy mop.

As he tossed his sack onto the table, he stared at Rose as if he were beholding a heavenly angel. *She should be seated on a dais,* he thought, *not sitting at a soot-stained hearth beneath the timbers of a kitchen.*

Her skin was as white as cream, with pink-tinted cheeks, not the florid complexion that was the fate of so many redheads, and her form was lean and shapely. Her feet, though clothed in deerskin slippers, looked small and delicate as did her hands, indicating that she was not of the tough peasant stock of the south. Her dress was a tawny wool that would have appeared drab on any other woman, but on the maid, it looked as vivid and rich as purple velvet.

"Beware of pretty wenches, Daggot," Gertie warned, seeing the direction of his gaze. "A priest once told me that even the devil can look like an angel. And if you ask me, she's the spawn of hell."

He walked to the hearth and picked up a fresh log from the woodpile, shoving it onto the fire. The flames hissed and spit as he spread out his hands, warming them in the burst of heat. "Don't mind them, Rose," he said kindly. "'Tis jealousy that fuels their tongues. They know you don't belong here among the likes of them."

"But I do," she insisted. As she stirred the broth, she stared into the fire, her eyes intense and far away. "I do."

"Don't let that sauce boil!" Cook called to the girl. "Where is the saucer? This wench cannot cook. She will curdle the master's tongue."

"The saucer died last spring of the plague," the rotisser mumbled.

The girl stood up, surveying the kitchen scene as if she were the mistress of the castle and not the lowliest of servants. "Perhaps you should stir the sauce yourself," she said to Cook, causing his eyes to ignite in outrage.

"You witless peasant!" He advanced toward her, and she drew back against the wall, dropping her spoon in fright. Meaty hands reached out for her neck as if he meant to choke her. "Watch your tongue or I'll boil you in that sauce."

"That'll give it the flavor of vinegar," Gertie huffed.

Just as he was about to grab her, Daggot lurched forward, wedging himself between the two of them in an attempt to protect her. As the portal opened, snow blew into the kitchen, causing the servants to turn meekly from the scene, anticipating a harsh reprimand from the castellan for not attending to their tasks. He liked Rose and always seemed to show up in time to rescue her from their bullying.

He filled the doorway now with his broad girth. "I need the kitchen wench," he bellowed, his voice rattling the shutters of the windows. A day's growth of beard shadowed his face in patches of dark and gray. His head, which was totally bald, was covered in a turban, and he wore a tunic of fur over his wool doublet. "The chamberlain is ill. I need the girl to prepare the master's bedchamber."

"You mean *adorn* the master's bedchamber." Gertie smirked. "Take her. She's of more use in the bedchamber than ever she was in the kitchen." Her remark was followed by a low rumble of laughter among the servants.

"Come with me," he ordered, and the girl quickly obeyed.

Sidling past the cook, she followed the castellan from the kitchen and out into the corridor. In only her shift, dress, and buckskin slippers, she shivered with cold as they strolled down the long passageway from the west tower. They passed the empty chambers that once housed the earl and his wife and the great hall where the master dined and held his court. As they entered the south tower, a dank smell filled her nostrils. It was very dark, and they could barely see their way as they wound up stone steps to the solar where the lord's bedchamber was located. How she longed to see this chamber where even a great warrior must at times be vulnerable.

Her teeth chattered with cold and excitement as the castellan opened the door. Shafts of pale light fell from windows that were high and arched. The shutters were open, and she was surprised to see light filtering in through glass panes. It was unusual to see glass windows outside of chapels, and she was disgusted by Cornwich's taste for luxury. He cared nothing about people living in poverty but only about his own lavish needs.

Stepping into the room, she glanced at the roaring fire and the fresh rushes that had been strewn over the floor. It was a room, warm and welcoming, she noted, that elicited a sense of calm.

Next to the fire was a wooden tub filled with steaming water. The master's bed was not there, but his chair was placed beneath a shaft of light like a heavenly throne. It was made of oak, intricately carved, with a feather cushion of rich green damask covering the seat.

The castellan paced the room, smelling the air and stepping lightly on the rushes, testing their freshness. He walked to a wall tapestry and examined a loose thread, then carefully patted it back into the woven fabric. Eyeing the tub, he quickly approached it and covered it with a wooden lid, sealing in its warmth.

His eyes fell upon the girl, studying her slender form as

meticulously as he had studied the chamber for cleanliness. As he walked in a circle around her, he noted the slope of her breasts and the rounded curve of her hips.

"You came to me before winter with no references," he reminded her. "I hired you though I knew you not." Clamping his hands on her shoulders, he looked down upon her with a worried expression. "I am placing all of my trust in you on this day. I wish you to bathe the earl. You must please the master, do you understand?"

"Aye," she said dully.

She understood all too clearly. He was placing her in full view of Cornwich, a tasty morsel for him to sample before his supper. She shuddered in revulsion. It was why the castellan had hired her, to tempt his master when he returned so that he could receive his favor. Laughter almost bubbled up in her throat. What a surprise the old goat would find when he entered his chamber and gazed into the eyes of his whore.

"If you do well tonight, I'll not forget your spirit, Rose. I'll reward you, I promise."

She forced a smile, hoping to reassure him.

As he left the chamber, he cast a last uncertain glance over his shoulder, then quietly closed the door behind him.

The silence settled in around her, and she placed her hand against her chest, wondering if she would ever be able to calm her wildly beating heart. The creaking of chains alerted her that the drawbridge was being lowered over the moat. Horses stamped across the wooden planks of the bridge, and her heart jumped with the pounding of each hoof. The master was home.

Above the din she heard the whistling of the north wind blowing snow and sleet down into the southern realm through the crevices of the fortress. But she was warm; her cheeks were flushed, and a mist of perspiration dampened her brow. Soon she would be face to face with Philip De Proileau, Earl of Cornwich, and there was much for which he would answer.

Chapter Three

The chamber grew so warm that for a moment Rose was reminded of spring and the orchards of the convent, the apple trees blossoming in April, their petals white and soft. When the blooms fell, they would cover the ground like drifts of snow.

She thought about her mother dead these many years, and the little nun who had tried to take her place. Like black shadows the nuns moved through her mind. Their sanctuary had nourished her body but not her spirit. They had not harnessed the hatred in her soul. She could have remained in the convent and become a nun, but she couldn't bear the idea of living a cloistered life. There was no charity or forgiveness within her. There was only her desire to escape to Glenwood Castle and reclaim her rightful place in society.

The sound of footsteps on the stairs vibrated through her mind and shook her from her daydream. The master was climbing the stairs, and he was not alone.

"I'll bathe before supper," he said from beyond the door. "There's no need to call my henchman. He's ill with a cough. I'll attend myself. If you'll be so kind as to have the pages bring up my trunk, Daggot."

Daggot, she thought with a start. The master had only just arrived, and already Daggot was trotting at his heels.

But the earl was sending him away. The henchman was ill. He would be unprotected. Good.

She scampered behind the master's chair, kneeling so that she would be completely concealed from his view. When the door opened, she peeped out and noticed the long shadow that fell across the floor. He was tall, a near giant of a man, much taller than she remembered.

As he strode into the chamber, he removed his beaver hat and dropped it to the floor. She heard a thud and suspected that it bore a jeweled brooch. Easing out a tad, she spied him, his back to the fire and his brown hair falling across his shoulders in soft waves. As he unfastened his fur-lined cloak, he revealed the dark green houppelande underneath. It was embroidered with gold thread, and the sleeves were trimmed in fur. At the sight of his obvious wealth, her anger grew hotter. For years she had survived on the bland food and bare threads of the convent while he had enjoyed roasted swan and fine garments.

Carefully he laid his sword on the floor, then pulled off his damp boots. As he walked to the fireplace, he shook the moisture from them, then set them down to dry. Rose cowered behind the chair and peeked out cautiously as he unstrapped his dagger from his lower hip then placed it gently on top of the rushes.

Her mouth went dry as he slipped off his hose and laid them next to his boots. Stripped down to his doublet, he filled her vision with a godlike image. The shirt was a pale gold color that fell to midthigh, revealing the muscles of his calves. They were thickly corded, sculpted from years of training. As he glanced up at the arched windows, she saw the profile of his bearded face, a young face, strong with the features of a Roman. In frustration, she realized that this man, whoever he was, was not the Earl of Cornwich.

As if sensing movement, he whirled about to face her.

"God's blood," he gasped, nearly stumbling back in surprise. "Who the devil are you?"

"A maid, sir," she said, quickly rising from her hiding place.

His eyes absorbed the sight of her, traveling the length of her silky hair and down her dress that ended at shapely ankles. With a calm understanding, he seemed to realize her purpose. "Why didn't you speak when I entered the chamber?"

"I meant no harm." She looked up into his eyes and was startled by the intensity of them. They were the color of a summer sky. "I was sent to prepare the earl's bath. When you entered the room, I was frightened. You are not Lord Philip. I must go now."

"No." He raised his hand to stop her. "Wait."

"Please, sir, I must leave," she said meekly and blushed at the sight of him in his doublet. "I was sent to bathe the earl, and you are not him. The castellan will be very angry if I do not leave at once. He will need me to attend the earl."

"Are you Cornwich's whore?" he asked bluntly.

"No," she answered, then realized her folly. If she had said yes, then she would have gained her freedom from this room.

"Then the earl has little if any need of you." His eyes were fixed on hers, his face rigid as if he had never beheld a sight so beautiful. "He will be occupying another chamber for the night. And he has a host of servants to attend him. In the morning he will be leaving Glenwood Castle. So he will not need you on the morrow, either. I am your new master."

Her eyes widened with bewilderment.

"I am David D'Aubere, the Earl of Lynchburg, the husband of Cornwich's daughter."

She stared at him stupidly, her mouth dropping open. "You are *what?*" she demanded, then quickly caught herself. "Pardon me, sir. You are the earl's son-in-law?"

"She will be arriving soon," he said in a tone that was both hopeful and hesitant. "I was married by proxy. I will meet her tonight for the first time."

She nearly choked. "I wish you good fortune, milord.

With your permission I will take my leave now. You see, I *am* Cornwich's wh-whore, and I must go to him."

"No," he said sharply. "You were sent here to bathe the master and so you shall."

Never, she wanted to spit at him. "Aye, milord, i-if that is what you wish," she replied, still dazed by the revelation that he was the new Cornwich.

"Tell me your name," he demanded.

Her eyes shifted to his manhood, which was well defined beneath the woolen fabric. "My name?" she repeated as she searched her memory that for a moment eluded her. "I am called Rrrr . . . Rose, sir."

"For your beauty, no doubt," he said, raising his arms to his sides. "Well, Rose, remove my doublet. I grow weary of it. After wearing armor for months, I cannot get used to this fragile garb. I feel a bit too vulnerable in it."

You are vulnerable, she thought and glanced at his dagger on the floor by the fire. *You don't know how much.* With one swift motion she could slice open his throat.

So, he thought her a whore. Well, she smiled dryly, why not play along with the fool. She would lure him into the tub, then gut him like a squirming fish.

As she removed his doublet, she felt his eyes glowing down at her, hot as embers. The muted light softly touched his skin and glistened along his thickly furred chest where the hair formed a V shape down to his groin.

Looking away quickly so that he would not see the flush on her cheeks, she walked to his bath. With trembling fingers, she removed the lid, then picked up a bowl of dried rose petals and sprinkled them across the surface of the water. The rising steam misted her face, and wisps of hair began to curl in the dampness, sticking to her cheeks and forehead.

Glancing up, she was stunned by the sight of him naked. He was walking straight toward her, without clothes, without weapons, without shame, totally vulnerable, completely trusting.

What fools men are, she thought in amazement as she

watched him step into the steaming water. *Like stags, their lust obliterates their caution.*

Picking up the soap, she began to knead it between her palms, trying not to let it slip through her shaking hands.

He sank into the tub, shuddering with pleasure as the water rose up to his chest and enveloped his sore muscles. Leaning his head back against the rim, he closed his eyes in relief.Slowly he slipped below the surface and let the water saturate his hair, then he sat up, shaking his locks like a wet lion.

"Oh!" she cried in indignation as he flung water across her.

"Lather the mud from my hair," he commanded, scooping the hair back from his face. "Must I tell you everything that you are to do? I would swear that you had never bathed a man before."

She obeyed with simmering displeasure, soaping her hands until she had worked up a rich foam. She set the soap aside and massaged his scalp until his hair was thick with lather. Groaning in pleasure, he relaxed beneath her warm and gentle touch. His breath deepened as he allowed her to lull him into a near half-sleep. As she wiped her hands on her dress, she watched the driblets of suds roll down across his forehead and into his eyes. Quickly he brought up handfuls of water, splashing his face and hair to rinse away the soap.

"You witless wench, are you trying to blind me?" he cried as he dug the heels of his hands into his eyes. Peering through stinging orbs, he saw only a blurred view of his chamber, then a bright slash as his dagger came down straight toward his heart. He was out of the tub in an instant. As his arms flailed, searching for his assailant, the room whirled darkly around him.

"You cursed witch, you've blinded me. And now you think to kill me!"

The rushes softened her steps so that he knew not where she stalked and could only turn in awkward circles, grasping at nothing. A sharp slash caught his left shoulder, and he spun toward it. Catching her wrist in his hand, he sent the dagger skidding across the floor. Fingernails dug into his face, and he grabbed the offending hand so tightly that she was certain it was being wrenched from her body. Clasping both of her wrists in one iron grip, he forced her to her knees.

"Bloody whore!" he cried and dragged her toward the tub. "I will drown you."

His free hand grabbed the back of her hair, and she felt herself thrust forward, her face shoved down over the tub, the steam misting her eyelashes.

He held her there, waiting for his vision to clear. He wanted to look into the face of his assailant. He wanted to watch her die. As his eyes began to focus, he listened for the whimpering, the cries for mercy that would surely come. But to his surprise, there was no sound from her.

As she stared into the water that would be her grave, she felt no emotion, only an acceptance. Her courage impressed him, for he'd never dealt a death blow to a woman before, and her reaction was not what he would have expected. His own men, whose powerful strength was legendary, would not have shown such courage.

"Every prisoner is allowed last words before execution," she said, stoically. "Shall I not be granted the same courtesy?"

Yanking her head upright, he stared into her face. "Why did you try to murder me?" he demanded, clenching her hair tighter.

"I feared you would violate me. I am not a whore. I am only a maid. I told you I was Cornwich's whore because I thought it would aid my escape from you."

He eyed her furiously, wanting to shake her until her teeth rattled loose. Water ran down his chest as he rose, pulling her up with him.

"If you do not wish to bed me, then all you need do is say so," he seethed. "I am not a rapist."

"I am sorry, sir," she said coldly. "I knew not your intentions."

He thrust her from him, and she fell against the floor with a soft thud, scattering the rushes as she slid to a halt. "Who are you?" he demanded. "You say now that you are not a whore. But you are no servant, either." His eyes bore through her as he scrutinized her clothing. "You speak like a lady, but you dress like a peasant. Your hair is sweet smelling and your teeth are white. But you wear buckskin on your feet."

She said nothing, only stared mutely up at him.

Slowly he began to circle her like an angry wolf, a low growl of warning emitting from his throat so that she dared not move. "Your manners are too good for a common wench. You do not belch or spit or claw at fleas. Yet you wear a coarse dress." He straddled her between his massive legs, his face looming over her. "Who are you? And why do you wish me dead?"

She looked up at him without answering. His skin shimmered with moisture, and his powerful arms and thighs flexed as he waited. This would be her last sight on earth, she realized, the new Cornwich, naked and wet, his manhood shrunken and nestled amid dark curls, his eyes, red and swollen, yet glowing with victory. At the corner of her vision she spied the golden handle of his dagger half hidden in the rushes. Reaching out, she grasped it and wielded a grazing blow to his belly.

He caught her wrist and snatched her to her feet. Raising his hand he brought it down in a bruising slap across her cheek. The dagger spun from her loosened grip as she reeled backward and landed hard against the floor. Tears filled her eyes, but she blinked them back. She would not show weakness before this monster.

"Who are you?" he demanded. "Tell me or I will beat you senseless."

"You will not need to beat me." She rubbed her cheek that bore the fiery imprint of his hand. "You have won the battle."

He stood with arms folded, bewildered by the hatred in

her eyes, the magnitude of which he had never seen on the face of a male opponent.

"Who are you?" he repeated slowly.

Lifting her eyes to his, she stared at him through thick lashes. Her chest heaved, causing her breasts to brush ripely against the fabric of her dress.

There was a mystical quality about her that unnerved him. A passion in her that was rare indeed among even the finest of noblemen. And her beauty, he thought, his chest tightening, her beauty was unsurpassed by even the mythical goddesses of Rome. By God, he feared she was bewitching him. She was a siren, an unearthly nymph sent to lure him to destruction.

"Who are you?!" he cried. His tone was nerve-shattering, like a great bell tolling her defeat.

She had tried to kill the master, a death penalty offense. There was nothing left for her to do but tell him the truth and hope for his mercy. If it was granted, then her end would be swift.

"I am Riley Snowden," she said. "Enemy to Cornwich. I am the last of my family, but . . ." She paused, for her speech was beginning to falter. "I am as my father was, a worthy opponent."

He stepped back in befuddlement. "You?" he stated in disbelief. "You are Riley Snowden?"

"Aye, sir. I ask that you bestow on me a merciful death as I would have certainly bestowed upon you."

For a moment, he stared at her, speechless, then threw back his head and laughed in hearty release. "Lady Snowden." He bowed mockingly. "I did not expect my most formidable enemy to have such a comely face. Cornwich never mentioned to me that you are a woman."

"Why should he?" she asked, unamused. "He sees my family as a herd of beasts, without souls, much less gender." She placed her hand against her cheek and savored the cool of her palm against that burning flesh. "My being a woman makes me no less formidable a foe. My father trained me as he trained my brother in weaponry and war."

"Oh?" He smiled down at her as she lay against the floor. "Then your father should have trained you better with a dagger. You were too easily disarmed."

"'Twas my woman's shift that stayed my step so that I was not quick enough."

He could not help but grin with amusement at her clever excuse. Reaching up, he combed his fingers through his hair, which was still threaded with foam, and briskly rubbed his scalp, scattering the wet strands about his face. "Then you should have forfeited your lady's honor and stripped naked. I would have enjoyed such a lovely sight even if it had been my last on earth."

She rose to her knees, her fists balled at her sides. "You are a wild beast of the fens!" she cried. "Kill me, bastard. I wish not to remain in your presence."

Turning his back to her, he strolled to the window, stepping into the grayish column of light. A pale aura caressed his hips and illuminated the moisture along his thighs. "No, I will not kill you," he said as he scratched his beard, thinking. "You are of far greater importance to me alive. The Duke of York is dead, but the war is not over. Should the Yorkists win, I shall need a prisoner to barter."

His words struck her, leaving her shaken and numb. "Richard is dead?"

"By my own hand, Lady Snowden." He glanced back at her, his eyes icy with indifference. "His head is mounted on a pike on the gates of York as surely as you are my prisoner."

"I am not your prisoner!" she cried, wanting to tear at her hair in anger and grief. "I will slash my own throat before I'll live in your Lancastrian dungeon."

"Then I shall bind your hands for the duration of your imprisonment for you are valuable goods to me. I'll not have you harming yourself."

She paled at his words, and the tears she had fought against spilled from her eyes, shaming her. Why wouldn't he allow her an honorable death?

Her tears surprised him, and he faced her awkwardly.

Having never seen tears on the face of an opponent before, he knew not what to do about it. "If you promise me on your honor that you will not harm yourself, then I will not bind your hands," he offered.

"I promise," she whispered, more fearful of being bound than of dying.

"Louder," he ordered, "so that God and all the saints will hear you."

The thought of being bound was like a knife through the heart of her courage. "I promise!" she shouted tearfully.

He stared at her, and for a moment she thought she saw a flicker of compassion in his eyes.

"I will lock you in the dungeon, but you will be well cared for. If you behave, I'll move you to one of the upper floors of the north tower." He smiled at her grimly. "Should the Yorkists win, the new monarch will return your family's estates to you. And I will exchange you for a royal pardon."

"Have you so little faith in your cause?" She laughed through her tears and felt a wicked sense of delight when she saw him grimace. It was true, she realized, he lacked faith in his own cause as any warrior would who fought for an incompetent king and a greedy queen. "The Yorkists will win," she taunted him. "But I will not last long enough in your prison for you to benefit. When the servants find out that I am a Snowden, they will kill me to please Cornwich."

Anger flamed in his eyes, and he took a menacing step toward her. "Cornwich will be leaving in the morning, and I doubt that he ever returns. I will consummate my marriage to his daughter tonight. And everyone here will be under my authority, not his."

"And if the Lancastrians win?" She flung the question at him. "What shall my fate be then?"

He folded his arms across his chest, one eyebrow winging upward in contemplation. "If you are well mannered, then I will banish you from England. I will send you back into exile in France. Defy me, and you will never again have your freedom. Do you understand?"

"Aye," she said thickly. She glared at him, wanting to laugh at his arrogance. He could not keep her alive if she did not wish it. She need only obtain a touch of wolfbane, and her life would be over. His "valuable goods" would be dead.

For the first time he realized that he was still naked and walked to the chest. Pulling out a drawer, he removed a towel and wrapped it tightly around his hips. Her eyes followed him as he walked to the portal, his legs dark with hair and damp. Opening the door, he shouted for a henchman.

Daggot appeared almost at once. What was he doing so near the solar? Riley wondered. It was unlike him to stray too far from the stables and kitchen. Had he hovered near to keep an eye on her? To protect her, maybe? Or was he hovering near the earl, hoping for an opportunity to gain his favor?

She felt humiliated as she was hoisted to her feet by Lynchburg and handed over to the groom. Daggot stared in shock at the red mark on her cheek.

"Take her to the dungeon," Lynchburg ordered.

"The dungeon, milord?" Daggot gasped.

"Is that not what I said?" His eyes smoldered with anger, daring the groom to defy him.

Daggot nodded and swiftly pinned Riley's arms behind her back in a grip so soft that it was barely felt. He led her down the stairs and out into the light of day, where knights, squires, and horses still filled the bailey. The dreary light of winter fell with a dull glow against their armor.

As the men eyed her curiously, she was marched across the grounds past the chapel and the barracks.

Looking up at the sky, she saw that it was heavy with clouds, portending snowfall by evening. She drew the cold air deep into her lungs and smelled a whiff of poultry roasting in the kitchen. It would be the last time she would see daylight or feel the fresh air for months, perhaps years.

Her legs stiffened at the thought, causing Daggot to gently push her forward. As they entered the north tower, she felt the darkness and stale air pressing in around her, smothering her.

"I will bear it," she whispered. "I will bear my imprisonment and not shame my father's name."

They started down a long and narrow stairwell, and the sound of their footfall against the stone steps echoed into the blackness. In the distance she could hear the dripping of water and the pattering of tiny feet across the stone floor. The air was so damp that it left beads of moisture on her face and so dark that she could barely see. Surely she would die before winter was over, she hoped.

Daggot released her and pulled a candle from a leather pouch at his waist, taking several minutes to light the wick. The feeble light permeated the dungeon with a soft glow. At the edge of the light she saw the raised portcullis and beyond it a wall where iron chains hung. He led her to that horrid wall and handed her the candle.

"I'll bring you fresh straw," he promised, his voice laced with pain. "I'll pull the portcullis closed and bring a torch. There'll be light in the outer corridor."

"Thank you," she said, unable to suppress the shivering that gripped her body.

"And I'll bring you a blanket, too."

He glanced behind him to make sure that they had not been followed. "Why does this visitor act so rashly with you?" he asked. "What did you do to rile him?"

Her green eyes glowed with anger above the flame of the candle. "He is no visitor but our new lord, the husband of Cornwich's daughter."

"What?" he cried. "Cornwich has a daughter?" His face contorted with confusion. "I've never heard a word spoken of her." Squinting his eyes, he searched his memory. "I knew Lord Philip had sons, although they were never here. They were fostered in London, but we heard often of their progress. A daughter?" He shook his head. "There's never been any mention of her."

"It does not matter, Daggot," she railed in disgust. "She is your mistress. And you will hear often enough of her now."

"And this is how they will treat us?" he scoffed. "What cause has this man to so abuse a Christian woman, a servant in his house?"

"I defended my honor in his presence," she said, which she knew to be the truth. She was defending her honor as a Snowden and the honor of her family.

His face grew taut and pale, and he ground one fist into his palm. "I will kill the bastard," he said halfheartedly. "I will kill him and set you free."

"No, you mustn't," she urged and placed a calming hand on his shoulder. She was determined that vengeance would be hers alone. "Daggot, you are so young. You know not the ways of an angry lord. In the morning he will be contrite, and I will go free." She tried to smile, but all she could muster was a slight twitching of her lips. "You must not kill him. Such an act would endanger your soul and your own life." She gently patted his shoulder. "And I am fine till morning. Do not worry. Please."

He dropped his arms to his sides with a groan of defeat and stared down at the stone floor. He could feel the cold through the soles of his shoes. "You will be all right?"

"Aye," she assured him.

Glimpsing the raised portcullis, he felt racked with anguish. How he hated having to pull down those bars and imprison her when her only crime was having acted nobly. "I will tell no one that you are here," he informed her, his voice wavering. "I'll not have the servants gossiping about you anymore."

"You are most kind," she said, "but I fear that many men saw us cross the bailey and enter this tower."

"They will not breathe a word against you. You will not suffer their gossip any longer. I will not allow it." His words belied the helplessness in his heart.

Reluctantly he backed away from her until he'd passed

beneath the portcullis. With a grimace he reached up and pulled down the iron grate, caging her like an animal.

"I will take care of you, Rose," he promised. "If the master doesn't free you soon, then I will come for you. And we will escape."

"Aye." She nodded hopefully. "I will count on you for that."

Chapter Four

"Where is my bride?" Lynchburg demanded. "I thought she was to arrive tonight."

"Be patient." The old earl sighed. "She is here. But she is resting. You must understand how overwhelmed she feels. The news that she is married was very sudden."

Lynchburg sat at the lord's table between his father-in-law and the chaplain, elevated above the great hall on a dais. He was clean shaven, and his hair was brushed back from his face revealing features that mesmerized the eyes of every serving maid in the room.

He wore a yellow houppelande which brought out the dark tone of his skin. The sleeves were trimmed in fur and hung longer than his arms, ending in knots that rested in his lap. The fabric had been slashed from shoulder to wrist to reveal the long inner sleeves of his silver doublet. Dressed as a bridegroom, he waited to meet his bride.

Overwhelmed, is she? he thought. He could understand her shock, but what noblewoman would ignore her duties and fail to face her husband at her wedding feast? She could not be suffering too greatly from the loss of her brother. They had not been raised together. It was unlikely that she had any memories of him.

As he looked down on the knights and administrators assembled in the great hall, his eyes were sharp and probing, his posture erect. He had the look of a king overseeing his subjects. Every man present took note that this was no weak lord but one who would be obeyed without question.

Long boards had been placed upon trestles along the sides of the hall to make tables for the knights. Tapestries covered the stone walls, and a large screen painted with images of angels stood in front of the door.

In the center of the hall a fire blazed, its smoke rising up through a hole in the roof. Several banners of Cornwich hung from the rafters and fluttered in the draft. Musicians performed from the gallery while a juggler walked through the hall, tossing raw eggs into the air and catching them. As Lynchburg surveyed the feast with growing discomfort, his face grew dark and hard.

After weeks on the battlefield he should have been famished for a banquet, but the earl was not hungry. He thought only of his wife and the humiliation her absence was causing him. For her not to join him was a breech of manners, not to mention duty, that he would not easily forgive. He wanted to be a good husband to her, but first he must establish his authority over her. How could he preside over a castle if he could not command the respect of his own wife? Obviously she had been pampered for too long. The nuns had been overindulgent with her, and now her father was giving her her way on this day of all days. Why, he wondered in growing agony, was she being so damned difficult?

Servants paraded from the kitchen with platters of roasted swan and pastries in the shape of St. Catherine filled with morsels of peacock in a rich gravy. A server placed a succulent pastry on each of their trenchers, serving Cornwich first, then the younger earl.

He thought about the Snowden wench in his dungeon, her auburn hair cascading down her back and her tears falling freely now that no one was near to watch. He would move her on the morrow to a higher level in the north tower. It was her health that concerned him, or so he tried to convince himself. He must keep her alive to ensure his future should the Yorkists win.

God, he'd never seen a woman as beautiful as her. The image of her took shape in his mind like a taunting apparition, her lovely form and face, her green eyes sparkling like pools of water in the sunlight, her lips red and full with a hint of a pout. But he must not think about her; he must think about the woman to whom he was married. In an attempt to divert his thoughts from his prisoner, he eyed the religious scenes depicted on the tapestries. Be damned, he thought miserably, but the wench's vision would not leave him. She had bewitched him, robbing him of his ability to think clearly.

She is my enemy, he reminded himself, *and would conquer me, rendering me as blind and as impotent as Samson.*

Grabbing his wine goblet, he brought it to his lips and drank deeply. Only the numbing effect of wine could take his mind off his captive, but after finishing three goblets, he realized that the drink had only set her vision aflame. It was burning slowly and steadily all the way down into his loins. Not even a concoction from the mythical gods could have cooled his desire for her at that moment. Nothing but his own death could have ended such a longing.

Wafers were brought out, powdered in sugar and cinnamon, but he waved them away. He was in no mood for sweets. Sitting in the great hall, his hall, filled with his men, he felt alone like a man who is in a foreign country, a man who is unwhole.

"I hear you locked up one of my kitchen wenches," the old earl commented, lifting a morsel of swan to his mouth. "My castellan is upset that he was not allowed to handle the situation. He fears for his position."

"'Twas a personal matter," the earl replied. "I will deal with her on the morrow. Your castellan is not to blame."

He shrugged and waved his hand, deflecting the conversation. "Do as you wish. 'Tis none of my concern."

A minstrel stepped forward on the gallery and began to strum his lute, singing a song of war and victory. Lynchburg wanted to strangle him. To be seated on the dais with only his father-in-law and a priest on his wedding day was a humiliation of which he'd had enough.

Slamming down his wine goblet, he brought the festivities to an abrupt silence. The minstrel ceased his strumming, and the knights quieted, their wafers poised midway to their mouths.

"I wish to see my bride now," he demanded.

The old earl swallowed his wafer and wiped his hands on the tablecloth. "She is in prayer," he announced loudly. "But she will receive you."

"She will receive me?" Lynchburg asked incredulously, pushing back his stool. What foolishness to allow a woman to be so disrespectful. "If she will receive me," he said sardonically, "I shall be most grateful."

The old earl stood and finished his wine with one gulp. Setting down his goblet, he wiped his mouth on the back of his hand and motioned for his son-in-law to follow him.

A cheer went up from the knights as the two men strode from the great hall. Only the chaplain remained silent, his eyes, knowing and apprehensive, followed the two men until they had disappeared into the blackness of winter.

Lynchburg found the night a welcome relief from the hall, where the smell of smoke and unwashed bodies made the air stagnant. As he approached the east tower, his fury quickened his pace. His wife would learn to save her prayers for morning mass. Of that he was certain.

The heavy wooden door creaked open, and the two men stepped inside. "This way," the earl said as he entered the dark stairwell. There was only one mounted torch to light their way, and Lynchburg was surprised that Cornwich did not stop to light a candle. It was as if he preferred the blackness that surrounded them.

Their feet scraped against the stone stairs as they wound up the tower past loopholes and shuttered windows. Lynchburg could have sworn that this passage was rarely used. The air was so thick with dust that he felt as if he would choke on it. A knot tightened in his stomach, his every nerve sensing a trap.

When they reached the third level of the tower, Cornwich paused before a closed door and turned to face his son-in-law. "Your marriage was an alliance," he reminded him. "You knew not who your bride was."

"True," he agreed. "But I wish to know her now."

The earl opened the door into a corridor that was lit by a single torch. They were leaving the tower and entering the uppermost floor above the chapel. Lynchburg was certain that the chaplain and his servants lived on the second level along with the earl's administrators. With the solar in the south tower and the earl's old chambers located behind the great hall, he was bewildered as to why this barren portion of the castle would be used by the earl's daughter.

In the dimness he spied a nun seated at a doorway. She was elderly and so shrunken that her wimple seemed to weight her down.

"My lord," she greeted the old earl softly and rose from her perch. "It has been many months since your last visit." Pausing in curiosity, she eyed the young Lynchburg.

"I wish to see my daughter," he said curtly.

The nun lifted a key from her belt and strained to see if she was inserting it properly into the lock. Lynchburg wanted to snatch it away from her and unlock the door himself. He was in no mood for her sluggishness, his only desire being to yank his wife off her knees and drag her to her marriage bed. Pushing open the door, she stepped back to allow the men to enter.

This is most strange, he thought. *Why is the girl locked in a room, and why is a nun positioned outside the door like a guard? Do they fear she will run away? Is she that displeased with her marriage arrangement?*

"What is this about, Cornwich?" he asked as he stepped into the chamber.

A candle burned on a corner table, casting a feeble glow across the room. It was a spacious room, he noted, heavy with shadows that hung in a dark veil over a mattress.

"Behold your bride," Cornwich said as he remained beyond the sphere of light.

Quickly Lynchburg walked to the bed and knelt beside it. Gazing down on the feather mattress, he saw a tiny girl curled up beneath a fur coverlet. Her eyes were closed in sleep, and her dark hair was scattered in oily strings across the cushions. Taking her face in his hands, he felt the cold stickiness of her flesh. Her features were as placid as death, and she was so thin that her cheekbones protruded unnaturally. Although he had been told that she was eighteen, she looked to be no more than ten. There was an odor about her as if she had soiled herself. Staggering to his feet, he nearly lost his balance.

"She is ill." He turned accusingly to Cornwich. "This is leprosy!"

"Nay, 'tis not, I swear it." Cornwich stood rigidly, fearing to take his eyes from his son-in-law. "She has been an idiot since her birth. She was born weeks before her time, and her mother died laboring to bring her into the world." His face deepened in sorrow as his eyes flitted to the huddled form on the pallet. "She was very tiny when she was born and made no cry or movement. I decided to put her to death, but the chaplain would not sanction such an act. So I placed her here. The church has cared for her since her infancy."

For several moments Lynchburg gazed in horror at his bride. "Why did you not tell me of her deformities?"

"Would it have made any difference to you?" His words lashed out at him from the darkness. "You wanted the estate, not the wife."

He knew that Cornwich was right. He had wanted the estate, but he wanted a family as well. He had wanted heirs, a son to someday inherit the sword of D'Aubere. Since the night of his marriage, he had assumed without question that he would have children and provide a future for himself and his family.

"Who knows about her?" he asked.

Cornwich swept his hand toward the door. "The chaplain and nuns who live in these chambers. The nuns are a known presence here, but they are cloistered. The chaplain brings their meals each day and provides them with whatever they need. I had to give the church a handsome piece of land to buy their silence."

Narrowing his eyes, Lynchburg blinked into the shadows that shrouded his father-in-law's face. "How much did you have to give the queen to buy hers?"

"Until your marriage at Wakefield, she asked nothing of me," he replied honestly. "Jeanette was just a pawn to be used when the time was right."

The candle sputtered, burning lower as the shadows darkened around them. "She has the mind of an infant," Cornwich explained glumly. "I hear that she clings to the nuns at times and seems to enjoy their affections. But she does not speak. For the most part, she sits and rocks, oblivious to the world around her. You must keep her a secret," he implored him. "I cannot have my enemies find out about her. They will attack my lands, thinking God to be on their side." He glimpsed his daughter and flicked his hand at the huddled form. "Were we not raised to believe that only the devil can produce such a creature as this?"

Lynchburg began to pace the chamber, his mind racing. "I will keep her a secret," he muttered. "I will say that she wishes for solitude, study and prayer. No one will ever know about her condition."

Cornwich stepped back, his form etched darkly against the torchlit corridor. "Now you see why I so desperately needed my sons."

"I am your son now!" he shouted. "It will be as the queen commanded."

"I need more than a son, David," he said firmly. "I need to secure the future of my estates and my title. I need a grandson."

Lynchburg could not believe what he was hearing. "A grandson?" he scoffed.

"You cannot legally inherit my title and neither can this girl," he explained. "Only my grandson can claim the title of Earl of Cornwich. I want my blood to inherit all that I have."

Lynchburg sputtered in disbelief. "But I cannot . . ." He

stared at the tiny, knotted figure. "Surely you do not expect me to bed this poor, pathetic creature."

Cornwich looked at him, his eyes becoming impassive, his manner detached. "You must."

"I cannot!" He shook his head, feeling staggered by the hopelessness of the situation. "How is she to bear a child? She cannot be capable of it."

"She is woman with a womb. On the inside she is no different from any other woman. I must have an heir." He remained in the doorway, barring Lynchburg's escape.

"I cannot," he repeated, advancing toward his father-in-law. "I cannot consummate this marriage. 'Tis not possible."

"You will," Cornwich warned in an equally challenging tone. "Or I will have this marriage annulled."

"What?" he shouted.

"I will have the marriage annulled. And you will be left with nothing." He stepped into the circle of light, facing his son-in-law. "And do not look to your queen for help. She will not interfere in a matter before the church. She has my land in the north. That's all she wanted from this affair."

Lynchburg drove his fingers deep into his hair, his brows lowering like stormclouds over tempestuous seas. "You betrayed me, Cornwich. You and the queen. You both betrayed me."

The old earl smiled bitterly. "You betrayed yourself. What you see before you is your reward for your greed. You will give me an heir within the year, or I shall end this farce." He watched him through the shadows, taking careful aim with his words. "But do not worry about where you are to go when you leave here. I am certain that the queen will welcome you back into her service."

Lynchburg felt as if he'd been dealt a blow from a mace, breathless and stunned. "All right," he agreed helplessly. "I will give you an heir. But . . . surely you know that this is an abomination."

"Is it?" Cornwich asked. As he watched his son-in-law, his manner became less guarded, his eyes hopeful. "You must believe as I do that she has remained alive for this purpose. To bring new life, pure life, into this world." The earl clamped a firm hand on his shoulder as his eyes slid briefly to Jeanette. "Do not fear for her, David. She has been heavily drugged. She will not be aware of what you do to her." Releasing him, he gave his back a pat of encouragement. "I will leave you to your wedding night. Fill her womb. Give me a grandson."

As he left the chamber, he closed the door quickly behind him.

Lynchburg stood in the deathlike stillness of the room, wondering what to do. As he sat down on the feather mattress he sighed, feeling the weight of his task crushing down upon him. If he did not produce an heir for Cornwich within the year, he would lose everything.

Giving Jeanette a sidelong glance, he felt a swell of pity in his heart. Her skin was almost translucent, and he could see the tiny web of red lines across her cheeks. "God have mercy," he said, making the sign of the cross over her face. There was no way he could have sex with this girl; he knew he could not.

Pulling the blanket up to her neck, he tucked it under her chin. "Do not fear," he whispered. "I would never harm you. I have brought this nightmare upon myself, and I must see my way through it." But how, he wondered, would he ever be able to appease his father in law and in so doing, ensure his own future as a nobleman? Sitting in the bleakness of the chamber, he rested his face in his hands and peered stonily into the darkness through the bars of his fingers.

Riley was roused from sleep by the sound of approaching footsteps. She sat up on her pallet and stared into the darkness beyond the portcullis, hoping that Daggot was coming to bring her a trencher of supper. As the visitor drew nearer, her hope quickly died. The footsteps were too heavy, too menacing.

When she saw Lynchburg materialize from the darkness, she felt her heart begin to pound with fear. Once again she was daunted by the height and breadth of him and swore inwardly that she would not be intimidated by this man. Or at least that she would not show it. As he came to a halt at the iron grate, she stared at his clean-shaven face, the strong jaw and shocks of blue that were his eyes.

Had he decided to execute her? she wondered, not wanting to know the answer.

Picking up the torch from its iron frame, he held it up to see her better. Her hair was a blaze of fire down her back, and her eyes were as bright as a dewy mead.

"May I have an audience with you, milady?" he asked, but it was not a question. It was a command made in a mocking tone.

She tucked her legs up under her and smoothed her dress over her shift. "Very well," she said, "seeing as how I have no choice in the matter."

He wet his lips, his eyes searching her face, his manner hesitant. "I wish to discuss the conditions of your release. I said before that I wish to exchange you for a pardon should the Yorkists win. But I have changed my mind. I wish to ransom you instead."

She laughed, and her laughter was musical, a gentle trill that fell lightly against his ears.

"You wish to ransom me?" She placed her hand against her chest in a gesture of feigned disbelief. "I am sorry to disappoint you, but I have nothing to give you as ransom. Parliament had my family's lands confiscated. When my brother died, my mother and I were living in Lyon. We had just enough money left to buy our way into a convent."

"You do have something you can give me, milady," he retorted, the large fingers of one hand closing possessively around the bars. "Your ransom is a child. I need a male child from you."

Her gaze froze into ice as contempt filled her. Surely he was jesting. "Why do you need a child from me? What's the matter with your Lancastrian bride?" A mirthless smile touched her lips. "Does she have two heads? Is she a withered hag, flatulent and ghastly?"

"My wife is none of your concern," he snapped, causing the flames of the torch to flutter. "I need a child, and you will give me one. That is, if you ever hope to regain your freedom."

Her eyes glowered at him. "No," she said, letting the word drip slowly from her lips. "I will not be your whore. I would rather die in this prison than birth your Cornwich bastard."

He snorted, and his eyes flashed with frustration, reminding her of an impatient stallion. "Don't you see? Your ransom will be to your benefit."

"Please explain to me how my birthing a bastard will be to my benefit." Folding her arms across her chest, she waited for his reponse.

"You hate Cornwich and wish to take revenge on him, do you not?"

Her gaze cooled, and her brows lifted appealingly. "Aye," she said.

"My wife is sickly and cannot bear children. I must produce an heir for Cornwich within the year, or he will end the marriage." He leaned closer to the bars and steadied his gaze on her. "Listen to me. If you give me a child, then your blood will inherit Glenwood Castle and the earl's title. The blood of Cornwich will be gone from this earth forever, and in its place will be the blood of Snowden. Years from now, as he lay dying, I will go to him and reveal our ruse. Those will be the last words that he ever hears, milady. I promise you that."

The offer intrigued her but at the same time repelled her. She appeared to mull over his words for several minutes until he rattled the bars with impatience. She was enjoying making him wait.

"Can I trust you?" she asked.

"By all that's holy," he uttered, tightening his hold on the iron grate. "I am a man of my word. As soon as the child is born, I will send you back to France."

She sensed his desperation and decided to paw it like a playful kitten. Why not torture him as he had tortured her in this cell? she decided. She would begin to give in, but then she would retreat. "I marvel at your cleverness, Lynchburg. And your greed. How can I resist such an offer?" She listened to his breath of relief, then raised her eyes to his in bland dismissal. "However, I must refuse you."

"'Tis a perfect plan," he blared in frustration. "I will keep you hidden from the servants. No one will know that you are the mother of my son. My wife will also remain in her sickroom. I will dismiss the nuns who minister to her and place only my most trusted servants in her chamber." He shifted his weight uneasily as the bars grew damp beneath his hand. "I will tell people that she is with child and in confinement. When the child is born, I will send her to an abbey in Scotland or Wales. I will announce that she is dead." He stopped, seeming to have run out of words.

Her chest swelled with an air of superiority, knowing that she was the one in control, not him. Savoring the long silence, she fixed her gaze on him and repeated slowly. "I will not bear your bastard."

He slammed his fist against the portcullis and marveled that she did not leap with fright. Even his stoutest men jumped when he roared. Yet she sat calmly, smiling up at him, relishing the helplessness in his eyes.

He recognized her game and was determined to end it.

"If I promise to give you more freedom during your imprisonment, will you agree?"

Ah, he is a persuasive man, she thought. *He offers me more freedom whether there is a child or not as long as I will try to conceive. 'Tis a tempting offer, but I do not wish to be his handmaiden.*

She remembered the Bible story of Abraham's handmaiden, who bore Abraham a son because his wife was barren. Then Abraham's wife conceived, and the handmaiden was pitched out into the desert along with her bastard to die. What if she bore him a son and then his wife conceived? What would happen to her child? She shuddered at the thought of his fate.

"Milady," he said, startling her from her thoughts. "Do we have a bargain?"

More freedom meant more opportunity to escape, she realized, if she could avoid conception. If she could not, then she would bear a child for the Lancastrain army and be returned to the convent of St. Pierre les Nonnains. Only this time her stay would be permanent. Lynchburg, with his new wealth and power, would ensure it. Grace was free, but the favors of the church were at a cost, and Lynchburg would gladly pay their price to be rid of her.

"Milady?" His tone was tinged with desperation. "I must have an answer. And be assured, I will not ask again."

No, he would not give her another chance, she knew. She must act now, say yes, and escape to fight again for York. Or say no and possibly perish in this dungeon. Of course, he knew her answer would be yes, beast that he was, forcing her to give up her honor and virtue for her freedom.

The thought of his muscular body bearing down on her nearly crushed the breath from her lungs. Could she endure it? she wondered. Or would she rather remain in this cold, dank prison facing endless isolation and eventually madness?

Oh, yes, he knew her answer would be yes, she realized, fixing her eyes sullenly on his. He wanted to strip her naked and use her, extract his heir from her loins, then put her away forever. He wanted to force her to give him the only thing of value that she had left, knowing all the while that she was nothing to him, less than the greyhounds that slept in the great hall, less than the mice that foraged in the kitchen at night. She inhaled deeply, her chest swelling with anger. The only life-force that remained within her was her lust for revenge against them all.

"Yes," she agreed.

Chapter Five

Lynchburg set the torch back in its frame and raised the portcullis, lifting the shadows of the bars from Riley's visage. As he advanced toward her, she pressed her back firmly against the wall, terrified of what he was about to do. She had never been touched by a man before, and the thought of this powerful warrior initiating her into forbidden acts turned her courage to dust. To show fear was to surrender her spirit to him, and she was determined never to do that.

"I am not afraid of you," she said derisively.

His dark, muscular form cast a long shadow across her body. "Good," he replied with a note of kindness. "I admire a woman with courage. And you are the most courageous woman I have ever met."

He stepped into the half shadows of the cell and began to remove his clothes.

Courage, she thought. It was the trait that had made the Snowdens remarkable for so many generations. And she was the last of her family line. Would she fail in displaying that which had made her family so great?

She squared her shoulders and flung a defiant glare at him, then just as quickly looked away. She was stunned by the sight of his manhood, erect and flushed with passion.

"Take off your dress," he quietly ordered. He wanted to

plunder her breasts with his tongue, to set fire to the unexplored territory between her thighs, to conquer her.

She stood up, and her knees wobbled, causing her to grasp for the wall. As he reached out to steady her, she recoiled from him, not wanting to be touched by him. She wanted only to get the deed over with as quickly as possible. Taking hold of her dress, she shakily pulled it up over her head and cast it to the floor. In only her shift, she felt vulnerable and embarrassed.

The light flickered across his face, and his eyes glimmered like the sparks falling from the rushes of the torch. The curve of her hips enticed him, and he wanted to rip the shift from her. But he would be patient, he told himself, very patient, for undoubtedly she was a virgin.

Hesitantly she tugged her shift from her shoulders and lowered it down her arms until she revealed the pink tips of her breasts. She closed her eyes, wishing for a puff of magic that would render her mindless until this ordeal was over.

When he saw the fabric slipping away from her silken skin, his breath stopped. He caressed the soft mounds of her breasts and felt her trembling beneath his hands.

"I will be merciful," he assured her, his breath warm on her face. "I will not harm you."

"Nor I you," she said, although the very idea was ludicrous. She was as powerless as a lamb in the jaws of a wolf, and she knew it. She was about to trade her most valuable possession, her virtue, for her freedom. There could have been no greater ransom than if he had asked of her her life.

His lips kissed a warm trail down to one soft peak, and she gave a small cry of shock as his mouth closed hotly over her nipple. Rolling the soft bud on his tongue, he gently pulled it and felt it stiffen. His tongue lingered on that cool, virgin flesh, and he was pleased to feel her body relaxing, becoming more pliant beneath his touch. Her nipple hardened in his mouth, reaching into the warm sanctuary of his body.

"You are my enemy!" she cried. "I submit to you only as a prisoner of war."

His hands slid along the satin skin of her belly and moved lower, slowly freeing her hips from the shift. She sucked in her breath as she felt the cool air sweep across her, then the cold, rough tips of his fingers touching her where she had never been touched before.

"You may plunder my body, but you shall never claim my spirit," she said.

"Lie back on the pallet," he directed her. His eyes looked feverish and faraway.

She lowered herself onto the straw and curled up on her side, not wanting him to see her nudity or to touch her again in that most secret place. As he gently parted her legs, she covered her face with her hands to hide her embarrassment.

His fingers stroked the moist lips and slipped into the soft pinkness of her womanhood. A pleasure was radiating from his touch, and she was appalled by this unexpected sensation. His weapons were his hands, his lips, and they were weakening her far more than any wound or illness or loss of blood ever had. She was slipping away into a haze of bliss. Surrendering! She gasped as his fingertip met the hard knot of her sex, turning her loins to liquid and threatening to dissolve her in their molten heat.

Taking her hand in his, he guided it to his shaft, swollen and pulsing against his belly. At first she resisted, then relented and gripped him hesitantly. She was surprised and frightened by the hard feel of his rod and the dark, velvet tip. Not knowing what to do, she pulled him toward her, and he arched his back in painful ecstasy.

He must wait, he knew and eased his member from her grip. Lying down next to her, he propped himself on one elbow and slid his hand down the narrow valley of her waist and up over the swell of her hip, caressing the smooth flesh.

Her skin was beautiful, pale and flawless, luring him into her even softer, warmer domain. As his fingers slipped inside of her, he brought a startled cry from her lips and felt the slick tightness of her hidden corridor. She tried to push his hand away, but stopped, knowing that if she fought him, he might hurt her.

Withdrawing his hand, he smiled at her, comfortingly, his eyes soft, blue fires. "I will be merciful," he murmured as he gently rolled on top of her.

She turned her face away from him, not wanting to look into the eyes of her conqueror, not wanting to understand the desire that was stirring inside of her.

The tip of his manhood teased her swollen lips, stroking and gently prodding until his shaft eased into her. She was tight, but her passion had lathered her slightly, promising to make this conquest sweeter than anticipated. A moan escaped his lips as a wave of pleasure seized him. Her flesh was white hot as he pressed deeper into her, conquering her inch by inch until his full length almost filled her. He stilled at his task, arrested by her maidenhead and allowed her time to adjust to the level of pain she was experiencing.

She raised her hips to ease her pain and squeezed her eyes shut as he pushed into her, breaking through the thin tissue of resistance. An explosion of fire seared through her, but she did not cry out or try to push him away. It was worse than she had ever imagined it could be, and she wished only to escape the pain and fire in her loins.

His face contorted as his body writhed against her in agony. Never had he felt such intense pleasure and pain as he tried to hold back his seed. He pumped faster now, harder, oblivious to everything but the pleasure that was cresting inside of him. With a piercing cry he drove into her, his body rigid, and his seed spilling in a hot flood. All of his life and energy seemed to flow out with it. Collapsing beside her, he buried his face in her pillow of auburn hair.

As she lay next to him, listening to his labored breathing, she grasped the soft strands of his hair that rested against his shoulders. After nearly murdering her only hours before, his lovemaking had been tender at first, then mercifully quick.

He is a paradox, she thought, *this roaring lamb.*

She had never dreamed that she would couple before marriage, for the nuns had warned her that to do so was a deadly sin. And now she had coupled though it were a sin and not even for love or lust but for freedom. The act had been painful. And that would be her penance, she decided. But it had been mingled with pleasant sensations that had left her loins trembling. His lips upon her breasts had actually made her feel a hunger deep within her sex, and it baffled her that she could feel pleasure at the hands of her enemy.

Rousing up, Lynchburg glanced down at her sleepily and took a strand of her auburn hair between two fingers.

"You are the most beautiful woman I have ever seen," he whispered as he brought the strand to his nose, inhaling the fragrance of roses. It felt as soft as the petals of a flower against his flesh. Reluctantly he sat up, his eyes drowsy with sleep. He felt befuddled, lost.

"I must go now," he murmured.

Slipping on his hose, he pulled them up over his hips and fastened them at his waist.

She grabbed her crumpled shift from the floor and covered her body with it. Her stomach was mildly cramping and flecks of blood appeared on the straw. Seeing the source of her pain, he turned away. He had never taken a virgin before, and the realization shamed him. Odd that she would have endured the act so serenely, he thought, but then again, she was unlike any woman he had ever known. She was almost spiritual, a wood nymph, a woman of extraordinary sensuality. Her body, though virginal, had not fought him but had yielded naturally to his.

He pulled on his doublet and houppelande then strapped his belt around his waist, mentally warning himself to beware of this bewitchment. "Do not think that you can rule me through my cock," he said roughly. "You are still my prisoner. Nothing more to me than that."

Her anger nearly choked her as it rose up like a bile in her throat. "Nor do I care to be anything more to you than that," she hissed. "You are nothing more to me than an instrument of my revenge."

He stared at her for a shocked moment, unable to comprehend that she had just spoken to him in so vile a manner. As he gazed down at her, a glint of admiration sparked his eyes. "Milady," he chuckled, "I should punish you for that remark, but I cannot. I am too amazed that you do not fear me."

Her eyes met his in a touch of cold velvet, and his laughter faded as the mute fury in her face sobered him.

"I ask that you not speak to me again in so baneful a manner," he sighed as he pulled on his boots. "I am, after all, your gaoler. It would not go well for you if you were to annoy me."

Skulking to the portcullis, he pushed it up, then paused, reminding himself that he had taken her prisoner, that he had demanded a child as her ransom, and had taken her virginity. She had every right to lash him with her tongue. Glancing back at her, he wondered if he should offer her some words of comfort, but quickly thought better of it. Naked and alone in the dying light of the torch, she looked like a siren on the rocks. One who would rob him of his wits and lure him to destruction. He must never weaken his guard around this woman, he realized, else there would surely be a blade embedded in his back.

The night would feel good to him after this episode. He needed the wind like ice thrown in his face to awaken him from this spell.

"Good night, milady," he said thickly. "Sleep well."

The chains squealed as he lowered the portcullis until the iron grate clanged against the floor.

She stared at him, saying nothing, her eyes fastened on him like leeches threatening to draw out his very soul. He could not imagine the intensity of her hatred for him. Briskly he stalked from the dungeon and mounted the stairs, taking them three at a time.

With heavy steps he trudged across the frozen ground to the barracks. There was nothing he wanted more right now than the company of his men. They could bring him back to the reality of war and save him from this bewitchment. Entering the barracks, he saw his men dipping their bowls into a barrel of ale. Aye, he thought gladly, ale was what he needed. To be drunk was what he needed, nay reeling drunk. He grabbed a bowl from atop a trestle table and dipped it into the frothy liquid. Bringing it thirstily to his lips, he drained it quickly, then plunged it back into the barrel.

"Come and join me, David." He heard Cornwich's summons and turned to see the old earl sitting by the brazier, the flames sending up flakes of ash wafting about the barracks.

"It does a man good to be among his army," he called to Lynchburg.

"Aye," he replied absently. "It does a man good."

He thought of the fiery-haired vixen who would suffer on the morrow with a soreness between her milk-white thighs. "Damn her," he muttered and gulped the bitter concoction. Why could he not for a moment get her out of his mind?

He walked to the portal and shoved it open, peering out across the bailey. It was nearing time for the guards on the parapets to change, and he would send his finest archers to replace them. Only his best men would be assigned to protect this fortress.

Nearby he heard the horses naying softly in the stables and the blessed crackling of the barracks fires. Along with the spent feeling in his loins, the smells and sounds of the castle gave him a mild sense of peace. "Aye, it does a man good," he repeated as he walked to the brazier and sank down next to his father-in-law.

"It went well?" the earl asked. "You took her maidenhead?"

"Aye," he replied.

The old earl nodded, staring at his son-in-law much too

intently for Lynchburg's comfort. "My daughter, she is . . . well?"

He shrugged. "As well as when I found her."

The old man nodded again. "I am pleased that you have satisfied your husbandly duties."

Lynchburg grunted and rose, feeling a need to escape the scrutiny of his father-in-law. Walking back to the portal, he glanced out across the bailey and watched a plump woman carrying a platter of food toward the north tower. His eyes narrowed when he saw the weight of the platter. No doubt there was swan upon it and pastries and wafers. He would have to move the girl as soon as possible. He did not know these servants and trusted none of them.

"What of you, sir? What are your plans?" he asked.

"I will be leaving in the morning with my men. They are camped beyond the castle tonight, and I will sleep there with them. 'Tis the only way to keep them out of the stews of the village."

Lynchburg smiled, relieved to hear that the old man was leaving. "Are you returning to the north?"

"Aye, I need to return with haste. The queen has need of me." He stood up and lumbered over to the barrel to replenish his bowl. "The Lancastrian army will be moving south like locusts. As soon as they cross the River Trent, they will sack every village until they reach London. I must control the troops, for Margaret will not do it." He scooped up a bowl full of ale and brought it to his lips, noisily slurping the amber liquid. "She allows them to loot because she cannot pay them. I will have to control them and keep them on the road to London. Otherwise they will turn from being soldiers to being rapists and thieves." A belch rumbled up from his chest and he smothered it with his hand.

"We must conquer London soon and free Henry from the Tower," Lynchburg said as he watched the old woman disappear through the portal of the north tower.

"Aye," he agreed, raising his bowl for emphasis. "And I must convince Margaret of that. But the queen has no money. It will be difficult for her to take London with an army both small and starving." He drained his bowl and dipped it back into the barrel. "A siege would take months, and her men could not survive the winter. Margaret will wish to wait until the spring to attack the city. She will want to feed her troops off of the fish and game of the forests."

Lynchburg watched and waited for the woman to emerge. What was she doing in there, he wondered, feeling a growing uneasiness.

"The Scottish troops will aid us if we act now."

"Aye." The old earl nodded and sucked at the taste of ale on his teeth. "But the task will still be difficult. London may soon have a new monarch. Young Edward, York's son, is in Wales gathering an army." He swished the ale in his bowl and brought it thirstily to his lips, lacing his mouth with foam. "Soon he will ride into London at the head of his troops like a king. He will replace his father as usurper. I fear that under his leadership the Yorkists will be greatly strengthened."

Lynchburg puffed at that thought. "Edward is naught but a boy. He cares only for pleasure."

"True, he hunts and whores. But he is also a warrior to be feared." His eyes were red rimmed from drink but deep with wisdom and warning. "We must keep him from London, David. We must take the city now. Or else."

"Or else what?" Lynchburg frowned, his eyes remaining fixed on the north tower.

"Or else Edward will drive us from all of England as his father drove us from the south. We cannot delay until the spring. By then he will have installed himself as king in London." He stared down sadly into the bottom of his empty bowl. "I fear that even now Margaret is negotiating with the French. She will sell Calais to the French king to gain his allegiance."

"No." He shut his eyes, and slung his bowl to the ground. "If 'tis true, I will kill the bitch. I will not allow her to give away another acre of English soil."

"You will be nowhere near her." He wagged his finger at him in paternal sternness. "You will stay here and guard my interests. And sire my grandson. I will handle Margaret."

He wanted to roar at the old man. He was a warrior, not a steward. How he itched to ride into Wales and lead his men into battle against the usurper, Edward. He would slay him as he'd slain his father. He would mop up this rebellion once and for all.

"When the time comes for my daughter to deliver her child," the earl mentioned hesitantly, "you must go to the village of Gersham. Ask for the healer, Elda. She must serve as Jeanette's midwife."

Lynchburg thought he detected a ragged edge to the old man's voice, a tinge of emotion. Glancing back, he saw a flush on his cheeks and wondered if it was caused by overindulgence in drink.

"Elda," he murmured in agreement. *Now I am in charge of procuring midwives,* he growled inwardly.

Staring beyond the bailey, he wondered why the old woman had not emerged from the tower. Probably entertaining the witch, he thought, remembering her silken skin and bright green eyes. Those eyes burned through him yet. They were of a hue unknown to him before today, deep and cool.

Riley, he thought, an ache in his loins. The wind swept across the bailey kicking up loose straw and blowing it against the castle walls. The world seemed empty to him. Even now with his fortress and his new wealth, he felt racked with greed for the one thing he could never truly possess. His enemy.

At the sound of footsteps, Riley rose from her pallet and crept up to the portcullis. The shadows of the corridor were as deep and dark as the sea, and she gripped the cold bars in her hands, wondering who this visitor might be. Soft steps echoed from the darkness, and she breathed in relief, realizing that it was a woman who was approaching, not a man.

Old Gertie padded into the torchlight, carrying a platter laden with food. Shuffling to a halt, she placed it on the floor and knelt to raise the bars. Riley got down on the floor to assist her, but together they hadn't the strength to budge the portcullis.

Gertie cursed as she sat back on her heels and examined her throbbing palms.

"Did Daggot tell you I was here?" Riley asked. "He said he would tell no one."

"He didn't tell me," she said, rubbing her palms gingerly across her dress. "The castellan did. He's in a black mood because of this. He says he's in charge of the servants, not Daggot. It should have been him who locked you up."

Riley grasped the bars and strained mightily until she had raised them just enough for Gertie to push the platter through.

She chuckled. "Better eat it before the rats do."

Riley sat cross-legged on the floor and grabbed a pastry, biting ravenously into it. The crust crumbled and spilled flakes of pastry down her chin, followed by a dribble of rich sauce.

"What did you do to be punished like this?" Gertie asked, tucking a loosened strand of hair behind her ear.

"I tried to kill the master," Riley replied, her words muffled with food.

She washed down the pastry with spiced wine and tore a chunk from the loaf of bread with her teeth.

Gertie nodded, having expected that answer. "So he knows who you are."

"Aye," she mumbled grimly. "He thinks I am the last Snowden."

Gertie tilted her head back and set her jaw at a stubborn angle. "You were so sure that you were going to succeed. The time was not right, Riley. You must know your enemy before you attack him." She flung her hands up in frustration. "But you had the impatience of youth."

"There was no time to know him," she retorted, nearly choking on the bread. "I had to be rid of him before he could consummate his marriage and further Cornwich's blood. I would have succeeded, but my dress stayed my step." She held up an imaginary dirk with one hand as she bit furiously into the bread. "I got soap in his eyes and grabbed his dagger. I could have killed him. I was so close."

"Maybe 'twas more than your dress that stayed your step." Gertie eyed her suspiciously and folded her arms across her chest. "He is a handsome man, Riley. Maybe your vision was more clouded with lust than his was with suds."

Riley looked through the bars at her, slowing her chewing as she fought the anger that welled inside of her. "I will forgive you for that insult, cousin. But only because I know how angry and disappointed you are in me."

"Angry and disappointed?" She sighed. "Nay, I am burdened beyond endurance. Now I shall have to get you out of here." She clasped her hands around the cold bars as if to emphasize the weakness of flesh against steel. "And it won't be easy. I was here six months before you, and I know what a strong fortress this is. I've searched the castle thoroughly, and there are no tunnels. When we escape, we'll have to go down the garderobe and out across the dry moat."

"Enlist Daggot's help," Riley said eagerly. "We can escape tonight."

"No." She shook her head. "We would freeze to death before reaching London. We must wait until spring. I'm sorry, cousin, but there's no other way."

Tossing her bread aside, Riley wiped her mouth on the back of her hand. "You don't understand," she said helplessly. "He wants a child from me. By spring I may be ripe with his bastard."

"What?" she asked, her brows furrowed in shock. "To punish you?"

"No, not to punish me. His wife is sickly, and he thinks to spring his heir from my loins. 'Tis a sweet plot and would gain my revenge on Cornwich. But, Gertie . . ." She paused and pushed a curling red tress from her face. "If I have his child, I give another soldier to the battlefield. How can I birth a baby, knowing that he will grow up to slaughter or be slaughtered? How can I nurture a child in my womb, knowing that he will grow up to be my enemy, the enemy of his own mother?" She sipped from her bowl of spiced wine and glimpsed at her cousin hesitantly. "It would be unnatural. Besides, he might grow up to be an even worse monster than his father." She shook her head at the hopelessness of her situation. "Lynchburg is an enemy far more powerful than any we thought to face here. He killed Richard."

"Richard is dead?" Gertie gasped, disbelieving. She covered her mouth with her hand, feeling a stab of nausea.

"Aye and by Lynchburg's own hand."

"My child," she breathed, "this man is of the devil."

"He is," she agreed, dusting her mouth with her fingers. "But in the end there can be only one victor. And it will be Richard's son, Edward. I know that he will come forward to lead the cause." She picked up a morsel of swan and popped it into her mouth. "Never has there been so noble a son to take his father's place. Edward will make a splendid king."

Gertie reached through the grate and gripped Riley's hands anxiously. "You can help him become king, Riley. You have the power."

She drew back in amusement as she chewed the swan. "What power? I am in prison and may soon be pregnant with the bastard of my enemy. My only hope is to escape before I can conceive."

"No." Her eyes brightened hopefully. "You must gain Lynchburg's trust so that he will tell you secrets in bed. He will come to you night after night, and you must charm him as Delilah did Samson. Discover the Lancastrian battle plans. When we escape in the spring, we will take his secrets to the Yorkists in London. The Lancastrians will be destroyed. And we will have whatever we wish from King Edward." She shook her gleefully, delighted at her own cleverness. "You will have the husband of your choosing and Cornwich's lands, too, if you so desire."

Riley gazed at Gertie with the patience of a mother listening to a child's fantasy. "Bah, 'tis a feeble plot. The earl will tell me nothing. If I become with child, then he will have nothing more to do with me."

Her eyes narrowed slyly. "You will not become with child, Riley."

Pulling her hands from Gertie's grip, she waved her away. "If he beds me, I *will* become with child." She picked up another morsel of swan and shoved it into her mouth.

"You can prevent it. I will bring you a pouch of hempseed from the kitchen. 'Tis kept in the pantry for crushing to make oil. When eaten, it causes the womb to become barren."

Riley eyed her in warning. "If Lynchburg discovers it, he will kill me."

"Nay," Gertie said softly, running her hands along the grate. "What does Lynchburg know of hempseed? He is a man, and all men are worms to be easily ensnared in webs of deceit. You will succeed." She chuckled. "And Edward will succeed. The Snowden name will be restored to its rightful place of wealth and honor. And England will again be ruled by a true king instead of a whimpering weakling."

"You speak with such assurance." Riley sighed. "Riley the giant slayer. Riley the kingmaker. I'tis lovely to my ears, but I think it best for me to escape from Lynchburg."

Gertie scowled at her, and her fingers coiled around the bars like thick snakes. "You summoned me to France, remember? And I went gladly. 'Help me, cousin,' you mewled on my shoulder. 'I wish to fight, for I have nothing else to live for but the restoration of my family name.' " She splayed her hands across the grate framing her cousin's jailed visage. "More than anything I wish to have my dead husband's name restored. So I put my faith in you, Riley. I spent my last farthing to bring you back to England. Now here you are, the last Snowden, strengthened by the blood of your slain kinsmen, the last hope of removing our attaintment. If you are not up to the task, then surrender now. And go back to France!"

Riley's eyes widened with apprehension. "Please don't be angry with me, cousin," she pleaded. To return to France, penniless, homeless, without family or future, was unthinkable. She realized that she would rather die in England fighting for the honor of her family, than return to France in hopelessness.

"Oh, Gertie, I am sorry for my cowardly thoughts. Please forgive me. I do want to stay and fight. I will not surrender."

"Well, then." Gertie leaned back on her heels. "You must do as I say. Deliver Lynchburg's army into the hands of his enemies. And hope that God speeds our dear Edward to the throne."

Riley raised her bowl of spiced wine in a shaky salute, then brought the bowl hesitantly to her lips.

Chapter Six

In the morning, Riley awoke to the smell of fresh-baked bread. It caressed her nose and lifted the veil of sleep from her eyes.

"Wake up, Rose, I brought you breakfast."

She squinted one eye up at Daggot, who was kneeling before her, holding out a loaf of bread and a bowl of steaming oatmeal.

"Oh, Daggot, that smells lovely," she said, sitting up. As she reached for the bread and bowl, her blanket fell to her waist, and her hair tumbled haphazardly about her shoulders. "I have never felt so famished."

"You slept well enough. It took me a while to wake you."

She pulled off a chunk of bread and dipped it into the oatmeal. As she bit into it, the taste sent ripples of pleasure through her.

"What else is there to do in a dungeon but sleep? There is no light here, no sense of time. I shall go mad if I remain in this rathole much longer."

Daggot's face brightened, and he smiled at her, proud to be the bearer of good news. "You are to go free this morning. The earl told me to escort you to his solar."

She felt a catch of fear in her heart. "Is the earl waiting for me?"

"No, he has ridden off with the steward. He's looking over his estate."

"Of course," she said smugly. "'Tis *his* estate. For a while, anyway." She licked a dribble of oatmeal that ran down her finger.

"I am to lock you in the solar. And no one is to know that you are there."

Her brows arched slightly in question. "Why did he order you to do this? Why not one of his own men?"

"I am one of his men now," he said proudly, straightening his back. "I have sworn my loyalty to him. And he has promised me land if I serve him well."

"'Tis good that you have given your allegiance to this man?" she asked.

He nodded in happy agreement, and she imagined the great Lynchburg offering this boy some parcel of sod, and Daggot scampering like a puppy to lap up these crumbs from the master's table.

"I asked him if I could guard you."

Pulling off another chunk of bread, she dredged it through the oatmeal. "And he allowed it though he does not know you?"

"At first he was suspicious of my intentions. But I told him that I wished to prove myself to him. What . . . I really . . . wish"—he stumbled over his words, lowering his head in embarrassment—"is to be near you, to protect you. I fear that he plans to try to dishonor you again. Why else would he want you locked in his solar?"

"Do not interfere with him, Daggot," she warned, stuffing the bread into her mouth, "do you understand?"

"Aye, I mean no." He gave her a puzzled frown.

"If he beds me, then so be it. For your own sake, you best stay out of his way."

"But what of his wife?" he whined. "I hear that she remains cloistered by choice. Why does she not attend him? I don't understand her reluctance."

"She cannot abide the beast," she grunted between chews.

"Why can she not abide him?" He held out his hands in question. "The maids seem well enough taken with him. Even ol' Gertie says he is a handsome man."

"The maids are taken with every man. And Gertie's eyes are dim with age." At the thought of him locked in the arms of one of the maids, a cold anger crept through her. "'Tis a weak lord who does not rule his passions," she muttered.

"He is not weak," Daggot quickly disagreed. "He is part stallion, part wolf. He is like a wild thing, long hair and feral eyes." His face displayed his boyish exuberance. "A man like that cannot long withstand the confines of a castle. You should have seen him when he rode out this morning. 'Twas as if he could not ride hard enough to leave this place behind."

She bit into the bread and chewed it slowly, thoughtfully. "And what about you, Daggot? Do you wish to be like him? A wild thing?"

"Aye," he said. "I wish to prove myself in battle so that I can become a knight."

The image of an awkward boy like Daggot wielding a sword on a battlefield was almost comical. She reached out and stroked his cheek, bringing a flush to his face.

"'Tis a shame the world cannot be conquered by love. You would be of the highest nobility." She smiled at him sadly and dropped the last bit of bread into the bowl. "I wish to leave this dark place, Daggot. Take me to the monster's lair. At least there I can bask in the warmth of a fire."

"Do not fear the master," he said as he assisted her to her feet. "When he spoke of you, his tone was gentle. If he beds you, he will be"—he paused, unsure of what to say—"patient with you."

"I shall pray so," she said, sweetly.

"I will not hold it against you, Rose, if you lay with him. He will tire of you soon, and then I will offer for you."

She looked at him in shock. "Daggot! I did not know the depth of your feeling for me."

His face flushed a deep scarlet as he scuffed one foot across the floor. "'Tis as deep and as vast as God's heaven," he blurted.

"Oh, Daggot," she said, dusting the crumbs from her hands, "you do not even know me. Nor would you wish to." She gave him a wary glance. "There is much I must tell you about myself someday."

"I do not care about your past," he said, timidly plucking a crumb from her sleeve. "I know not what you did before you came to Glenwood, and it does not matter. I will accept your past whether it be pure or brimming with sin. You may tell me all now, and it will be forgiven."

She pressed two fingers against his lips. "Hush, sweeting. Someday you will know everything there is to know about me. I promise. And when that day comes, I will reward you for the kindness you have shown me." She would give him several acres of her choicest farmland, she decided. Smoothing the wrinkles from her skirt, she preceded him from the dungeon like a queen leading her most loyal attendant.

When they entered the solar, she was surprised at how different it looked from the night before. The bed had been assembled next to the fireplace, and she marveled at the size of it. The silk mattress stuffed with feathers was large enough to sleep five men, and high enough for at least two cots to be stored beneath it. The room had a masculine smell to it, an odor of musk and smoke. It was Lynchburg's scent, she realized, remembering the warmth of his skin and the smell of his hair against her cheek.

She could imagine him slumbering in this massive bed, his shoulders naked and glowing softly in the firelight. Warm and comfortable. A flicker of need glimmered deep in her heart. Suddenly aware of her own stale smell and dirty clothes, she ordered Daggot to prepare a bath for her at once.

Within the hour she was stepping into the tub, the steaming water embracing her calves. Daggot, having fulfilled her request, had left her alone in the vast and quiet room, locking the door behind him. As she sank into the tub, the water felt glorious as it rose up over her flesh. She grasped a bowl of dried rose petals and smiled in pleasure at the scent of the flowers. Sprinkling them across the water, she closed her eyes as the fragrant steam enveloped her face.

She picked up the cake of soap and plunged it into the water, then ran it up and down her arms, the clean feel of it tingling along her skin.

Lynchburg, she thought with a flutter of fear and excitement in her heart. He was her enemy, but his touch had opened a door slightly, just enough for her to glimpse pleasure at his hands. The thought of another journey into intimacy with him made her burn with anticipation. And guilt.

A knock on the door startled her, and she held her breath, knowing that it could only be Daggot.

"Daggot?" she called, shyly.

"'Tis Gertie," came the abrupt reply.

"Gertie!" she cried, scrambling out of the tub. As she ran naked and wet to the door, soap bubbles rolled down her arms and legs. "I cannot let you in. I have no key."

"Nor would I expect to find a prisoner with a key," she quipped. "I have your hempseed. 'Tis in a pouch and flat enough I can slide it under the door."

"Then do so, cousin," she whispered in relief. The water ran down her thighs and calves and pooled on the floor. When the pouch appeared at her feet, she snatched it up.

"'Tis attached to a string so you can tie it to your waist. Hide it beneath your clothes and have it near you always."

"Thank you, cousin." She shivered as gooseflesh spread across her damp body. "How did you find me?"

"I followed Daggot. I knew that pup would lick the master's hand to gain access to you. Be careful that you do not destroy the boy with your mockery of sweetness. Should Lynchburg discover the boy's feelings for you, he'll slit his throat from ear to ear. He wants his bastard inside of you, not another man's. Give him no reason to doubt you, Riley, or you destroy our hope of defeating this Lancastrian fortress."

Her hand touched the door, the wood rough against her palm. "Gertie, have you heard any news of Lynchburg's wife?"

"The Lady D'Aubere has secluded herself is all I've heard. That's to her advantage I'm sure. Who would want to be married to a monster?"

Riley thought of his hands, large and warm, caressing her breasts, his lips traveling along her skin. "Who indeed." She coughed slightly to hide the tremble in her voice. "He told me that she is sickly."

"Perhaps she tried to poison herself to avoid her fate."

"Enough," she moaned and leaned her forehead against the door. She wished that she had not mentioned the girl. "Gertie, when you were married, did you enjoy coupling?"

"I bore it," she said. "Why do you ask?" Her voice was sharp with suspicion. "Do you enjoy it? Do you lust for that whoreson?"

"No," she said quickly.

"'Tis good. Because lust is a deadly sin. Keep in mind, cousin, that Edward will soon be king. He will not be kind to a woman who lusted after his father's murderer."

She closed her eyes in frustration. "I don't feel desire for Lynchburg," she insisted, yet her heart was infused with a strange need to see him again. "'Tis just that the act was not so bad. 'Twas painful but also . . . pleasant."

"Ya bawdy wench," Gertie seethed. "If you want a man in your thoughts, let it be young Edward. When he becomes king, he'll need a wife. Who better than the woman who betrayed his father's killer? Keep that in mind, my child. The truest revenge against Lynchburg will be for you to sit as a queen on the throne of England. While Lynchburg thinks to plant his bastard in your womb, you are keeping it pure for a prince. Think about the future of your family, Riley—a Snowden on the throne of England. 'Tis a sweet thought, is it not?"

It was a sweet thought, but one turned sour by her heart.

She did not want Edward for a husband, although she admired him as a fighter and believed in him as a monarch. She wanted a husband in time, but one who would give himself wholly to her. Young Edward was not that sort of man. At eighteen, he had already established a reputation for wenching that exceeded that of most seasoned men.

"Leave, Gertie, now before we're caught," she pleaded. She wanted to speak no more of Edward. Marriage to such a man would be unendurable.

"I will leave," she snorted. "But remember, my lady, keep your thoughts on politics, for that is the stuff of survival, not lust."

"I will," she feebly promised. Opening the pouch, she shook out three seeds and popped them into her mouth, chewing them swiftly.

"Saint Catherine, close my womb, I pray," she said silently, feeling a cold dread seeping through her. If Lynchburg found the hempseed, even Saint Catherine would not be able to help her. Or Gertie. Or Edward. She would be all alone, held accountable by a man who would surely be merciless.

With trembling fingers she tied the pouch around her wet flesh and mouthed another silent prayer.

Gertie ambled down the tower steps and into the corridor that would lead her back to the kitchen. It was bad enough that Riley's father was too weak to survive the Battle of St. Albans, she moaned inwardly, and had allowed himself to fall beneath De Proileau's sword. But then Riley's brother had acted so recklessly that he had gotten his family banished from England. And now Riley was lusting after the enemy!

She had brought the girl back to England to help the Yorkist cause. She had put great faith in her along with the last of her meager wealth. And what had been her reward? Riley had not only gotten herself captured, but she was beginning to feel desire for her gaoler! She muttered angrily under her breath as she shuffled into the kitchen. "Weaklings, the lot of them." Thank God she was strong, strong enough to keep a young girl's heart from the allure of love and lust. She would remind Riley, harshly if necessary, where her loyalties must remain. She had spent too many years without an identity, living under the protection of her brother. Her husband's name had been stripped from the records of England as had all references to the Snowden family. Attaintment was worse than death, for it had rendered her a nonentity. In the eyes of England, all who bore the name of Snowden did not, nor had they ever, existed.

"And who will right this wrong?" she asked herself woefully. "A little stripling of a girl whose appetite for blood is too quickly fading."

Chapter Seven

Lynchburg and the steward rode into the bailey, guiding their horses through the muddy snow. The sun was low in the sky and had set the clouds afire with bands of crimson red. The sunset reflected in the sludge as they rode toward the great hall, and the air filled with the smell of baking bread and roasting squirrel.

Lynchburg was tired of riding, having surveyed the estate enough for one day. He had visited the mills, the bakehouse, the brewery. Images of the day filled his mind and made him shift restlessly in his saddle. He longed to train with his men, to feel the sword and lance in his hands, and to test his skill against that of his finest officers. This lumbering pace of castle life was maddening.

He stared up at the south solar and imagined Riley sitting by the fire, her hair plaited in a long braid down her back and a blue velvet gown clinging to her shapely form. How he wished he could seat her beside him on the dais of the great hall. If only she had been his wife instead of the lifeless Lady De Proileau, he would be a contented man. Damn fate, he cursed as the hooves of his missodor slapped against the ground.

Chickens flew across his path, and a young girl, catching sight of him, herded them quickly toward the coop beyond the stables. A boy who was shoveling snow paused to stare at the riders. Frightened, he gripped his shovel as if needing to draw strength from it. As Lynchburg rode past the stares of his servants, he felt no sense of welcome here.

"What troubles these servants?" he snarled. "They stare at me as if I am the devil come to claim their souls."

The steward reined in his horse at the entrance to the great hall and waited for the grooms to attend them. "They do not know you or the Lady D'Aubere," he said as he dismounted. "They thought they were to have a new mistress, but they've seen no sign of anyone." He took a deep breath, dreading the conveyance of rumor but accepting it as his duty. "They gossip that you murdered your wife on her wedding night. That you murdered another, too. The young kitchen wench with the fiery hair."

Lynchburg scowled down at the grooms as he dismounted. One stepped forward to take his horse but avoided his eyes as he did so.

"My wife is in study and prayer," he addressed the steward, but announced it loudly enough for all to hear. "We wish for a child soon, and she calls upon God and all the saints to make it so." The lie lay like a stone in his heart. "If the servants have nothing better to do than gossip, then fill their days with work. Their tongues will be too tired to wag." He pulled off his gloves as he strode toward the east tower, taking deep gulps of icy air, hoping to cool the anger that burned within him.

As he climbed the steps to Jeanette's chamber, a mood descended over him as bleak and dark as the evening air. He had surveyed all of his territory and possessions this day, saving this crumb of a girl for last. She had been drugged on her wedding night, her true condition kept from him. Now he would see for himself the extent of her mental deformity.

As he entered the corridor, he noticed that her chamber door was ajar and the nun's stool was empty. He pushed against the door, sliding it open slowly, and blinked into the darkness. *Why must the room be as dark as a cave?* he wondered.

The girl was sitting on the floor, hugging herself and gently rocking to and fro. Her childlike face was blank, her eyes shadowed by dark circles.

The old nun was seated at a table and nodded a greeting to Lynchburg as he entered. Working her flint, she quickly lit the candle beside her. "Good evening, my lord. We were just finishing our prayers. Please come in."

Upon seeing Lynchburg's giant form, the girl wailed loudly and scampered to the nun, clamoring into her black robed arms.

"Now, now," the old woman cooed to her as she began to stroke her hair. "Don't be afraid. 'Tis the Earl of Lynchburg, your husband, coming to visit us."

The girl moaned piteously, her face contorted, and clung to the woman's shoulders.

"She will quieten in a while," the nun assured him. "She is unused to seeing anyone other than the chaplain and the other nuns."

Lynchburg stood rigidly, his eyes hard. "Is there anything that she needs?"

"Aye," the nun said with a kind smile. "She needs a miracle, sir."

His brows shot up as he gave her a glance of reproof. "Then give her one. You are a daughter of the church. Does the church not boast of miracles?"

"I pray for her daily, sir," she quickly uttered. As she continued to stroke the girl's head, she placed a gentle kiss upon her brow.

Curling into a knot, the girl acted as if she were trying to disappear into the woman's robes.

"The chaplain will bring us our supper soon. Will you join us?"

He stepped back, his booted feet scraping the stone floor. "Nay, I cannot stay. I just wanted to see for myself whether or not there was any hope for her."

"There is always hope, my lord," she said sweetly. "Lady Jeanette, go and give your lord a kiss."

She huddled deeper against the nun and buried her face in her hands.

"Go on," she gently prodded her, but the girl would have nothing to do with it.

"Why do you ask her to kiss a man who terrifies her?" he demanded.

The nun patted the child's head and sighed wearily. "I was only attempting to assure her that you are no threat to her, sir."

"How can she be assured of anything living in the dark like an animal?" He glanced up at the shuttered windows. "On my next visit I want to see the shutters open and light flowing into this room. 'Tis no wonder the girl has no wits about her."

"Aye, sir, we will do whatever you ask of us," the nun said agreeably. "I, too, believe that sunlight would be good for her. 'Twas her father who ordered the darkness. He was afraid that someone might see her at the window."

"Cornwich is gone," he grumbled, "and his darkness goes with him. She's old enough now. Anyone seeing her at the window would think that she is one of your order." He turned to leave, but his step was stayed by the nun's halting plea.

"My lord! If you truly wish to help her, then give her the miracle she needs."

Lynchburg glanced back at her, his eyes brightening with interest. "How am I to do that?"

"A pilgrimage." As she spoke, she cuddled Jeanette like a squirming infant. "If you would allow me to take her on a pilgrimage, she would surely be cured."

Closing his eyes in disappointment, he turned back toward the door. *The sick are always going on pilgrimages, thinking sin to be the cause of their illnesses,* he thought direly. *And here I stand hale and hearty, the executioner of a prince. I am the crack, nay the abyss, in their theory.*

"I will think on it," he said, but there was little promise in his tone.

As he stepped into the corridor, he came face to face with the chaplain, who was carrying two bowls of steaming broth. For the first time, he noticed how small and dark the man was.

"My lord," he greeted him, surprised, although Lynchburg suspected that he had been standing beyond the door, listening long enough for him to be aware of his presense. *Or else this war has made me suspicious of everyone*, he chided himself.

"May I walk with you down the corridor, sir?"

Lynchburg drew up every ounce of patience left within him and nodded in assent. As the two men walked slowly, the smell of the broth filled their heads with an almost repugnant odor.

"Is that what you plan to feed the girl?" he asked tiredly. "Can she not stomach a decent meal?"

"Aye, but she does penance by eating little," he explained.

"Penance!" he cried, astonished, and halted their slow progress. Turning to stare at the man, he searched for some sign of mockery. "Do you jest?"

"No, my lord," the chaplain replied somberly. "In order to obtain forgivness from sin, she must prove remorse."

Lynchburg stared at him, speechless, wondering if he should pitch him headlong from the highest tower window. The man was mad. "What sin did that helpless creature ever commit? She was born with no mind. How could she have ever had an evil thought in her life?"

"She may be innocent, sir, but evil can still inhabit her body. The sins of the fathers shall be visited upon the children, or so the scriptures instruct us. Her condition is a testimony to the inherent nature of sin."

"That is distorted wisdom," he said, shocked.

"Sir." The chaplain lowered his head respectfully. "Your words could be construed as blasphemy. Would you like to come with me and make your confession? I understand you have spent much time on the battlefield and need to purge your heart."

"No," he replied, his voice low and harsh. "I trust no man so well as that. When I confess, it will be to God alone." He drew himself up to his full height, displaying an even more immense and imposing figure. "Take that soup away and bring the girl a proper meal. I'll not have you starving my wife."

"As you wish." The chaplain glanced at the soup, his eyes dimming with disappointment. "I wished to speak to you on the matter of her care."

" 'Tis I who will speak to you on the matter of her care," he interrupted and was pleased to see the look of immediate resignation in the man's eyes. He wanted no trouble with this priest. "What is it you truly want? More money?"

"Aye, for a pilgrimage, of sorts," he responded haltingly. "I wish to take Lady Jeanette to the bishop to be examined by the church. They can best determine . . . healing measures."

He glared at the chaplain so coldly that the man felt as if he'd stepped out into an icy rain. With a violent shiver he turned away from the earl. "Perhaps we should discuss this another time, my lord."

Lynchburg nodded a wordless assent. *Perhaps we will*, his eyes seemed to say. The silence tightened painfully around them as they stood, pondering whatever threat the other might pose. Lynchburg was in authority over the castle, but the chaplain had the backing of the church, and they could be a cumbersome lot, Lynchburg thought glumly.

"I will check on my wife often." His voice broke through the quiet with the sharp tone of warning. "And I will determine for myself what 'healing measures' need to be taken."

When Riley became with child, it would be necessary to remove Jeanette from the care of this priest. He would find an abbey where she could be safely housed, and he would be bothered no more with this misguided cleric.

• • •

As Riley sat in the master's chair, she gazed into the fire that flamed brightly in the hearth, blackening the stack of logs. Daggot had brought in a trunk filled with gowns, chemises, and hose, a wardrobe intended for Lynchburg's wife. He explained that the trunk had come from the old solar behind the great hall and had belonged to the late Lady De Proileau, who had died there in childbirth. The steward had ordered him to take the trunk to the earl's bedchamber for the new mistress's use.

Since her dress and shift needed to be cleaned by the laundress, Riley had decided to don one of the garments. It had been years since she had been attired in silk, and she relished the look and feel of it. There was no harm in wearing one of the dresses for just a few hours, she assumed. Besides, Lynchburg might like her in it and insist that she keep it. It would be wonderful to have a new dress after years of wearing rags.

For her chemise, she chose a yellow silk with long sleeves and turned back cuffs. Her overdress was a green velvet belted beneath her breasts with a band of jeweled leather. The hemline was trimmed in yellow ribbon, and she had plaited the same color ribbon into the weave of her hair. Her long braid coiled around her head like a crown held in place by ivory pins.

At her feet was a basket containing a mound of fleece. As she pulled out strands of fibers, she rubbed them between her hands and threaded them through a spindle. Daggot sat on the floor by the fire, strumming a lute as he watched her.

"You can make my surcoat when I go to war," he suggested.

He talks like a husband, she thought as she began to twist the spindle. "This thread will be used for my embroidery. If I make enough thread, you must bring me a loom," she said, attempting to change the tender tone of his speech.

His fingers moved deftly over the strings and played a

tune that was sweet and lulling. "I will bring you whatever your heart desires, my Rose."

She glimpsed him from beneath raised brows. His face was pretty enough to be a woman's, she noted, far too soft to be a warrior's.

He stopped playing the lute and set it down next to the hearth. "I will fight the whole army of York to win you." Rising awkwardly to his feet, he stumbled a few steps, then knelt before her, laying his head in her lap.

She begin to twist the spindle faster. "Daggot, you must go now before Lynchburg returns. I wouldn't want him to catch you here. He would be very angry with you."

She stretched out her arm, maneuvering around his head to free another length of fleece from the ball. She felt sorry for him, knowing that her feelings for him would never match those he held for her.

"I will leave, but my heart will remain with you." He smiled up into her eyes. "My love will surround you like a protective shield."

"Sweet boy," she humored him. "You are my champion."

He grabbed her hand, startling her as he brought it to his lips in a passionate kiss.

The door creaked open, and she felt a cold draft stir the air. Snatching her hand away, she pushed Daggot from her lap. Lynchburg's shadow fell across them like a death shroud as Daggot scrambled to his feet, coming face to face with blue eyes that were more feral than an angry wolf's. Panic stricken, he shrank away.

Lynchburg towered above them, allowing the silence to thicken until it was near to choking the both of them. Spying the lute on the floor, his first impulse was to grab it and smash it against the wall. Closing his eyes for a moment, he fought to control his rising temper.

"I offer you land in exchange for your loyalty, and this is how you repay me?" he addressed Daggot. His voice shredded the stillness of the room. "By giving your heart to a woman who is my prisoner?"

His eyes, dripping with ire, shifted to Riley. "I give you a soft imprisonment, and this is how you thank me? By charming your guard into being your champion?"

She dropped her spindle into her basket and hurried to assist him out of his cloak. Her fingers brushed across the hardness of his shoulders, reminding her of how very strong he was.

"Oh, no, milord, 'tis not what it seems," she said breathlessly. "There is bathwater in the tub. Shall I have Daggot warm it for you?" Gingerly she shook out his cloak and spread it before the fire to dry.

"Why?" he asked with animated concern. "So that you can try to cut my throat again?"

"S-Sir, she is innocent," Daggot stammered. "D-D-Do not hurt her, please."

Lynchburg tossed the boy a withering glare. "You are my henchman. You belong in the corridor, guarding my chamber, not sitting at my hearth with your head in the lap of my prisoner. Get thee to your post!" he barked.

Daggot stumbled from the chamber, shutting the door behind him. He was free, but Rose was not, and he prayed fervently for her safety. If she were harmed because of him, he would not be able to bear his guilt. He would rather face the lord's wrath himself than have her endure it. But Lynchburg had ordered him back to his duties and undoubtedly would deal with him later.

"Take off that finery," Lynchburg ordered. His eyes fell upon Riley in accusation. "Those clothes belonged to the late Lady De Proileau, mother to my wife. The steward told me that he had ordered them brought here from the old solar. And you made free use of them to tempt your guard."

She started to retort angrily that she had done nothing of the sort, but thought better of it. It would be folly to fuel his anger. She would accept her punishment whatever it might be, and hopefully Daggot would be spared.

Besides, the earl was beginning to look more tired than fearsome, she noted. His eyes were hooded and his face grim beneath a shadow of beard.

He leaned against the wall, watching her as she unfastened her dress and lowered it to the floor. She was a stubborn wench to act so brave, he thought with admiration. Any other man would punish her all the more for her pretense, but he found her show of courage appealing.

Untying the silk string of her chemise, she pulled the flowing fabric over her head, and let it drop to the floor. In mounting embarrassment, she ungartered her hose and rolled them down her calves, kicking them off. She attempted to cover her naked body with her arms, but abandoned the effort, knowing that the darkening room would serve that purpose. Glancing up at him she tried to gauge his mood, but she could not. The setting sun had left him invisible except for the reflection of the firelight in his eyes.

"What is that?" he asked, eyeing the pouch that was tied at her waist. "You did not have that before."

She shrugged and gave him a wavering smile as her heart thundered painfully. "Aye, but I did have it last night. I removed it before you came. I had thought to go to sleep and had put it aside in the straw." She tried to talk slowly so that he wouldn't hear the tremor in her voice. "'Tis only a pouch. It contains nothing. Would you like to see?" She started to open it, but he shook his head.

"No, I do not wish to see it," he said. "I wish to see your hair." His voice had softened to a raspy murmur.

Reaching up, she quickly unpinned her hair and unwound the braid from its coil. Loosening the weave, she freed the strands and scattered them freely over her breasts in ripples of reddish gold.

There was a longing in his eyes the like of which she had never seen before on a man's face. "Lie down on the bed on your stomach," he said, an urgency in his voice.

She climbed up onto the bed and lay down across the twill cover, the pouch pressing into her stomach. The air was cool against her naked skin, and she welcomed it. Her heart was pounding so hard that she was flushed with heat.

As his hand gripped her buttock, she felt the roughness of his palm against that tender flesh.

He stared down the length of her to the dip of her back and the white mounds of her derriere. He knew that she had never fully experienced pleasure, had only tasted it, but tonight, he was determined to gratify her. He would prove to her that he was her master and there would be no other.

His fingers slipped down between her soft cheeks and found her womanhood. As he stroked her there, he felt her heat and heard her breath quicken. She was ready for him, her lips already moist and swollen. Was it Daggot's nearness that had caused this passion to brew? he wondered darkly.

Gently he slid his finger into her hidden corridor, massaging the wet flesh. It was a sweet torture, and he would not release her from it until he had heard a groan escape her lips. As he slipped his finger between the pink folds of her flesh, he felt her swelling bud of womanhood. Her body arched, inviting him to enter her, but he refused the invitation. Instead, he withdrew his fingers, leaving her shuddering with frustration.

As he stroked her nether lips, he felt the quiver of excitement coming from deep within her.

"Oh," she breathed loudly as he slipped his fingers into her nest of curls and began to tease her with gentle friction. She felt a pulsing in her loins, and her nipples grew hard and elongated, pressing into the twill fabric. Her mind became inflamed with desire, and she felt as if her heart was consuming her entire body, turning it into one throbbing mass. Her hips twisted slightly as a tingle radiated from deep within her.

She sought him now in mindless obsession, her thighs opening wider to receive him.

He increased his pace until her moans filled the chamber. The glossy elixir of her body bathed his fingers, and he knew that she was fast approaching her peak. Her skin took on a pink hue and was misted with a fine sweat, reminding him of a dewy rose at dawn. As his fingers thrust and wiggled inside of her, her body began to shake with spasm after spasm of jolting pleasure. Her cry rose up, piercing the quiet, and her buttocks lifted, her hidden corridor sealing to his fingers, pulsing and brimming over with a hot lather.

Like a breaking wave, she collapsed onto the bed, her hair spilling across the cushions, her face flushed and her eyes closed as if she were stunned.

Slowly so as not to hurt her, he withdrew his fingers. The room was completely dark now but for the dying glow of the logs. He pulled the curtains shut around the bed and lit a candle.

Strolling to the door, he opened it and walked through the antechamber into the corridor. Daggot stood guard beyond the door, his back straight and his eyes fastened rigidly on the tower stairs.

"Daggot," he addressed him firmly. "Your duties are over for the night. Go to supper and then to your bed."

"Sir," Daggot responded, a slight tremor in his stance. "May I speak with you?"

One brow arched sternly upward as Lynchburg eyed the groom. "Aye," he consented, a glow of reluctance in his eyes.

"Milord," he whispered, so frightened that he could barely speak. "I was wrong to neglect my duty and will suffer the consequences of my wrongdoing. But Rose is innocent. I wish no harm to come to her."

"No harm did," he said. His eyes were cooler now, his demeanor calmer. "I do not fault you for loving her, Daggot. But 'tis not to be." He reached out, his hand still wet with her passion, and gripped the boy's face. "She is mine. Do you understand that?"

Daggot swallowed hard, fighting back tears. "Aye, milord. She—she is yours." His heart was breaking, and the pain felt as if it were splintering his chest.

Lynchburg released him and patted his shoulder paternally. "Take you to your bed and think no more on her."

"Aye," he agreed and turned to flee.

"Daggot?"

He froze. "Milord?" he responded weakly.

"Take that trunk back to the old solar. I will tell the steward that 'twas not needed."

"As you wish."

He held up his hand, stopping him. "Then go to the barracks and summon my officers to the great hall. I wish to meet with them at once."

"Aye, milord." He nodded as he hurried into the bedchamber. He could not look at the curtained bed that imprisoned Riley. Hoisting the trunk into his arms, he slunk past the earl and exited the chamber.

Lynchburg shut the door behind him, then walked to the bed with a heavy gait. Snatching back the curtain, he found Riley lying naked and curled on the bedspread, her breath still panting.

"Please do not harm him," she pleaded and watched in alarm as the color rose in his cheeks. The glow of the candle lengthened the shadows beneath his eyes and gave him a surreal appearance.

"Do you love him?" he demanded.

She laughed nervously. "I love him as I would a puppy or a butterfly."

He glared down at her and contemplated delivering a few painful smacks to her naked buttocks. "He is not a puppy," he stated gruffly. "He is not a butterfly. He is a man. Do not toy with his heart in hopes of gaining your freedom."

Freedom, she thought. It was not a very alluring thought at the moment. She was warm by the fire and satiated with pleasure, her every nerve purring with contentment. "Aye, milord," she agreed.

"You will earn your freedom when you pay your ransom. You will not gain it at the cost of a good man. Now, leave me."

She raised up on her elbows and stared at him, befuddled. "Leave?" she asked, her voice strained. "You wish me to leave? Where am I to go?"

"You will return to your kitchen tasks. I will be leaving tonight, and I don't know how long I'll be gone. You will work in the kitchen and say nothing of me to anyone. If the servants ask you where you've been, you will tell them that you were imprisoned but are now pardoned. Is that clear?"

She slid from the bed, her bare feet padding across the rushes. He had claimed her so easily and just as easily had cast her aside. Sullenly she snatched her wool shift and tawny dress from a peg on the wall.

At least they are freshly laundered, she thought and held the clean fabric against her skin. Its fresh smell would soon perish in the grease and smoke of the kitchen.

"I will return to the kitchen if that is what you wish," she said, her voice trembling with anger. "And when summoned I will come to your bed like an obedient whore."

Grabbing her arm, he spun her around to face him. "You are not my whore," he corrected her. "You have not been elevated to that status. You are my prisoner. The kitchen may not well suit you, Lady Riley, but 'tis a far sight better than the dungeon. Do you not agree?"

She tried to pull away from him, but his grip was like iron.

"I warn you, I am not Daggot to be manipulated by your clever tongue and your black heart. I am a soldier at war. I am your gaoler and your master until the day your ransom is paid."

He released her, and she felt the blood rushing back into her arm.

"I well understand my position, Lord D'Aubere," she said crisply, rubbing her arm, "and the terms of our bargain." After slipping on her dress, she ran from the chamber without even a backward glance at him.

Striding into the great hall, Lynchburg mounted the steps to the dais and waited for his officers to arrive. They came quickly, the red-haired Irishman, Roark, followed by Sir

Miles Stanton and Sir John Lambrey. As they joined him on the dais, he called for wine.

Gertie shuffled forward with a silver goblet for the earl and bowls for the three officers. She poured their wine, then hastily retreated into the shadows.

Lynchburg raised his goblet. "God save the king," he mumbled.

"God save the king," the others repeated, lifting their bowls.

"I am glad you called us together," Roark began. He sipped from his bowl, staining his rust-colored beard with wine. "The winter is harsh, and I fear for our men. They will grow bored here. No battles, no tournaments. We must challenge them else they will lose their luster."

Lynchburg set down his goblet and idly fingered the rim, a listless gesture that puzzled the men. "They will not remain here long enough to lose their luster. There is no threat of harm to this fortress. I have made a thorough check of the area. I saw nothing amiss."

"Shall we rejoin the queen's forces then?" Miles asked eagerly.

Lynchburg rubbed his hands across his eyes and thought for a moment. "No, she has not summoned us, nor will she until she is near London. Edward is in the Welsh Marches recruiting an army. Soon he will receive word of his father's death. Then he will hear that the Lancastrians are marching toward the capital." He scratched the stubble on his cheek, then propped his elbows on the table, resting his chin in his hand. "He will try to reach the city ahead of us. Once there he will proclaim himself king."

"Then he will murder Henry in the Tower," Roark predicted bleakly.

Lynchburg smiled at that remark. Did these warriors know nothing of politics? "Nay, he won't murder Henry. It would be folly to do so. Most of the magnates are still loyal to Henry. If Henry dies, then the Prince of Wales will be king in their eyes. And the little prince will be a far more effective ruler than his father." He lifted one eyebrow and stared pensively toward the center of the hall where the fire burned low. "No, Edward will not murder Henry, but he will plot to murder the prince. Once the boy is dead, then executing Henry will be a matter of little significance."

"What must we do to stop Edward?" Roark asked.

"We must ride to Wales," Lynchburg replied and took a slow sip of his wine.

"But we do not know how great an army he has recruited." Roark held up his hands in bewilderment. "His army may far outnumber us."

Lynchburg shifted his gaze to him and stifled the urge to clout him with his wine goblet. "Am I a fool to lead my men against an unknown foe? We aren't riding into Wales to attack Edward. We are riding into Wales to recruit Lancastrians for the queen's army. That will hinder Edward's recruiting efforts and detain him longer in that country." He finished his wine, and Gertie hurried forward to replenish it. "By the time he reaches London, it will be too late. The queen will have the city under siege."

The three men nodded in agreement.

"When do we ride?" John asked.

"Tonight. I care not to remain another night within these walls of hell."

The men looked at one another, their eyes alight with curiosity.

"Your wife does not please you?" Roark asked, and the other two men looked on him in shock. Only an Irishman would be so brazen as to ask the earl such as a question as that. "I hear that she is in constant prayer," he continued innocently. "I, too, married a woman who wishes to be nearer to God than to me. 'Tis a lonely union, although there are three of us in it."

Miles frowned and rolled his eyes. "I have the opposite problem. My wife wishes me nearer to God than to her. Twice she's tried to kill me."

The men snickered at that comment, and even Lynchburg managed a smile.

"You should make her fear you, my lord," Roark suggested, thumping his fist on the table. "Respect is born from fear."

Miles scoffed and gingerly cupped his bowl. "Nay, my lord, give her a child. That will turn her attention to more earthly matters."

Roark set down his bowl and splayed his hands across the table as if preparing to rise. "Let us rouse the men and prepare the horses."

"Wait," Lynchburg urged. "There is another man I wish to take with us. The groom, Daggot."

Roark laughed. "That peasant boy who licks your boots?"

Lynchburg shot him a look of warning, one brow sharply arched. "He is no peasant. His father owned his own farm. The boy was educated by the parish priest. He wants much out of life, and I like the ambition I see in him."

Miles raised his bowl, draining it in one final gulp. "Any pretty maid can dream a dream, but only a man can seize it on the battlefield. I question his skill as a soldier."

"As do I," Lynchburg said with a sly grin. "Soon I will know if he is as skilled with a sword as he is with a lute. For now, he will be my henchman, and he will learn from the other men."

The men glimpsed one another uncertainly. "What if Edward engages us?" Miles asked. "The boy will die. You mean to destroy him?"

"No, I mean to make a man of him." He set his goblet down with a thunderous clap. "He has been too long in the company of women. He gives his heart like a puppy to any skirt that trails past him. He needs to run with the wolves for a while."

"What if he will not go?" Miles asked.

"He will go," he stated, his tone afire with confidence. "He has sworn his allegiance to me. He will go."

The night ahead would be long and the ride difficult, Lynchburg knew, but it would be a welcome relief from his domestic nightmare. As he walked out into the bailey, he spied the east tower where his wife resided, then his eyes darted to the south tower where his prisoner had spent the afternoon, twisting her spindle like a spider. He was glad to send her back to the kitchen. Drudgery would keep her busy, and her reappearance would quell the rumors that he had murdered her.

He had no fear of her escaping. She would entertain the idea, surely, but there was no way out for her, not until the snows melted. By then she would be heavy with child. Calling for his squire, he headed toward the stables.

Chapter Eight

Three weeks later

T he master is returning!" the herald shouted as he rode past the gates and into the bailey.

Riley could hear the clanging of a bell, warning the castle folk that the master and his retinue were fast approaching. Although she was tired, her heart lurched at the thought of seeing Lynchburg again.

For hours she had been scrubbing the floor of the great hall beneath the glare of the castellan. Her knees were red and sore from incessantly kneeling on the hard stones, scrubbing with a stiff brush.

"I have not knelt this long since I last did penance," she said smartly.

The castellan scowled at her, his beefy hands propped on his hips. "There is no penance harsh enough for the likes of you. I trusted you to care for the master, and you put soap in his eyes."

"And he put me in a dungeon. Was that not punishment enough?" Angrily she scoured the floor and felt her dress growing heavy with water. "I shall catch my death of cold down here," she fumed.

"Good," he said, his eyes skimming her. "Then we shall all be free of the curse of your presence."

Rearing back, she pitched the brush at him. It spun through the air and grazed his forehead, causing his head to snap back from the blow. "Then scrub the floor yourself, sirrah. I will not be treated worse than a dog."

He grabbed his forehead and checked his palm for blood. Seeing none, he shook his finger at her face. "The master will hear about this. You'll pay for your willful ways. Now get thee to the kitchen and wait there."

She hurried into the kitchen, glad to be free of her intolerable task. As she sank into a corner by the fire, she felt tired and cold, and her knees were throbbing. The servants were too busy to notice her as they prepared the evening meal, turning the air thick with the smell of wine and spices.

Shouts from men in the bailey alerted her that Lynchburg's band of Lancastrians was arriving, and she shivered in anticipation. It had been weeks since she had last seen him, and the thought of his return caused a strange longing inside of her.

"I do not miss him," she scolded herself. "I would rather fear him than miss him." But no matter how hard she tried, she could not fear the touch of his fingers on her most secret places or the soft warmth of his lips on her breasts. But it was more than just his sensuality that she missed. She missed his nearness.

She wondered what it would be like to share with him the simple intimacy of companionship—a game of chess, a pleasant conversation, an early-morning hunt.

Battle plans. Political secrets.

The intrusive thoughts shook her brief contentment. The secrets she longed to discover were not those of his army, but the ones buried beneath the steel plates and rough chainmail of his shielded heart.

Who is the man beneath the warrior's facade? she wondered with a faint smile.

Gertie dropped a sheepskin coat into her lap and jolted her from her daydream. "The master returns," she whispered. "Go out and listen. Find out what you can of Lynch-burg's journey."

The confusion of feelings swirled inside of her until she felt dizzy. Even though she was drawn to him, she knew that it was her duty to hate him, her mission to betray him. She could no longer breathe in the crowded and noisy kitchen. Pulling the coat about her shoulders, she strode out into the snow.

The sun had set an hour earlier, leaving the bailey dark. Only the flames of torches lit the grounds as riders gal-loped past the gatehouse. She heard the horses hooves and saw the air filling with the white fog that flowed from their nostrils. As she strolled along the stone walls, she watched the men dismounting, their shadowy figures layered in furs and cloaks. Soon the bailey would be overflowing with mounted knights.

Leaning against a wall, she watched the dark and shift-ing forms and wondered hopefully if Lynchburg were among them. Grooms were emerging to take the horses to the stables, and knights were tromping past her, heading for the great hall. One of the men pushed back his woolen hood, revealing a mop of black curls.

"Daggot!" she cried, stopping him in midstride.

As she grasped his arm, he almost sputtered in fright. "Rose! What are you doing out here in the cold?" Looking fearfully toward the gate, he pulled his arm from her grip. "Go inside, please."

"I heard you went with Lynchburg into Wales." Strands of red hair wound across her face in the wind, and she gen-tly brushed them from her eyes.

"Aye, I rode with his army. I am his henchman now." He sidestepped away, putting a distance between them. "You shouldn't stand so close to me. If the carl should see us, he would be suspicious."

She planted one hand firmly on his shoulder, halting his escape. "I wish you no harm, dearest. I only wish to know if your journey was profitable? Was Edward detained?"

"What do you know of Edward?" He stepped back, detaching himself. Without waiting for an answer, he strode toward the great hall.

"I only know that Lynchburg wished to detain him," she said, scurrying to catch up with him. "Was our lord successful?"

"Aye." He paused and turned to face her, his eyes beaming with reverence. "Lord David recruited an army of Welshmen so that there were very few left for Edward to recruit."

She grasped his arms, hoping to anchor him to the spot if only for a few more moments. "Will Edward be able to fortify London with such a small army?"

"I don't know." Gently he pulled away.

She was puzzled by his unrelenting attempts to avoid her. After only three weeks with Lynchburg's army, he had become a knight exemplar, the very soul of unwavering loyalty. "What is Lynchburg's next move? Will he ride after Edward?"

"He will await the queen's orders," he said as he turned away and headed for the portal.

"Where is the queen?" she called after him.

He stopped and glanced back at her in bewilderment. "Why so many questions about things that do not concern you?"

"Rose!" It was the castellan's voice, and she leaped at the sound of it.

Looking back at Daggot's boyish face, she saw a sharpness in his eyes. His personality had lost the softness of innocence, and there was a maturity in his stance. His posture was that of a confident man.

"In trouble again?" he asked, his face breaking into a smile.

Good God, she thought, *he looks amused!*

The old Daggot would have escorted her into the kitchen, pleaded with the castellan, helped her. To her distress, the new Daggot strolled into the great hall, leaving her abandoned.

Running through the portal of the kitchen, Riley felt the castellan's fleshy fingers lock onto her elbow.

"The master is returned," he stated matter-of-factly. "Now you'll account for your shrewish ways."

She could hear the barks of greyhounds and the raised voices of knights as they began filling the great hall. Above it all she could hear Lynchburg's voice, strong and commanding.

The castellan snatched her down the corridor and thrust her into the chamber. The floor was muddy from boots tramping across it, and she thought angrily of the hours she had spent scrubbing it only to have it ruined.

On the dais the earl sat in his white doublet and scarlet houppelande, and her heart thrummed at the sight of him. His hair was brushed back, and his face was bearded beneath eyes that looked fatigued. Still he was a magnificent-looking man.

She gave a small cry of surprise as the castellan wrenched the coat from her shoulders.

"You'll not be hiding in sheepskin like some innocent lamb," he blared, flinging the coat to the floor.

As she watched helplessly, he made his way to Lynchburg's side and whispered in his ear.

The noise from the crowd was deafening, and the earl slammed his fist down for silence. The room grew quiet except for the thudding of a greyhound's paw against the floor as she scratched her ear.

"What has that wench been about?" he asked tiredly. His eyes swept across the room until he found her. The torchlight filled her red hair with sparks of fire, and his eyes could not help but soften at the sight of her.

Her heart tripped, and she fought the urge to smile nervously back at him.

"She has been obstinate and violent," the castellan announced.

He reared his head back and looked up at the man in bemusement. "Violent? How so?"

"She pitched a scrub brush at my head and clipped me good."

There was a low rumble of laughter among the men, causing the castellan to color in embarrassment.

"Better a brush than a dagger, my good man," the earl commented with a grin.

"Aye, milord, but I wish to have her punished," he insisted.

"Then do so. Why do you bring this tiresome case to me?"

Gertie hurried forward and poured wine into his goblet.

"Because I wish to turn her out."

Lynchburg stared at the castellan, his face displaying a trace of concern. "That would be a death sentence." Lifting the goblet to his lips, he sipped the warm wine. "Can her dismissal not wait until spring?"

"No, milord. By spring she will have brought down the very walls of this castle with her incompetence."

He nodded, mulling over the castellan's suggestion. "Then I suppose I must dispose of her. But I will not turn her out into the snow and wind. I will take her to a pagan village on the morrow and sell her into service to the heretics."

The men laughed loudly and even the chaplain had to smile.

Why must he publicly humiliate me? she wondered. *First the servants in the kitchen deride me, and now I must be subjected to this. Have they no sense of honor? Well,* she thought, *if humiliation is Lynchburg's sport, then he will find himself outmatched.*

"I protest, milord!" she shouted, bringing startled gasps from the crowd.

The chamber fell into silence, and the earl's smile faded into shock. Slowly he rose from his chair and eyed her in glowering contempt.

"How dare you speak to me without permission."

Her hair spilled wildly across her shoulders, framing her face in a glory of fire. Her chest heaved, eager to spew

out venomous words, and her fists clenched at her sides. "I
will speak my mind with God's permission!" she cried.
"There is a higher authority than you, Lynchburg, though I
know it amazes you to hear that truth."

There were muffled gasps among the crowd.

"I will not stand here and be made a mockery of," she
continued. "If I am to be banished, then so be it. I will walk
out into this winter's night and be gladly banished. The
cold air would be of more comfort to me than your
warmest fire."

His eyes sealed on her, molding to her very soul as she
stood her ground, refusing to be silenced. She had nothing
left to lose to this man but her life. And if he wanted that,
too, then so be it.

She had been a fool to long for him, to nurture a fantasy
of companionship. It would be wiser to make a pet of a
snake than a companion of Lynchburg. *Years of loneliness
have driven me to this madness,* she thought.

"I will turn her out," the castellan offered eagerly.

"No," Lynchburg snapped. "I will handle this matter
personally."

He gazed at her with an air of vindication. "Take her to
the dungeon," he ordered the castellan, "and if she gives
you any trouble—bind her hands."

"No!" she cried as the castellan strode through the
crowd. He grasped her arm and pulled her from the hall.
"Do not bind me."

As he pushed her out through the portal, she saw the
ashen face of Daggot.

His eyes were as filled with anger at her as they were
with pain. "Why did you rile him?" he demanded in more
of a manly tone than she had ever heard him use.

Before she could answer, she was dragged away. Nausea clawed at her stomach as the castellan led her back to
the dungeon. *Why,* she thought angrily, *didn't I cut my own
throat or pierce my own heart rather than be taken prisoner?* As she was shoved back into her cell, she sank to the

floor, fighting a sense of defeat that threatened to over-
whelm her.

She would survive, she decided, rallying her determination. She would survive, and someday she would ask King
Edward for these lands and make of all of them ragpickers.
She would be the mistress of Glenwood Castle, and the
castellan would bow to her will. Someday, she thought
with a sniff as the portcullis slammed shut, and the darkness blanketed her in a deepening silence.

She was so tired from her day's work that she quickly
fell into a deep sleep, but her dreams were soon interrupted
by the very real and angry voice of the master of Glenwood Castle.

Chapter Nine

"Wake up, 'tis time to depart." The harsh tone ripped through Riley's sleep, jarring her awake.

She opened her eyes and spied Lynchburg standing over her, his legs splayed and his furlined boots reaching up to his knees.

No wonder he is such an effective warrior, she thought. *The sight of his powerful build would shrivel the courage of even the finest soldier.* As she threw off her blanket, the air pierced her with cold, and she trembled visibly.

"Here," he said, dropping a cloak of black wool to the floor. It was a thick garment lined with rabbit fur, and she eyed it warily. It looked to be full of fleas.

"Thank you, milord, for tossing me this bone," she said caustically. "Shall I raise up on my hind legs and lick your hand?"

"You will feel my hand if you don't get moving." His voice was steady and hard, his stance unyielding.

She sat up, rubbing the sleep from her eyes, and felt for the small pouch of hempseed at her waist. "Where are you taking me?" she asked.

"That is not for you to know," he replied.

"I demand to know." Folding her arms stubbornly across her chest, she sat back on her heels. "I will not budge from this perch until you tell me."

"Need I remind you that you are my prisoner?" His voice, though controlled, rang against the walls. "You will be appreciative for that cloak, and whatever else I, in my eminent mercy, choose to bestow on you. But you will not demand anything of me."

She clamored to her feet, kicking the cloak from her. "I will not wear a cloak offered to me by so vile a man. I will walk out into the snow and die of cold before I touch the flea-ridden rag."

He grabbed her arms and pulled her to him, raising her up onto the balls of her feet. Her face tautened as she bit back a gasp, refusing to allow him to see her pain.

"You will put on that cloak. And you will follow me out into the bailey. Or I will drag you there."

She squirmed away from him, freeing her arms. "Tell me where you are taking me," she said quietly, refusing to rub her burning flesh. She would not yield to his power. "I am only asking to know my destination. Is that such a difficult request?"

He reached down and snatched up the cloak, wrapping it around her in one swift movement. Before she could cry out in protest, he had picked her up and hoisted her over his shoulder. As he headed down the corridor, her head banged against his padded back.

"Where. Are. You. Taking. Me?" she asked, her words broken by his strides.

They mounted the stairs into the main passageway and burst from the tower into the rosy light of dawn. His feet crunched against the ice as he crossed the bailey and, with a thud, deposited her into the back of a wagon. As he threw a deerskin blanket over her, she uttered an oath.

"If you make one more sound," he warned, "I will nullify our agreement." His face looked dark against the sunlit sky, his eyes raw with determination. "I will send you to Cornwich wrapped in that deerskin like a piece of meat thrown to a wolf. Do not challenge me on this."

She did not doubt him, monster that he was, and held her tongue.

He climbed onto the wagon and snapped the reins, causing the mare to lurch forward. Beneath the blanket she could feel the wheels rattling over the drawbridge then bumping along the rutted road of Northampton. Wrapping the blanket tighter around her, she lay like a puppy buried in its mother's fur. Only now that she was hidden from his view did she gently massage her arms where the ache was already fading. She wished she could raise up just enough to see where they were heading, but she didn't dare provoke him any further.

The air grew colder, and she realized that they had moved out of the light of day and into the forest. Pushing back the fur, she spied a canopy of trees overhead, their branches gray and bare against the winter sky. Bravely she raised up on one elbow and watched Lynchburg steadying the reins of the mare.

Thin streams of light fell through breaks in the trees, and the air was filled with a haunting mist.

"Where are you taking me?" she asked.

"Down a peg or two," he replied.

With an exaggerated sigh she clutched the blanket up under her chin. "That was accomplished when you threw me into a dungeon and bedded me."

He glanced over his shoulder at her, his face showing his astonishment. "How you twist the truth like sheep's wool into yarn. If you had not tried to kill me, you would not have been thrown into a dungeon. And you agreed to be deflowered. We made a bargain, did we not?"

"Aye, we did," she said glumly. "You demanded a babe as my ransom, and I agreed to pay it. When King Edward finds out about that, he will deal harshly with you."

He pulled on the reins, bringing the horse to an abrupt halt, and turned to face her. The fire in his eyes was white hot in the snowy air, and she felt herself cringe as if burned. She wished that she could slide back under the cover and retreat into the past before she had uttered those words.

"That boy is not your king," he said, his breath as white as steam.

As much as she wanted to hurl an angry retort at him, she knew that doing so would not help her cause. If she were ever going to gain his secrets, she must be a temptress, and a temptress had a honeyed tongue, not one that cut like a blade.

Lowering her eyes meekly, she took a deep breath and thickened her determination. "I am sorry for my serpent's tongue," she apologized.

His fierce eyes smoldered with suspicion. "You are a woman of many moods, Lady Riley."

"No, milord," she said sweetly, keeping her eyes downcast. "I hiss like a cat only when I am frightened or have been caged. When I'm treated kindly, my moods are most pleasant."

Slapping the reins, he jolted her back into the bottom of the wagon. *Swine,* she thought, pulling the cover up around her.

"Now that we are alone and there is no one to hear, I am taking you to Buckhall," he said. "'Tis Cornwich's hunting retreat."

There would be servants there. She could get a message to Gertie. "Thank you milord," she said. Sitting up, she gripped the side of the swaying wagon. "It will be nice to feel a roaring fire at my feet again."

"We won't be staying at the manor house." He steadied the reins as the horse plodded down a narrowing path. "There are servants there who will talk. Instead we'll be in one of the cottages bordering the estate. And it will be just the two of us."

"What need have we of servants, milord?" She rested her hand lightly against his shoulder. "We will get along well enough without them."

Gingerly he brushed her hand away, and she saw the deep scars etched across his knuckles. "Your gentle mood astounds me," he said. "I trust it not. I suspect 'tis a ploy to divert my attention so that you can plant a blade in my back."

She laughed lightly as if he had just expressed the most ridiculous thought she had ever heard. Looking at his back, she tried to picture a knife embedded there, but to her dismay, she could only picture her fingers caressing the naked flesh between his shoulders.

Lying down in the wagon, she pulled the deerskin up to her neck and closed her eyes, trying to block him from her vision. Even in her innermost darkness, his form took shape. She wondered briefly what it would be like to kiss him, to feel the potency of his touch when given in tenderness. Her eyes flew open, and she realized that she was becoming his prisoner in more ways than one for his essence was beginning to penetrate the sealed borders of her heart. By wanting his companionship, she had wanted him to *like* her, to reciprocate feelings she was apparently harboring for him. And now she was wanting a kiss given in tenderness? What next? she chided herself. A marriage proposal?

With a groan of self-loathing, she pulled the deerskin over her head, smothering her thoughts.

Within the hour they had arrived at their destination, a timber-framed house made of wattle and daub. The thatched roof was a deep gold color and the outer walls were gray with mud. It was hidden within a copse of fruit trees and surrounded by thick holly shrubs.

Grabbing two bags of clothes and supplies, she hopped down from the wagon. As she walked up to the cottage door, she could smell the musty scent of the interior and wondered how long it had been since anyone had lived here. There were no windows, and she imagined the inside to be dark and cold. "Another prison albeit a more palatable one," she speculated aloud as she pushed the door open and stepped inside.

A charred circle of stones outlined the fireplace in the center of the floor. A wooden table stood against one wall, and straw was banked against the other to form a bed. It wasn't much different from the spartan crib she had endured at the convent.

When Lynchburg stepped into the room, he had to duck his head to keep from striking it on the doorframe. Standing just inside the door, he was silhouetted against a shaft of soft daylight, and the sight of him caused a strange comfort to stir within her. With his bow and quiver of arrows gripped in one hand, he had the appearance of a protector, a provider. It had been a long time since she'd had any sense of home and hearth, and her memories drew her back to her father's manor in Kent, the winter hunts with her father in the deer park and long nights nestled in his arms, listening to her mother's stories by the fire. Her throat constricted with sorrow at the memories of her lost family.

She set the bags down on the table and waited, wondering if she would finally receive some morsel of kindness from her conqueror, some small gesture to ease her captivity.

Looking around, he nodded in satisfaction as he hung his bow and quiver on two pegs beside the door. "This will do," he said. "We'll only be here long enough for me to plant my seed in your belly."

Was there no warmth within him? she wondered angrily. *Why would he not toss her some crumb of kindness so that she need not feel so alone?* "My lord," she ventured, her voice straining to hold back her pain. "I have lost everything to this war. If you must plant your seed in my belly as you say, then I ask only for some small show of kindness." She knitted her brow at him, her green eyes pleading. "No seed grows in winter, sir. The coldness of your heart will kill your seed as frost does a fertile field."

He gazed down at her with a quiet and contemplative air. Crossing one arm over his chest, he propped his elbow on his fist and brought his hand to his chin, scratching along the stubble of his cheeks. "So I must be kind to you or else . . . you will be barren? I have never heard of this condition in women. Is it particular only to you?"

She detected the amusement in his tone and felt defeated by it. Would he mock her even now that she must plead for his warmth? She bowed her head, feeling small before him. "There is no castle enclosing us, no servants watching us, and no army surrounding us." She kept her eyes fastened on the floor, unable to look at him for fear she would see laughter on his face, and the guarded center of her would shatter into weeping. "We are alone now—two human beings each in need of what the other can give. Should wc not have a truce?"

He angled his head to better see the expression on her lowered face. "A captured prisoner does not offer a truce, my lady, but a surrender. A truce is a compromise. A surrender is complete submission. And I will accept nothing less from you."

She gritted her teeth in mounting rage. "Must you speak only in terms of battle?" Her words seemed to hiss through her teeth. "Can you not speak from your heart?"

"I guard my heart, Riley, as I do my lands and all else of value to me. What is it you want?" he asked, tersely.

"Some small show of affection," she murmured, her breath catching anxiously on each word. "Is that too much to expect?"

Shc walked to the straw pallet and sank down upon it, resting her head in her hands. How could she have asked him for affection, she wondered, miserably. She may as well have asked it of a wolf. Besides she should be used to her solitude by now. It had been over a year since she had held another human being in her arms and that had been her dying mother at the convent.

She closed her eyes, a sudden tear of grief escaping down her cheek. There had been no last words exchanged between them nor had there been in years. Her mother had been silent since the night they had been driven from their home.

Riley could still hear the horses galloping across the grounds toward the manor house, their powerful hooves charging through the blackness of night, and her mother's hysterical screams as the sheriff read the order of attainment.

Her screams had not been directed at the Lancastrians or at the sheriff or at his armed guards, but at Riley's brother.

"You have undone us all!"

Those were the last words her mother had ever spoken. She had been a kind woman, a woman of peace who had deeply loved her family. *And how like my father and brother I am,* Riley thought bitterly. She closed her eyes tighter, but another tear squeezed past that sealed portal.

Lynchburg stood stiffly, enduring an awkward silence. *By God,* he thought, *the girl weeps and for what? Affection? What childishness is this?* He stepped toward her cautiously as a wolf sniffs about a trap. An angry and defiant prisoner was easy to handle, but a weeping one was quite beyond his realm of experience. He wondered what he should do? To hold her would be a dangerous gesture, a signal of weakness. But if they were going to be housed in this small space for an indefinite period of time, then her constant melancholy would drive him insane. If an embrace, albeit brief and tepid, would end her moping, then he would provide it.

Despite his warrior's instincts, he eased toward her.

She lifted her head when she felt rough fingers stroke her cheek. At first, she wanted to spring back, but there was such warmth in his callused hand that she felt drawn into its comfort.

"I admit that I am a cruel man, Riley." He cupped her face in his palm and shuddered at the exquisite softness of it. "The need to survive brings out the beast in us all." Taking her hands in his, he lifted her to her feet. Such small hands were completely swallowed up by his own. "But I am still capable of certain human traits." Slowly he opened his arms to her, and she fell into his protective embrace, feeling strangely free. There were no servants to spy on her, no Gertie to rage at her for her weakness. The burdens of loss and imprisonment seemed to flow out of her as his powerful limbs enfolded her in a beautiful, dark warmth. She nestled her head against his breast, inhaling the spicy smell of the forest that lingered on his cloak.

There was strength in his touch, and she sensed that it came from deep within him, not just from the physical locking of arms. There was a thread of caring that was binding him to her. His face dipped closer, his nose catching the scent of her.

How long will I be able to avoid surrendering to him in

this close and rustic environment? she wondered. Already her hatred had given way to her need for his strength and embrace. And her emptiness was crying out to be filled. Closing her eyes dreamily, she let her mind drift on the pleasant current of the moment until it struck the rock hard image of Gertie.

You summoned me to France, remember? And I went gladly. 'Help me, cousin,' you mewled on my shoulder. 'I wish to fight for I have nothing else to live for but the restoration of my family name.' More than anything I wish to have my dead husband's name restored. So I put my faith in you, Riley. I spent my last farthing to bring you back to England. Now here you are. You are the last Snowden, strengthened by the blood of your slain kinsmen, the last hope of removing our attainment. If you are not up to the task, then surrender now. And go back to France.

She drew back horrified, realizing that Gertie had sacrificed everything to bring her back to England to fight, not to surrender to a child's need for love. "I will not surrender. I am your prisoner, milord," she blurted as she moved away from him. "And I must get used to my station."

Dropping his shoulders, he rolled his eyes in frustration. "You ask for affection, then you turn away from it?" He huffed as he began removing his houppelande. "You are like a spoiled child who weeps for a toy, then throws it down." Yanking off the garment, he cast it aside and pulled at the buttons of his doublet.

She wiped her damp cheeks, her heart pounding as the fabric slipped away from his shoulders, revealing his naked back. As his doublet fell to the floor, she glimpsed his muscled buttocks and his thighs that were shadowed with dark hair beneath his hose.

"I am sorry, my lord. 'Tis just that I didn't expect to enjoy your embrace so much," she struggled to explain. She knew that Gertie would be furious if she had witnessed this scene. She could have pretended to surrender to him. That was what Gertie would have wanted her to do, to obtain a closeness that would have brought her nearer to his secrets.

But instead she had driven him further away. It was the feel of his arms, the masculine cushion of his chest that had held back her deceit, she realized. How could she betray him when he was offering her a solace so genuine that it had melted her pretense and had laid bare her deepest needs?

He crossed the room and, picking up a satchel from the table, pulled out a bundle of clothes. They were not fine clothes, she noted, but a shirt of plain wool that had been dyed green with vegetable dyes and a tunic of brown linen.

As he pulled on the shirt, she noticed that it was buttonless with a loose neckline, the type worn by farmers. The tunic came down over his head and covered his back, falling to his knees. He girded it at the waist with a leather belt then slipped a large brown hood over his head. She marveled that he was even more handsome in the peasant garb than he had been in his finery.

"May I have a change of clothes as well?" she asked, holding out the skirt of her dress. "I fear that these foul rags are not fit for the eyes of a lord. Do you not wish for me to burn them?"

"Aye," he replied absently. "Burn them whenever you please. You need no clothes at all for the purpose that you serve."

So, their relationship would be nothing more than sparring words and cold sex, she thought sullenly. And that was her fault. She had asked for affection, and he had given it.

He would not do so again.

"Have you ever loved anyone, Lynchburg?" she asked, startling herself by posing the question.

He glimpsed her warily, the glint in his eyes penetrating the darkness of the room, reminding her of an animal crouching in the night. "I love honor and all who embrace it."

"That is a politician's answer." She sighed, tucking her hair behind her ears. "Will you not speak from your heart?"

"I have been too busy defending England to woo women," he grumbled and picked up his knife, strapping it to his waist. "I've never had time for such foolishness."

"A man who thinks love is foolishness is already a fool."

He grabbed her roughly, lifting her from the floor so that her face was even with his own. There was a power emitting from his eyes that intimidated her into silence. Her body hung in his embrace like a sack of grain, painfully drained of its strength.

"Stop playing your child's games with me, wench."

Before she could respond, he had abruptly set her back on her feet. "I begin to think you wish to have my heart," he accused her. "And not on the end of a dirk." Peering at her intently, his eyes bored down on her until she turned shyly away. "Is that your ploy? To gain my heart as your victor's prize so that I will be your fool? As Samson was Delilah's?"

She felt a paralyzing shock of fear, for he had used the same analogy that Gertie had used before sending her on this mission.

With a half grunt, he walked to the portal and opened it as if he were leaving. Pausing, he turned back, having remembered something he needed to tell her. "You have not been interrogated as a prisoner of war, a failing of mine which I must remedy."

She blanched at his words and watched him calmly stroll from the cottage, his final statement filling the air with a deathlike ring.

Interrogate me? she thought frantically. *What did he mean by that?* He would not harm her, she was certain, for he needed her to conceive his child. What answers would he demand from her, and what methods would he use to obtain them? As she waited in the dimness of the cottage, her fear became intense, almost maddening. Would he bind her and question her relentlessly until she revealed all? Would she be forced to confess Gertie's part in her scheme? No, she would never tell him anything about Gertie, bound or not. Perhaps there would be no questioning, she tried to convince herself. He was merely enjoying making her suffer in a prison of fear and uncertainty.

When he returned with the firewood, she was waiting with a pale smile. He piled the wood in the charred circle and began to work with his flint to start the blaze. The sparks took root in the sticks, and the flames began to crackle as dusky shadows danced about him.

"Do you wish me to prepare a meal for you?" she offered kindly, hoping to divert him from any thought of interrogating her.

He stood up, dusting his hands. "No, I don't wish for you to cook. The fire is to keep you warm."

"But I must cook for you," she insisted, looking about the room. "There are no servants here."

"Nor is there anyone here deserving of them," he replied. "I will cook. First I must hunt else there will be nothing to put in the pot. If you're hungry, look through the supply bags, and you'll find bread. When I return . . ." He gave her a brief and knowing glance. "You and I will have a lengthy . . . conversation."

Ducking through the doorway, he headed back toward the woods. She ran to the door and watched. Slinging his bow over his shoulder, he strode into the surrounding woods, leaving a trail of rustling branches in his wake.

She searched the bags until she found a dry crust of bread but ate very little of it. She had not felt such anguish since she was a little girl, waiting for punishment after inflicting some mischief on her nurse and not knowing what her fate would be—a lecture or boxed ears. If only Lynchburg had told her what to expect, the waiting would not be intolerable.

Tossing the bread aside, she sat down on the straw pallet and ran her fingers through the chaotic tangle of her hair. The dungeon had been bad enough, the lack of fresh clothing insufferable, the mockery inhuman, but now she must wait in a darkness of ignorance.

Looking down, she saw the dirt stains on her woolen dress and a louse crawling along the sleeve of her shift. With a cry of disgust she pulled the garment from her before the creature could infest her hair. She was tired of her own failures and of her treatment that was less than that of an animal.

You need no clothes at all for the purpose that you serve, Lynchburg had said as if she were no different from a wild creature that prowled the surrounding forests. Well then, she decided, she would become like an animal and live only in what God had provided her. Nothing would be better than filthy rags swarming with vermin. Her mind was wrought with confusion and swelling with panic. Peeling off her dress, she ripped it in half and tossed it into the fire. The smoke billowed up from the burning fabric and rolled upward toward the holes in the thatch.

She kicked off her deerskin shoes and shoved them under the straw mattress. When she had pulled off her shift, she tore it into pieces, then slowly fed it into the fire. The smell of burning wool filled the room with a horrid stench. Wrapping a blanket around her, she settled down near the flames and waited for her gaoler to return.

He will have no time to question me, she thought with a shudder, *for he will be too busy searching for a dress to clothe me, a clean dress, not lice-infested wool. I will no longer be food for vermin or the victim of inhumane treatment.*

Her eyes flickered open, and she realized that she had dozed off. *The sun must be low in the sky,* she thought groggily. The cottage had grown very dark, and the fire was nearly out. As she sat up, she had the strangest sensation that the floor of the cottage was vibrating with a steady thud. Standing up on weak legs, she walked naked to the door and opened it a crack, feeling the cold air stinging her body. A rider was charging up the forest path, and she slammed the door shut, throwing her back against it.

Now what? she wondered. Hurriedly she grabbed the fur-lined cloak and wrapped it around her. Snatching up the blanket, she ran to a corner and laid down, burying herself beneath the heavy layer of wool.

A horse galloped into the yard and halted.

"Lynchburg! Lynchburg!" the rider shouted as he slid from his mount.

It was an unfamiliar voice.

"Lynchburg!"

She heard boots slap against the snow-wet ground as the man walked toward the cottage, then the sound of his knuckles rapping harshly against the door. Her every nerve seemed to spring at the sound.

What if he comes into the cottage? she wondered miserably. *What if he throws back the blanket and finds me?*

"Merriweather, my friend."

It was Lynchburg's voice, and she nearly wept in relief.

As the door creaked open, she peeped out from beneath the rim of her blanket and saw two men standing in the doorway. Lynchburg carried a swollen sack, and she assumed that it was filled with fresh game. His hair was strewn about his face, and his eyes shone through the strands like a sunny brook through the brush. She had never seen him look happy before, but at the sight of this visitor, his face radiated joy.

"Aye, my good man," Merriweather greeted him and clasped his arms around him in a bear hug.

The two men were of equal height, and she could tell that Merriweather was the older of the two. His hair was flecked with gray, and his face bore the lines of age.

"What brings you here?" Lynchburg asked.

He glanced inside as if searching for someone. "I asked for you at Glenwood Castle. Your henchman, Daggot, directed me here. Are you hunting with your new bride?" He emphasized this last word with a mischievous wink.

"Aye," he said, and turned quickly away from his friend. "The land is good for hunting. What news have you of Henry's army?"

Riley saw that Merriweather's eyes were suddenly shadowed with discouragement. "There's time enough for that. Can a man not get a bowl of spiced wine after a long ride?"

"Come into the cottage," he invited him and stamped his boots against the stone stoop, breaking the mud from his soles.

As Lynchburg strolled through the cottage door, he

dropped the sack on the floor. Three furry rabbit heads slipped through the opening, coming almost nose to nose with Riley. She held still beneath the fur cover, not daring to even breathe.

"Where is your bride?" Merriweather asked, his eyes darting about the tiny cottage. "I see not so much as a hair ribbon to hint of a woman's presence."

Lynchburg laid down his bow and quiver of arrows. Grabbing a wineskin from the bag of supplies, he poured a bowl of wine for his visitor.

"She must be hunting. I'tis a fine day for hunting," Merriweather observed. "There must be many stags in these woods."

Lynchburg's face turned to stone as he handed him his bowl, saying nothing.

He eyed his friend carefully. "Are you happy with her, David?"

Lynchburg looked as if the sun were setting in his eyes, turning them the deep violet color of the sky at dusk. "She is a good woman," he replied.

"Does she please you?"

"How can she not?" He smiled sadly at his friend. "She is as meek as a lamb. Now, tell me why you've come. What word have you of Henry's army?"

He took a deep sip of wine and swallowed noisily. "It grieves my heart to tell you."

Lynchburg stiffened at that response, his gaze deepening with concern. "Do so anyway," he urged.

Raising the bowl to his lips, he took another swallow of wine, then snorted, clearing his throat. "Queen Margaret sent Jasper Tudor to fight the Yorkists at Mortimer's Cross. Edward won the battle."

"What?" He looked as if he could not stomach what he was hearing. "God's blood! Was Tudor killed?"

"No, he is at York and is yet safe." He stared down at the stones of the floor, unwilling to watch the anger and shock that was about to cloud his friend's face. "His father was captured. Edward beheaded the old man in the market at Haverfordwest."

"Owen Tudor is dead?" he said, disbelieving. "King Henry's stepfather is dead?"

"Aye," he nodded, his eyes remaining downcast. "He laid his head on the block—that head that once leaned against the breast of a queen."

The image of the old man executed by traitors twisted inside of him, and he drove his fingers deep into his hair. "I must go to Margaret."

"Aye, she sent me for you. You are to meet her troops at St. Albans outside of London."

"Good. If she is going to St. Albans, then she has agreed to take London. My father-in-law will be there as well." He ground one fist into the palm of his hand. "Together we can drive the Yorkists from the capital and free Henry from the Tower. How many men ride with her?"

"A few hundred, no more than that."

He nodded thoughtfully. "I will assemble another five hundred from Glenwood Castle and meet you at St. Albans."

Tipping up the bowl, Merriweather sucked up the last swallow of his wine and tossed the bowl onto the table. "We will meet again then in a day's time," he said, wiping his mouth on the back of his hand.

"Aye, in a day's time," Lynchburg assured him.

The two men embraced, then Merriweather went quickly on his way.

Riley remained huddled unseen in the blanket, her heart aching. The Lancastrians were going to attack London and try to capture the city. It was her duty to keep Lynchburg from going to St. Albans. Without his leadership the Lancastrians might not win.

"You can come out now," he called to her as he glanced toward the lump in the blanket.

Throwing off the heavy cover, she sucked in the fresh air. "I was near to suffocating, I was. Buried alive."

"I apologize for your brief discom . . ." He stopped and began to back up, his boots scraping the floor like a befuddled boy. "Riley, had I known that you were so eagerly anticipating my arrival, I would have returned home without haste."

Pushing long tresses from her face, she looked up at him and saw the reflection of the fire burning low in his eyes. In horror she remembered that she was naked, her breasts exposed to his view. Embarrassed, she pulled the cloak across her chest, covering herself.

"There was a louse on my dress," she said, squirming uncomfortably beneath his gaze. "Besides, you told me that I needed no clothes at all for the purpose that I serve. Now that I am naked, you must fetch new clothes for me, clean clothes, not scratchy, lice-infested wool."

He cocked his head at her as his eyes roved hungrily along her slender form. "I think I shall keep you naked," he said. "I like you better this way. Besides, I'll have no fear of you escaping."

She wilted in embarrassment. "P-Please milord. To be naked all the time would be too humiliating, not to mention unhealthy." She clutched the cloak tighter about her. "I could catch cold. I beg of you, go to Glenwood Castle or to the village. And bring me some fresh clothing."

"Would you feel better if I took my clothes off, too?" he asked. Grinning wickedly, he removed his cloak.

"Nay, do not," she pleaded, but he was already pulling off his tunic, revealing the hard outline of his shoulders. The sight of his nudity scintillated down her every nerve, and she shut her eyes tightly. She didn't want to see him naked. She didn't want to want him.

"Look at me," he ordered.

Her eyes flew open, and her senses reeled at the sight of him. He was naked with his back to the fire, the flames casting a crimson aura around his body. She wanted to feel his arms around her again, the rough brush of his whiskers against her cheek. She wanted him.

"Let it drop," he implored her, his manhood rising with heated passion.

She obeyed, letting her cloak slip from her shoulders.

"If I tell you what to do to pleasure me, will you do it?" he asked.

She nodded fearfully, yet felt a tremor of excitement within her.

"Take my shaft in your hand," he gently ordered, sinking back on the pallet of straw.

Kneeling between his legs, she slid her hands up the hairy terrain of his inner thighs to his manhood. She gripped it and began to stroke it, her fingers warm and soft, producing a powerful effect.

Closing his eyes, he allowed her touch to consume him, and all of his strength was drawn into that lengthening, thrusting shaft. He could not help but smile at the idea of this slight girl rendering one of the queen's warriors as weak as a feather in the wind.

The golden curve of his throat was tempting, and she leaned forward, kissing his neck where the scent of pine lingered along his skin. He opened his eyes in pleasant surprise as she nibbled his throat, leaving a trail of warm kisses down to his breastbone. He felt too weak even to breathe. Laughing helplessly, he raised his hands as if he would push her away.

"Milord," she admonished him. "You are ticklish."

He took her waist between his hands, his fingers spanning its slender breadth, and pulled her on top of him.

"Aye and in all the right places," he said, his eyes gleaming. "I want you to sit astride me. Can you do that?"

"Aye," she said, feeling a quiver of need. Taking his shaft in her hand, she began to ease it into her as she lowered herself down onto his lap.

Arching his back, he felt her heat sear him and a simmering pleasure flood through his body. When the full measure of him was inside of her, he cupped her buttocks in his hands and began to raise and lower her, showing her the rhythm that he needed.

The friction felt warm and made her knees go weak as she grasped his chest, kneading the muscles in her hands. He was powerful like a mythical beast, his muscles taut and hard as stone. Although the room was cold, a sweat soon misted her brow.

She rode him gracefully, her body rising and falling against his shaft, her eyes glistening in anticipation of that moment when life would render up its purest joy. Quickening her pace, she pressed her hand against her swollen loins and moaned at the heightened intensity of her pleasure. Her senses were melding into one powerful sensation. There was no longer any grief or vengeance or war. There was only she and this man, rising above the din and smell and rancor of the world.

To her frustration, he lifted her from his shaft and tossed her onto her back. Lowering himself against her, he pressed his chest to her naked breasts until she could feel the thudding of his heart deep within him.

"Take me," she wanted to plead but bit her lip to stop herself. The last thing she wanted was to admit to him that he could conquer her in this way. He was still her enemy.

He teased her with the tip of his cock, rubbing it playfully between her nether lips. Moaning, she tried to pull him into her, but his body was unyielding. Just as she felt she would go mad with desire, his manhood filled her sweetly, hungrily. He stilled at his task, letting her feel the hard length of him embedded within her, driven like a banner into conquered territory.

"Am I your master?" He grinned down at her.

"You are my captor," she breathed. "I am your prisoner."

"Am I your master?" he asked again, and withdrew his manhood to the borders of her sex. She was throbbing, starving for his seed to be released.

"Aye," she panted, gripping his buttocks. "You are my master."

The grin faded from his face, and he entered her fully, bringing a cry of passion from her. "My lady," he said, concerned. "Do I hurt you?"

"Oh, no." Her words shivered past her lips. "'Tis just that I feel you so thoroughly."

He lowered his head, and she felt his lips softly fluttering against her neck, followed by his warm, moist breath. "What does it feel like?"

"Magnificent," she breathed.

Thrusting into her, he heard her scream, a sound so wild that it could have emitted from the depths of the woods. She clung to him, her breath hissing between clenched teeth.

"Do you wish to feel more?" he murmured.

"Aye, I do," she pleaded as she writhed beneath him.

He thrust harder, causing her passions to flame wildly through her until they ignited in explosive release.

With one final thrust he released his seed and filled her with new and intense sensations. She felt her body melting into the straw beneath her, then the coolness of his skin, wet and clinging to her own.

Sagging against her, he could feel the wild pulse of her heart. "Am I your master?" he whispered in her ear.

"Aye," she said, dazed. "And I am yours."

"Aye," he agreed.

He rolled off of her and reached for her hand, wanting to feel the silken touch of her fingers nestled in his own, wanting to bring them to his lips in a lover's caress. With his other hand, he lifted a strand of her hair to his nose and inhaled the scent of roses. He was acting intoxicated as if he'd drunk too much and was in a languid state of repose.

It was near impossible to get up, to stagger to his feet like a satiated simpkin and look about the room in a haze of confusion. "I must go to the village and fetch you some clothing," he murmured. "For as long as you are naked, I will have you. Which means that I may forsake all else and never leave this cottage again."

He pulled on his hose and realized with a deep yawn that if he was to appear in the village he must dress the part of a lord. As he donned his fine doublet and houppelande, he watched his prisoner drifting off to sleep.

Sitting down next to her on the straw, he gazed at her, his eyes lingering on every feature. Her mouth was the color of roses in full bloom in the warmth of spring, nourished by the sun. Her face was as pale as fine pearls, and her hair was aglow like polished copper. Picking up the deerskin blanket, he gently draped it over her so that she wouldn't chill.

"The village," he thought tiredly. Surely there would be some lass who would hand over a dress or two for trade. But what would he give her in return? Rabbits? he thought, eyeing the sack in the corner. The peasants could not hunt the land because it belonged to the lord. Rabbits would be a prized relief from chicken and salt bacon.

"A dress," he said with a contented sigh. "My country is at war, and I am out bargaining for a lady's dress. Any man would think me a crazed fool." He stared down wistfully at the sleeping girl. "Or a besotted one."

This cannot be, he thought, scratching the stubble on his chin. *I cannot be enamored of this wench.* Standing up, he grabbed his cloak and swung it around his shoulders. "Saint George, deliver me from that destructive a curse."

As he headed out the door, he snatched up the sack full of rabbits and began to whistle low the memory of a minstrel's tune.

Chapter Ten

Riley awoke to the smell of roasting rabbit, her naked skin warm beneath the blanket. The straw mattress poked her through the fabric, and she shifted onto her side trying to find a more comfortable spot. Lynchburg was squatted before the fire, turning a rabbit on a spit as the flames crackled, and the air filled with spirals of smoky warmth. She smiled fondly at the sight of him. His haunches were thick and sinewy beneath his hose, powerful enough to guide a warhorse in battle while his hands were occupied with the mace and sword. His brown hair fell down his back and nestled between his shoulder blades, beckoning to her to comb her fingers through the soft strands.

"Did you bring me a dress?" she asked sleepily. Reaching out, she slid her fingers down his spine in a long, leisurely stroke.

"Nay, milady," he replied and removed the spit from the fire.

Sitting up, she pulled the cover up over her breasts. "What do you mean, 'nay'?" she asked angrily.

He laid the rabbit on a stone to cool and unsheathed his dagger. "I went to a farm nearby," he explained, wiping the blade on his sleeve. "The family is very poor. 'Tis winter, after all. They had nothing to spare. But I gave them two rabbits anyway."

"Why didn't you go into the village?" she asked accusingly. "There are weavers and spinners there. And perhaps a peddler with fine cloth for sale."

"There was no time." He swiftly sliced a thigh from the rabbit. "'Twas dark."

"Are you afraid of the dark?" she asked in exasperation.

"Aye." He shrugged, turning to her with a smile. The blue of his eyes stunned her, and she looked away as if she had just glanced into light that is too bright.

"You are lying, sirrah," she said, her lips turning down in what he considered to be a very luscious pout. "You wish me to be naked."

"I wish you to be naked?" He laughed. "I was not the one who tossed your clothes into the fire."

She clamored from the bed, wrapping the blanket around her. "Please go back to Glenwood Castle and bring me a fine dress."

The smile faded from his face, and his cheeks darkened with anger. "I cannot go back to the castle to fetch a dress. No one must know that we are here together." Turning back to the fire, he sliced the other thigh from the rabbit. "I am suppose to be hunting, and you have been banished to a far-off village. Remember?"

"I need clothing!" she cried in frustration, her hair tumbling about her shoulders as she wound herself tighter into the cocoon of her blanket.

He gave her a look of idle indifference. "You are a prisoner, milady. Prisoners do not have fine clothes."

"Prisoners who are members of the nobility are allowed to have clothing befitting their station," she pleaded. "I need something to wear."

"You need nothing but to be on your back in my bed." He laughed, reaching for her, but she leaped away.

"How much more must I endure from you?" she cried. "I have no freedom. I haven't a stitch of clothing. I haven't even a gillyflower to set upon my table. Only a whoreson, a beast, would treat a woman so shabbily."

Her words faded into a vacuous silence as the room took on a dark cast. She felt as if she were trapped in the open with a violent storm threatening to break from the clouds. Her blood chilled as she watched him rise to his feet, a blue vein bulging from his neck. Backing away, she suddenly felt cornered in the small cottage.

"Whoreson, am I?" he bellowed. "Be careful what names you cast at me, witch, or your words may become reality." Picking up a stool, he threw it against the far wall, shattering the wood. "I can be a whoreson." He grabbed a bag of flour from the table and slung it to the floor, sending up a cloud of white powder. "I can become the monster you claim me to be." He kicked the table, toppling it over onto its side.

"I am sorry," she said and truly she was.

He glowered at her, his eyes red and wild as he spoke in a voice that shook with anger. "I will not be flayed by your tongue anymore." He pointed toward the fire. "Now sit down by that fire that I built for you. And eat the supper that I prepared for you. And stop calling me names!"

"Yes, milord," she whispered.

Her eyes searched the floor for the roasted rabbit. Seeing it unscathed, she walked through the cloud of flour to retrieve it. Picking up the blackened meat, she tore off a piece with her fingers and tasted it. It was unseasoned and bland. Licking the grease from her fingers, she eyed Lynchburg across the room. His anger had touched her passion with a spark of excitement.

She wanted him in a carnal way and could not deny it. The memory of him pressed hungrily against her, his manhood easing between her thighs made her feel weak with longing. But she could not love him, she tried to convince herself. He was incapable of evoking love. He was her enemy. He was married! No, she sighed as she tore the tender meat from the bone, she most certainly could not love him. Swallowing the morsel of rabbit, she tossed the stripped bone to the floor.

The cottage grew darker until she could see only the dying embers of the fire and the outline of Lynchburg's broad shoulders as he sat, cupping a bowl of wine in his hands. A draft filtered in through the roof, touching her face with fingers of ice and causing the flames to flicker.

"Go to bed," he quietly ordered. "'Tis cold in here. You should be under more blankets."

Not wanting to witness any more destruction this night, she obeyed him. She climbed onto the straw pallet, and pulled an extra blanket over her as she watched him. He rose from his perch, his shadow drifting across her, and began to move restlessly about the cottage.

She remembered his threat to question her, and the fear it evoked, his fingers biting into the flesh of her arms, and the pain he caused. She remembered the beauty of his embrace, the pleasure of their sexual intimacy and the comfort of his nearness. How could she fear him and yet be drawn to him? She should despise him, yet she wanted him. *How can this be?* she thought. *I must be going mad.*

Throwing off the covers, she crawled from the bed and rose unsteadily to her foot. As she walked naked across the chilly room, he watched her as a man might watch the approach of a wild animal, unsure of its intent. Kneeling beside him, she rested her hand on his shoulder.

"I am sorry, David," she spoke softly and saw the stern glow rise in his eyes.

"You are not my equal," he reminded her coldly. "Do not use my familiar address. You will call me 'my lord.'"

"My lord," she began again. "'Tis cold in the bed. Will you come lie with me? I need your warmth."

He cocked his head at her in question. "You are lonely for me?" he asked in a low, cautious tone.

"Nay," she said with a shake of her tousled head. "I am cold." She ran her hand down his arm and fondled it gently. "I wish to feel you beside me."

"Then you are lonely for me," he said, his eyes slanted in accusation.

"Aye," she confessed with a roll of her eyes. "I am lonely for you."

He stood up, sweeping her into his arms and carrying her to the pallet as if she were prey about to be devoured. Never had she felt so deliciously helpless. There was an animal scent to his tunic that fueled her desire.

"You want me?" he asked, seeing the flush sweep across her cheeks.

"I wish to lie in your arms," she whispered weakly. "It comforts me."

He laid her on the pallet and stepped back to remove his tunic and hose. As he crawled naked into bed beside her, he felt strangely comforted, too. Nestling against her, he felt the velvet warmth of her flesh and a need to possess her, protect her.

"You must get up," he ordered, and she sat up quickly, confused by his directive.

He shifted to the other side of the pallet and guided her to his left. "You cannot sleep to my right," he explained. "That is my sword arm. And I may have need of it during the night to protect us."

She smiled and buried her face against his neck, her breath tickling him until he laughed.

"Go to sleep," he commanded. Grabbing her head, he pushed her down into the crook of his arm and threw one leg over her slender torso. "I must ride early in the morning and I need to rest."

"Might you ride tonight?" she asked invitingly and placed her palm gently against the curve of his back. His manhood had already hardened to iron and was pushing hungrily against her stomach, causing him to bite back a curse.

"Is it your ploy to win this war by exhausting me?" he muttered, almost incoherent with need.

"Aye," she replied, her breathy tone like a wind to his fire.

The heat leaped angrily within him, demanding release. As he rolled over on top of her, he felt her body supple and moist, opening to receive him.

"Exhaust me," he challenged her. His hand slipped between them and found her moist thighs spread wide for his entry. His rod slid easily into her, and he shuddered as pleasure engulfed his senses.

Groaning beneath him, she pulled him harder into her. "I can exhaust you," she assured him. "Give me a rhythm to match the beat of my heart, and you will be exhausted."

She was soft and lush, her sex drawing him into her pulsing wetness. *You exhaust me already,* he thought, *assaulting my senses with your warmth and beauty.* He thrust into her, his heart racing as he transcended all human experience and rose to an apex of unparalleled pleasure.

"I should ride you for real," he gasped. "Turn you over onto all fours and propel you to a fine finish." His thrusts became fierce as he increased his pace.

She ran her tongue along her lower lip, her mouth succulent and darkening to a deep reddish hue. Her eyes were filled with such intense desire that they appeared feverish. She was out of control, her head tossing on a pillow of auburn silk and her sex thundering within her. It was too much to bear. Her center began to break apart, then shatter into a thousand flaming fragments.

As her climax faded, the fire within her burned to glowing embers. Yet lingered. She opened her eyes and looked at him, at the naked emotion on his face. Their loins were spent. But she felt a fullness in her heart. She had seen affection in his eyes, true affection, the yearning of one human being for another.

As he lay down beside her, his breath raced and the hard lines of his chest rose and fell in rapid succession. There were no words spoken between them. Both had seen the look of the other in the aftermath of their release. It had been an unguarded moment, dazed with gratification.

"Go to sleep," he ordered gruffly.

Resting her cheek against the warm damp flesh of his

chest, she could not help but smile. "Aye, milord," she said
sweetly.

Closing her eyes, she wondered if she were already
dreaming.

As the light of morning seeped in under the door, she
awoke and rolled herself tightly into the blankets. Sitting
up, she realized that she was all alone. The fire had died to
glowing ash.

With a deep yawn she looked at the mess Lynchburg's
anger had wrought the night before and felt a twinge of regret. She had called him a whoreson and a beast, but she
couldn't remember why she had called him those names.

Standing up, she swaddled herself tighter into the warm
blanket and crossed the room, leaving her footprints in the
flour. As she gathered up the pieces of the stool, she heard
a horse trotting up to the door. *Lynchburg,* she thought and
felt a nervous spring in her heart. She tossed the broken
stool into a corner and righted the overturned table, pushing it back against the wall.

He walked through the cottage door, stamping the mud
from his feet at the threshold. A smile of mischief creased
his face when he spied her, and she puzzled over his boyish grin. He was holding both hands behind his back, and
she had to lean to the right to see what he was hiding. Skidding away, he laughed and backed against the wall.

"What are you hiding behind your back, milord?" she
asked, enjoying this unusual burst of merriment.

With a sweeping gesture, he presented her with a yellow gillyflower.

"Oh!" she cried, taking the flower from his grasp and
holding it delicately in her hand. She glanced up at him,
and her eyes struck him like moons from which clouds
have passed. It had been months since she'd seen a flower,
and she had wanted desperately to see one. And now her
enemy had presented her with one as if she were his true
love.

"I will put it in a pot," she said, her voice misty with

emotion. "So that it will last all winter." Lifting it to her nose, she breathed deeply. "It has a sweet smell."

"'Tis the symbol of faithfulness in adversity," he said quietly.

"Are you offering me a gift of peace?" she asked.

"If you will accept it as such, and refrain from calling me whoreson and beast in the future."

She laughed and dipped her nose into the flower again. So sweet a scent was dizzying. "Aye, I will accept it as such. And I will not call you names anymore." She walked to the table and laid the flower on the rough, wooden surface.

He brought out his other hand, and she was delighted to see that it held a shift and dress.

"Oh, 'tis beautiful!" she exclaimed.

She took the gown and brought it to her cheek, nuzzling the soft fabric. It had been dyed yellow and was of a much better quality than the one she had burned.

"I found a spinner. She was willing to trade a gown and shift for game from the lord's forest."

She felt her heart swell with happiness and turned her back to him so that he wouldn't see the moisture in her eyes.

Clutching the clothes to her breast, she let the blanket drop to the floor.

At the sight of her naked derriere, his face softened with desire. Her auburn hair cascaded down her back, tapering to a point just above her dimpled buttocks. Her bottom was round and firm, and he eyed it with bold admiration. As the shift came down covering her, he felt an ache of disappointment.

She pulled the dress on over her head, and he stepped forward to assist her, tugging it down across her hips and smoothing it into place over her backside. Reaching down into her shift, he brought out her hair and let it spill through his fingers. It looked chestnut brown in the darkness of the cottage, the tresses rich and healthy.

As she turned to face him, she saw the passion radiating

in his face. He seized her, taking her by surprise in an embrace that was so passionate it was almost fierce. His mouth came down on hers, and she felt his tongue slip past her lips, tasting the sweetness of her mouth. She had never been kissed before, had never imagined the sensations a kiss could ignite. Hungrily, she took his lips in her own and feasted on the warm terrain of his mouth. Drawing back, she looked up at him with an expression that was hopeful yet pained. Confusion seemed to dance in her eyes as a longing drew her back to him like an invisible thread pulling them together.

Her mouth met his again in a tender, probing heat. Reaching up, she caressed his neck and followed the long slope of muscle down his back. As his mouth bore down on hers, his arms tightened around her, and she felt an urgency in his kiss. She wanted him desperately, not just his body but his heart, his soul.

"Oh, milord, tell me that you care for me. Not just for my womb and what it can provide you."

He looked at her silently, his eyes guarded.

Tell me that your kindness is not just an illusion, she wanted to scream. *Tell me that your passion comes from your heart.*

His silence was a torment to her, and she wondered if she could have been mistaken about what she had seen in his eyes the previous night. She could not bear the possibility that she meant nothing to him.

"If you wish to bed me then do so," she snapped, pushing away from him. "But I will only lie there and show no passion for you. You who would use me and ask a bastard child of me as my ransom."

He took a deep breath before he spoke, steadying his voice to address this latest insult. Was his caring not evident in his actions? he wondered, wildly. Did it not matter that he had given her a dress and a flower?

"Do not blame me for your fate, Riley Snowden. It was by your own design, not mine. It was you who slipped into my fortress. It was you who tried to kill me in my blindness. Your punishment could have been your life."

How she hated being reminded that he was in control of her, that he could end her life if he so chose. "I regret ever returning to England!" she cried softly. "I should never have returned here seeking vengeance." Walking to the table, she snatched up the gillyflower and clutched it to her chest for comfort. Tears welled in her eyes as she brushed her fingers across the soft petals. "I am paying the price for my wrongdoing. I was foolish in my anger, hungry for vindication, and mad with loneliness."

Turning to him, she gripped the flower loosely in her hand. "Your life has brought an appeasement to my heart far greater than any your death could have provided. I was wrong to try to kill you. But can you not understand my state of mind at the time? Can you not forgive me?"

His eyes began to seethe with frustration. "I understand only battle, Riley. I have given you a peace offering. Now be content with that and do not ask more of me."

The flower slipped through her fingers, and she grasped for it as it fell. Fumbling to catch the stem, she only knocked it farther away. A gasp escaped her as she watched it drop into the hot ash of the fireplace. The yellow petals sputtered and melted in the heat.

Lynchburg's rage boiled over, reddening his face as he reached her in two steps. Grasping her arms, he shook her roughly. "I give you a gillyflower, and you cast it into the fire!"

"'Twas an accident," she breathed tearfully, but he would not listen.

"I have tried to please you, yet you play the bitch with me." His grip tightened, and she gasped at the pain in her arms.

He had been a fool to care for the girl, and he raged at that soft inner core within him that would dare to love a woman. Feelings like bad weather came unbidden and unstoppable, he knew, downing even the staunchest trees.

She would become a chink in his armor if he did not fortify his heart against her.

All along he had felt a dread ruffling the edge of his contentment, an uneasiness, however slight, that was warning him not to allow his prisoner to dull his instincts. But feelings were powerful adversaries, lowering his shield of resistance and luring him into a state of complete vulnerability. With a cry of anguish, he released her and whirled toward the wall, slamming both his fists against it.

Backing away, she felt her pouch slip from her waist and fall from beneath her dress. As it tumbled across the floor, she lunged for it, scooping it up in both hands. With trembling fingers she fastened it around her dress.

"Give that to me," he ordered. "If you will cast my gift into the fire, so then I will cast in your every possession behind it."

She cried out in despair as he yanked the pouch from her waist, breaking the string and causing the hempseed to spill onto the floor.

"What the devil is this?" he asked, watching the tiny seeds bounce against the stones and roll into the crevices of the slabs.

She stood back, hugging the wall behind her, her chest heaving.

Bending down he picked up a seed and examined it closely. "What is this?" he asked again, holding the seed between his thumb and forefinger. "You told me the pouch was empty, but you lied. Do you plot to poison me?"

"No, milord, 'tis only seed." She wanted to sound calm, but her voice rose to a higher pitch. "'Tis seed to plant in the spring."

"Seed to plant in the spring?" he asked, disbelieving. "Have you gone mad to tell me such a lie as this? Do you think me a fool?"

"'Tis only marigold seed, milord, I swear it."

"Marigold seed?" He rolled the tiny ball between his fingers.

"Aye, marigolds are always needed," she insisted. "For

cooking. For medicine. 'Tis nothing better to use against the plague."

"Who gave you this seed?" he asked as he swept up the seeds with his fingers and sprinkled them back into the pouch.

"I had it with me always," she lied. Her lips trembled, and she bit into her bottom lip to hide her fear.

Rising to his feet, he clenched the pouch in his fist. "You fear something, but I doubt 'tis plague. I will ride into the village. And I will find a wise woman to tell me what this seed is used for. If you had it in mind to poison me, then God have mercy on you."

She looked toward the door, her every instinct screaming for escape. Seeing the direction of her gaze, he gave her a warning look. "I will fetter you until I return."

"No!" she cried. "Please do not bind me."

"Then tell me what this seed is used for," he demanded, thrusting the pouch at her.

She closed her eyes, looking away. If she told him, he would beat her. If she didn't tell him, he would ride into the village and find out from someone else. When he returned, he would beat her anyway. Let him work to find his answer, she decided.

"Who works with you?" he asked, his eyes keenly fixed on her, hardening to a wintry gray.

She felt stunned by his question as if the breath had been knocked completely out of her. "Edward," she blurted. "He sponsored my return to England. He is my cousin, on my mother's side." Her lies came out in short, staccato breaths, almost like hiccups. "My mission was to kill Cornwich. In return, when Edward became king, he would restore my father's lands to me."

Lynchburg tilted his head in appraisal, studying her with an air of cool detachment. Was she confessing, he wondered, or lying? "Be glad that you did not succeed," he advised her. "Killing for land settles rather unpleasantly on one's conscience. Trust me on this. I know."

Grabbing her wrists, he half-dragged her to an oaken

beam and bound her hands in leather strips. Taking one long thong, he slipped it through her bonds so that she was on a leash and tethered to the beam. She would not be too uncomfortable, he determined, for the leash was long enough to allow her to sit or lie down if she so chose.

"I will return within the hour. If you are right about these seeds, then I will release you. But if you have hidden them from me for some evil purpose . . ." He clenched the pouch tightly in his hand. "Then you will regret it."

He stormed from the cottage, and she heard him mounting his horse. She could imagine the horse's hooves kicking up snow as he headed at full gallop toward the village. She would have precious little time to escape.

The wind whistled through the thatch, and the smoke from the dying fire danced in the draft. Pulling at the bonds fiercely, she burned her wrists as she twisted against the leather. As she grew colder, she felt the tension in her bonds beginning to ease. Wiggling one wrist and then the other, she managed to pull one hand free. Quickly she picked at her leather clad wrist, stretching the thongs and loosening the knots until her other hand was out.

Reaching under the mattress, she retrieved her shoes and slipped them on. She had to make her way back to Glenwood Castle. She had to find Gertie and get the two of them safely to London before the siege began. Once inside the city they would be under the protection of Gertie's brother, Geoffrey, and thankfully, she thought, this mission of vengeance on which she had so foolishly embarked would be over.

Grabbing her fur-lined cloak, she wrapped it around her shoulders and headed out into the cold morning air. If she could make it back to Glenwood Castle, she would steal two of the lord's horses, then she and Gertie would ride all night to the safety of London.

Chapter Eleven

Lynchburg sat astride his mare, lumbering down the old Roman road toward the village of Gersham. The thought of Riley's slender wrists bound in leather restraints tore at his heart.

Her image filled his mind like a mist in the forest, bewitching and beautiful. No woman had ever affected him so profoundly as his prisoner. His prisoner, he reminded himself, who was clouding his judgment. Instead of fighting for his king, he was bartering a rabbit for a gillyflower just to please her. And she had cast it into the fire, singeing his heart along with it. Damn her.

Gripping the pouch tightly, he muttered a curse and eyed the village up ahead with a troubled air. He would not turn back; he would go forth and discover Riley Snowden's intentions whether fair or foul. He would keep his warrior's wits about him and would not surrender his power to her. Never would he be like Henry, a fool ruled by a woman.

The sunlight filtered through the clouds and fell in misty swirls of light along the road. A dog charged at his horse barking at the mare's hooves and scampering back and forth across its path. In the distance he could hear the bleating of sheep in the sheepfold and the slow banging of a hammer.

As he crossed the bridge into the village, an old woman emerged from the alehouse.

"Good morning, milord," she called up to him as she pulled a sheep skin over her shoulders. He noticed that most of her teeth were missing, and her face was craggy with age. "Would you like to sample our ale, sir?"

"Nay, I thank you," he said, surveying the village. The air was foul with the smell of a nearby dung heap and the odor of the ponds. "I am looking for a wise woman."

"She's near the duck pond." The woman pointed down the road. "Her name is Elda. If ye be seeking a cure, she's the one what has it. She's cured many a dying man and beast. Keep going past the sheepfold till ya see the pond. Her cottage is there."

Clutching the pouch, he thanked her and rode on. When he arrived at the cottage, he dismounted immediately before he could change his mind. He supposed that the woman inside was as putrid as the stench of the village and as worn and yellowed as the walls of her home. Best to get this over with quickly. Pounding on the door with his fist, he waited for the crone to answer his summons.

When the door opened, he was surprised to see a youthful face staring up at him with eyes as bright and dark as a bird's. She was tall with an erect stance and a blond braid that rested against her shoulder like a ribbon of gold.

"I am the Earl of Lynchburg," he introduced himself, "the new lord of Glenwood Castle. Husband to Cornwich's daughter."

She hesitated a moment before bobbing a curtsy of respect, her dark eyes stunned.

"Are you the wise woman of this village?" he asked gruffly.

"Aye, my lord," she said. Her voice was so soft that it could have been borne on the wings of a butterfly. "Come in."

He stepped into the warmth of the cottage. The open fire in the center of the room caused the shadows to flicker and dance, and the air seemed filled with spirits. A single candle sat on the trestle table along with pots and plants and everywhere a spattering of dirt. The air was scented with herbs and dried flowers.

"I will state my business and be done," he said, though there was something inviting about this chamber. It was peaceful and quiet, and his soul was drawn to it.

"I know your business, sir," she said. "It has been many years since I have seen the Lady Jeanette. How does she fare?"

His eyes slid to hers, sealing on her with predatory force. She felt staggered by the anger that emitted from his face.

"What do you know of the Lady Jeanette?" he demanded.

She quickly walked to the fire to distance herself from him. Kneeling beside it, she picked up a stick and began to stoke the flames. "Forgive me, my lord. I did not mean to anger you. I assumed that Lady Jeanette was the reason for your visit."

Lynchburg stood, saying nothing, his silence a command in itself. She knew that he waited for her to answer his question.

"Many years ago a plague broke out," she explained as she nervously poked at the fire. "Many in this village sickened. A few died, but most of the sick I cured. When Lord Philip found out about it, he summoned me to Glenwood Castle." She moistened her lips with her tongue and turned her gaze up to his. They were lusty eyes, he noted, half-hidden beneath feathery lashes. "He took me to his daughter's chamber and asked me to cure her. I told him I could not. But I would try to make her better." As she spoke, her eyes turned bitter, and she jabbed at the fire. "I could have helped her, but the chaplain turned the earl against me. He told him that sickness is caused by sin and can only be cured through prayer. Any other method of healing is considered by the church to be of the devil."

Lynchburg nodded, beginning to understand. He re-

called Cornwich's mentioning a healer named Elda, the
only woman he trusted to be his daughter's midwife.

"The chaplain convinced Cornwich that if he employed
me, he would be selling his soul to Lucifer. So he banished
me from the castle."

"Why did you not counter the chaplain's argument?" he
asked. "Plead with Cornwich?"

She lowered her eyes to the fire and gazed into the curling flames. "A priest is a powerful man, my lord. The
church has often tried healers for witchcraft. Many of us
have been burned at the stake. It does not matter that I am
innocent. The chaplain warned me that he would suffer no
threat to the church's authority."

Lynchburg let out a long sigh of fatigue. "Can you help
the girl?"

Her eyes brightened with hope as she rose to her feet.
"Aye, my lord. She needs to be brought out into the sunshine. That and fresh air will drive the bad humors from
her body. I think she can learn things—how to comb her
hair. Perhaps even how to feed herself."

Lynchburg rolled his eyes with impatience. The healer
spoke of inane activities. Was there no true help for the
girl?

"Have you ever spoken of her to anyone?"

"And incur the earl's wrath?" She almost laughed at
such an outrageous question. "No, my lord. The earl has
my loyalty, as do you. He was a kind master." She smiled
shyly and cupped her slender waist in her hands. "He was
not so fearful for his soul that he did not visit me often. I
eased the pain of his loneliness." Her lashes fluttered
provocatively over dark eyes. "How may I serve you, my
lord?"

Opening his fist, he presented the pouch to her. "Tell me
what this seed is used for," he commanded.

Her white fingers closed enticingly around his and
slowly slid the pouch from his hand.

As lovely as she was, he felt no desire for her. His
thoughts were only on Riley, the woman he'd tethered in

his cottage, the woman who consumed his every thought and who had brought him to such frenzied passion that he had feared he would die in her arms.

She opened the pouch and shook the seed out into her hand. With a seductive swagger, she walked toward the fire, her braid swaying against her back.

"I will leave a rabbit I've killed in payment for your assistance," he offered.

"A rabbit," she said with mock interest. "Nothing else?" Her voice was soft and husky.

He knew the meaning of her words, the invitation they imparted.

"No," he said sullenly. "The rabbit is all that I can give you."

She examined the seeds, letting them roll around in her palm. As she knelt by the hearth, the fire glowed along the whiteness of her neck and turned her eyes to black coals. After a moment's pause, she said, "'Tis hempseed."

"Hempseed," he repeated. "So 'tis not marigold seed?"

"Marigold seed?" She laughed. "Nay, 'tis hempseed."

Hempseed, he thought sickly. Riley had lied to him. "And what use might a woman have for hempseed?"

"You know as well as I." She shrugged her slender shoulders. "A woman might plant it to grow hemp. Or crush the seed for oil."

"What else?" he asked, his breath quickening. When she did not answer, he became angry. "What else?" he shouted, causing her to jump at the sound of his tone as if she'd heard the crack of a whip against her stone floor. The light fled from her eyes and was replaced by fear.

"'Tis used for sex," she said quietly.

"What do you mean?" His eyes were puzzled, searching. "Would a woman use it to increase her pleasure?"

"No." She rose to her feet, holding out the pouch to him. "A wanton might swallow hempseed. It closes the womb."

He felt stunned and dizzy as if she had just struck him with a large stone. "No," he said, half-breathing. The blood pounded in his ears, deafening him. The bitch. "No," he roared and slapped the seed from her hand. She leaped back, her eyes wild with fear.

"I—I am sorry," he said, dazed. She was not the object of his pain, and he would not take his anger out on her. There was only one who was deserving of that.

Slamming out of the cottage, he could barely see his way. His vision smoldered with fury, and the world swirled around him. As his mind reeled, he wondered if this was what it felt like to be driven completely mad. Swinging up onto his mare, he snapped the reins and headed back into the forest.

"Why did she do it?" he wondered aloud and grabbed the silky mane of his horse. *Why?* he thought, until the thought threatened to rend his mind in two. She had agreed to have his babe as her ransom. She had agreed, damn her! He kicked the mare until the horse was in full gallop through the snow.

Ducking the low limbs of trees as if they were the lances of attackers, he cursed himself. He should be in the field training, not in a cottage giving gillyflowers to a traitor. He needed the heat of battle, the fight to rid his mind of the faithless bitch. He needed to face an opponent in black armor mounted on a missodor. Now there was an opponent he could understand, not one who lied and plotted behind his back.

The lady was unreadable. She was ice and fire, too cold one moment and too hot the next, like a blazing torch at night beneath the glow of a winter moon. How could she hate him yet become a fiery vixen in his bed? It made no sense. By God! he shouted within himself. No one betrayed him without regret! No one.

Spying a cottage in a clearing, Riley ran toward it. If only the clouds would start to snow again and hide her footsteps. She need only pray and God would make it snow, for if ever there was a pilgrim in trouble it was she. As soon as she could make it to the cottage, she would warm herself by the fire, she decided, and enlist the help of the family within. After all, she was a noblewoman, a Snowden in Yorkist territory. Who wouldn't want to assist her?

She plodded across the cobbled ground to the door and banged on it with her fist. The family's stone oven stood open, its interior black with ashes as if it had been recently used. When no one answered her knock, she thrust open the door and found the cottage empty. The fire was nearly out, and she assumed that no one had been at home for some time.

Where could they have gone in the snow? she wondered. *Probably to the village to purchase flour or baked bread.*

A woman's dress hung on a peg and a man's ax lay on a table along with a bow and a quiver of arrows. She would love a cup of cider right now and a warm stew, but there was none to be had.

As she walked to the table, she shivered with cold and rubbed her hands briskly together. A sack lay on the table, and she opened it to see if there was anything inside to eat. She found two rabbits, newly dead. Poachers, she realized with a smile. Good. They were stealing rabbits from Lynchburg's land.

She was starving and needed something to eat if she were going to make it the rest of the way to Glenwood Castle. She needed warmer clothes, too, and eyed the dress on the peg. It was thick and wool and would be very warm. If she should take it, what would she do with her own clothing, she wondered? She couldn't leave her shift and dress as trade. Lynchburg might stop here and know that she had passed this way. It would be better if he found her clothes on the road and thought her dead. Just like the story of Joseph in the Bible, she remembered. Joseph's brothers had sold him into slavery, then had torn and bloodied his clothes so that his father would think that he had been killed by a wild animal.

Quickly she pulled off her shift and dress and stood naked before the low fire. Her skin was aching from the cold as she pulled the woman's woolen dress on over her head. It was a shapeless sack, brown in color with loose sleeves that hung past her hands. Very unfashionable but very warm, she decided as she draped her cloak over her shoulders.

Spreading her dress and shift over the table, she laid a rabbit on top of them and picked up the ax. Swiftly she brought the blade down cutting the rabbit's throat. Blood spilled out onto her clothes until they were fairly saturated. Poor dear folks, she sighed inwardly as she pushed aside the carcass and rolled up her soiled dress and shift. Someday I will repay them for the losses that I have caused them this day. Fleeing the darkened room with her bloodied bundle, she ran back out into the cold.

A light snow was beginning to fall, and she thanked God for it. It would fill in her footsteps and hide her trail from Lynchburg. The thought of him made her shiver even harder. He would be furious when he found out that she had lied to him about the seed. He would track her down like a hound on the trail of a deer; she was certain of it. She must get to London as soon as possible and seek the protection of Edward.

She began retracing her steps through the snow back to the main road. Her buckskin shoes were soon soaked, and her feet were growing wet and numb. As she hurried through the skeletal forest, the branches clung to her cloak, and twice she had to stop to free herself. It was as if the forest was detaining her, working on the side of the Lancastrians, she thought dismally.

Sliding to a halt, she unrolled her bundle of bloody clothes and tore the garments to shreds, scattering them about. Holding on to one sleeve, she picked her way through the branches and down to the road. She would leave this last piece where Lynchburg would surely see it and think her killed by wolves. Wringing the sleeve from her hand, she began to run, hoping to reach Glenwood before the snow grew worse, before night fell and before she slowly froze to death in her flight.

Chapter Twelve

Gertie stirred the sauce that was bubbling in the cauldron over the kitchen fire. Lifting the ladle, she stole a taste. It was squirrel broth heavily spiced, and she planned to eat her fill of it before serving it to the earl's administrators. Night would be falling soon, as if it mattered. The day and night looked nearly the same to her in winter. The snow had started falling at midday, and the cold had kept her close to the fire all afternoon. Her skin was red from the heat and her lips slightly parched.

She was alone in the kitchen, the others having left their tasks to attend evening vespers. For no other reason than to get off their feet for an hour, she assumed. She would rather steal from the stewpot than sit in a cold sanctuary.

When the door opened a crack, she took no notice, thinking it was one of the servants returning early or huntsmen bringing her more animals to clean, more work to do.

"G-G-Gertie," Riley stuttered as she flung open the door.

Gertie whirled about and gave a little shriek at the sight of her young cousin. Her lips were blue, and her cheeks were very pale. Flakes of snow glimmered in her hair, and her body was nearly convulsing with cold.

"Riley!" she cried, then quickly put her hand to her

mouth as if she had let slip a curse. "I mean, Rose, get over here by the fire."

She grabbed a poker and stoked the fire until the flames leaped angrily.

"You are near to frozen," Gertie said, her voice an anxious whisper. Taking Riley's hands between her own plump ones, she rubbed them until she was certain that the blood was flowing through her veins again. "Where have you come from?"

Her teeth were chattering so hard that she could not speak.

"Eat this," Gertie said, ladling some broth into a bowl, "before the cold robs you forever of your voice."

With shaking hands, Riley accepted the steaming bowl and brought it to her lips. She shuddered as the hot broth slid down her throat and into her stomach, warming her. Gertie pulled off her wet shoes and placed them on the hearth to dry.

When Riley raised her toes to the fire, she felt nothing. Her feet were numb, and she prayed that they would thaw quickly. "I ran away from Lynchburg. He will find me soon if I stay here. We must . . ." She shivered and sipped again at the broth. "We must steal two mounts and flee to London tonight."

"Why did you run from him?" Gertie asked, her eyes growing round and luminous. "Have you obtained secrets from him already?"

"No, no." The thought of her betrayal twisted inside of her. "He found the hempseed, and by now he knows why I had it."

Gertie lifted her hands to heaven as if beseeching God. "I should have never brought you back to England. I should have known that you were too young and inexperienced to handle the Lancastrians."

"I am sorry, Gertie," she said, her voice stuttering with cold. "I have failed the cause of York."

Gertie turned toward the pot and began to stir the broth. "No, you haven't. Not yet. There is still a chance for you to aid the Yorkists. You must wait here and face Lynchburg. You are still a valuable prisoner to him."

"Face him!" Riley shouted, nearly dropping her bowl. "Are you mad? I have betrayed him. I have run away from him."

"Then ask his forgiveness and try to be better." She brought the ladle to her lips and sipped it. "Convince him that you will have his child. And continue to listen for his plans. In the spring we will escape."

"I already know his plans." She held the bowl up to her chin, feeling the warm steam on her face. "The Lancastrians are gathering at St. Albans and plan to lay siege to London." She looked at her cousin helplessly. "We can no longer wait until spring. We must leave tonight, or we won't be able to get into the city."

Gertie angrily tossed the ladle into the pot. "Are you mad? How are we to steal two of the master's horses? Then just leisurely ride out of the castle gates, gates that are heavily guarded."

"'Tis nearly night. If we dress as huntsmen, then we can ride out, and no one will recognize us. We can obtain their clothes from the laundress's pile. And boots, too, from the cobbler's shop."

Gertie eyed the girl in a huff. Tucking loose strands of gray hair up under her veil, she scowled at her. "As soon as you finish that broth, get a sack and fill it with roasted squirrel. I'll fill two wineskins and fetch our disguises from the laundry. If we are to ride out before night, we must hurry."

Riley wanted to throw her arms around her cousin, but instead she hungrily sipped the broth. The sooner she finished, the sooner they could depart.

As the sun set, the light of dusk fell in thin veils through the clouds, turning the snow in the bailey a lucent white and deepening the shadows of the walls.

When they entered the stable, they spied two young boys huddled beneath a blanket, playing dice. The boys took no notice of the two huntsmen who swiftly prepared their mounts. Riley grabbed a child's bow and quiver of arrows that hung near the door and swung up onto her mare. In growing aggravation she watched as Gertie stepped up onto the mounting block and struggled to lift her short leg over her mount. Riley kept her horse between Gertie and the boys, hoping that they would not notice.

When Gertie was finally astride, they trotted out into the bailey and headed for the gatehouse. The sky was aglow with the orange light of dusk, and Riley looked skyward to see a flock of black birds winging their way through the clouds.

"They are free, and so shall we be," she whispered to Gertie.

"Aye," she answered uncertainly, her knuckles white as she gripped the reins of her mount.

They meandered through the gate, attracting only a brief glance from the guards at the gatehouse. Their hooves hammered against the drawbridge, and Riley felt her every nerve lying raw and open. Looking out across the snowy fields of Northampton, she kicked her horse to a faster gait. It would be a cold and long night, but within a few hours time they would be safe within the Yorkist court.

An owl hooted, its call piercing the night. The ground was hidden beneath a rolling mist, and the trees, tall and silent, stood like guards over an ethereal plain. The horses plodded slowly down the road as Riley sat slumped over her mount, her head bobbing sleepily. Snatching awake, she looked into a darkness deeper than any she had ever experienced. Her limbs ached, and she was exhausted. More than anything she longed to stretch out on a pallet in front of a crackling fire and sleep long and deep. Her head nodded as she drifted off again.

"We're lost," Gertie sputtered, her voice seeming distant and ringing. "I can't see a thing in this blackness. The only way I know 'tis snowing is that I feel it on my face."

"'Tis snowing?" Riley murmured through a yawn.

"Aye, 'tis snowing, cousin. And 'tis near midnight and my fingers are frozen to the reins of this animal." She looked around her, her eyes trying hopelessly to pierce the veil of night. "You and your schemes. By morning we'll be frozen dead in the snow. And it won't be Lynchburg who finds us. It'll be the wolves first. Then the squirrels will finish off what's left. They'll chew our knuckles like they was acorns."

"I'm sorry I brought you to this," Riley fretted.

"'I'm sorry,'" Gertie mimicked her angrily. "'Tis all I ever hear from you. Never 'Today was a victory, Gertie' or 'I've slain the enemy, Gertie.' Only 'Gertie, I'm captured. Gertie, we must run for our lives.'" She looked around and hunkered deeper into her cloak. "At least our plight can't get any worse than this."

A thud sounded against the rump of Riley's horse and sent the animal whinnying in pain. It reared up on its hind legs, and Riley screamed as she felt herself being pitched off. She tumbled through the air and fell headlong into a bank of snow.

"What the devil is the matter now?" Gertie yelled, reining her mount to a halt. With much effort she clung to her horse's neck and lowered herself to the ground. "Are you all right?"

Riley clamored to her feet, dusting the snow from her clothes. Her horse continued to buck while Gertie's mount tossed its head and pranced nervously.

"Something struck the mare," Riley said, trying to peer through the darkened woods.

"Nothing struck the mare," Gertie insisted, her nerves taut. "She's just high-spirited is all. We're moving too slowly. Let us mount up and ride faster."

The wind moaned through the trees as if the spirits of the night sensed the presence of intruders. Riley swallowed against a sick fear that was rising inside of her. "Aye," she agreed. "Let's mount up and ride faster."

"Yer not going anywhere," a voice called from the darkness. It was a deep voice pinched with a whine.

Riley protectively grabbed her cousin's arm and pulled her close to her. "Who are you?" she demanded.

They heard the shuffling of many feet and soon realized that they were surrounded by as many as five men, ruffians bundled in furs with their bows drawn and arrows pointed directly at them. One swaggered forward, and Riley squinted her eyes as she strained to see his face. He was not a very big man, she noted. In fact, he appeared to be smaller than herself. Her eyes scoured him and saw that he carried no weapon.

"I am night and stars," he answered, "and clouds and wind. Now empty yer purses."

Gertie quickly untied the wineskins from her mare and tossed them to him.

"Two fine wineskins," he said, disappointed. "What else?"

Riley untied her pouch from her horse and tossed it to the ground at his feet. He bent to retrieve it and peered inside. "Roasted squirrel. Is that all ye have? Wine and food? 'Tis a mean night for a picnic."

"We are on our way to London," Riley said, trying to deepen her voice and straddle her legs like a man. "Now let us pass."

He walked in a wide circle around the two women. "What do ye think, boys? Two hunters going to London at night. Only the cold air has had a strange effect on them. It's turned them into women."

The other men snickered as he circled back around. "Why, pray tell, are two women dressed as hunters going to London in the middle of the night?"

"Maybe we're thieves, too," Gertie said and struck her chest with her fist.

He mulled over that comment. "Maybe ye are. In which case I shouldn't steal from ye. There's honor among thieves."

Walking toward Riley, he swiped the beaver hat from

her head. She cried out as her hair fell to her waist, framing her body in a fiery mane.

"I bet yer a fine-looking wench by the light of day." His face twisted into a crazed smile. "Fine-looking without them men's clothes."

She stepped back and glanced fiercely at the other men who were closing in around her. She could fight off one man but not all five.

"You are waylaying the cousin of the future king," she said sternly. "I am Riley Snowden, the daughter of Lord Robert Snowden, cousin to Edward, Earl of March."

"So yer a liedy," he drawled, and the other men began to laugh.

"Aye," she said proudly. "I have business with Edward in London. I beg you to let us pass. If you do, I will see to it that you are well rewarded by the king."

"Oh, I think I'd rather be well rewarded right now." He smirked. "I've never lain with noble blood before." Grabbing her cloak, he tore the garment as he yanked it from her.

She struggled against him, but he gripped the front of her tunic, pulling it over her face. Her arms were caught in a tangle above her head, bound fast in the twisted wool. Pulling against him in a tug of war, she fell free of the tunic, then leaped to her feet. Her cloak and tunic lay in the snow, and she stood in only her shirt, her heart beating so fast that she could no longer feel the cold. Kicking him, she was uncertain of her target until she saw him doubled over in pain. Her booted foot must have struck him in the stomach. She kicked again, aiming for his chin, and heard a sharp crack as her heel met the bone of his jaw. Staggering backward, he spit out a tooth and caught the blood that ran down his chin. To her amazement, he seemed undaunted by his pain.

As he grabbed her, he pressed his face against hers, and she retched at the rancid smell of his breath. His teeth were yellow and rotting, and she realized that one of his eyes had been put out. There was nothing there but a dark, empty space. Opening her mouth to scream, she felt him go rigid against her and heard his scream of surprise. He slumped forward into the snow, pinning her beneath him. She tried to push him off of her and saw the arrow jutting from his back and his clothes growing dark with blood.

Before she saw it, she heard it, the snorting of a beast emerging from the night, its breath filling the darkness with a white fog. The missodor appeared first, then the warrior on its back swinging a mace. It whizzed through the air and smashed the skull of one of the men. He fell, his head a mass of blood and shattered bone. The other men dropped their bows and scattered, stumbling away into the forest.

As Riley shoved the man's body off of her, she sat up and stared bleary-eyed into the frosty night. The warrior dropped the mace and dismounted quickly, his steps swift for a man so large. As he loomed above her, she saw the face of Lynchburg and wondered if she were dreaming.

"Are you unharmed?" he asked.

"Aye," she said, stunned by the sight of him. His eyes were those of a tortured man.

He was not even winded from the fight, a fight that she quickly realized was not over yet. The air around him seemed to vibrate with his fury. Could she make it to her horse, she wondered, then knew in an instant that she could not. He barred her way, the breadth of him unscalable.

He loosened his belt, and she heard the leather sliding across the fabric of his houppelande. Did he mean to bind her again, she wondered? To do that which she hated more than anything? As she tried to scramble to her feet to run, he reached down and grabbed both of her wrists, holding them tightly in one unbreakable grip.

Doubling his belt in one hand, he raised it high in the air, then brought it down with a loud snap across her backside. It stung through the thin shirt but did not hurt. He swung the belt again, harder this time. Her back arched from the blow, and she gave a small gasp of pain. A third time the belt cracked against her posterior, and she felt her knees buckle. She was so tired. She could not fight him. The fourth and final blow burned away her resistance, and she crumpled to the ground.

Releasing her, he turned to Gertie, who was red-faced with fear. As he advanced toward her, he snapped the belt against his thigh.

"She made me come with her!" Gertie cried, her voice cutting the air. "I didn't want to do it. I caught her stealing your horse. And—and I told her that I was going to tell the steward." Her voice was infused with panic. "She took a knife to my throat. She said I would have to come with her." Her eyes narrowed angrily at Riley, who was crumpled on the ground. "You didn't beat her enough for what she did to me."

"Gather up those weapons and mount up," he ordered Gertie. Turning to Riley, he pointed at the mare. "Get up and get on that horse."

She rose slowly, rubbing her abused posterior and headed for the mare. As he watched her, he was filled with pain. Here she was, unhorsed, beaten, and nearly dead from exhaustion and all because she wanted to escape him.

"Why did you run from me?" he cried, all the ache in his soul spilling out with his words.

"Because I knew you would beat me when you found out what the hempseed is used for."

He grimaced at her words and stared at her bitterly. "Why did you lie to me about that? Why did you betray me?"

She grabbed the neck of her horse and swung herself up onto her mount. "Because you are my enemy!"

"Did I not bring you fresh clothing? Did I not feed you? Did I not fetch a gillyflower just to please you? What other prisoner has ever been treated so kindly?"

Her anger rose through her pain and fatigue. "My back-side burns now from your kind treatment. I only took the hempseed because,"—she paused, knowing that she could not tell him the whole truth—"because I feared that you would kill me as soon as the child was born."

He fastened his belt around his waist and scooped up her tunic and cloak. Throwing the garments up to her, he mounted his missodor.

"I told you I would not harm you. I told you I would send you back to France when the child was born. Am I such a monster in your eyes? God's blood, woman, you betrayed me and ran from me. And all you got was a whipping."

"Because you still have need of me to bear your child!" she yelled back, causing her mare to jump. Tears burned her eyes and spilled hotly down her cheeks. Turning her face away from him, she donned her tunic and pulled her cloak tightly about her shoulders.

"And you will yet, milady," he said harshly. "You will yet." Slapping the backside of her horse, he sent it into a gallop, then followed in angry pursuit.

Gertie dug her heels into her horse and lurched down the road, praying that she would be able to keep up.

Chapter Thirteen

Riley awoke as the scent of roasting rabbit drifted beneath her nose. Shifting under the furs, she stretched out her arms and legs and blinked into the morning light. The fire was crackling heartily, and Lynchburg was perched on his haunches turning a rabbit on a spit. The fire cast a warm glow across his face and reflected deep in his eyes.

"Good morning, milord," she greeted him, pushing up onto her elbows.

"'Tis nearly afternoon," he muttered. He lifted the spit from the fire and set it aside to cool.

Her mouth watered at the sight of the meat, brown and steaming. Beyond the flames she spied Gertie huddled in her fur-lined cloak. Her hair was disheveled, and her cheeks were smudged with dirt.

"I did not try to wake you," he said, slicing the thighs from the rabbit. He handed one thigh to Gertie and the other to Riley. "I thought you needed the rest."

Riley tore at the meat with her teeth, so hungry that she didn't care that it was too hot to eat. "Where are you taking us?" she asked, fanning her mouth.

His eyes flitted coldly to hers, then returned to the rabbit. Biting into the loin, he tore the meat from the bone and chewed it slowly. "Wherever we go, we must take this serving wench with us," he said, glimpsing Gertie. "Now that she knows of our plan to conceive a child, I can never allow her to return to Glenwood Castle."

Gertie paused, holding the thigh midway to her mouth, and stared in mute horror at Lynchburg.

"Of course you can send her back," Riley suggested as she eyed Gertie sullenly, remembering her admonishment to Lynchburg that he had not beaten her enough. "Just cut out her tongue so that she can't talk."

Gertie glared at her, her mouth opening to voice her outrage, then just as quickly tightening into a silent frown. Riley gave her a smug smile of victory, pleased that she had angered her. She knew that Lynchburg would not harm her.

"I have no intention of sending her back with or without her tongue," he grumbled. He pulled another strip of meat from the backbone and offered it to Riley. "She will remain with you and be your servant."

As Riley accepted the meat, she gazed at Gertie through half-lowered lids. "Thank you, milord, for breakfast. I will thank you for the servant if she proves herself capable."

"Are you going to do the same to her as you did to the gillyflower?" he asked, eyeing her askance. "Cast her into the fire as you do all my gifts?"

"That was an accident if only you would believe me," she insisted.

"You would also have had me believe that you were a serving wench named Rose. And that the hempseed was really marigold seed." He gave a mild "humph" as he eyed her keenly. "I'd just as soon believe the devil as you."

She saw the bitterness in his eyes and was oddly encouraged by it. His anger should be past, and he should feel only indifference now. But there was frustration on his face, the look of a man who wants what is just beyond his reach.

Thoughtfully she wiped the grease from her lips with her fingers, then licked them gently, an innocent move that tweaked his passion.

He wanted to touch her in that moment as the sunlight broke through the clouds, setting off sparks in her hair. If only the old wench were not present, he would take her now, here in the forest by the fire. A coarser man would take her anyway, he thought with a smirk. It would serve her right to be debauched before this hag who had suffered a miserable night because of her. Gazing briefly at the woman, he felt a gloating satisfaction that Riley had taken her, of all people, hostage. Due to her age and obvious lack of experience with horses, they had been unable to reach London. The old crone could barely stay astride a mount.

"How did you find me?" Riley asked, breaking into his thoughts.

"I followed your tracks until the snow filled them in. 'Twas then that I found the strip of cloth." The memory sickened him as he recalled picking up the stiff strand of yellow wool and seeing the blood. He had nearly gone mad with grief. "Then I realized that you were too clever to allow yourself to be food for wolves. I rode to Glenwood Castle and found out that two huntsmen had left the grounds and had not returned." He cast his bone into the fire, causing the flames to hiss and spark. "I suspected to find you on the road to London."

"And so you did," she said.

"Do not ever run from me again," he warned. To think that she could have been killed, maimed by thieves, pricked painfully at his heart and conscience.

"I promise I will not," she vowed but saw the lack of trust in his eyes. With a small shrug she continued. "The hempseed is gone. My betrayal is revealed. I have no choice but to accept my fate."

Her words wounded him, for he wanted to be more to her than just a fate that she must accept. But that was impossible, he knew. "We must hurry," he said gruffly. "We have wasted too much time already." He scooped up snow in his massive hands, then dropped in onto the fire, dousing the flames.

"You have not said where we are going," she reminded him.

"To St. Albans."

"What?" She threw off the fur cover, displaying her calves, slender and shapely.

His gaze was drawn to them, and he felt his groin stiffen with desire for her. *Damn the witch,* he thought. Would she never cease tormenting him?

"No!" she pleaded. If she could keep him away from St. Albans, then the battle would be lost. "I must go back to the cottage. You cannot take a woman—two women—into battle."

"I would have been at St. Albans by now if not for you," he said angrily, tossing more snow onto the fire until it fizzled out. "I have no more time to waste on you. I ordered my men to depart from Glenwood Castle at first light. They will be expecting me to join them today at the queen's camp. The war is nearly over, and I wish to finish it quickly." He stood up, wiping his wet hands on his houppelande. "As soon as we take London, Edward will be defeated. And this madness will be over."

The possibility of a Lancastrian victory had never entered her mind. If King Henry won, then she would be left with nothing. Lynchburg would have his child from her, then he would send her back to France. A look of disgust settled on Gertie's face as she watched Riley with a relentless scrutiny, her eyes, so full of judgment, bearing down on her.

"The madness will not be over!" Riley cried pleadingly. "My suffering will not be over."

"Nay, it will be worse if you don't get moving." The wind blew through his hair, scattering strands across his face. His was an unyielding face, with blue eyes steadily blazing.

She wanted to club him in that instant, to pierce his stone exterior and see if there truly was a human heart beating in his breast.

A whizzing sound broke the air, passing close to her ear.

Lynchburg reeled backward, then spun around and fell to his knees, a streak of blood snaking down his face. Like a great downed tree, he toppled over and sprawled motionless on the ground.

Gertie leaped to her feet, pointing toward the woods. "'Twas a rock!" she squealed. "I saw it. 'Twas thrown from the woods. Someone aimed at him with a slingshot." She almost cackled as she danced from one foot to the other. "'Tis as sure a mark as was made by David. Come on, cousin, now's our chance to escape."

Riley felt her breath catch as she knelt beside the earl, gently turning him over onto his back. A blue lump was swelling around a hole in his forehead. Leaning down, she pressed her ear to his chest and was relieved to hear a steady heart beat.

"He's not dead," she said thankfully.

"Zounds, woman, but you sound like you're happy about that," Gertie whispered hoarsely. "Why do you tarry? We must hurry."

He was as still and pale as death, and Riley bit down on her bottom lip to stop it from trembling. "No," she said, wiping the blood from his face.

"Come on, Riley! Whoever did this is nearby. Most likely he wants to rob us."

Riley unsheathed Lynchburg's dagger from his hip and gripped it in her hand. Running to the mare, she lifted her bow and quiver of arrows from the saddle, then motioned for Gertie to follow her into the woods.

"We can't leave the horses," Gertie whispered, outraged.

"'Tis the horses the thieves want, not us." Grabbing Gertie's cloak, she pulled her into the tangle of limbs and brush. "If we aren't on the horses, then the thieves won't come after us." She paused several yards from camp and crouched down behind a tree, watching through the barrier of limbs.

"What are we waiting for?" Gertie hissed. "We must flee!"

She pressed one finger to her lips in a plea for silence as she watched three men wander into the camp. They carried no weapons, and Riley suspected that they were the survivors from last night's failed robbery.

Raising her bow, she balanced an arrow on its site and peered down the shaft to the tallest of the intruders. He was bearded and filthy, wearing a coat of deerskin. Drawing back the bow, she trained her arrow on him as he approached Lynchburg's body. With his booted foot, he kicked him in the ribs.

"I got him good, boys!" he crowed, his face breaking into a toothless grin. "He's out cold as a lamb." Walking to the missodor, he ran his hand along the hilt of the sword that was strapped to Lynchburg's saddle. "'Tis rubies. I told you 'twas rubies." He giggled and clasped the hilt, quickly unsheathing the sword. "Aye, if we ain't rich today."

The other two men moved toward him warily, their eyes constantly scanning the woods. "What about the others who were with him?" one asked, his breath whistling past toothless gums.

"Don't worry about them," the tall one snorted and spit on the ground. "They was only women. 'Twas like tossing a rock in the chicken coop and watching the hens scatter. They're halfway to London by now."

The ogre looked out of place with that fine sword, Riley decided and pulled the bow taut. Her vision was filled with him, with his breath clouding the air like the rising stench from warm manure. Releasing the string, she saw a flash as the arrow flew through the air and pierced his chest. The shaft impaled him, and a stream of blood shot out from his back. At first he appeared startled and looked down in bewilderment at the shaft that protruded through his chest. He gripped the arrow in a stunned and fruitless effort to remove it, then his face contorted in agony as he fell to the ground, writhing with spasms. His fellow thieves, still weaponless from the night before, dived to the ground.

Riley was shaking so hard that she had trouble steady-

ing the next arrow. Drawing back the bow, she took aim at
the second man who was crawling briskly away. She drew
the bow taut again and, with a snap, launched the second
arrow. It vanished into the air, coming to rest with a re-
sounding thud through the thief's midsection. It ripped the
breath from him and drove him face-first into the snowy
ground. Immediately his body grew still. The third man
fled into the woods. For several moments she waited for
him to reemerge from the forest. When he didn't reappear,
she crept toward camp, whispering to Gertie to stay put.

A low groan emitted from Lynchburg, and he began to
stir, lifting his hand to his bloody forehead. He opened his
eyes but could see nothing through the blinding pain of his
head. When his vision began to clear, he spied an arrow
pointing directly at his face. Reaching for his dagger, he
found nothing there, and he cursed his stupidity. How
could he have allowed himself to be bested? he wondered.
Why had he not heard a twig snap or a branch rustle, some
telling sound that an intruder was near? But he had been a
stupid man since the first moment he had laid eyes on
Riley Snowden. She had invaded his very soul.

He sat up slowly, gripping his head. "What have you
done with the woman?" he moaned. "If you have harmed
her, you will not live, weapon or no."

"The woman is safe."

It was Riley's voice easing through his pain.

"Riley?" he asked. His eyes began to focus, and he saw
that the culprit who pointed an arrow at him was Lady
Snowden herself. "Did you attack me?" His heart grew
heavy at the thought until it began to sink into the pit of his
soul like a stone.

"No, milord," she answered, lowering her bow. "Your
attacker lies there by your side."

He looked to his right and saw the dead man, his body
still now but for a slight twitching. In amazement he
looked up at her. "You killed him?"

"Aye, two of them. They are the same band of thieves

who attacked us last night. I am certain of it. They meant to murder you and steal your sword."

Forgetting the pain in his head, he looked around hastily until he saw the sword beneath the dead man's body.

"Thank Christ for it," he breathed. "'Tis all I have left of my father." Pushing the body away, he clutched the sword and dragged it closer to him.

As he staggered to his feet, he touched the lump on his forehead.

"We should return to the cottage," she suggested. "You mustn't go to St. Albans in this condition. You may need trepanning."

"Trepanning!" he shouted then grabbed his head as the pain rent his skull. "If a surgeon comes near me, I will cut his throat with his own scalpel. You speak too much of going back to the cottage." He closed his eyes to shut out the light that had become unbearable. "I am beginning to think you wish a tryst with me."

She smiled brightly, but in his agony he did not see it.

"Aye, a tryst. Let us go back to the cottage," she suggested gently, "for a tryst."

He opened one eye and glared at her. "I thought you would want to go to St. Albans. You wanted to escape to London, did you not? You will never be closer to that city than St. Albans. Tell me truthfully, why do you wish to go back to the cottage?"

"For your health," she said, though it was phrased more as a question.

He rubbed his head as he spoke. "What nonsense is that? I have no time to stand here and dawdle with you. Prepare a poultice of snow for my head while I saddle the horses. And find that old woman."

As he walked to his horse, he stopped suddenly, realizing that she had killed two men to save his life. *No,* he told himself, *she had done it to protect herself.* But she could have killed him, too, yet didn't. She had pointed her arrow directly at him but had not released it. *Why?* he wondered. What message was she trying to convey to him?

He turned to her and saw the vision of a warrior goddess with eyes of deep green and blowing hair. Raising the bow, she drew back the string and released the arrow. It flew past his shoulder nearly nicking his arm and disappeared into the outer fringe of the woods. A bloodchilling scream pierced the forest followed by loud cracks as a body fell, breaking branches in its path.

Lynchburg looked toward the trees and saw a man dead, the arrow through his neck. In his hand was the slingshot that had nearly killed him. No doubt he had been aiming it at him again; this time with more deadly accuracy.

As he turned back to the clearing, he stared at Riley, in awe of her skill. "Thank you, milady," he whispered.

Her face, flushed from her effort, looked shaken by her own feat.

"I told you that my father trained me," she said.

He nodded with a strange expression on his face. He'd never been more dumbfounded in his life. "I'm glad I met you first in the bedchamber and not on the battlefield. For 'tis no doubt in my mind who the victor would have been."

She smiled shakily, and her eyes glimmered with pride at his compliment. "I will make you a poultice of snow now," she offered. "And fetch the old woman."

"Riley," he stopped her as she turned to leave. "You may keep my dagger. I rather like having you protecting my back."

"As you wish, milord."

She was still smiling as she wandered into the woods. A hand reached out like a claw, grasping her by the throat and dragging her to the ground.

"Gertie," she rasped through the old woman's painful grip. "What has come over you?"

"I should be asking you that question, ya lusty bitch." She clenched her throat tighter until Riley felt her face turning red. "Why didn't you kill the whoreson? 'Twas our chance to flee."

"I don't know," she said, prying Gertie's hand from her throat.

"You not only spared his life, you protected him."

"I was protecting us." She struggled to her feet, shoving the old woman away.

"Kill him now, Riley. Raise your bow and aim it at his back."

She backed away from her, distancing herself from her harsh command. "I cannot."

Gertie shook her fists at her in anguish. "I brought you back to England because you wanted to destroy the House of Lancaster. You wanted to fight. 'Twas your right you said to take your revenge. Well, vengeful wench, why aren't you doing it? The opportunity is now. Seize it. Else I'll swear you are a traitor to your cause."

Riley stared at her, lost.

"Think of the rewards we will reap from Edward if you kill the man who murdered his father," she urged.

"If I kill him, then I cannot find out the Lancastrian secrets," she argued weakly.

"What secrets?" Gertie squealed in a high-pitched whisper. "His only secret is that his heart is drawn to you."

Riley looked back toward the clearing where Lynchburg was rolling up the blankets and tying them to the horses. The sunlight fell across him like a gray veil so that he seemed half hidden in a mist. Could Gertie be right? she wondered. Could he truly be drawn to her? She watched his hands, large yet dexterous, tying the ropes securely to the saddle, and she wondered, *Is love something that this great lord can even understand?*

"Kill him," Gertie urged.

She could not obey her cousin and avenge her family. It was as Gertie had said. She had become a traitor to the Yorkists. She was falling in love with the very man whose cause she had hoped to destroy.

Perhaps he was drawn to her. The thought danced like light through her mind, titillating her. After all, she had seen emotion in his eyes the last night that they had made love in the cottage. And he had presented her with that lovely gillyflower. Surely it was a rare gesture from so hardened a warrior.

"Get that dreamy look off of your face, girl," Gertie fumed. "You are young and unschooled in men. A woman taken in by a handsome man is a vain fool. Look to your cause, Riley. Serve your cause and your king. Does not Lynchburg serve his?"

"Aye, I do serve my cause and my king by keeping Lynchburg alive." She fumbled with her words, hoping to placate her cousin. "When Edward finds out that Lynchburg executed his father, he will want his own revenge. Just as I wanted revenge on Cornwich for killing my father."

Gertie propped her hands on her hips, her eyes steaming. "Fine. Have it your way. You lust for him. Do not deny it." She raised one finger in warning. "Mark my words, young lady. His heart is made of stone. He is battle-scarred and heavy-handed. He is not Daggot, a young pup to scamper after a woman. He is a warrior who knows only how to destroy."

Riley looked at her cousin, at the seriousness in her eyes and the wisdom therein. "You are right," she said, feeling as if she were being shaken from a dream. "You are right, but I will not decide his fate. I will leave him to Edward." Shaking the snow from the folds of her cloak, she headed back toward the clearing, feeling foolish for ever having entertained the thought that Lynchburg might love her.

They reached St. Albans by midafternoon through a billowing snow. As they neared the camp, Riley saw the ring of supply wagons surrounding acres of canvas tents. She pulled her hood farther down over her face, hoping the soldiers milling about would think her a boy in her hunter's clothes. The last thing she needed as she rode nearer to the queen's tent was for someone to recognize her as Riley Snowden, enemy of the Crown.

When she saw the royal tent of yellow canvas, she stiffened in fear. It was where all prisoners would be taken and quickly condemned. Further away was Lynchburg's tent, much smaller than the queen's but large enough to house the earl, his personal supplies, and his bed. Daggot stood outside by the fire waiting, his manner brightening as soon as he recognized his master.

"I have partridges boiling in a pot," he called out. "Are you hungry master?"

"I am." Lynchburg gingerly rubbed his thumb across his forehead. "What about the foot soldiers? Have they eaten?"

Daggot's mouth sagged open as his eyes focused on his master's wound. "I don't know, milord. The queen told them to hunt the woods."

Lynchburg rolled his eyes in anger and heaved a sigh that was a voiceless curse. "There are not enough rabbits in these woods to feed all of these men. Go to my personal supply wagon. There is salted pork left over from Christmas. Give it to the men. There'll be a battle soon, and I want them strong."

"Aye, milord." He nodded, still staring at the bruise on his forehead.

"And take the women inside," he ordered as he dismounted, handing him the reins of his missodor.

Daggot looked at the two women, unsure of who they were. He saw only large hoods covering their faces and thick tunics beneath their cloaks. "Women?" he asked, but the earl was already striding through the snow on his way to meet with the queen.

Riley hopped down from the mare and brushed past Daggot, ducking into Lynchburg's tent. She pulled off her hood and shook out her long hair.

"Rose!" Daggot exclaimed as he followed her inside. "What are you doing here?"

"I am a servant of the Earl of Lynchburg," she stated flatly. "Where else should I be but with my master."

A brazier burned brightly in the center of the chamber,

filling the tent with a blessed heat while outside the snow pattered against the canvas walls.

Daggot's eyes slowly filled with adoration as he watched her hair streaming down her back. "You cannot serve him in battle. You are a woman. You should be with the queen."

"No," she gasped and whirled to face him. "The queen must not know that I am here. No one must know that I am here. I am content to be Lynchburg's servant and no one else's."

He looked at her queerly. "Would you not welcome a position with the queen's household?"

"Be quiet, you fool," Gertie scolded as she entered the chamber. She glowered at him as she rubbed her hands briskly together for warmth. "While you seek to advance this wench's position, you risk losing your own." Pausing at the brazier, she held her hands over the flames. "Didn't your master ask you to fetch salted pork for his men?"

"Gertie," his mouth formed the word, but he could not speak.

"You left his horse unattended in the snow. If I were your master, I'd give you a good beating for your negligence."

Turning on his heel, he scampered out of the tent.

"So, you are pleased to be Lynchburg's servant, eh?" She glanced at her cousin. "Pray tell, how do you serve him? You don't stay out of the dungeon long enough for that." Pulling off her hood, she ran her fingers through her coarse hair. "He does not need you to cook for him. He does that well enough for himself. 'Tis the way of a man who fears poisoning. He does not need you to bathe him, either. He no longer trusts you for that. He's got Daggot to pitch his tent and scrub his horse. And a squire to wash the blood from his hands after a hard day's work." Glaring at Riley, she propped her plumb fists on her hips. "He has a wife, too. A wife joined to him in a holy union."

"I understand that," she whispered harshly. "Now leave

me be." Walking to the brazier, she stood beside Gertie, warming her hands over the flames.

Gertie leaned near her ear. "We are within walking distance of London. We are within reach of our freedom. We could this night be in the bosom of our dear King Edward. What say you, cousin? There are no chains binding you. At least none that I can see. It will soon be spring and time for planting the seed of Snowden in the court of York."

Sitting down on the rush strewn ground, Riley huddled into her cloak. She laid her head on her knees and wrapped her arms around her legs as if she could burrow into hiding from Gertie. Her heart was binding her tighter than any chains.

"No, we must wait," she pleaded. "We must wait."

Gertie's words came back to her, tantalizing her like a summer breeze. *His only secret is that his heart is drawn to you.*

She smiled at that thought, rolling the words over in her mind. *Love cannot long hide itself,* she reasoned. *If he does love me, he will soon confess it. If he does love me.*

She felt Gertie's eyes boring into her and the heat of her presence.

"You are a child, Riley Snowden. You are no soldier. You are nothing more than an innocent easily swayed by a man's attention."

Riley closed her eyes, refusing to look up, not wanting to meet Gertie's angry stare.

Throwing up her hands in frustration, Gertie kicked at the floor of the tent. "You were reared a Snowden, always focused on your path in life. Never distracted or deterred by foolish whims. You wanted to kill Cornwich. You wanted Lynchburg's head to present to your king."

It was true, she knew, but now the thoughts of death were repugnant to her. Now the only victory prize she wanted was the love of her enemy. When had she become so feckless? she cried within herself.

"What do you hope to gain from Lynchburg?" Gertie

asked. "Love? Can you be so naive as to truly hope for that?"

She heard Gertie kneeling beside her and felt her hand like a claw pinching her shoulder. "We must leave this place, the sooner the better."

"I must think it through," she answered.

Her grip tightened, truly hurting her. "Think it through, then, Lady Snowden. Think it through to the very core of your heart—the heart given to you by your father. He perished five years ago at the hands of Philip De Proileau."

Riley gritted her teeth as her mind churned around the memory like a rising storm. "Must you invoke my father's name?"

"Aye, for his blood cries out for vengeance. And you turn a deaf ear to him."

"My mother never wished for vengeance," she whispered.

"Your mother was weak, embracing her fate like a martyr," Gertie spewed out her anger as she pushed Riley from her. "But you, Riley, I thought you were made of stronger stuff than that. You can either follow your mother to a silent end or rise up with the warrior spirit of your father and bring us to victory."

As the cadence of her voice faded, Riley lifted her head into the darkness and silence of the tent. Such choices had already brought her to the brink of disaster. She could be neither her mother nor her father, she realized. In her fight to reclaim her name she had lost her heart, the core of her identity. Only with Lynchburg could she feel again the richness of life, the extreme of happiness. And know who she was.

"I will think on it," she said again, but her mind was already made up.

Chapter Fourteen

Lynchburg stepped into the inner chamber of the queen's tent and stood waiting for her acknowledgment. She sat at a mahogany table with the Earl of Cornwich on her left and the Dukes of Somerset and Exeter on her right. The air was filled with a bluish smoke and the smell of burning wood chips in the brazier.

In the half-light of the tent, she looked youthful and soft. Her robes of purple satin seemed to swallow her small frame, and the gauze veil of her headdress flowed down across her shoulders. Her auburn eyes studied Lynchburg in airy displeasure as he sank to one knee before her.

"You are late," she snapped. "I had anticipated your arrival a day ago."

"I beg your forgiveness, Your Grace," he said with his head bowed. "I was waylaid on the road to London."

She made a little face as she turned back to her men. "You must be getting old, Lynchburg, if you cannot efface a band of ruffians with greater speed than that."

He remained on his knee in silence for a full minute before she spoke to him again. "Rise," she said with a ragged sigh. "I should never have sent you off to be married. Had you been with me at Mortimer's Cross, we would not have lost that battle. Sit." She patted the table, indicating an empty seat beside her. "The king's stepfather is dead. And so is Sir John Throckmorton. And so are nine other Lancastrian gentlemen. Executed by Edward of March, all of them. He will not stop now. He is in a rapture because of that victory."

"Where is Edward?" Lynchburg asked as he took his seat.

"God only knows." Cornwich shrugged apologetically, then winced at the sight of his son-in-law's head wound. "Even our best spies have lost track of him. All we know is that he is not yet in London."

"You should have seen him at Mortimer's Cross," the queen fumed. She pressed her palms together and tightly interlaced her fingers. It was a nervous gesture that Lynchburg had never seen her use before. "He was a giant in golden armor, a jeweled coronet on his helmet. On the day of the battle three strange lights appeared in the heavens, an omen of his victory." She rolled her eyes in exaggerated disbelief. "So now he thinks he is being guarded by angels. He has even put three suns on his banner. He calls it the sun-in-splendor." She fanned out her fingers in mock awe. "Everywhere he goes the people flock to him as if he is the Savior."

"But the magnates are still loyal to Henry," Exeter assured her.

"That means nothing," she snapped. "Edward is gaining the loyalty of the merchants. They are wealthier than most of the nobility. The magnates will follow the merchants. They need them as husbands for their daughters." She looked to Lynchburg for help. "When the nobles see the wealth of England shifting toward Edward, so will they. What should we do?"

He folded his arms on the table and drew a deep breath. "We are prepared to attack the Yorkists at St. Albans. Let us do so. We'll drive out the Yorkist troops, then leave the village in peace." He held out his hands as if offering her the only solution. "There will be no looting, nothing to alarm the citizenry of London. Then we will enter the city peacefully."

"What if London closes its gates to us?"

He shook his head, giving her a look of reassurance. "If we leave St. Albans in peace, London will not close its gates. They will have no reason to fear us."

"What if they do?" the queen asked firmly. "London can withstand a siege for months. But what about my troops? How will my men live through a winter's siege?"

"As armies always have." He smiled at her patiently. "On the inspiration of their leaders."

Her tight frown vanished, and a gleam of amusement brightened her auburn eyes. She glanced into the faces of her assembly, and her fingers fluttered toward the door, inviting them to leave. "I must speak with Lynchburg and Somerset in confidence," she announced. "Please leave us for now."

Begrudgingly Cornwich and Exeter stood up and bowed before backing out of the tent. It angered them that only Lynchburg had a way of softening the queen's temper. As they left, they could not disguise the disgust and jealousy on their faces.

The queen reached out for Lynchburg's hand and gripped it in her own. "You are my greatest treasure, David, outside of my husband and my son."

Somerset glowered upon hearing those words.

"I am honored by your compliment, Majesty," he said.

She slid her fingers up to rest a placating hand on his arm. "I am truly sorry about your marriage arrangement. I ordered it only because I thought it best for you."

He shook his head to ward off the conversation. "I will deal with it. Do not concern yourself about it."

"We must plan our strategy to take London," Somerset groaned loudly, bringing their minds back to what he considered to be more pressing matters.

Ignoring him, the queen kept her eyes leveled on Lynchburg. "What do you propose, David?"

He searched her face for some sign of reason. How could he make her understand that victory was slipping from her grasp?

"Send word to the mayor that we wish to enter London in peace," he suggested.

"The mayor will not negotiate with us." Somerset eyed Lynchburg, amused. "He is Yorkist. We must seize power, not beg for it."

"We will offer him hostages to hold us to our word," Lynchburg urged them.

The queen held up her hands for silence. "We will not negotiate with the mayor or lay siege to the city." Lowering her hands to the table, she clenched them in tight fists. "I must strengthen my army with an alliance, not deplete it with a siege. And Somerset is right, we cannot beg for power." Glancing toward the door, she motioned for them to bring their stools closer to her. "I have sent an envoy into France to tell King Charles that Edward of March plans to invade his country," she whispered. "I am asking him to ally himself with the Lancastrian dynasty in order to ensure peace for both our lands. The Yorkists can fight off the Lancastrian army but not the entire army of France. When the mayor hears that the alliance has taken place, he will know that the Yorkists are defeated. He will surrender the city to us."

"An alliance with France is too uncertain," Lynchburg said. Her words had chafed his nerves, and he could not hide the anxious tone in his voice. "How do we know that the French king will agree to it? We cannot risk months of negotiations with France only to have them reject an agreement."

Somerset nodded. "I know my cousin, Edward of March. As soon as he is proclaimed king, he will send his own envoys to Charles to negate our every word."

"I will have my French alliance," she insisted. "'Tis the only way to secure my husband's throne."

What is she plotting? Lynchburg wondered, remembering Cornwich's prediction that she would trade Calais to the French in return for their aid.

"I will only do what is best for England," she said, a note of comfort in her voice. "Do not fear."

He knew that he would be a fool if he did not fear her. She had been raised a queen, and she would not be toppled from her throne no matter what the cost. He studied her face, the delicate jaw and slender line of her neck. How fragile she looked, yet how very dangerous she was. She thought to strengthen her rule by diminishing her lands.

If her troops discovered that she planned to give up Calais, they would kill her. Then the country would be ruled by her son, the little Prince of Wales, a rash boy who had inherited his mother's passion for ruthlessness. The war would continue, and another generation would carry on the battles of an ever-weakening country.

She lifted her brows and watched him intently through eyes that were almost black. "You look troubled, David." Placing her warm hand against his cheek, she slid her fingers along the thick stubble of his beard.

"Forgive me, my queen, but I am tired." He stiffened, wanting to recoil from her touch. "With your permission, I will take my leave."

Smiling weakly at him, she patted his arm. "Go then, David, and rest, for I shall need you strong in the days ahead."

With a hurried pace he rose and left the tent, preferring the icy breath of winter on his face to the warm touch of her fingers.

When he entered the inner chamber of his tent, he found Riley sitting in front of the brazier. She was nestled in a heavy blanket, and her hair spilled in a shining mass over her shoulders. Having removed her tunic, she was wearing only her wool shirt. It opened down her chest, revealing the milk white of her throat and the slant of her breast.

As she gazed up at him, her lashes fluttered over sea green eyes that threatened to draw the darkness from his soul.

Another woman wanting something from me, he grumbled inwardly. Removing his cloak, he tossed it over a trunk and walked to the brazier to warm his hands over the fire. "Why do you play the temptress with me?" he demanded. "What do you want? Another new dress? Another gillyflower? What can I offer her ladyship that she may destroy?"

A small ache tightened in her chest. "I wish nothing from you," she said. "I thought to give you something—some respite perhaps."

Respite, he thought with a grunt. *I am going to lose this war, and she thinks to show her breasts to me and give me respite.* His eyes like sputtering coals blinked angrily down at her. *If only I had arrived at camp sooner, I could have spoken with Margaret alone, convinced her to follow my plan. But I was chasing after this traitor while my country was falling from my hands.*

"My lord, your anger bewilders me." She sighed, pulling the blanket higher up on her shoulders. "I truly wish nothing from you. Except your trust."

He gazed back at the fire, then shifted his eyes to hers in a sidelong glare. There was innocence in those green orbs, he noted, and, even more amazing, sincerity. "Trust is not given, Lady Riley, 'tis earned."

Her eyes filled with hurt at his words. "Did I not earn your trust when I saved your life? I could have killed you myself, but I didn't. Have I not proven my trustworthiness?"

"No," he answered sharply. She had saved his life, but for what true purpose he could not be sure.

"There is much I must tell you," she said. Standing up, she let the blanket fall away from her. She was naked beneath the oversized shirt, and he felt his heart thump against his chest. It was the effect she had intended, he knew. Even if he looked away, he would be unable to shield himself from her sensual power. Her scent, her soft beauty overwhelmed him, igniting a primeval need for her.

"If your purpose is to seduce me into promising you my complete trust, then your ploy is most welcome," he said roughly.

Like a swooping hawk, he lifted her into his arms and

carried her to the bed, dropping her roughly against the covers. Her heart began to pound as his lips came down on hers, hungry and searching. Unbuttoning her doublet, he jerked it from her breasts and gripped the rose-tipped mounds in his hands. Her nipples grew hard, puckering with desire as he bit down the soft slope of her throat, then buried his face in the round firmness of her breasts. Nuzzling one ripe nipple, he kissed the stiff peak, his mouth like a fire against her skin.

She moaned as he teased and tasted the plump bud, his hands caressing the satin skin of her belly. Seeking her other nipple, his tongue flicked across the protruding tip, sending a fiery current through her loins. As his hand slipped downward, he found the soft wet curls of her woman's mound and felt her opening to his touch like a blossoming flower.

"I am going to kiss you," he said hoarsely. "Truly kiss you."

She felt puzzled, uncertain of his meaning for he had been kissing her and kissing her skillfully.

His lips moved along the flat of her stomach, his kisses sending out ripples of excitement from each spot they touched. Lowering his mouth to her, he kissed the pink rose of her sex. The shock of his hot tongue dipping into her flesh caused a tiny cry to emanate from somewhere deep within her. Her whole body melted into a mist as his tongue caressed the swollen kernel hidden within her womanhood. The heat of his breath, mingled with his searching tongue, left her keening with ecstasy.

"Please, my lord, shouldn't you undress?" she asked with breathless urgency.

Quickly he slid from the bed and began to disrobe. His eyes were feverish, and already a glow of sweat glistened upon his skin. "You may not have my trust, Lady Snowden," he claimed weakly, "but all else within me is yours to possess."

Her eyes stroked his thick thighs, the muscles that were well defined and taut, and his manhood that was pressing against his furred belly. She wanted to possess him and to be possessed by him, to become one with him in a shared rapture.

"Right now 'tis not your trust that I crave the most," she admitted.

He laughed huskily as he mounted her, parting her legs with his own. Driving his manhood into her, he heard her cry out and smothered it with his mouth. His tongue caressed hers, and the stubble on his face burned her tender cheeks.

She wrapped her legs around his waist and clung to him, her nails gripping his back as he filled her. He abandoned himself to her, thrusting into her with a swelling desire so intense that he was soon lost in a blinding storm of passion. He would give her anything at this moment. His trust, his heart, his life.

She grabbed his buttocks, forcing him to slow down. He would please her, she decided, but at a more leisurely pace. He obliged her and slowed his thrusts though it increased his pain for her. He wanted to release his seed in a fiery bliss, but he would linger a while longer if that was what she wanted. She moaned softly beneath him, her body rising to meet his while her inner flesh, like an undertow, drew him deeper into her.

Her eyes flew open, but she saw only a silver haze as a spasm racked her violently, singeing down her every nerve. Waves of pleasure swept through her, one cresting atop the other, each one shattering the one before with more heightened sensations. The pleasure that fired her blood sent a rush of heat sweeping through her, enveloping her until her climax stunned her with a bolt of ecstasy.

When the quaking within her loins began to subside, she lay beneath him, shuddering for breath.

He withdrew from her, giving her time to regain her senses, then he would enter her again and finish his own pleasure.

She rolled onto her stomach and gripped a cushion, clutching it to her face. Never had she felt anything so intense and so wonderful. Her heart was racing, and her breath panted from the exhilaration she had experienced. Her mind was a befuddled mangle of half-sleep and waking dreams of Lynchburg. *Could there be any greater lover than this man?* she wondered.

He ran his hand along the curve of her buttocks and saw a faded red stripe caused by his belt. The sight of it jabbed his heart with a pang of guilt.

"I am sorry that I whipped you."

Pressing her cheek against the pillow, she faced him and saw the ache in his eyes.

"I am crude in my ways," he explained, unused to making apologies. "Vulgar and coarse. I was hurt that you had betrayed me."

"Hurt?" she asked in surprise. "I can understand your being angry but not hurt."

He looked at her as a man does who has just let slip a confession. His anger turned inward now to his self-betrayal, to his traitorous heart that was drawn to his enemy. "I was hurt by your cruel trick with the hempseed." He hesitated. "Because I had begun to grow fond of you."

"Fond of me?" she asked, a challenge in her voice. "Or fond of my bed?"

"No." He shook his head as he peeled a strand of hair away from her face. "'Tis not just your bed that I want. Though your charms there are sweeter than any I have ever sampled in the past."

She felt overwhelmed with joy. It was as if springtime had broken in her soul, flooding her with warmth and light. He was about to confess his feelings to her!

Rolling into her arms, he clasped her tightly beneath him and gripped her mouth in his own. His passion flowed into her, swelling her loins with fresh fire.

"I wish we had known each other in a time of peace," she ventured, gently and folded her arms around his neck. "I might have been tempted, just a bit, to give my heart to you." She gave him a teasing smile. "That is, if you had proved yourself worthy of me."

He peered at her, his expression heavy with love. "In a time of peace I might have wooed you, milady. But only if the dowry had been very impressive."

"Oh, you cur!" she cried and struck his chin playfully with her fist.

Nipping her knuckles with his teeth, he laughed down at her, his hair falling about his face in glorious disarray. "Now, now, there'll be none of that. I'll not have my mistress cuffing me."

Mistress. The word struck her like a lash across her face driving the joy from her mood. She realized that their play could never be anything more than debauchery, carried out in secrecy, for Lynchburg was already married, committed for life to another.

"What's wrong?" he asked, kissing her turned cheek with soft, gentle caresses. "What bad humor is befalling you, dearest?"

Dearest. She looked at him helplessly as if seeing him beyond an impenetrable barrier. "I wish I could have been the Lady D'Aubere," she blurted, her words coming out in a gush of emotion.

His marriage fell like a black shroud over his happiness, and a desperation clouded his eyes. "I am married, 'tis true. But to a woman who does not even know that she's in the world."

Riley quirked her brows at him. "I thought she was sickly."

He scoffed. "She is beyond sickly. We were not able to consummate the marriage."

Her eyes widened, absorbing the shock of his words. Taking his face in her hands, she cupped his cheeks and felt the stubble of his jaw prick her palms. "Your marriage has never been consummated?"

"Never," he said with a slight shake of his head. "Nor did she ever speak any vows to me. We are not married in the eyes of God, only in the eyes of the queen."

Sliding off of her, he lay on his side, breathing in the scent of her hair. "When I found the strip of cloth on the road and thought you dead, all reason left me. I was like a madman." He took her hand in his and intertwined his fingers in her own. "Now I realize that 'tis not my wife's estate I care about." He kissed the tips of her fingers. "I will gain lands someday, somewhere. But greed is not the soul of my humanness. I crave a life for myself, Riley. When the queen apologized to me for my marriage arrangement, I told her that I would deal with it. But in my mind I thought that—perhaps I should have the marriage annulled."

She was shocked by what she was hearing.

Tumbling on top of him, she let her hair fall about his face, causing his nose to twitch. "Tell me you love me," she teased, ending her last word with a kiss. His lips were warm and yielding, fueling her passion and causing her loins to swell painfully.

"Should not trust come before love?" he asked. "I cannot trust you, Riley, until you surrender to me. Abandon your cause and pledge your loyalty to me forever. Or else there can never be anything between us but suspicion."

She rested her cheek against his chest and felt the vibrating drum of his heart. "I am tired of warring with you," she confessed. "What good am I, even as a Yorkist queen, if I deny my heart? It is the heart that is the soul of our humanness."

She hesitated for only a moment before she slid from the bed, kneeling beside it. *Let the dead seek their own vengeance,* she decided with a welcome finality. *I am a useless vessel to them now.* What a relief it was to let it go, to lay down the sword and embrace life. She felt as if she were emerging from years of a dark confinement.

"I surrender to you, David D'Aubere. And I pledge my loyalty to you from this day forth." Gathering his hands into her own, she brought his signet ring to her lips and kissed it, sealing her oath.

He gazed at her in surprise, his eyes filling with amazement. "Then take my heart," he said, tweaking her chin. "And make it into something better than what 'tis."

"Is that your idea of a confession of love?" she asked, perturbed.

As he pulled her back onto the bed, he snuggled her against him. "Woman, I gave you what I have never given another and yet you want more."

She lifted her eyes to his, hopeful and waiting, but the confession she had hoped to hear did not come. He would not tell her that he loved her.

Wrapping one arm around him, she laid her head against his shoulder, savoring the feel of him, the smell of his skin, and the sound of his breath near her ear.

"Will you petition the church for an annulment?" she asked hesitantly.

"Aye," he murmured. "As soon as this war is over."

If you are still alive, she thought desperately.

"Why must we wait for this war to be over?" she asked, her eyes filling with bewilderment. "Why can't we leave this war behind? We can go to Wales or France, far from these battlefields." She brushed her hand along his forehead, smoothing the hair from his face. "What do we care anymore if York or Lancaster rules this bloody land? 'Tis not worth your life or mine, not any longer."

He grabbed a tress of her hair that lay against his chest and felt the silken strands against the calluses of his fingers. "But I do care about England. 'Tis my past, my ancestry, my blood. I cannot abandon this land and its people to Margaret of Anjou."

She furrowed her brow at him unable to comprehend his meaning. "But I thought that's what you wanted, for her to continue to rule."

He shook his head in disgust. "I have come to believe that she has no love for this kingdom. She only wants power for herself and her son. If we do not take London soon, she will negotiate with the French king to sell him Calais."

"What?" she gasped.

"She will trade Calais for a French alliance," he repeated, blandly. "Margaret will have her crown, and France will gain a valuable piece of our country."

"Why then do you not join Edward of March and fight against her?"

He sat up and plumped his pillows, then propped his back against them. He wished he could explain to her the concept of honor, but at the moment it defied logic even to him.

"I have pledged my allegiance to Henry, and I cannot go back on my word." The sweat glowed across his broad chest as he stared dully at the dying flames in the brazier. "I once thought Henry to be God's appointed king. But now I don't know if any man could hold such high esteem in God's eyes. I must stay here and convince Margaret to take the city. Else this war will drag on until this country is too weak and sick to fight anymore. Then our enemies from other lands will invade us, and England will be no more."

She brought her lips to his, silencing him and tasting the sweetness of his mouth. "Speak no more of this to me," she pleaded. "If we cannot escape this war for good, then let us do so at least for these next few moments."

He wrapped his arms around her and rolled over on top of her. Slipping his tongue past her lips, he explored the moist warmth he found within. His manhood was throbbing, aching to burrow deep into her soft heat. As he pressed his shaft into the folds of her flesh, a delighted gasp sprang from her lips. Gripping his buttocks, she pulled him deeper into her. She was swollen, hungry for him as he sank against her, and for several minutes, he thrust slowly, savoring the white heat of her loins.

Lifting her knees, she rose to meet his thrusts until the heat washed through her, flooding her with swells of pleasure. He cried out as he felt her hot juices flowing down his shaft. His face contorted in rapture, and he tossed his mane like a wild stallion. As he collapsed against her, he wondered if he were dead. How could he have survived the shattering passion that he had just experienced? He felt weak, his body damp with sweat and his energy spent. Reaching out, he entwined a strand of her hair around his finger and brought it to his nose. Still it bore the scent of roses.

"My wild rose of York," he murmured sleepily as he nestled into her arms.

She moaned softly, feeling the delicious warmth and wetness of his skin. Entangled in each other's limbs, they drifted off to sleep, little caring what the morning would bring.

The canvas door parted, and a shadow stole into the tent. Stealthily it moved nearer to the foot of the bed, then hovered for a moment before receding into the night.

"So, milady likes the master's bed," Gertie mumbled as the snow swirled about her. "Well, then, I shall make it into a bed of thorns, and therein shall she perish."

Chapter Fifteen

Riley awoke as the first ray of dawn slanted across the canvas tent. The blanket felt so warm against her naked skin and the feather mattress so soft that she faded back into sleep. Reaching out for Lynchburg's warmth, she felt only the cold, bare linens. With a start she sat up, pulling the covers up over her breasts. A shadow had suddenly appeared at the foot of her bed, and she scooted back against the headboard, her heart pounding.

With a rush of relief she realized that it was only Gertie who was watching her.

Standing beside the flames of the brazier, the old woman glowered with fury. "What a fine sight you are," she snarled. "Naked in the monster's bed." She cocked her head at her and folded her arms across her chest. "Did you find out anything? Were any secrets told to you last night? Or were you even listening?"

Riley climbed down from the bed and walked shivering and naked to the trunk. Her hair streamed down across her breasts, covering her to her waist. Taking out her man's doublet and hose, she began to dress.

"I'm giving up the fight, Gertie." She slipped the doublet over her head, pushing her arms into the oversized sleeves.

"What did he say?" she demanded. "What makes you think the cause of York is lost?"

Riley fastened a belt around her waist and picked up her hose, shaking them out. "Margaret will enlist the help of the French by promising them Calais."

"The bitch," she growled. "When her plans are revealed, she will be killed by her own army."

Riley pulled her hose up over one leg and yawned deeply. "No, Lynchburg will sway her from her plans. He wishes to convince her to take London quickly, before Edward has a chance to arrive."

Gertie stiffened, and her eyes grew round with fear. "If they take London, they will defeat us."

"If they ally with France, they will defeat us." She sighed, no longer caring. "I have surrendered. I suggest you do the same. I will speak to Lynchburg on your behalf, but we must go to him together." She finished gartering her hose and looked up to find her cousin gone.

Running into the outer chamber, she reached Gertie just as she was about to bolt from the tent.

"Where are you going?" she cried, latching on to her arm.

"You may be defeated, but I am not!" she cried. "I will go to London and deliver Margaret's plans to my brother, Geoffrey."

"No, you mustn't," Riley said, shocked that Gertie would take such action. "The soldiers will kill you if you try to leave the camp."

She eyed her young cousin curiously. "What are you talking about, girl? I could walk out of this camp, and the soldiers wouldn't notice, much less care."

"But you shouldn't attempt it," she beseeched her. "You are too . . . old. And the weather is . . . very foul. You must remain here."

She lifted her chin slightly with an air of suspicion. "You've never lacked faith in me before. Wasn't it I who first went to Glenwood Castle and scouted the fortress?

Wasn't it I who rode off into a winter's night with you to London?"

"But your flight requires a horse," she nearly wailed. "And you cannot ride a horse. You know that is your weakness."

"I will set out on foot. 'Tis not a long journey. I will be there within the day."

"No, you will be caught." Riley gripped both her shoulders, pulling her further into the tent. "Please, cousin, I am only trying to protect you."

"Protect me?" she challenged her, pushing her hands away. "Is it me you wish to protect? Or the Lancastrians?"

Riley paced to the farthest corner of the chamber, hoping to escape her question.

"Answer me!" Gertie shouted.

Turning to her cousin, she twisted her hands in misery, remaining silent.

"So now the truth is revealed," Gertie seethed. Her face reddened with anger, and she clenched her fists in balls of rage. "You love the monster. He pleases you in your bed. You wish to forsake your rightful place, your father, and all your kin to sit upon the cock of your enemy."

"Be quiet," she pleaded. "You do not know what you are saying. You do not see what I see in him. He is noble and kind."

Gertie stared at Riley in outrage, her eyes wide with astonishment. "Aye, he was kind when he punished your backside with his belt. That much I saw. He was kind when he imprisoned you in his dungeon. You are blind with lust for the whoreson."

"I would not call him that if I were you," she muttered.

"He is a whoreson, and I will speak the truth. You were once his prisoner, milady," she reminded her. "What are you to him now?"

"Silence!" Her eyes shone with a defiance that startled and sickened the older woman.

"Aye, I will be silent, for I no longer trust you. You have turned from Edward and become Lynchburg's whore."

Riley advanced toward her, menacingly. "Do not dare accuse me of such."

"I accuse you of nothing, milady. I only speak the truth." Spinning on her heel, she stormed from the tent.

As she ducked through the doorway, Riley started after her. Throwing back the flap of the tent, she saw a burst of sunlight and felt a jolting pain as Gertie's fist slammed into her jaw. Staggering backward, her knees buckled and the tent faded into black.

Gertie hurried across the campground, running straight into Lynchburg. Catching her wrist in one massive hand, he pulled her upright before she could topple over.

"Get back to that tent," he ordered.

She noticed that he was pulling a prisoner behind him. The man's hands were bound behind his back, and a rope was secured around his neck from which a leash had been fastened. The young soldier eyed Gertie, his eyes filling with recognition, then he shifted his gaze to the tent from which she'd run.

Gertie paid little attention to the prisoner, her eyes settling on the earl in a murderous glare. "I will no longer serve your whore," she hissed.

Rushing past him, she sprinted across the campground showing amazing spryness for a woman her age.

"I hope your men are more obedient to you than your women," the prisoner smirked.

Lynchburg shook his head as he stared after the fleeing woman, wondering what Riley had done to provoke such rancor. "I'd rather have a thousand men under my command than one woman. They have no physical strength, but their wits are formidable. Their tongues slice deeper than a sword."

A knight approached, and Lynchburg handed the prisoner over to him.

"Take him to the tent erected as gaol. I will question him shortly."

The knight nodded and led the prisoner away.

Lynchburg breathed deeply, inhaling the spicy fragrance of pine and the crisp tang of the winter air. It had been a long morning. He'd set out before dawn with several of his men to hunt. Instead of finding a stag, they'd found a Yorkist camp of scouts and had taken them by surprise, asleep in their tents.

He looked to his own tent and thought of Riley naked in his bed, her hair scattered across the cushions, turning copper red in the rising sun. As he pulled off his gloves, he headed for his tent and the pleasant warmth he hoped to find there.

Riley was pacing in her hunter's clothes, rubbing her sore jaw when he entered.

"My lord," she spoke nervously, then stammered as if unsure of what to say. "May I prepare your breakfast?"

"You can't cook," he said, noting her anxious tone.

"There is partridge left over from last night. I can fetch it for you."

He smiled, feeling helpless in her presence. No woman had ever made him feel weak in the knees, but this one had a remarkable power over him.

"I will breakfast later with the queen," he said kindly. "We will attack tomorrow, and there is much to be done before then."

She ran to him and flung her arms around him, feeling the hardness of his chest and the raw strength of his arms as they encircled her. "Please, I beseech you, my lord, let us leave England this day."

"I cannot." He gently pushed her away. Holding her at arm's length, he gazed into her eyes and wondered at the turbulence he saw there. "I cannot desert my country, my men. 'Tis not possible. This is not so troublesome a battle. Do not worry for my safety."

"I-I have something to tell you," she said, her face coloring in fear.

"Lynchburg!"

It was the queen's chamberlain, and the earl stiffened at the sound of his name.

"How I abhor hearing my name on the lips of a fool,"

he said with a frown. "I must go, Riley. The queen awaits me." He stroked her face with his rough hand. "I will return as soon as I can."

"David, wait," she pleaded, but he put his finger to her lips, silencing her.

"I can wait, but the queen cannot." Briefly he kissed her forehead, then embraced her, swallowing her up in the love and warmth of his arms.

As he left, she wanted to cry out for him to stop, but her courage faded. Her fear twisted inside of her, threatening to shred her nerves. What would he do when she told him that Gertie was her cousin, and that she was on her way to London to reveal the secret he had imparted to her? She groaned and rubbed her throbbing temples. Maybe she didn't have to tell him anything. Gertie was gone. A runaway servant, so what? No one would care. If she did manage to bring harm to the Lancastrian cause, Lynchburg would never know. Would he? She paced the tent as time dragged to a stop and a sense of doom thickened around her like a suffocating smoke.

When the sun began to set, Lynchburg pushed back his stool and stood up on legs stiff from inactivity. He had sat for hours with the queen, Exeter, and Somerset drawing out their battle plans and now he must question the prisoners. He had thought it best to question them first, but the queen had said no. It would take hours to get any answers from them if at all, and she didn't want to waste valuable time. As darkness settled and their plans were finalized, he knew that he must face this unpleasant task. His boots crunched across the frozen ground as he headed toward the makeshift gaol.

When he entered the tent, he saw that the prisoners were bound separately instead of in one bundle as he would have wished, but no matter, he decided. They had been more comfortable than he would have desired, which would make them less ready to talk. He sank to his haunches and stared into their faces, their eyes. They were tired and hungry, and all but one avoided his gaze. The one who had spoken to him earlier was returning his stare with fervent curiosity.

"Lord David," he ventured, "if I may be so bold as to ask, how did you win over the Lady Snowden? I thought her loyal to the Yorkists."

Lynchburg eyed him, darkly. "How did you know Lady Snowden was here? Did she come to you?" The anger was already boiling up inside of him at the thought. If Riley had consorted with this enemy during the day, she would answer for it.

"I recognized her in the camp this morning."

He looked at him, quizzically. "When?" he asked.

"When we first entered. You told her to return to her tent, and she refused."

He quirked his brows in utter befuddlement. "That was not Lady Snowden. That was a serving woman."

Now it was the prisoner's turn to look befuddled. "That was no serving woman. That was Gertrude Snowden, widow of Charles Snowden. He was the nephew of Lord Robert Snowden, who was attainted years ago. She is sister to Lord Geoffrey Seward, Earl of Bellville."

His eyes clouded with rage as the realization bore down on him. She was Riley's kinswoman, a traitor, an enemy who had infiltrated his castle and now his camp. As much as Riley had softened toward him, her heart was still as hard as granite. She had played the tender lover while plotting behind his back to destroy him. She had even pretended to surrender to him! He had told her secrets last night and as unthinkable as it seemed, she may have told them to Gertrude Snowden. *Was that why the old woman was running from the camp this morning?* he wondered. *Was she in London by now, awaiting Edward, telling everything to all who would listen?*

He wanted to bash in the head of this infidel. Unsheathing his sword, he raised it high over the neck of the prisoner. With one swipe he could kill him and silence his rebel tongue forever. But his hand froze in midair. He was weary of bloodshed, betrayal, and war. With an anguished cry, he lowered the sword to his side.

The prisoner stared up at him, disbelieving. "Will you not kill me Lynchburg?" he taunted him. "I thought you were a warrior, a soldier of the queen. Where is your spirit? Has Margaret rendered you as impotent as Henry? Is it her way with all men?"

"Silence, sirrah!" he cried. "You toy with your life, you fool." He turned and left the tent, holding the heavy sword at his side.

He'd been betrayed by men, even the queen, but nothing had ever ripped his heart like this. As he advanced across the field, he lifted his sword and swung it in a wide arc, slicing the air. Near the center of the camp was her tent, her canvas prison where she lay warm and protected, he thought in disgust. The fury burned his eyes as he set his sights on that tent, its canvas billowing in the wind. No siren's song was luring him this time, only contempt and a mad lust for revenge. He sliced the air again with more force than he had ever used in battle. The sword made an evil sizzling sound as it cut the air.

Yorkist witch, he thought. *You will never betray me again.*

Chapter Sixteen

Riley had busied herself preparing a bath, boiling water in pots, and pouring it into the wooden tub Daggot had brought from the supply wagons. Stirring the water with her fingers, she dreamed of Lynchburg's skin wet and sleek beneath her touch and of his muscles yielding beneath her palms. She would bathe him until he was totally relaxed, then she would reveal her dark secret to him. Her crime would not matter because he had given his heart to her.

"Say no more," he would whisper. Running his finger gingerly along the curve of her jaw, he would bring her mouth to his for a kiss. "All is forgiven."

She emptied the last bucket of water into the tub, then carried the empty bucket to the outer chamber.

The flap of the tent flew open, and for a moment she thought that it had been blown back by a gust of wind. A darkness filled the doorway like storm clouds, blocking out all light, and the flames of the brazier fluttered wildly.

Stepping back in fright, she stared at the tall form of Lynchburg, his legs splayed and his arms thick with muscle. His breathing was audible as he stepped into the tent and yanked down the flap, shutting out the sights and sounds of the camp. Raising his sword in both hands, he held its blade down, and, with a mighty heave, drove it deeply into the ground.

He knew. Somehow he knew. She backed into the inner chamber, and he followed her step for step until she felt the canvas wall of the tent molding to her back. "Do you wish me to bathe you, milord?" she asked, her voice cracking.

He glowered at her until she felt her skin catch fire. "Aye, boil me in your witch's cauldron. 'Tis no less than I deserve." In silence he stripped off his cloak, then his clothing until he stood before her completely naked.

His chest was as solid-looking as a marble statue's, his arms bulging with muscle and his shoulders strong and well rounded. Her eyes traveled down his furred chest to the flat terrain of his stomach, then to his slender hips that melded into sinewy, powerful thighs.

"Study me well," he said through clenched teeth. "Do you see any mark on me? Do you see a gash or gaping hole?"

"No, milord," she said timidly. The wound on his forehead had faded, and she saw no other.

"Then why do I ache as I have never ached before?" he asked, his voice deathly quiet. "Why do I feel as if all life has drained out of me?"

"Are you wounded?" Lifting her hands, she implored him. "Tell me."

"First you betrayed me with your hempseed. That I could understand, even forgive. But then you came to my bed willingly. You were tender and passionate." He paused, closing his eyes as if the words were too bitter to speak. "You surrendered to me! Never have I met a woman as warm and sensuous as you. As capable of pleasing a man as you. I thought that you would not betray me again." A great sigh escaped him, and he opened his eyes, which were damp and dull. "I thought that we had put aside our feud."

"We have." She stepped closer to him, softly, no longer afraid.

"Who is the serving wench, Gertie?" he demanded. "Who is she!"

His words grated across her ears, causing her to shudder in pain. "She is my cousin, Gertrude Snowden," she confessed. Her heart had become a boulder, plummeting through her. "I could not tell you of her. I did not want her harmed."

He raised one hand to his temple as if struggling to understand. "I would not have harmed her."

"You would have imprisoned her."

"I would not have killed her!" he cried. "I would not have tortured her. She would have been well cared for. Where is she now?"

His voice lashed her like a cold wind, watering her eyes and staggering her words. "I—I do not know. She left this morning, and I have not seen her since."

"Was she going to London to warn the Yorkists of the queen's plans? The plans that I so stupidly revealed to you?"

She blanched as his angry tone turned evil. "I begged her not to go. I did not order it. She acts of her own accord."

He held his head in his hands as if he were ill. "You could have told me. I could have stopped her."

"I tried to tell you, but you were busy with your queen. I was going to tell you as soon as you returned."

He turned away from her and stepped into the tub, sinking into the warm water. Wetting a cloth, he pressed it to his eyes and laid his head back against the rim.

"Get out." The words sputtered out of him like the dying flame of a candle. "I wish never to look on you again. Go to Daggot. Tell him to house you in the supply tent."

She watched him, unmoving, the cloth pressed to his eyes.

"Please, David. Do not send me away."

"Go," he said, and she heard the finality in his voice.

He does not mean it, she thought wretchedly. *He cannot mean it.* She waited for him to recant. Why would he not listen to her? she wondered as she stood wooden with expectation. And despair. Was it because she had lied to him so many times? she answered herself snidely.

Shuffling toward the door of the tent, she felt only self-loathing. She should never have mentioned the queen's plan to Gertie. And worse than that, she should never have fallen in love with David D'Aubere. It was not possible for enemies to find happiness together, she realized numbly. There were too many wounds from the past, too much to hide. She stepped out into the evening air, brisk and gray, and realized that she did not have her cloak. Wiping a tear from her eye, she decided not to go back for it. What did she care if she froze to death? She had destroyed the heart of the man she loved. With heavy steps she made her way through the snow to Daggot and the ring of supply wagons that surrounded the camp.

All through the night she tossed fitfully, the pain of her loss racking her like a fever. Her heart burned for Lynchburg, and she longed desperately to hold him again, to sleep in his arms and feel his need for her. A sense of hopelessness knifed through her until she wondered if death would not be better than this life of grief and pain.

As the sun rose, she heard footsteps shuffling through the snow, and she prayed that it was Lynchburg seeking her out, wanting to forgive her. If only he would, she would prove to him her trustworthiness. She would dedicate her life to it. Eyeing the canvas wall of the tent, she watched as a dark form took shape.

"David?" she whispered.

Her hope turned to profound disappointment when Daggot answered.

"Get up," he called, "and prepare to ride. The earl has commanded it."

She sat up, her joints aching from so many sleepless hours on the floor of the tent. "Ride where?" she asked shakily as she tucked an auburn tress behind her ear. "Where is Lord David?"

"He has ridden out to meet the Yorkists. He has asked me to bring you to the field."

Her first thought was that she was being exchanged, handed over to the Yorkist army in return for a Lancastrian prisoner. A dread filled her at the thought, yet she knew that it could be true. Lynchburg despised her now and would want to be rid of her. Had he not said that he wished never to see her again?

Pushing off the quilt, she shivered in her doublet and hose. She slipped her feet into her boots, then bound them tightly with strips of leather. Her hose were loose, and she retied them, knotting them above her knees.

"I am ready," she said, but for what she did not know.

Her hair fell in tangled waves down her back, and she quickly combed it with her fingers.

As she stepped out into the morning's gray light, Daggot handed her her a cloak and a hood to hide her hair.

The weather was cold and bleak, matching her mood as she donned the cloak and quickly swung up onto her mount.

Glancing behind her at the camp, she noticed that most of the soldiers were gone. Their fires were smoldering piles of ash, and the tents were quiet and empty.

"Put on your hood and cover your hair," Daggot ordered. "And stay behind me. You won't get hurt."

Get hurt? she wondered. Pulling her hood on, she swept her hair up under it. "Where are we going?"

"To St. Albans to watch the battle," he said. "The master wants you to witness the loss of your cause."

"My cause," she sputtered. "You know who I am?"

Daggot's eyes fired at her like blazing arrows. "Aye, he told me that you are Snowden, the most loathsome of my master's enemies. He wants you to watch your army's defeat."

"Oh, he does, does he?" she snapped. *So this is how he will take his revenge on me,* she thought. *By making me watch as he obliterates the army I had once hoped to assist.*

Daggot's horse, sensing his master's anger, tossed its head and sidestepped nervously. "You do not realize what a kind lord and master you had. When you are in Edward's clutches, you will know what you have lost. But by then it will be too late."

"What are you talking about?" she asked, but he had already turned and was riding away. "Am I to be exchanged to Edward?"

Kicking her horse to a full gallop, she pursued him. "I demand to know what you are talking about!" she cried as she caught up to him.

He pulled on the reins, slowing his horse and turning his mount to face her. "My master will gladly give you over to Edward when the time comes. Perhaps Edward will reward you by taking you to his bed—Yorkist whore."

"I am not a whore," she retorted, her fists gripping the reins tightly.

Daggot's eyes narrowed to angry slits, and his tone was thick with venom. "You are a whore, Mistress Riley, as surely as your Edward is a rutting buck. His reputation as a despoiler of women is legendary. And for his crown you threw away the love of a man."

Her chest felt heavy, and tears glistened in her eyes. "How do you know that David loves me?"

He stared at her, his eyes dimming at the memory. "I have known it since the night he caught us together in his chamber."

She wanted to tell Daggot that she had never wanted to lose Lynchburg's love, that she still loved him and always would, but she knew that he would not believe her.

He galloped across the fields that were buried in snow and headed toward the bluff that overlooked the tiny village of St. Albans. She pursued him, reaching the bluff and reining her mount to a halt beside him. Looking down, she was stunned by the sight below. Hundreds of men were preparing for battle. More than two hundred knights in black armor sat astride warhorses with their lances, maces, and poleaxes strapped to their mounts. Foot soldiers blanketed the field wearing layers of deerskin or leather jackets stuffed with tow. In their hands were billhooks and half-pikes. Archers were mounted on horseback, and at the front of the lines, noblemen in Dutch plate were riding missodors.

"Where is the Earl of Lynchburg?" she asked anxiously.

He pointed across the field to three horsemen riding

along the periphery of the battlefield. "He is riding with Her Majesty and the Prince of Wales."

Riley stared at the tiny woman on a mare, buried in an ermine-trimmed cloak and hood. By her side was a small boy, also in an ermine cloak, who was riding a magnificent-looking stallion. The woman was pointing toward St. Albans as if giving orders, and Lynchburg was nodding at her every word.

His sword was strapped to his horse along with his mace, and she wondered worriedly if his weapons would be enough to protect him. If he should be unhorsed, his heavy armor would hinder his escape.

The queen turned away from him and rode slowly to the periphery of the field. Swinging down from his horse, Lynchburg freed his sword and mace and walked through the rows of foot soldiers to the head of the battlefield. To her horror she realized that he would not fight on horseback or remain at the rear to protect the queen and prince. He was heading toward the very front lines of war. She wanted to scream at him to stop.

The Yorkist troops were assembling at the village's boundary, and they appeared to match the Lancastrians in strength and number. A man in Dutch plate rode along the front line of the Yorkists as he took his place at the head of his troops.

"Who is that?" Riley asked, wondering if he were Edward.

"Lord David told me that these troops are being led by the Earl of Warwick," Daggot said. As if reading her mind, he added, "Our spies have already informed us that your Edward is not here."

She cringed as the Yorkist and Lancastrian troops charged onto the battlefield, their piercing cries ringing through the air. The mounted archers rode to the south of the field and launched their arrows into the advancing rows of Yorkists. A hail of arrows hissed through the sky and rained down, thudding into the bodies of soldiers and into the shields of others. The clatter was deafening as the foot soldiers from both sides met in a thunderous clash. Poleaxes clanged against armor and soldiers screamed in pain.

In the foray she lost sight of Lynchburg, then saw him again, near the front of the field. He swung his mace, smashing the armor of a soldier and knocking his helmet from his head. With his sword, he knocked down an advancing enemy and quickly ran him through.

Riley wanted to ride into the battle and fight beside him, protect him, and help him. Another hail of arrows flew into the Yorkist ranks, driving them back.

A warrior staggered across the field, unhorsed by a blow from Lynchburg's mace. He drew his sword and aimed a slicing blow at the earl's head, but Lynchburg ducked and drove his mace into the man's belly, crushing his armor. He fell to the ground, his blood turning the snow crimson.

"Dear God," she prayed aloud, "please make this stop."

She had never seen Lynchburg's skill before, had never witnessed his vocation of death, and this grisly display of might stirred within her a sickly mixture of horror and awe.

As the clouds began to dissipate, the sun glimmered across the ground in patches of light. Everywhere were fallen men in pools of blood. Horses, having lost their masters, galloped aimlessly across the field.

The mounted archers lit their arrows and prepared to fire them into the village. Lynchburg saw them and waved at them to stop.

"Don't burn the village!" he cried, causing them to lower their weapons. "Henry is within!"

A soldier rode up behind him, wielding a mace, and Riley screamed out in warning, though through the noise of battle he could not hear her. He turned with his sword raised and toppled the rider from his horse. Springing to his feet, the soldier unsheathed his own sword and steel clashed against steel as the two men fought, circling each other. Riley spurred her horse forward, hoping to join the fight, but Daggot grabbed her reins and held her back.

"Release me," she ordered. "I must help him."

"I do not understand you," he smirked. "You would help the man you had hoped to destroy? Have you had a change of heart?"

"Shut up, you fool. You know nothing about me, about us."

He looked at her, his eyes unreadable.

"I did not betray him to the Yorkists," she explained, trying to pull her reins from his grip. "I tried to stop my cousin from going to London, but she went against my wishes."

"You are a liar, milady." He smiled darkly and gazed back across the field. "Your treason has already been revealed. And your cause has failed. Look to the south. Your army is retreating."

She looked down and saw the Yorkist troops fleeing with the Lancastrians in pursuit. Lynchburg was sheathing his sword and trudging through the muddy snow toward the village. Prisoners were being dragged through the muck, and squires were hauling chains to bind them.

"Come," Daggot said, "we must return to camp. The Yorkists have met their fate."

Holding the reins of her horse, he steered the animal northward. She glanced behind her in time to see Lynchburg striding into the village, his scabbard flashing at his side. For years she had been told what to do and when to do it. First by her father, then by the nuns of Calais. By God, she thought, casting a fiery glare on Daggot, she would not submit to the commands of a groom.

Snatching the reins from his hands, she turned her mount toward St. Albans and charged down the bluff heading into the village. Her hood fell into the wind, releasing her hair in a cloud of red on gold. As she sped downward, her cloak fluttered out behind her, giving her the appearance of an angel in flight.

The road leading into the village was choked with men hoping to pillage the town. Many of them were knocked aside by her mount as the horse slowed its pace and waded into the crowd. The men were shrieking in victory and stumbling toward the shops and cottages, trampling everything under foot. She heard the sound of a door being broken down, the wood shattering. Her ears rang from the deafening shouts of the soldiers and the screams of women and children.

Lynchburg moved through the crowd, his eyes tired and angry. He knew that he could not control a mob such as this. As his eyes scanned the rioters, he spied Riley riding into the village as if she were unaware that she swam through the very fires of hell.

"Dear God," he muttered and battled his way back toward the gates of the village. Reaching the mare, he grabbed her reins and struggled to guide the horse down the street that was swollen with crazed soldiers.

"David!" she cried, seeing the crowd crushing in around him.

Leaping up onto the horse, he pulled the reins from her tight grip and steered the animal toward a stable on the far side of the village. Within minutes they were safe within its walls.

She clung to him as he pulled her from the horse, grasping fistfuls of his cloak in her hands.

"What on earth possessed you to ride into the village?" He shook her roughly. "You could have been killed by those men. They are like wolves in a frenzy from the smell of blood."

"I had to see you, to tell you that I did not mean to betray you."

"You say that now that the battle is won. Now that the Yorkist cause is defeated." His eyes were as blue as a clear morning sky, and she melted in the heat they emitted. Twisting from his grip, she sank to her knees before him.

"I am not lying," she whispered. "I beg your forgiveness on my knees." Reaching up, she grasped his hands and brought them to her lips. "Would I humble myself before you like this if I were lying?"

"Get up," he pleaded and grabbed her elbow, lifting her

to her feet. "We have no time for this. I have to find a way to get you out of St. Albans."

A giggle reached his ears, and he snatched around, his eyes scanning the empty stalls. Motioning for her to stay put, he drew his sword and crept toward the back of the stable. When he had reached the last stall he paused, lowering his sword to his side.

"A lady fair was dancing, dancing , dancing. A lady fair was dancing one fine day," a thin voice sang.

Riley walked quickly to where Lynchburg stood and raised up on tiptoe to see over his shoulder. A tiny man was crouching in a corner, and she noticed the childlike innocence in his face and his boyish stature. His brown hair was curled over his ears, and his eyes, a deep brown, rolled as if searching for something unseen. His mouth was small and puckered, and his nose appeared too long. She thought him an idiot, frightened by the battle, who had taken refuge in the stable.

Sheathing his sword, Lynchburg went down on one knee, his head bowed. "Behold your king, my lady," he introduced her.

Henry pulled off his shoe and began to count his toes through his hose. "One, two, three, four, five." He giggled delightedly.

Lynchburg set his elbow on his knee and rested his chin in his hand. "Lady Riley Snowden, may I present to you Henry VI, King of England and France and Lord of Ireland."

She curtsied stiffly although she suspected that homage was not what he needed at the moment.

"Your Majesty," Lynchburg greeted him in a voice inordinately loud, Riley thought. "You must come with me at once." He held out his gloved hand to the king, but Henry scrambled away, huddling deeper into the corner of the stall. "We cannot delay your departure," he ordered sternly. "Get up now and come with me, Sire."

Henry looked at him with eyes that were puzzled and fearful.

Riley felt a twinge of pity for him and wondered at the great Lynchburg, who could command an army but could not deal with one simple-minded man. *Men,* she thought with a huff, *they know only how to shout and cajole. They know nothing of diplomacy and grace.*

She smiled sweetly at the king and approached him slowly. Settling down next to him, she gently took one of his hands in her own. "Your Majesty, you cannot stay here," she said softly. "You must come with us. We will take you home. Would you like that?"

He nodded briskly and held on to her hand as they rose together.

"He will come with us," she said to Lynchburg, giving him a reproving glance. "Come, Your Grace."

Putting one arm around the king, she led him from the stable. Lynchburg grasped the reins of the mare and followed, shaking his head in wonder at her skill.

"Put your hood back on," he advised her as they stepped out into the open. "It would not behoove this mob to attack a woman, even if she is with me. They are out of control." He sighed heavily as he glanced around. "And I do not wish to have to kill my own men."

Riley quickly pulled her hood on, not wanting to witness any more battles this day. Keeping to the boundary of the town, they made their way on foot back to the village gates. When they arrived at the main road, Daggot was waiting, his horse steaming and his face flushed.

"Lord David, I . . . she . . . she ran from me," he blurted.

"I know," Lynchburg said with a shrug. "'Tis her way. Take her on your horse back to camp, and I will mount and ride with the king."

Daggot's eyes grew wide and glassy in reverence. "The king! Your—Your Majesty," he said, bobbing his head, unsure of what to do.

The king stared about as if he could neither see nor hear. "A lady fair went dancing, dancing, dancing, a lady fair went dancing one fine day," he sang as he caught a snowflake on his finger. Grinning, he watched it melt.

When they arrived back at camp, Lynchburg dismounted and assisted the king from the mare. "You will have to come with us," he said to Riley, worriedly cutting his eyes at her. "I fear the king may not proceed without you."

She slid from Daggot's horse and pulled her hood tightly about her head as she followed Lynchburg and the king to the queen's tent. Henry kept casting glances over his shoulder, making sure that she was near him. As Lynchburg lifted the flap of the tent, he motioned for Henry to enter, but the king shrank back, frightened by the sound of the wind beating against the canvas walls.

"Your Majesty," Riley urged, feeling a nervous clench in her stomach. "You must enter. Your wife awaits you."

"Lady fair, lady fair," he half-sang, half-hummed as he strolled into the tent.

Riley entered but remained outside the main chamber where the queen was waiting. Surrounded by guards, she sank to the floor and kept her head bowed like a humble squire, hoping and praying that they would not see through her disguise.

As Lynchburg entered the chamber, he saw the queen seated on a thronelike chair, her young son standing by her side and the Dukes of Exeter and Somerset standing behind her.

"Henry!" she cried, springing from her chair. Lifting her long skirt, she ran to him and threw her arms around him. "Henry," she said, kissing him on both cheeks.

The prince stood back, eyeing his father with a black contempt.

"Dearest"—her voice shook with excitement as she turned toward her son—"come and greet your father. He has been freed from the Yorkist prison."

The boy approached with slow, reluctant steps and hugged Henry with arms that were limp from lack of emotion. There would be no show of love from him, Lynchburg realized, for he was too much the warrior prince to feel affection for his demented father, a man with whom he had nothing in common. Unlike the meek Henry, the little prince was fearsome. He was reputed to train constantly with weapons and with a fierceness unnatural for a child of five. War was all he ever talked about.

"Your Majesty," Lynchburg addressed Queen Margaret. "Begging your pardon, I must tell you that the men have sacked St. Albans."

"I know," she said with a dismissive wave of her hand. "I told them to sack every town in southern England if need be. 'Tis in lieu of payment."

"Forgive me, Your Grace, but such actions will cause London to panic. They will close the gates of the city. They will not allow us to enter."

Exeter and Somerset exchanged worried glances. "The city gates are already closed," Exeter stated. "Edward of York will arrive at any moment with his troops. The mayor and aldermen of London have sent word to us. They will give the city over to his protection."

"Not if we take it now!" Lynchburg nearly shouted. *Damn fools,* he thought. *To tarry is to lose everything.* "Edward of March has not yet arrived. We must negotiate with the mayor to admit the royal court."

"The Londoners are frightened," Exeter explained. "They threaten to riot if we enter. The mayor will not open the gates."

"My troops are famished," the queen interjected. "The winter has been cruel, and they are nearly starved." She gazed at Henry with a calm smile and patted his hand reassuringly. "We must return to York."

"We cannot retreat," Lynchburg implored her. "Not now that the war is nearly won. We need only take London to claim victory."

The queen glared at him, letting him know that she would not endure this argument much longer. "My troops cannot survive the months of waiting until London surrenders. What will they eat? We need to retreat across the

River Trent, where we have plenty of food. We will attack London in the spring." She dropped her voice to a whisper. "By then we will have gained the aid of the French."

"No!" he cried, digging his fingers deep into his hair. How could he make them understand? If they retreated now, the war would be lost. Edward would arrive, and along with Warwick he would strengthen his forces. He would crown himself king at St. Paul's Cathedral. He would begin his own negotiations with the French. By spring he would be charging toward York in ruthless pursuit of the Lancastrians.

"The magnates of England are behind Henry," the queen said sighing with growing impatience. "You know that."

"You need the allegiance of the merchants, not the magnates." His eyes met her cold stare with equal determination. "London is the wealthiest city in Christendom. Without it, you will never control England." His eyes shifted to Somerset, who flashed him an arrogant smile. It was, after all, his plan the queen had chosen, not Lynchburg's. "The magnates cannot give you London," he warned. "They can only give you their loyalty. And that is as changeable as the wind. Do not put your trust in them. They will be Edward's men in the end, if they are not his already."

"By God, you've gone too far, Lynchburg!" Somerset shouted, his hand grasping the hilt of his sword.

"Stay your hand, Somerset," the queen pleaded. "David," she spoke softly, drawing his full attention by using his familiar address. "Come with me to York. I need you to help me draw my battle plans."

Henry began to giggle uncontrollably and sank to the ground, his small form rolling over onto his side. His shoulders shook as his eyes danced about the tent.

"No." Lynchburg raised his hands in refusal and backed away from her. "There will be no battle plan. The war is lost."

"Nonsense. I should have you drawn and quartered for such treasonous prattle. We will defeat Edward of March and take London in the spring. Until then we will send Edward a message of his own pending doom." She turned to Exeter and Somerset. "Who are our prisoners?"

"Lords Bonville and Rosemon," Somerset replied. "And Lord Geoffrey Seward."

Riley gasped at this news and quickly clasped her hand to her mouth. Lord Geoffrey was Gertie's brother.

Lynchburg glanced toward the door as if suddenly aware of her nearness. His eyes filled with irritation that she had made any sound at all.

"Bring them to me," the queen ordered, her eyes glowing cruelly. "I want them beheaded at once, and their heads mounted outside the city gates." She folded her hands in self-satisfaction and rested them against her stomach. Her repose was regal, arrogant. "Let that be the first sight Edward sees when he rides into London."

"No," he said. "We must not execute them. If you need money, you must ransom them, Your Majesty."

Her eyes sparked at him. "Ransoming them will prove nothing to Edward but that we are broke!"

"Of course, Your Grace," he submitted with a brief bow. "I will bring the prisoners to you at once. But would it not be wise to execute them at night? It would be a shame for their last sight on earth to be the light of day. Is not the sun the banner of Edward? Why not rob them of their symbol of hope and make them die in the darkness that they have wrought?"

Riley could not believe what she was hearing. This man whom she had grown to love was going to execute her cousin's brother.

"As long as their heads greet Edward when he rides into London, I care not when they die," the queen replied dryly. "As soon as the sun sets, you must bring them to my campfire. My son and I will watch their executions."

He glanced down at the little prince whose eyes burned through him. An evil smile twitched at the corner of the child's mouth.

"As you wish, Your Grace," he uttered and bowed as he

backed away. Leaving the tent, he motioned for Riley to follow him.

"Where are you going?" she whispered frantically. Catching up to him, she strode with him out into the afternoon light.

"Back to the battlefield to collect my horse and attend my wounded," he murmured. "Go to my tent and wait there."

"Are you really going to execute those men?" she cried angrily.

He stopped and turned to glare at her as if her questions annoyed him. "What choice do I have in that?" Pulling himself up onto the mare, he kicked it to a gallop and rode hard from the camp.

He may have no choice, but I do, she thought. She could change the fate of at least one of those prisoners. *But how?* she wondered, glancing helplessly toward the tents of the knights. Which of the hundreds of tents housed Lord Geoffrey, and how would she ever be able to free him? Her hopes began to dim as she realized the impossibility of her task. Standing alone on the grounds, she felt the icy wind stinging her cheeks and her own sense of inadequacy haunting her. She had been useless throughout the war, powerless to stop her father's death in battle. Or her brother's death from hopelessness and destitution. Or her mother's death from a broken heart. Inhaling deeply, she turned toward the tents and looked upon them with new resolve. She had not saved her family or even avenged them, but tonight she would at least save the life of Geoffrey Seward.

Chapter Seventeen

"Y̶ou there," Riley called to a young squire who was busy tossing pine logs onto a fire.

The boy looked at her from across the flames, his eyes watery in the winter air. He wore a hood over a thatch of brown hair and a deerskin jacket over his wool doublet. The smoke rose into the air, shielding her from his curious gaze.

"I am servant to Lord David D'Aubere," she explained, attempting a low, masculine tone. "He wishes to know where the prisoners are housed."

"In the tent yonder." He pointed behind him. "Don't he know where the gaol is?"

She strode toward the tent, catching sight of the guard at the entrance and wondering uncomfortably how many more guards might be within. As she approached the man, she saw that he was very large with a long scar down the side of his face and a callous look in his eyes. Her steps faltered, and she felt her resolve beginning to weaken.

I must go through with this, she told herself. *I cannot let Lord Geoffrey die.*

He watched her in silence until she felt her flesh prickle beneath his stare. Could he tell that she was a woman beneath her boy's clothes? Was she about to be seized and hauled before the queen?

"Lord David D'Aubere wishes to question the prisoner Bellville," she announced, a slight tremble in her voice.

Jerking his head to the side, he muttered. "Go in, boy." His eyes were red and swollen, and his breath reeked of ale.

Lifting the canvas flap, she ducked inside. It was cold in the tent, there being no fire, and the air smelled of soiled straw. Several men were chained and stripped of their armor. Wearing only doublet and hose, they were shivering in the frigid air.

Lord Geoffrey looked up as she entered, blinking into the brief burst of light. He was not the handsome earl she remembered from her childhood, but an aging man with gray hair and deep lines etched in his face. As he stared up at her, there was no recognition in his eyes.

Three guards were seated on the floor, gambling. They paused at their game and glanced up at her, irritated by the interruption.

"Lord David wishes to see Bellville at once," she announced, hoping that they wouldn't notice her quaking knees and the nervous crack in her voice.

"For what?" one of the men asked. He rose to his feet and swayed slightly. He had been drinking, too, she realized. Good.

"He wishes to question the prisoner," she answered.

"He does, does he?"

Another man smacked his fist against his palm. "I wouldn't want to be questioned by Lynchburg. I was hit by him once. I thought I'd been struck by a poleax."

The three men laughed roughly.

"Get up!" the drunken one yelled to Bellville and kicked him in the ribs. Riley bit her lip to keep from yelling at him to stop. "I'll drag your worthless hide to Lynchburg myself." He yanked the prisoner to his feet and shook his chains to ensure their sturdiness.

Hobbling out into the icy wind, Lord Geoffrey shuddered as the cold air seized him.

Will we get out of this alive? Riley wondered as she led the way to Lynchburg's tent, listening to Geoffrey's faltering steps and the rattle of his chains followed by the guard's drunken shuffle. Her body was shaking more from fear than from the cold, and her mind began to buck against her plan. It felt as if all eyes were upon them as they trudged across the camp. She had to see it through. She was past the point of retreat. As they strode into Lynchburg's tent, the guard glanced around, seeing no one.

"Where's your master?" he asked sternly.

"I'll fetch him," Riley said, her mind grasping at her hastily thought-out plan. As she backed toward the door, she spied a pile of firewood and breathed deeply, steadily, trying to calm her racing heart. Picking up a small log, she swung it high and cracked it against the back of the guard's skull. The blow sent him sprawling facedown on the ground. Crying out in alarm, Lord Geoffrey toppled to his knees, tripped by the chains around his ankles.

Quickly she grabbed the key that hung from the guard's belt and unfastened it with fingers that were trembling violently.

"Who—who are you?" Lord Geoffrey asked, breathlessly.

"I am Riley Snowden." Sliding the key into the lock, she twisted it, snapping the iron cuffs from his ankles.

"No, my hands first," he begged. "My hands."

"Oh, of course," she panted, flustered. Jamming the key into the wrist irons, she freed him from his bonds. The chains were tangled about his feet and together they swiftly unwound them.

"Riley," he said, when his legs were at last free. Reaching out, he cupped her face in his hands. "I have not seen you since you were a small girl."

"No time to get reacquainted," she warned. "You must flee. Help me take the clothes from the guard. You will change identities with him and escape."

He rolled the guard over and untied the belt from his chain mail. As he tugged off the man's garment he spoke hurriedly. "Your cousin, Gertie, is at my townhouse in London. I saw her for only a moment before I left with

Warwick's forces." He held the chain mail up to his chest, gauging its size. "She told me that she had been with the Lancastrians."

Riley felt a shiver of fear as she pulled the belt from beneath the guard. "Has she told you anything about Lynchburg? And me?"

"No," he answered, pulling the chain mail on over his head. "I had no time to talk with her. I will question her at length when I return."

She wrapped the belt around his waist and fastened it securely.

"You should have seen her when she arrived in London," he continued. "She was ragged and nearly frozen. All these months I thought her in France."

She retrieved the guard's knife and tucked it into a loop of his belt.

Grasping her hand, he stopped her and scrutinized her face. "What do you mean, did she tell me anything about Lynchburg and you? What are you doing here?"

"There's no time to explain," she said as she stepped past him and poked her head through the opening of the tent.

She saw only a few knights and foot soldiers milling about the camp. Most of them would still be reveling at St. Albans. Slipping back inside, she viewed Lord Geoffrey with a meticulous eye. He looked very much like the guard in his chain mail and wide leather belt.

"You must cover your hair," she said, running to Lynchburg's trunk. She opened it and pulled out a chain mail coif, then tossed it to him. "Put this on."

He obeyed, and pulled the coif down over his head, adjusting it across his forehead.

"Hurry, and Godspeed," she whispered, frantically pushing him toward the door.

"What about you? Shouldn't you come with me?"

"Aye," she realized. "I suppose I must. But we cannot leave together. It would draw suspicion. Go to the River Lea and wait for me. I will meet you within the hour. If I am not there by that time, you must go on without me."

"No." He shook his head, grasping her shoulders. "I will not leave you."

"Don't be an idiot," she admonished him. "Just do as I say."

"At the River Lea, then. I will see you within the hour." With a look of resignation, he turned and strode from the tent.

At last she could breathe again. Looking down, she saw the lifeless form of the guard. Kneeling beside him, she put two fingers to his neck and felt for a pulse. He was alive, but when he woke up he would have a terrible headache. And she would meet a terrible fate unless she, too, escaped. Lynchburg would not harm her, she knew, but he would not be able to save her from the queen's wrath. Or from the bloodthirsty little prince.

Pulling her cloak tighter around her, she headed out into the wind. It was nearing dusk, and she knew that even if she made it to the river before the wolves caught her scent, she'd have little chance of finding Lord Geoffrey in the darkness. It would be best to hide in the woods and climb up into the high branches of the trees for the night. In the morning she would set out for London on foot as Gertie had done.

When Lynchburg returned to camp, the hour was nearing midnight. The moon had risen, half obscured by winter clouds, and the fires were burning low, casting golden lights across the ground.

The queen had expected him to execute three prisoners at sunset, and although the hour was late, he would have to fulfill her orders before he could take his rest. Hopefully the delay would have given her time to think, to reconsider ransoming them. He was so tired of bloodshed.

He reined his horse to a halt and dismounted. No more death tonight, he hoped, rubbing his eyes wearily. He only wanted the cool touch of Riley's fingers on his chest. He wanted to feel the cold tips of her breasts between the heat of his lips. Aye, he had forgiven her, but he had not forgiven himself. Closing his eyes, he breathed in the bitter air of winter. He had been reckless to repeat the queen's plan to her, and she had been equally reckless in repeating it to Gertie. He had given her his heart, then in the aftermath of their passion, he had let slip a well-guarded secret. Never again would he be so stupid as to allow his emotions to cripple his judgment.

"My lord?"

He opened his eyes in irritation to see the queen's chamberlain standing before him. His fur-lined cloak appeared to weight down his skinny frame, and his smile seemed strained. It was his way when he had bad news.

"What is it?" the earl asked tersely.

"The queen wishes to see you at once."

He handed his reins to the chamberlain and walked across the campground, his feet leaden as he shuffled through the snow to the queen's tent. She would chastise him no doubt for his lateness, and he would endure it as he must.

Stepping through the opening, he felt the guard's eyes following him suspiciously. He wondered why more men were not guarding her. Where had they gone? He had seen Cornwich, Somerset, and Exeter returning to St. Albans, but the queen's guards had not been with them.

A torch was mounted on a support beam, and its warmth filled the inner chamber, yet an icy chill seemed to permeate the room. He noticed that the rushes had been kicked into disarray, and a wine goblet lay broken on the floor. Befuddled, he looked to his queen, then to the little prince who sat as still as a poised snake ready to strike.

"Your Grace," he greeted her, bowing hesitantly.

She stared at him, her eyes pools of shimmering light, reflecting a fury that could barely be contained. "Bellville has escaped," she said.

"Escaped!" His voice broke like thunder, and he felt a sickness stir in his gut. "How could a prisoner have escaped?"

"How indeed, Earl of Lynchburg? 'Twas your servant who freed him."

"A servant of mine freed a prisoner?" He half-laughed at the very idea. "Have I that clumsy an oaf in my employ?"

"No clumsiness," she said sardonically. Stepping closer to him, she studied him carefully. "'Twas a well-thought out plan. The girl has escaped with him."

Riley, he thought. He looked at the queen, his face contorting as her words pierced him. "No," he said. "It cannot be."

"Where is your wench?" she demanded. "And you needn't lie to me about her. Daggot has confessed everything."

"Daggot!" He felt his mind sinking into a tomb of fear. "You had him tortured," he accused her.

"Aye," she said with a lift of her brows. "But not for long. I have tortured women longer than that boy. One slap, and he babbled like an infant." She smiled in cruel amusement. "He told me that you brought the Snowden woman into this camp. A pretty maiden to be sure. But one who is most disloyal to the Crown."

A pain welled up in his chest threatening to crush him. "She is—*was*—my prisoner."

"You brought an enemy into this camp without informing me!" she shouted. The prince stirred slightly on his stool and fixed his steely eyes on Lynchburg.

"Aye," Lynchburg said deadly. The warmth had gone from his body, and he felt a darkness settling within him that was icy and vast.

She was gone. She had helped Bellville escape and was gone. She had betrayed him again, but this time there would be no forgiveness, only the queen's retribution.

The queen circled him, her eyes flashing as she surveyed him. "Tell me, Lynchburg, what tortures did you inflict on her during her captivity? Wine? Tasty morsels of swan? Flesh?" She stopped at his ear and whispered harshly, "Did you know her carnally?"

"Aye," he confessed, hating himself for being so gullible. Hating Riley, wanting to crush her. If she were standing before him now, he would . . . his thoughts stumbled to a halt. He didn't know what he would do. "I did know her. In her cell at Glenwood Castle," he murmured miserably, "in my father-in-law's bedchamber, in my tent in your camp."

To his surprise, she began to laugh, and the sound of it pricked his heart like a thorn being driven into a scabbed wound.

"David, David, you poor fool," she teased. "You are so like a man, strong and powerful. Yet easily swallowed up by a woman." She pursed her lips, muffling her laughter. "Did you love her? Surely you did. You kept her near you like a man whose passion is fresh. You were in love with her."

"Perhaps," he answered. "But no more. I will find her and punish her for this betrayal."

Her laughter died, and her eyes narrowed at him, cooling into spheres of ice. "What you call punishment, she would probably call pleasure. I will take care of this debacle myself, not you." She pointed a long tapered finger at him. "My men will find her and Bellville, and when they do, they will bring them back to this camp. And you will watch them die."

A desperation raged within him. *How could Riley have done this?* he thought sickly. *What madness had possessed her?*

"Forgive me, Your Majesty," he said, "but I should be the one to find her. She is my prisoner, and I will not be denied the opportunity to bring her to justice, *my* justice."

She took a step back and looked at him in outrage. The little prince quirked his brows at him, having never before seen anyone stand up to his mother.

"Are you defying my orders?" she ranted.

"Aye, Margaret, I am," he said, shocking her further by using her familiar name. He was tired of this woman and the hold that she had on him. He had bent to her will until he had broken in half. "Your orders are wrong and always have been. 'Tis because of you that this country is in turmoil. 'Tis because of you that your husband will lose his throne." The words were past his lips, and there was no taking them back.

He'd gone too far and could only plunge further into destruction. "You have bartered English soil for a cause that you do not know how to win. You have lost the war. You are no longer a queen. And I will no longer obey you."

"Traitor! I will have you arrested!" she shouted. "I will have your head."

He drew his sword and tossed it to her, causing her to scurry backward to avoid being struck by it. It landed with a thud at her feet. "Then come forward now and take it," he dared her.

"Guards!" she called. Two guards entered the tent and stood clumsily in her presence. "Arrest him!"

The guards looked at each other, then at Lynchburg. They didn't dare move.

He stepped toward her, and she quickly retreated. The little prince leaped to his feet and lunged for the sword, lifting it with surprising strength. He swung it, hitting Lynchburg in the side, but his padded houppelande deflected the blow.

Easily he disarmed the boy and sheathed his weapon. "I will take my leave of you, now and forever."

As she watched in shock, he turned his back on her without bowing and walked from the tent.

"Guards!" she shrieked. "Seize him."

The two guards rushed at him from behind. With ease he drew his sword and whirled to face them, causing them to leap back. Knowing that they could not best him, they stood apart from him.

With his eye trained on them, he mounted his missodor and kicked it to a full gallop, heading into the surrounding forest.

Riley awoke to the gentle light falling through the branches of the oak tree. She had trudged deep into the forest until the sky had gone dark, and she had lost her way. Climbing to a high, sturdy branch, she had slept fitfully through the night. The cold had threatened to freeze the blood in her veins, but she was still alive though very tired.

She had been unable to reach the River Lea, and she could only hope that Lord Geoffrey had ridden on to London without her. The city was several hours away, but the sky was clear. If the weather stayed fair, she could reach the city well before nightfall.

Climbing down from the tree, she sat on a low branch, then dropped to the ground. The fall jarred her, compounding the achiness in her joints.

Her stomach burned with hunger, and she scooped up a handful of snow, shoving it into her mouth. It would have to do for breakfast. How long had it been since she had last eaten? she wondered. As she traipsed through the forest, she thought of Lynchburg and the fury that would explode within him when he found out what she had done.

She felt light-headed and stopped to rest, leaning against a beech tree. Sunlight dappled the forest floor, and a breeze whistled through the branches of the trees, causing her to shiver uncontrollably.

He would come after her, and she would have to face his anger unless she kept walking. Pushing away from the tree, she meandered wearily through the snow. The wind howled across a nearby meadow sending up a cloud of swirling flakes from the ground and turning the air white. She heard the pounding of hooves or maybe it was the sound of her own heart. She was so tired that she thought she might be dreaming.

Out of the cloud charged a missodor, and she knew at once that it was him. He sat astride his horse like a god, his armor still in place beneath his fur cloak. The horse slowed to a trot as Lynchburg dismounted and walked toward her.

"Riley," he called as he reached her, grasping her shoulders. He held her upright when she would have swooned. "In the name of God, what have you done?"

"I have saved the life of my cousin's brother," she said weakly.

"And forfeited your own. The queen has ordered you captured and executed."

She felt her knees buckling, her body going limp. "You

have obeyed her orders well. I am captured. Now will you execute me, too?"

Her breath felt like fire against his cheek, and he noticed the glazed look in her eyes.

"No, I will not give you over to the queen." His hands grew heavy on her shoulders, and his flesh glowed eerily in the winter light as if his skin had turned to stone. "I have my own plans for you. And the queen will not deprive me of them."

She winced at his words, his sharp tone twisting inside of her. "David," she swallowed dryly. "I could not let you kill Geoffrey. Nor did you wish to kill him. Can you not be grateful that I saved you from more bloodletting?"

He scoffed, bemused, and dropped his arms to his sides, his gaze glancing off the surrounding forest. "Your reasoning baffles me, woman. If only you could have left the war to me. I could have seen us safely through it. I could have talked Margaret into ransoming those men."

She clutched his arms, bruising her fingers as she clung to his hard frame.

He stood stiff, unresponsive.

"I know you despise me. I do not blame you for that." The words rubbed rawly past her throat; her mouth was parched. "But 'tis the war that tears us apart. If only you would leave the country with me, we could find peace together."

His eyes were as gray as the sky, bled of all emotion. "Even as you talk of peace, you war against me. You have taken everything from me, Riley, even my army. And now you wish to take me from my country as well."

His words crushed the breath from her. Sliding down his chest she felt her cloak catch on his buttons and the life drain out of her. The world whirled about her, then faded into total darkness. The last sound she heard was the sharp sound of her name on his lips.

Chapter Eighteen

The missodor thundered across the drawbridge and through the gatehouse into the bailey of Glenwood Castle. The servants crept from their fires and watched in befuddlement as Lynchburg reined his horse to a halt in a spray of snow and mud. In one arm he cradled a lifeless form wrapped in his cloak. The servants stared at the slender ankle that dangled from beneath the fur, then at the face of the man who ruled them. His eyes, once a vibrant blue, were as dark as stone.

The chaplain rushed forward to take the still form from Lynchburg's arms, but the master held her tightly, refusing to hand her down to him.

"My lord," he spoke with urgency. "You must give me the girl. We must minister to her."

As if realizing for the first time where he was, he glanced down at the servants who were gathering around him. With great care he lowered the shrouded girl into the chaplain's arms.

Her head fell back against the man's shoulder, and he could feel her heat penetrating the blanket, warming him.

"Holy Mary," he whispered, "the girl is burning up."

Her lips were slightly parted, and her breath was coming out in gasps. Glancing at the steward, he frowned and shook his head. There was no way that this woman would live.

"Take her to the solar," Lynchburg ordered.

The chaplain did not feel the cold air as he crossed the bailey, for the girl was like a fire burning against his chest. The fever would kill her within the hour. Of that he was certain. No one this sick could long survive.

"Sir," the steward greeted him. "Where is your army? Where is your mesnie?"

Lynchburg looked at him with eyes that were empty and dull. "Go to the village of Gersham. There is a wise woman there who is known for her miraculous cures." As he dismounted, the servants backed away and maintained a safe distance from him. "Bring her to me at once."

"If that is your wish, my lord," the steward said uncertainly. Gersham was more than an hour's ride away. The woman would be dead by the time he returned.

"That is what I wish," he said, his voice crackling with nerves. "Or I would not have asked it of you. Take my horse. There is no time to prepare another." Dropping the reins, he headed toward the south tower.

He had thought he could hate her, that he could somehow forsake her, bring her back to Glenwood Castle and imprison her, make her think that he was leaving her to Cornwich. That was to be her punishment, he had decided. Then he would ship the incorrigible little waif back to France and abandon her forever. Even in the darkest moment of his anger, he had doubted his capability to carry out his judgment. How, he wondered, had she ensnared his heart so thoroughly that his forgiveness was becoming inexhaustible.

As the steward watched Lynchburg trudge across the bailey, he felt a flush of terror burning through him. There was only one malady that could ravage a body so hungrily.

"Who is she?" a maid asked him timidly. "What's the matter with her?"

"Is she a beggar he found on the road?" another asked.

"Nay," a groom whispered excitedly. "She's his wife, who followed him into battle."

Fools, he thought, *to puzzle over a frozen bundle of human flesh.*

"I will tell you who she is," he muttered. "She is the angel of death."

The servants gazed at him, their eyes clouded with innocence as they waited for him to explain his meaning.

"Within a fortnight we may all be dead. That girl has the plague."

A moment of shocked silence ensued, followed by screams as the servants began to flee, colliding with each other in their haste to escape. A woman grabbed a small child who was almost trampled underfoot. Swinging him up onto her hip, she rushed toward the gates. A man slipped on the icy surface, his feet flying up in the air and his back hitting the ground with a painful crack. A page stumbled over his fallen body and spilled onto the frozen mud.

Let them go to the village, the steward thought as he watched them scurry across the bailey, *at least there they may be safe. For a while.* Mounting the missodor, he prayed a silent prayer that he would be spared from so dark a fate as the plague. Crossing himself fervently, he rode out into the misting sleet.

The chaplain entered the tower, clutching the girl as he tramped up the winding stairs. When he entered the antechamber, he saw the castellan surveying the room, trying to determine if the maids had given it a proper cleaning.

"Who is that?" he asked gruffly, as he glanced over his shoulder at him. "What happened to her?"

The chaplain laid her on a straw pallet and pulled the cloak away from her face. "She's Lord David's mistress, I presume. Apparently, he has brought her here to die."

"To die!" The castellan leaped back and crossed himself. "'Tis the plague."

"Hush, man, there is no plague here."

Creeping up to the pallet, the castellan peered cautiously at the girl. "Jesu, 'tis the kitchen maid who was banished days ago."

"Aye," whispered the chaplain. He stared at Riley's face, white and still, her eyes shaded underneath with dark circles. "But I suspect she was banished no further than the master's bed. A comely face brings naught but trouble into a Christian home."

A moan escaped her parched lips, and she began to toss fitfully on the straw pallet.

"God has brought this fate upon her to warn us of the dangers of sin," he continued sternly. "Now behold the devil's handmaiden. Cast your eyes on her, for this is what becomes of a wanton. When Satan is finished with a sinner, there is nothing left but a wasted soul."

"Stop your prattle, sirrah!"

They spun around to see Lynchburg standing in the portal, his eyes blazing with fury. "I will not tolerate your self-righteous babble."

The chaplain slunk away from the pallet, his shock evident on his face. "My lord, you cannot mean to speak to me in such a manner."

"I will do more than speak to you, sirrah." He grasped the hilt of his sword. "I will draw my sword on you if you ever utter another hellish word against her."

Turning to the castellan, he glared at the man's ashen face. "Get thee from this chamber!" he roared. Sliding his sword from its sheath, he held it up at a threatening angle. "Go and stand guard at the tower entrance. No one shall enter this solar without my permission. Any man who does will die."

"Aye, sir." The castellan shrank toward the door, then bolted past the threshold and down the stairs.

Lynchburg turned to the chaplain, who scurried away from the pallet. In terror he watched as the great man stalked him until his back was wedged into the farthest corner of the solar and his chin was resting on the point of Lynchburg's blade.

"Kneel!" the earl roared.

The chaplain immediately dropped to his knees.

"If sickness is caused by sin, then by God you will pray for her until she is healed," he ordered. "Pray!"

"Aye," the chaplain said, his voice wavering with fear.

"Tell God that I am a murderer—tell him that I confess it!"

"Aye," he said and began intoning a prayer.

"Tell Him that I repent of it all." He lowered his sword to his side. "Tell Him that I need, that I beg for His assistance." He closed his eyes, fortifying his voice with a deep breath of stale air. "This girl is dying. And I cannot lose her."

"Aye," the chaplain said, repeating the words in prayer and silently begging for his own deliverance from this madman.

"Tell Him to restore her to me, and I will give Him all that I have left." He cast the sword aside. "Tell Him that I will not bear arms again. Tell Him He may send an angel to fetch my sword, and I will gladly surrender it." He backed away and knelt by the pallet, gazing helplessly into Riley's feverish eyes. "Tell Him all of that, and when you are finished, tell Him again. And then again."

He touched Riley's face, her neck, and swallowed against the panic that constricted his throat. "Is not a priest our link with God?"

"Aye," he rasped weakly from his small corner.

"If she dies, then you have proven yourself to be a poor link. And there will be . . . repercussions."

The man is deranged, the chaplain thought, his chest gripped with fear. Bowing his head, he sealed his clasped hands to his forehead and prayed with an intensity of which, under normal circumstances, only the saints would have been capable.

As day melded into night, Lynchburg remained by her side, never noticing the food that was brought in or hearing the young maid plead for him to eat. She prepared a pallet for him in the bedchamber, but he would not rest.

The chaplain continued to pray until his voice was worn down to a whisper. Only then did Lynchburg allow him to leave and take his rest.

Night brightened into day again, and the snow blew against the windowpanes. The young maid stoked the fire and brought in fresh blankets for the sick girl. At times Lynchburg dropped off to sleep only to snatch awake, fearful that in that breath of time Riley had been taken from him. The hours crawled past, but she continued to breathe, and each breath that shuddered past her lips gave him hope.

She is alive, he thought, *for one more moment she is alive.*

Night came and with it howling winds and a hail of sleet clattering against the castle walls. He laid his head against the fresh linen of her pallet and began to pray with all the strength within him that she would live. A hand touched his shoulder, and he looked up to see the steward standing over him.

"We were delayed by bad weather, my lord," he apologized, "but the healer is here now."

Lynchburg saw Elda in the doorway, silhouetted against the torchlight of the corridor, and his heart leaped with hope. The sight of her suffused him with new life and energy. Surely now Riley would be saved.

"You have done well," he thanked the steward.

"Has he?" Elda asked as she stepped into the candlelit room. She removed her heavy cloak and hung it on a peg by the door. Her long blond braid flowed down over her breast, and her dress of green wool molded to her figure. "I did not wish to come here, my lord. But I knew that I could not disobey your command." She looked at him, her face drawn with fear.

"You have nothing to fear within these walls," he assured her. "I will slay any man who tries to harm you whether he be cleric or count. You'll not be under any threat here."

Her features relaxed, softening at the thought of the

great Lynchburg acting as her protector. The very sight of him soothed her fears, swathing her in a sense of security. She turned toward the steward, her eyes with birdlike alertness freely studying him.

"Leave us, steward. Else you may become infected. And I do not wish to have an epidemic on my hands."

The steward nodded and quickly took his leave.

Elda walked to the pallet, her satchel hanging from one shoulder, and knelt beside the sick girl. Placing her fingers gently against Riley's neck, she felt for her pulse.

"She is alive," Lynchburg assured her, as if daring her to say otherwise. "She is sleeping."

"How long has she been like this?" she asked. Opening her satchel, she took out small bags of herbs and dried flowers.

"Three days' time." He could not control the catch in his voice. He had slept little and had eaten nothing since her illness had begun. His nerves were taut.

"I can give her barley water and dandelion soup." She rested her palm against Riley's forehead. "Marigolds will also help cool her fever."

He gripped Riley's hand tightly, feeling the heat of her flesh burning his palms. "Do whatever you must to cure her."

"It will take all of my skills, my every ounce of strength for the next few days." She shook her head uncertainly. "I will have to be with her constantly."

"I don't care if you are entombed here!" he bellowed. "You will cure her."

She stared at him for a moment, her lips pursed in anger, then turned away with a frown. "As I said, I will try."

"Tell me what you want, and if she lives, it will be given to you."

Her mouth twitched in amusement. Usually, she was offered coins, trinkets, sometimes livestock for curing the sick, but never a limitless gift. *How much could this girl's life be worth to him?* she wondered. *She is very beautiful, but she appears to be no more than a servant.*

"Whatever you ask," he reiterated. "Say it, and it will be given to you."

She was surprised by his generosity and determined to test the sincerity of his words. Her eyes slid around the antechamber until they came to rest on the sword lying next to the door.

Rising, she stood for a moment, then walked cautiously toward the sword, waiting for him to command her to stop. When he didn't, she knelt before it almost reverently. Reaching out, she touched the ruby-encrusted hilt and caressed the cold stones beneath her fingers. It would fetch a fine price in London, she mused.

"Your sword is very beautiful." She looked at him shyly. "I ask of you your sword."

"So be it," he agreed. "The sword is yours."

She smiled in pleasant shock. Should the girl live, she would be wealthy. And the girl looked young and strong. There was no reason to doubt that given proper care she would recover.

"Go to the kitchen and prepare an onion poultice at once," she directed him.

He stared at her queerly. "Onions?"

"I will lay it on her chest," she explained. "As the onion draws tears from our eyes, so does it draw out the poisons from our bodies."

Without delay he headed for the kitchen to prepare her concoction.

Perhaps I should have asked him for his castle as well, she thought with a chuckle.

Strolling back to the pallet, she settled down next to her patient and folded the blanket back from Riley's chest. Pressing her ear to her breast, she listened to her labored breathing and realized that she had arrived just in time. One more day and she would not have been so confident that she could save her.

"Who are you?" she murmured as her eyes glided over

Riley's ivory skin. Her breasts were beautiful, full and firm. Her nipples rose and fell with her breath like petals on a silver surface. "His lover? Has the great warrior, Lynchburg, surrendered his heart to you as easily as he has surrendered his sword to me?"

She dipped a cloth into a bowl of water and squeezed it out. Pressing it against Riley's forehead, she glanced back at the sword. In the candlelight the rubies seemed to wink at her.

She had disarmed him, and this girl had obviously softened him, evoking compassion in a man renowned to be ruthless. She wondered what Cornwich would think of his son-in-law. Surely he would consider him deranged.

She wiped the cloth along Riley's jaw, down her neck and along the full curves of her breasts.

"I once had a lover, too," she murmured, a sad smile touching her lips. She missed Cornwich, the feel of his arms around her on a cold, winter's night and his fond words whispered in her ear. He had been a good lover with the stamina of a much younger man, and he had visited her often when he was hunting at Buckhall. That is, until the war had taken him away. His absence had been an agony to her, but she had lived with the hope that someday he would return. That hope had ended with Lynchburg's marriage.

If only he could have given me Philip instead of the sword, she thought bitterly. She would have gladly preferred the heart of the old earl to any of Lynchburg's wealth.

The sun rose over the castle walls, streaming in through the arched windows of the bedchamber and spraying an arc of light through the open door of the antechamber. Elda did not notice, she was so intent on her patient. Riley had coughed through the night, expelling the poisons from her lungs. The onion poultice and marigold soup had worked, and now the sheets were damp with perspiration.

Lynchburg paced the floor at the foot of the pallet, relieved and weary. "You have great talent as a healer," he said. "I marvel at your skill."

She reached up and wiped a wisp of hair from her face. "You must marvel at what a frightful sight I am." There were dark circles under her eyes, and her face was pale and tired.

"Nonsense," he commented fondly. "When your patient awakens and sees you, she will think she is in heaven with an angel."

Her heart warmed at the compliment. "The fever is broken," she announced and listened to Lynchburg's joyous release of breath.

"Thank you," he said, his voice wavering as if he would weep. "To see her live is my only desire. Is she safe from death?"

"Aye," she said idly, wiping the girl's brow with a damp cloth.

She stood up to warm a pot of soup over the fire, but Lynchburg stopped her. Turning her to face him, he took the pot from her and set it down on the floor.

"You have not slept for two days, and I fear that this malady will overcome you as well." Planting his hands firmly on her shoulders, he gave her a stern frown. "Go and rest in the bedchamber. I will watch over our patient."

"I will sleep in time," she said, enjoying the feel of his strong grip.

"No," he commanded. "You will rest now. Or I will carry you to bed."

She smiled, and her breath quickened with pleasure. "I am a healer, sir," she said playfully, and pressed her palm against his chest. "You would treat your healer like a bag of meal?" The hard contour of his muscles made her yearn to touch him with greater intimacy.

"Aye, if she has no better sense than to argue with me." He swept her up into his arms, bringing a cry of surprise from her lips. The fragrance of her hair filled his head, and the yellow strands glimmered like silk beneath the glow of the candles.

Her feigned outrage quieted when she felt the raw strength of his arms around her and saw the beauty of his face so near her own. His scent, his strength, aroused a craving within her that could not be contained. As he lowered her onto the straw pallet, she encircled his neck in her arms and brought her lips to his in what turned out to be a tepid kiss.

Drawing back, she eyed him in disappointment. "What ails you, milord? Cold fish have more passion than what you display."

He released her and retreated to the portal. "I-I was only attempting to put you to bed," he stuttered, "not seduce you."

She sat up and touched the lingering feel of his lips on her mouth. "Forgive me for my forwardness, sir," she said, feeling truly puzzled. "I thought you found me appealing."

"Elda," he addressed her kindly. "There was a time when I would have found your charms very satisfying. But my heart rebels against me now." He glanced toward the antechamber. "There is only one woman whom I wish to claim in that way. I cannot feel passion for any other."

Her eyes grew sullen, and her heart filled with disappointment. *I have been so lonely of late,* she thought, *and the first man I find who can compare to Philip cannot be tempted.* She rose from the bed, her brow furrowed in thought. *If he were a bit drunk, he might allow me to lie with him for a little while.*

"Before I sleep, let me prepare you a brew of warm wine and special herbs to ward off the fever," she offered. "It would not do for your young maid to recover only to find her master ill. She would bear the guilt of your suffering."

"If you promise to rest afterward, then you may brew whatever concoction you wish," he joked. "I will drink it, though not gladly. I do not care for medicine."

She got up and walked to the antechamber, returning moments later with a cup of wine.

"To your health, milord," she said, offering him the cup.

He raised it reluctantly to his lips and downed the bitter brew. His eyes squeezed shut tightly, and he shuddered. Tossing the cup aside, he placed his hand against his stomach. "Your brew has set off sparks in my gut," he wheezed.

"Then come with me, milord, and let me put you to bed." Taking his hand, she led him to the pallet and helped him off with his houppelande. In only his doublet and hose he lay down, gazing at the ceiling, feeling as if he were in a near stupor.

"My eyes cannot focus," he said. "I feel as if I am drunk."

His eyes grew heavy, and his breathing became labored. "You have drugged me," he murmured, his speech slurred.

"No, my lord," she said, innocently. "You have not eaten or slept in a long time. I should have known the herbs would take effect quickly."

He could hear her words tugging at the periphery of his consciousness, and he struggled to open his eyes. As his mind slipped away, he slowly spun into darkness.

She watched him sink into a deep sleep of relief and exhaustion. Seeing him abed in only his doublet caused the ache in her heart to strengthen. How wonderful it would feel to lie against a warrior's muscular form again, to feel a powerful body next to hers.

Lowering her dress and chemise down her arms, she let the garments slip to the floor, pooling at her feet. As she slowly stripped off her hose, the candles flickered, their soft lights dancing across her skin. Climbing onto the pallet, she pressed her naked breasts against his chest and curled her arm around his shoulder, seeking the warmth she had so long been without.

At noon the serving girl entered the solar and saw Riley sleeping, her hair damp with sweat. On tiptoe she crossed the antechamber and entered the bedchamber. The fire was nearly out, and the room was dark. Elda moaned softly and rolled over, displaying her bare back to the maid.

"Lady D'Aubere," she mouthed the words.

Quietly she stoked the fire, then tiptoed from the room, not wanting to disturb the slumbering couple. As she left, she closed the door behind her.

Elda eased up and gazed over at the sleeping giant, his hair strewn across his pillow and his skin brown against the white linen sheets. His breathing was strong and even, and she knew that he would sleep a while longer.

Hurriedly she slipped into her clothes and stepped softly into the antechamber to check on her patient. Riley was cool to the touch and enveloped in a deep sleep. Retrieving her cloak, she draped it over her shoulders, then removed a small pouch from her satchel. As she made her way down the stairs and out into the bailey, she tied the pouch to her waist.

Snow mottled the ground, but the gray clouds had dissipated, revealing a deep blue sky. After days of low clouds joined to the land in a gray mist, the afternoon seemed painfully bright and clear.

The maid was walking to the henhouse to gather eggs when she spied the golden-haired woman strolling across the bailey toward the east tower. *Having fulfilled her wifely duties, she retreats,* the maid assumed. *So, the rumors I heard were true. The lady is half nun, half wife.* She had thought it impossible to be married to a man like Lynchburg and not be wholly possessed by him. *The only reason for her freedom must be that he does not like her very much.* Humming mildly to herself, she sauntered into the henhouse.

Elda entered through the east portal and made her way up the winding stairwell to the third level. To her surprise she found Jeanette's chamber unguarded and unlocked. Easing open the door, she saw the girl sitting on the floor rocking just as she had years before when she had met her for the first time. Suddenly a ruffle of black robes fluttered like the beating wings of a bat.

"Get out," the nun spat. She had been sitting beneath the window, hidden behind its bright shaft of light. Now she emerged with wings fully spread, her eyes as sharp as talons. "You are not wanted here."

The light wafted down upon Jeanette, illuminating the horror on her face.

"Not wanted?" Elda asked with a calm assurance in her eyes. "By whom? His lordship sent for me and I have come here under his protection." She walked to the mattress and settled upon it, untying her pouch from her waist.

The girl crawled into the nun's waiting arms and hid her face against the old woman's breast.

"Come to me, Jeanette," Elda invited her as she opened her pouch.

"She will not come to you," the nun cried, "you evil beast!"

Elda reached into the pouch and brought out a handful of colorful stones, placing them on the floor at her feet. After several minutes the girl eyed them blankly, then crawled hesitantly toward her. Picking up a stone, she smiled, and her eyes began to glisten with joy. Elda gave the nun a knowing grin. "You see, she did come to me. Would you like to see her sit upon my lap?"

"She will never do that," the old woman snapped.

Taking a stone from her pouch, Elda placed it between her teeth. It was larger than the others, prettier. Within minutes Jeanette was climbing into her lap and grasping at the stone in her mouth.

The nun let out a muffled groan. "Those are magic stones. You have charmed her with your black arts."

"And you have smothered her with your black robes," she retorted. "I have come only to see to her health. 'Tis what Lord Philip would wish." Gently placing her hand against the girl's womb, she felt the flatness of it. "Your husband has neglected you," she said, pleased. "'Tis kind of him to leave you be."

The portal darkened as a shadow swept across the threshold. Looking up, Elda saw the chaplain lunging toward her.

"*You* leave her be!" It was a voice that crackled like fire and sent a wave of panic billowing through her.

Jeanette dropped the stone and dived from her lap, scurrying into the arms of the nun. The chaplain kicked the stones aside as he reached Elda. Gripping her ear, his fingers felt like hot tongs searing her flesh.

"I heard that you were returned. Witch. Sorceress!" Snatching her from the bed, he dragged her from the chamber with such force that she was unable to gain her footing.

"Release me!" she cried and clawed at his fingers, her feet stumbling as if she were running on ice. "I am here by order of the earl."

Grabbing a torch from its wall frame, he proceeded down the corridor, dragging her beside him. "And I am here by order of the church."

She was pulled, struggling, down the tower stairs and into another corridor. The crucifixes lining the walls swept past her, each one striking her vision with a painful jolt. As she tumbled down the passageway, she felt as if she were freefalling with nothing to grasp on to.

Shoving her through a portal, the priest flung her to the floor. As she fell to her hands and knees, she gasped in pain and fright. Placing her hand against her throbbing ear, she glanced up to see that she was in a study, his study. His desk rose before her, inlaid with gold, smothered in bound manuscripts, and crowned with a crucifix of pure gold.

Behind her she heard the door slam, entombing her. The air seemed to swirl around her, sucking her into a dark and despondent core.

"What do you want from me, priest?" she gasped.

"I warned you not to ever return here, but you defied me. You came back. And you used your black arts to heal that girl."

"You had best release me from this room at once. Or I shall tell Lord David of this mistreatment. And he will make you suffer for it."

He glared at her with flinty eyes, his voice moaning as eerily as a cold, night wind. "I do not answer to Lynchburg, witch. I answer to the bishop, and he to the pope. I will write to him and tell him of your evil presence." He jabbed at her with the torch, causing her to scream as she scrambled to her feet to avoid the flames. "Do you wish to die by fire?"

"No!" she cried frantically, raising her hand as if to fend him off.

With a smirk of triumph, he set the torch in a frame and strode to his desk. "If you tarry here, the villagers will flock to you for healing." He glared at her, gaining some satisfaction from the rabbit look in her eyes. "I will show Lord David a miracle to outmatch any your magic has produced." He opened a drawer and brought out an engraved wooden box. Easing open the lid, he gazed at her, his eyes reflecting a golden sheen.

Scooping up a handful of coins, he held them up in the dusty air. "This is the money the steward set aside for the care of Lady Jeanette. The nuns wish to use it for a pilgrimage." He squeezed the coins in his fist. "But I intend to take this money to the bishop. With it we will buy the services of an exorcist."

"No," she pleaded. "Surely you know the girl is not possessed. An exorcist will only torture her, thinking he is driving out a demon. You cannot put her through such cruel treatment."

He spilled the coins back into the box, then grabbed a small folded parchment. "I have already written the bishop a letter detailing my wishes," he said, rubbing it between his fingers. "I shall send it to him on the morrow."

"No, you cannot bring such unspeakable suffering upon her."

Setting the box aside, he grasped his quill. "We must all suffer for salvation, Mistress Elda, including you." He snatched open his desk drawer and brought out a blank parchment. "I will pen another letter to the bishop. This one will be a warning against you. I will beg him to purge you from this land."

"No!" She lunged at the desk, grabbing the parchment

and ripping it from his hand. As she did so, he gripped her braid at the nape of her neck and forced her head back at an unnatural angle, bringing her helplessly to her knees.

Her hands fumbled across the desk until they found the golden crucifix, heavy and large. Raising it high in the air, she brought it down once, twice until she felt his hand release her. As she dropped the crucifix, she clamored to her feet and saw him falling away from her, collapsing onto his back, his arms spread out like a downed bird.

Grabbing the box, she fled from the chamber and ran as quickly as she could back to the earl's solar. Lynchburg was still deep in slumber, and there was no time to wake him and explain what had transpired. She had struck a priest, and the penalty for that would be excommunication, being cut off from the entire Christian community, beyond the assistance of almost everyone.

Retrieving her satchel, she stuffed the box inside of it and slung it over her shoulder. By nightfall she could be in London, safe from the chaplain and his bishop. She grabbed the sword and headed for the stable. Without the money, the priest could not hire his exorcist, and Jeanette would be safe, too. As soon as she was in London, she would give the coins to the poor or to one of the hospitals, anything to be rid of them.

When she arrived in the stable, she saddled a mare that looked young and ready to run. After wrapping the sword in fur, she tied it securely to the saddle. Like a man, she leaped onto the horse and straddled the animal, her hose white against the horse's brown fur.

As she approached the gatehouse, she abruptly reined in her mount. The guards were closing the gates, walling her in, and her heart hammered painfully in fear.

"I am the healer brought here by the Earl of Lynchburg!" she cried out. "Why do you close these gates? You must let me pass."

The guard shook his head firmly. "I cannot allow it. No one is to leave."

"Why?" she cried. "What cause have you to keep me

here? I have done nothing wrong." Tears of anguish filled her eyes as she watched the guards bolting the gates.

"There is an army without," he explained. "Many troops are gathered on the fields."

"Are we under siege?" she asked.

"I do not know. We have sent for the master. Soon he will tell us what awaits us."

Lynchburg awoke, feeling as if the blanket that covered him was made of stone. He could not move, he was so groggy. He crawled from the mattress and eased into his boots. His head was throbbing, but he knew that he must clear his mind and see to Riley. Stumbling into the antechamber, he found her sleeping, her face pale against her reddish cloud of hair.

He picked up the cold pot of dandelion soup and took it to the fireplace, setting it in the hot embers to heat. As a curl of steam rose up from the simmering liquid, he stirred it with a spoon and sipped it, shuddering at the taste. It was a bitter draught, but she would drink it, he determined. By God, she would drink it. If she was to get well, she would have to eat.

Sitting down next to her on the pallet, he dipped the spoon into the pot and pressed it to her mouth. The soup stung her parched lips, but she sipped it, swallowing thickly.

"Riley?" She heard her name as if from deep within a cave. "Riley?"

She tried to open her eyes, but she couldn't. It was as if lead coins were resting against her lids. Her lips parted, and she tasted the soup again. The softness of the bedcovers caressed her skin, and she felt cool and damp. A drop of sweat beaded on her forehead and trickled down her face, seeping into her hair.

"You must eat, Riley. You must eat or you will not get well." His voice was a whisper filtering through her mind.

The hot spoon touched her mouth again, and she sipped at it. Opening her eyes, she saw him as through a veil of light. His face was thickly bearded, and his eyes looked swollen.

"I have seen death often," he murmured as he stirred the soup. "But never have I feared death as much as I have these past few days."

She closed her eyes, lacking the strength to keep them open.

"You swept into my life like a raging storm."

The spoon touched her lips again, and she sipped it weakly.

"I did not want to love you, Riley. I wanted to defeat you, to conquer you, and to send you back into exile. But 'tis my own heart that is conquered. I could not tell you of my feelings for you. I thought a confession of love was a confession of weakness." He scooped up a milky swirl of soup and placed it against her lips. "But I confess it now. I am a weak man, after all. One who cannot walk alone in this world. I did not realize that about myself until I almost lost you. . . . I love you."

Lifting her hand, she touched his sleeve and felt his hand close around hers, then his lips suddenly kissing her fingers.

"Riley," he mumbled, cradling her hand against his face.

A pounding on the solar door sifted through her mind with a dreamlike echo.

"Lord David! Lord David!"

He felt jolted by the intrusion and angry. "Enter," he called, and the young maid rushed in, her face terror stricken.

"You must come at once, sir!" she cried. "You have been summoned by the guards. There are riders approaching."

Riley felt Lynchburg's lips press a kiss to her forehead. "I will return soon, my lady. 'Tis nothing to worry about. We have visitors is all."

She could hear him moving about the chamber, donning his houppelande and cloak, but she was too weak to open her eyes. As she drifted back into sleep, she heard his footsteps fading from the room.

He crossed the bailey with long strides, his stomach burning. The queen had pursued him and would lay siege to Glenwood Castle. She would demand his surrender and his life, for he was now as guilty of treason as Riley Snowden. *Let her do what she must,* he decided, *but she will not harm Riley.* He would hold off her army singlehandedly if need be until Riley could be smuggled to safety.

He climbed up to the ramparts and gazed out over the toothlike structure. A small legion of soldiers was gathered on the field. "'Tis a small army," he noted with some relief.

The steward climbed up beside him and raised his hand to shield his eyes from the sun. "Whose army is it?" he asked. "My eyes are not good. I cannot see their banner."

In the distance the earl spotted the blue stag against a red sun rising and smiled grimly. "'Tis the army of Philip De Proileau," he replied. "My father-in-law."

Chapter Nineteen

Two riders approached the castle, and Lynchburg recognized them at once. One was the Earl of Cornwich and the other was Daggot. They rode slowly beneath the fading canopy of midafternoon.

As he descended from the parapets, the earl called down to the guards to lower the bridge and open the gates. He stood in the bailey as the gates parted, revealing the bridge and the fields beyond. The wind whipped his cloak to the side as he waited with his legs braced apart, watching the men draw nearer. Cornwich stopped at the moat, refusing to enter, but Daggot rode forward.

Lumbering across the bridge, the boy kept his head low, trying to hide his face from his master. As he halted before him, he stared at the ground like a child condemned. Gone was his prideful air and his gleam of innocence.

"Dismount," the earl ordered, and the boy slowly obeyed.

The sight of him with his head bent beneath a burden of shame sent a glimmer of anger through Lynchburg. Daggot was young, and the road he had chosen was long and treacherous. Perhaps it was not the right road for him, he surmised, but the boy would learn to stand up straight upon it.

"Look at me," Lynchburg commanded. "Never turn your eyes from a man. 'Tis a show of weakness."

Daggot lifted his eyes timidly, and Lynchburg was relieved to see that no lasting damage had been done. He was bruised, and his right eye was swollen, but he would heal.

"I betrayed you," Daggot confessed, his voice unsteady. "I told the queen about Riley."

"So you did." His brows lifted slightly over eyes that were dark and searching. "Do you still wish to serve me?"

Daggot looked at him in surprise. "Aye, my lord," he said. "If you will have me, I will serve you with all my heart and to my death."

Lynchburg could not suppress the smile that tugged at his lips. He walked up to Daggot and rested his hands on his sagging shoulders. "Go tell Cornwich that 'tis safe for him to enter. Tell him that I will have food and wine for him in the great hall. I will join him in an hour's time."

Nodding his shaggy locks, Daggot mounted his horse and rode out of the bailey, acting as if he could not ride quickly enough to do his master's bidding.

The earl retreated to the solar to wash and dress for his confrontation with his father-in-law. Careful not to awaken Riley, he donned the purple houppelande that was embroidered with gold thread. Opening the chest, he took out a ruby ring and slipped it onto his finger. He knew that shortly he would be evicted from this land, but for tonight he was still the lord of Glenwood Castle, and he would look the part.

Cornwich sat by the fire in the great hall, clutching his fur-lined cloak tightly across his chest. He was cold from the long winter's ride, and even the roaring fire could not break his chill. As the sunlight slanted through the hole in the roof, it illuminated his aging features. He was tired, and the lines around his mouth and eyes were deep with anger. Uninterested in food, he had nearly choked on the bread, cheese, and salted pork that the serving girl had brought him. He didn't want to eat or rest. All he wanted was his son-in-law's neck locked in the vise grip of his hands.

To his fury, Lynchburg entered the hall looking like a prince. He was clean shaven and handsome, the light glinting off of the golden threads of his houppelande.

"How fares my estate, Lynchburg?" He waved his hand to stave off his answer. "Nay, do not bother to tell me. I have seen for myself. When I arrived, I went to check on my daughter. The nuns told me that she is still a virgin. When I went to the priest to make my confession, I found him knocked unconscious and the chapel's money stolen. When I entered the great hall, there was no one to serve me but a lone girl. My servants seem to have scattered."

Lynchburg blinked down at him in shock. "The priest was attacked?"

"Aye, by Yorkist infiltrators, no doubt. He has no memory of the attack. It may be days before he recovers his wits." His voice grew louder, ringing through the vast, empty space. "But before you explain this rampant chaos, I must speak to you on an even graver matter. The queen told me that you have withdrawn your allegiance to Henry."

Lynchburg held his gaze as he walked toward him with calm, deliberate steps. "I will no longer pledge my allegiance to a king who cannot rule. Or to a queen who is selling our country from beneath our feet."

Cornwich slammed his fists down on the arms of his chair. "Don't you understand what your madness has wrought? The nobles have learned of your decision. They have begun to abandon the queen, to scatter to the wind like a flock of startled birds." He pointed a long, crooked finger at him. "They look up to you, David. They follow you. And you are leading them from God's intended ruler."

Lynchburg paused before the fire and carefully scrutinized his father-in-law's face. "Is Henry truly God's intended ruler? He is weak and sick in his mind. You think to justify his reign by calling him God's appointed, but my conscience will not allow such blasphemy."

"You speak treason," Cornwich sputtered, his face taut with anger.

"I only speak what is in my heart. I can no longer serve Margaret. If others follow my lead, then perhaps they feel that 'tis right in their hearts, too."

Cornwich's face twisted in anger, and he pounded the chair again with his fists. "What is this dribble about hearts? You are talking like a besotted fool! The queen said that you brought the Snowden bitch to St. Albans." His eyes burned brightly, and he slashed the air with his hand. "How dare you consort with that last of a family of whores. She betrayed Her Majesty and set a prisoner free. And rather than hand a traitor over for execution, you deserted your men and your queen."

"Riley Snowden is not a whore!" he stated, his voice low and tense.

"She is a whore!" he shouted, rising to his feet. "She shares your bed and keeps you from your lawful wife. Your marriage was *never* consummated."

"I have rejected my wife," he said quietly. "And have chosen another."

"What?" The color flashed in Cornwich's cheeks. "How dare you betray your queen and your father-in-law. How dare you live on my daughter's dowry with another woman. I will not have it!" He shook his finger in Lynchburg's face. "You are an adulterer. And a traitor to the Crown. You and your whore will be taken from Glenwood Castle this hour."

Lifting his hand slowly, Lynchburg's brushed the earl's trembling finger aside. "I cannot allow that. Riley is ill. She must remain here until her health improves. When she is well, we will venture into Wales, and you will see us no more."

Cornwich grabbed the hilt of his sword, and Lynchburg's hand went quickly to his dagger.

"I care not if your whore dies," he growled. "The queen has ordered me to bring you back to York."

"So that she can lop off my head?" he asked with a mirthless half-smile.

Cornwich released his sword and let out his breath in a tired sigh. Pacing away from his son-in-law, he raked his fingers through his thin, white hair. "The queen does not want your head, David," he said flatly. "She wants you to ask her forgiveness."

Lynchburg arched one brow at him quizzically. "Her forgiveness?"

The old man turned to face him, his eyes dark and vacant. "She wants you to lead her troops again. She has returned all of your supplies." He swept his hand toward the door. "I have them beyond the walls—even your bed. She wishes to confiscate nothing from you. If only you will return to her, all will be forgiven. It will be as if your quarrel never occurred."

He raised his chin in question. "What about Riley?"

"She will be executed."

Lynchburg shut his eyes and felt them burn rawly against his lids. "Never," he spat.

"Turn her over to the queen," Cornwich urged. "What is she to you that you would sacrifice everything to have her?"

"She is my life."

"She is your death." Cornwich's eyes flashed in warning. "That woman has ensnared you with lust to lure you to the Yorkist cause. 'Tis the oldest trick in the Bible, and you are too blind to see it."

"'Tis more than lust. I plan to claim her for my wife."

Cornwich threw up his hands in frustration. "Then be damned!" he cried. "Take your whore to hell for all I care. If you do not return with me to York, then Margaret will ride against you. You have no troops here. You cannot hold this castle against her forces."

"Let her do as she must," he said. "Tell her that I await her."

Cornwich stared at him, disbelieving. He could not understand his son-in-law's stupidity at choosing Riley

Snowden, a penniless traitor, over his queen and his wife's dowry. To see that look of daring in his eyes was more than he could bear. He wished that he could drive his sword through this madman's belly, but he had promised the queen that he would bring him back alive. Now he must return alone and face her anger. Spinning on his heel, he stormed from the great hall.

When he reached the portal, he paused and peered back at his son-in-law through dim eyes. "Where is the healer, Elda?" he asked tiredly. "The old nun told me that she is here."

Lynchburg breathed in the harsh winter air that flooded in through the open door.

"She came here at my command," he replied, "to cure Riley. But she is gone now. I know not where."

His father-in-law's gaze grew heavy, guarded. "Does she work for Lancaster? Or for York?"

Lynchburg smiled, a dark eclipsing smile. "You're asking me to reveal to you the heart of the woman you sleep with?"

Cornwich's eyes flickered away for a moment of regret, then sought him again. "She has saved the life of Snowden, and for that she has failed me."

"She did not know whose life she saved," Lynchburg blared at him. "She is a healer who goes where she is needed." He eyed him, his gaze intense with warning. "And do not dare seek her out for harm. She is under my protection."

"I wish her no harm," Cornwich said quickly, his voice heavy with remorse. "I ask only that you find her and send her back to Gersham. She is not safe here."

"Find her yourself and see her safely home."

Cornwich looked at him, his face hard in the winter light and white with age. "I cannot desert my duties. My country is at war, and unlike you, I will stand by my king to final victory. Since 'tis more your habit than mine to chase after women, I shall leave the task to you." Turning his back on his son-in-law, he strode out into the snow.

Lynchburg released his hold on his dagger and walked to the doors, watching his father-in-law mounting his missodor. He would take the news of his refusal back to the queen, and soon her troops would be swarming over Glenwood Castle. There was still time to get Riley out, he speculated. Within a few days she would be strong enough to travel, then they would escape into the wilds of Wales.

*London, England
February 27, 1461*

Gertie paced the stone floor in the hall of Lord Geoffrey's London townhouse, her feet kicking the rushes aside as she walked. She was in a gown of scarlet velvet that felt too restrictive under her heavy breasts. Having grown accustomed to the loose peasant clothes of Glenwood Castle, she could not help but tug at the binding gown. Her ragged scarf had been replaced by a jeweled headdress that hid her hair beneath a long pleated veil of purple satin.

Where was her brother? she wondered as she followed a well-worn trail through the rushes. She had been waiting for hours for news.

At the sound of footsteps, the greyhounds roused up from the hearth and began yapping in greeting, their barking pricking her every nerve. Stumbling over each other, they scampered to the portal as Lord Geoffrey swung open the door. His face was flushed with happiness, and Gertie felt her heart spring with hope.

"What news have you?" she pleaded.

"Good news, my sister," he replied as he strode into the hall and removed his gloves. "Edward has arrived in London."

"God be praised!" she cried, throwing up her hands. "Our cause is won."

A manservant entered the chamber and removed Lord Geoffrey's cloak, folding it over one arm.

"The people thronged to see Edward as he rode through the streets," he said, handing his gloves to the servant. "He is fearless, our Edward. And it shows in his bearing." Strolling up to a table, he poured himself a goblet of wine. "The crowds idolize him."

"God has sent us a champion."

He set the pitcher of wine back on the table and smiled to himself as he lifted the goblet to his lips. "He will be proclaimed king within the week, and our future will be secure at last."

"Will it?" she asked worriedly and resumed her pacing, her long skirt dragging behind her. "As soon as Edward is proclaimed king, we must tell him of Riley's treachery. She is whore to the man who executed his father. She must be brought to justice."

"No," Lord Geoffrey said firmly. Sinking into his chair, he rested his back against red damask cushions and thought about his precious neck. He was warm now, warm and safe, and all because of Riley's courage. "I do not believe that Riley is Lynchburg's whore." Sipping his wine, he felt its warmth slide down his throat. "His prisoner, yes. But not his whore."

As she walked past him, her shadow drifted across his face. "I have seen enough to know that she is a very willing prisoner. She is as Lancastrian as Henry VI. She has sold her soul."

"'Tis because of Riley that I live. She rescued me, and I will do nothing to bring harm to her."

"Argh!" Gertie cried, her tone scalding him. "She may have rescued you, but she will soon be the death of us all." Angrily she kicked at the rushes on the floor. "What will happen to us when Edward finds out that Lynchburg murdered his father? When he discovers that Riley is Lynchburg's whore?" She paced the length of the hearth and back again, her fists clenching and unclenching. "He will have us all arrested and questioned mercilessly. When he finds out that we knew about Lynchburg's heinous crime yet said nothing, he will have us attainted."

When Lord Geoffrey did not respond, she paused to glare at him, her eyes ragged with emotion.

"A man who does nothing declares his own impotence!" she cried. "Riley has brought this fate upon herself. She could have been a queen, Edward's wife. Instead she chose to be mistress to a monster." Kneeling at his chair, she clasped his hand in her own. "She must be eliminated, Geoffrey, else her sins infect us all. If we tell Edward everything now, we will save ourselves. If we do not tell him, then we are dooming the Seward name to ruin."

Geoffrey pulled his hand from her grip and shifted uncomfortably in his chair.

"Go to him and convince him of our loyalty," she urged. "I know of a Lancastrian secret that could bring about their downfall." Her eyes brightened as she leaned nearer to his ear. "The queen is plotting to sell Calais to the French for an alliance against Edward. If you tell him this news, he will show us mercy."

He gave her an indulgent glance. "We have suspected as much for quite some time," he said patiently. "The French will not help Margaret. She will soon lose the war, and they know it. Your secret is no secret at all." He gulped the last of his wine and thought for a moment. "I will go to Edward and tell him that Riley is being held prisoner by Lynchburg. I'll offer a ransom for her return. We'll assure Edward that Riley is the helpless victim of this man."

"And what assurance will we offer Edward when he finds out the truth? His mind is as sharp as his blade. Never take that boy for a fool. To do so is to take your life into your hands."

"I will think on it," he promised, though she detected a falseness in his tone. "The day has been very long, and this wine is potent." Wearily he rubbed his eyes though he did not look overly tired to her. "I wish only for my bed."

"Then go to bed and sleep," she snarled at him as she struggled to her feet. "'Tis what men do best. You are all rats who prefer to burrow in darkness."

He waved her away in angry dismissal. "Don't rile me, sister, for my patience is thin." Giving her a sidelong glare, he scowled at her. "Don't forget that 'twas you who brought the girl to England, not me. 'Twas you who conspired with her at Glenwood Castle. If you had not financed her quest for vengeance, then none of this would have happened." He turned his face toward the fire and clutched his wine goblet as if it contained his very soul.

"I brought her back to England because I thought she would be the salvation of the Snowden name. Instead she has become the downfall of us all. She must be eliminated."

"I said I will think on it," he snapped. "Now leave me, sister, to my own thoughts." He closed his eyes, shutting her out as he rested his forehead in his hand.

"Your own thoughts are on saving Riley," she accused him.

He sat in silence, breathing in the warmth of the fire, ignoring her. There was no longer any doubt in her mind that she alone must betray Riley and seek Edward's mercy. But would she be able to succeed without her brother's help? she wondered. She had heard that Edward was an approachable man. She would go to him without Geoffrey's knowledge and tell him everything that had transpired over the past few weeks. Hopefully the boy who now called himself a king would show mercy to her and her brother. As for Riley, she would learn the lesson taught her in the convent, that the wages of all sin is death.

Chapter Twenty

Glenwood Castle
March 7, 1461

With the help of the young maid, Riley walked on un-steady legs to a tub that was filled with hot water. As the steam rose up from the water's surface, she smelled the scents of roses and herbs.

Loosening the drawstring of her gown, she pulled the linen garment from her shoulders and let it drop to the floor.

"The master bade me take good care of you," the maid chattered merrily. "I am the only serving girl left within these walls. All have fled, fearing the plague. But not I. I would never desert my master."

She gripped Riley's hand, steadying her as she stepped into the tub.

"Nay, but there is no plague here," the maid continued. "None but the plague of feeble-mindedness."

A shudder went through Riley's body as she sank into the water and felt its warmth tingling along her flesh. She had not bathed since her illness, and the water felt glorious as it rose up over her stomach and touched her breasts.

"Truth be told, the servants fear the master. Ever since he arrived, there's been nothing but bad luck for all of us.

First his wife was nowhere to be seen. Then you were sent away and Gertie disappeared. Then we thought the plague was upon us. Then the chaplain was attacked. There's many who thinks the new master brought an evil curse upon this house."

Picking up a sponge, the maid lathered it with soap and began to stroke Riley's shoulders.

"Is the water too hot?" she asked. "The master said he didn't want your flesh burned. He is most kind to his ill servants. Methinks I will get sick next winter to win his love."

I am not a servant, Riley wanted to confess. But she knew that she could not divulge her identity, not yet. If she did, her life would not be safe here. With her illness vanquished, the servants would be returning soon. She suspected that many of them were still loyal to Cornwich and would kill her to gain his rewards.

"The master is most kind," the maid repeated, almost as if to herself. "He had a trunk brought into the solar for you. There are pretty clothes in it. 'Tis a lucky servant who has such a kind master." She was lazy in her movements, lingering at her task as she rubbed the sponge down Riley's back.

Lost in a daydream, is she? Riley thought. *She is infatuated with her lord.*

"He is kind when kindness is deserved," she said. Taking the sponge away from her, she slid it up her chest and throat, leaving a white streak of suds. "If you cross him, he can be very unkind."

The maid dipped her hands into the water, washing the soap from them. "I remember when he imprisoned you in the dungeon. You had gotten soap in his eyes," she said idly. Wiping her hands on her dress, she stared pensively into the water. "I'd never have done that."

The girl really is fond of him, Riley thought. *He can do no wrong in her eyes.*

"I envy the Lady D'Aubere. Is she not a lucky woman?" Riley held the sponge tightly against her chest, her heart quickening. "What do you know of the Lady D'Aubere?" she asked.

She shrugged innocently. "She is cloistered near the chapel is all I know."

Riley slipped deeper into the water, feeling its warmth rise up her chest to her throat. "I have heard that she is very sick."

"Sick?" the maid questioned, a note of surprise in her voice. "Nay, she is not sick. She is healthy and hardy."

The weight of the water suddenly felt like a churning current as her heart began to skip. "What do you mean? Lord David told me himself that she is sick."

"Nay, she is very religious, never wanted to leave the convent." She scooped a petal from the water and watched it float down into the palm of her hand. "He has allowed her to remain cloistered as she wished. But she is a wife to him. I saw her in his bed only three days hence. And later that same morning I saw her strolling across the bailey heading back to the east tower." She savored the feel of the soft petal, then dropped it back into the water. "I hear that she prays constantly for a child. She'll remain in seclusion until God grants her prayer. Soon there will be a babe. We all pray for it."

Her words felt as sharp as the talons of a hawk clawing Riley's heart.

"Is the bath too warm?" the maid asked, puzzled. "Your face is burning red hot as a peat fire."

Riley brought her hands to her cheeks, cooling them with the bath water. "'Tis just the fever," she said.

"But you've had no fever for days," the maid corrected her.

Impatient to divert the girl's attention, she turned her ear to the door. "I think I hear Lord David coming," she whispered.

The maid clamored to her feet and smoothed her dress. Bundling up her tangled mass of hair on top of her head, she hastily covered it with a red kerchief.

Lynchburg entered the chamber just as she knotted the

kerchief at the base of her neck. Glancing at the maid, he gently ordered her out of the room.

"Can I be getting anything for you, sir?" she asked hopefully.

"Aye," he said. "Pack a supply bag with salt pork and wine and salted fish. I will pick it up from the kitchen."

"Aye, milord." She curtsied and padded from the room.

He walked toward Riley, his lips curving sensuously into a smile. His face was as soft and dusky as twilight, and his eyes were as blue as a smoky sky. Kneeling by the tub, he picked up the sponge and lathered it with soap.

"Why do you need supplies packed?" she asked, uninterested. "Are you leaving?"

"We will discuss it later," he said. As he began to stroke the ivory slope of her shoulder, he watched the water running in foamy rivulets down her arms. They were beautiful arms, too slender due to her illness, but unblemished and graceful. Leaning over, he kissed her shoulder, and his lips lingered on the cool dampness of her skin.

She felt his breath chill her flesh and fought the desire for him that was swelling painfully inside of her. Grabbing the sponge, she raised it over his head and squeezed it out. The water rained down over his face, startling him, and he began to laugh. Reaching into the tub, he plucked her from the water.

"Unhand me," she demanded and pushed against his massive chest.

As he carried her across the room, water streamed down across the floor.

"Not until I've had my revenge," he warned with a mischievous glint in his eye. "I care not for pranks."

He laid her on the straw pallet, but she rolled away from him, avoiding his grasping arms.

"You may be recently recovered, but you are as swift as a deer," he observed.

"And you, sir, are as black as the plague."

"Aye," he laughed, "and just as unstoppable. I'm looking for a maiden to die in my arms."

Picking up a towel, she wrapped it around her trembling body and backed away from him.

Lynchburg paused, a look of bewilderment shadowing his face. "Why do you hide yourself from me?"

"Why should I not?" she cried, clasping the towel tighter. "You are married."

His eyes turned to stone, and his jaw clenched angrily.

"Did you lay with your wife when I was sick in my bed? Does she pray for a child?"

He rolled his eyes heavenward and drove his fingers deep into his hair. "Servants," he seethed. "They are remarkable gossips."

"I only want the truth from you. Is she ill or is she not?"

"How dare you question me?" he roared. "You who have not befriended the truth in years."

She gazed up at him, her eyes wet and challenging. "I have lied at times in order to survive. But I have never given my heart falsely."

"My wife is ill." He held up a silencing hand as he turned away. "Leave it at that. The woman in my bed must have been your healer. She may have rested beside me, but I did not touch her."

She wanted to believe him, but she could not escape the doubt in her heart. "You said weeks ago that your wife was near death. Yet she lives? How can this be?"

"Silence!" he bellowed.

Her bottom lip quivered in anger, an anger that would not be restrained. "I will not be silent. You said that she was *near death.*"

"I said that she is beyond sickly, my lady. *Beyond sickly.*" He held out his hand to her. "I will help you dress, and then I will show you how she lies in her living tomb."

"No." She braced herself against the chair. "I do not wish to meet your wife. I could not bear it."

"You will meet her," he commanded gently.

"No." She slumped down in her chair, huddling in her towel. Her resistance was useless, she knew. If she didn't go with him, he would force her. As her eyes followed him warily, he walked to the trunk. Flinging it open, he reached in and grabbed the dress of green satin that had so enticed Daggot. It was beautiful and high-waisted with yellow ribbon sewn around the hem.

"Wear this," he said, handing it to her. Pulling out the long-sleeved chemise of yellow silk and soft leather boots, he thrust them at her. "And these."

She rose shakily and snatched the garments from him. Stepping behind the door screen, she began to don the elegant dress. Her body was still wet, and the clothes clung to her flesh. Her hair, still dripping, fell in curling tendrils down her back.

When she emerged, the sight of her caused his eyes to soften. Removing his cloak from its peg on the wall, he draped it over her shoulders and fastened it snugly up under her chin.

"You look like an angel," he said and stroked her cheek with his rough hand.

She drew away from him, unsmiling, her eyes sullen. "But I am not an angel, sir. I am a paramour."

"That is enough!" he shouted and grabbed her wrist, half-dragging her from the chamber.

"Please," she begged. "My heart cannot bear this truth." She was pulled down the stone steps and out into the crisp March air. The breeze on her face felt glorious after so many days of confinement in the solar.

"My heart has borne it!" he cried. "And so must yours."

A blacksmith's hammer rang in the distance like a bell tolling, and somewhere beyond the walls, sheep bleated hungrily.

She began to feel ill and feared that at any moment she would heave up the dry bread and cheese that she had eaten for breakfast. As a dizziness overwhelmed her, she began to cough in painful spasms.

He stopped and wrapped his arms around her waist, holding her to him until her coughing ceased.

"I am sorry," he said. "Lean on me and I'll support you."

Relaxing against him, she felt the solid muscles in his arms keeping her aloft. Chickens scattered from their path as they walked across the bailey, her waist supported in his iron grip. When they entered the tower, they slowly climbed the musty stairwell to the third level. Lynchburg placed his hand against the door, then paused to glance down at her. Her face was framed by darkness, and her eyes shone like verdant orbs in a dusky sky.

"I truly am sorry," he uttered, feeling a sharp pang of love and regret, "for all the suffering that I have caused you."

He pushed open the door, startling the nun who sat dozing in the corridor. "My lord," she greeted him in a voice newly awakened. Spying the young woman, she noticed that her eyes reflected pain. Whether physical or emotional, she could not tell.

"Is all well, my lord?" she asked, her eyes fixed on Riley.

He ignored the question. "How is my wife?"

"She is comfortable. She took some bread and broth this morning. Her mattress has fresh straw, and she has been bathed."

Riley began to pull against his grip, but to no avail.

"This is Lady Riley Snowden," he introduced her as he thrust her forward. "Her family has feuded for years with that of Lord Philip. She was once my enemy but is no more. Now open the door."

The nun was speechless, motionless.

"Open the door!" he barked, and she quickly stood up and fumbled with the key on her girdle.

As the door opened, Riley was repelled by the smell of the chamber and tried to pull away. Gently Lynchburg pushed her forward into the dark and putrid room.

"Behold my wife," he said.

She looked at the tiny form on the pallet. The periphery of candlelight fell across her so that she was cast in a half-moon of light. She could tell that the girl's eyes were closed in sleep. Her dark hair had recently been cut very short, much like a man's, and in the middle of her scalp had been shaved the figure of the cross.

"What think you, Lady Riley?"

She stared at the girl, feeling an ache of pity in her heart. It was as Lynchburg had said. The girl lay in a living tomb.

"Answer me," he urged. "What think you of my marriage made in hell?"

The girl stirred at the sound of his voice, and one eye blinked open sleepily, then closed again.

"God have mercy," Riley whispered.

"Christ have mercy," he responded, suddenly filled with a fierce repentance. "Is this not a fitting punishment for a man who took the life of a prince?"

She tried to slip away from him, but he grasped her waist and pulled her back against him.

"You called me a liar. Now, feast your eyes on the truth."

His arms encircled her like the powerful limbs of a bear, holding her within that bleak chamber.

"You cannot divorce her," she said, a waver in her voice. "'Tis your duty to take care of her."

She felt his body stiffen and sensed his growing desperation.

"She will be cared for," he said curtly. "Someday her father will place her in an abbey. He will sweeten their coffers so that she will never want for anything." His arms tightened around her, and the fragrance of her hair filled his head. "But I must be free of her." He buried his lips in that soft mass. "I must be free of Cornwich."

"Lord David. What is the meaning of this?"

They glanced up to see the chaplain standing in the doorway, his face a mask of fear and indignation.

"What sinful display is this?" His eyes roved down Riley's beautiful green gown, then up to Lynchburg's scowling face. "You parade your whore before your wife as would a man who has no conscience," he chastised him in a voice whisper soft. "Have you no fear of God, sir?"

The girl awakened, her mouth opening in a silent shriek as she rolled over and saw them hovering near her. The nun hurried forward and knelt to comfort her, hugging her to her breast.

"Have you?" Lynchburg asked. Gently pushing Riley away, he rested his hand on the hilt of his dagger.

"Please, sir, do not draw your blade on me again," the chaplain pleaded. "I am a man of God. I am unarmed."

Lynchburg drew his dagger and held the tip of it to the chaplain's throat. "I am a man of no conscience. You just said so yourself. I do not wish to harm you, but I will if I must. You see, I can be quite dangerous."

"Why—why do you threaten me?" he whimpered.

Reaching back, Lynchburg grabbed Riley's hand and pulled her to him. "I wish to be married to this woman. And you, sir, will perform the ceremony before the sun sets on this day."

"What?" she gasped and gazed at him in shock. "You wish to marry me today?"

"You cannot commit adultery," the chaplain sputtered. "'Tis against God."

"You are right. I cannot commit adultery because I was never married to Jeanette De Proileau."

The nun covered the girl's eyes and ears as if she could protect her from this painful scene.

"But you are married," the chaplain stated, shocked. "Lord Philip proclaimed it."

A sneer tugged at Lynchburg's lips as the tip of his dagger pressed deeper into the chaplain's throat. "Then Cornwich proclaimed a lie. Let us go to the chapel and proceed with the ceremony."

"But you are married," the chaplain insisted. "God bore witness to your marriage to the Lady De Proileau."

He wanted to laugh at the ridiculousness of that assumption. "I was married on a battlefield, my boots soaked in blood, my armor splattered with it." He slid the dagger up under the chaplain's chin and tilted his face back. "The blood of a prince dripped from my sword. And on the night wind the stench of death wafted into every cavern." One brow arched sharply in anger. "My marriage was never more than a verbal agreement nullified by betrayal. 'Twas never consummated."

The chaplain glanced fleetingly at Riley, hoping to see the same fear in her eyes that was surely evident in his own. To his frustration, he saw only a glimmer of joyful tears. "Does this lady truly wish to be married?" he asked. "I do not believe that she has answered your proposal."

Lynchburg shifted his gaze to Riley. "Well, milady, do you truly wish to be married?" he asked.

Her heart was pounding, and a rising warmth flowed through her body. Reaching out, she placed her fingers on the blade of his dagger and eased it away from the chaplain's throat. "Aye," she answered, feeling as if she were in a dream. "I suppose 'tis time we exchanged our bloodlust for lust of a different kind."

His eyes brightened like candles newly lit as he sheathed his dagger and offered her his arm. She grasped his elbow tightly and pulled herself to him, her head resting against his shoulder.

"Let us proceed with the ceremony," she said tearfully. "I am ready."

The chaplain's face was gray with shock as he led them to the chapel. "What will the bishop think of this?" he muttered, too low for the others to hear. *The churches money is stolen, a witch is on the loose, and now I am joining two people in an adulterous union. Oh, dear,* he thought, feeling as hapless as a beggar. *I shall lose my credentials for certain!*

As they entered the chapel, Riley's red hair, still partially damp, streamed down her back, and her eyes, although sunken from her recent illness, were as deep green as the foliage of summer. She was getting married, and the thought hung in her mind like a mist. Glancing up at Lynchburg's strong profile, she could not believe that this legendary warrior was about to become her husband. In the flickering light of the candles and the cool air of the chapel, they were proclaimed man and wife.

When they stepped out into the bailey, Riley felt a touch of warmth. For the first time she noticed that the snow in the bailey was melting, and a shimmer of sunlight was glowing across the stone towers. Spring was coming, bringing with it a warmth that they had been deprived of for far too long.

When they returned to the solar, they noticed that the shutters had been opened, and the chamber was filled with sunlight. The bedcurtains had been pulled back, and a heavy damask cover had been spread across the mattress. The flames in the fireplace danced and filled the air with the smell of burning pine.

"Are you cold, wife?" he asked.

"Aye, husband, but my heart is warm," she replied. Climbing up onto the bed, she gathered up the long skirt in her hands.

"Do you wish to rest?" he asked.

"Nay," she replied with a laugh. "I feel . . . resurrected."

He watched her, his heart heavy with love. "Then allow me to assist you out of that dress," he offered with a grin.

He unfastened her gown, then lowered it, exposing the white curve of one shoulder. Peeling away her chemise, he kissed her bare skin and let his lips blaze a trail down her naked arm. His kisses tickled her, and she fell back onto the bed, laughing helplessly.

Yanking the garment to her waist, he exposed her breasts to the cool air. Their peaks stiffened, and he hungrily took each one in his mouth, gently sucking the rosy tips. As his tongue stroked her, she felt her loins begin to warm with the slow fire of passion.

He took her face in his hands and kissed her deeply, lingering in the warmth of her mouth, his tongue seeking hers, tasting the sweetness of her.

Gliding her fingers down his neck and shoulders, she felt the corded muscles of his body. His manhood strained against his houppelande, and the rising hardness caused her to blush with excitement. Squirming out from under him, she pushed her gown and shift from her and kicked them from the bed.

"You must disrobe," she said, pulling at his belt. "I command it."

"You command it." He laughed.

"Aye, I am your wife now, and if you do not obey me, then I shall turn into a shrew."

"Nay, no shrew will rule me," he said, amused. "I have a way of taming a shrew." He got up from the bed and shed his clothes, watching a radiance rising in her eyes.

"Tame me then. For I cannot stand this raging wildness within me."

He lay down on top of her, his large body covering hers, and his manhood swelling to a long and hard fullness. "Do you want me inside of you?" he asked.

"I do, husband," she panted in his ear. "I do very much want you inside of me."

He pressed himself against the pink folds of her womanhood but would not enter her.

"Why do you tease me?" she cried softly. "Do you test the boundaries of my sanity?"

His hair framed his face in silken borders, and she wove her fingers through the thick strands, gripping them tightly, painfully.

"I test the boundaries of your passion," he replied.

"You are a monster, husband. Why do you not quench my thirst for you? Why do you make me wait?"

He grinned at her wickedly, his eyes pools of blue fire. "A little suffering is good for the soul," he growled seductively.

The sound of his voice stroked her every nerve, and she writhed beneath him, her loins pulsing for him.

"Are you ever to be a shrew, milady?" he asked, pressing the tip of his manhood into her throbbing flesh.

"Nay, never," she gasped. "I beg you to release me from this torment."

She cried out as he entered her, and, in response, she

raked her fingernails across his naked back. His thrusts pierced her, and she clung to him, swept up in the rush of blissful sensations. Seeking his mouth, she eagerly took his lips in her own.

"You are unlike any woman I have ever known," he murmured. "I am awed by the depth of your desire."

Lifting her legs, she wrapped her calves around him, urging him to ride her harder. His shaft was very large, and his thrusts became painful, but there was an edge of pleasure to the pain. A sweet tingling rippled up from her loins, and she fought to hold back her cresting pleasure.

"I must slow my pace, my love, else I satisfy you too soon," he said, kissing her.

"Aye," she panted. "Then I'll be hungry again before nightfall."

He smiled, his face flushed with heat as he pumped against her with a gentler rhythm. The massaging of her secret flesh lulled her into a dreamlike ecstasy. Moaning beneath him, she felt the first sweet taste of appeasement.

"I must have you," she demanded. Her nails bit into his buttocks as she lifted her hips, seeking the full length of him. "I must have you now."

He thrust harder, sending a warm current surging through her like a rising tide. When she reached her peak, her passion flooded her every limb with a raw ecstasy. Her cry of release shattered the silence of the chamber and echoed down into the passageways of the south tower.

Two hounds sleeping in the antechamber stirred at the sound and whined softly.

He drove into her, impaling her on his shaft and moaning as his seed burst forth. For a moment they hung suspended, their hearts pounding wildly, their limbs frozen in an agony of bliss.

As the haze began to subside, he gazed down at her flesh that looked too pale amid her waves of auburn hair. His mind was amazed. "Riley, you are more potent a lover as my wife than ever you were as my prisoner."

She laughed and pulled his head down, burying his face

in her soft breasts. "Do not ever punish me so harshly again by making me wait."

Lifting his face, he stared down at her through tousled locks. "The only way to tame a shrew is by making her boil a while in her own brew." He kissed her mouth lightly, teasingly, then brought his lips down hard against her own.

She opened her mouth to him, feeling the thrumming of her pulse deep in her loins. She was sated and sleepy, knowing that she was his now, not his prisoner, not his property to barter, but his wife to cherish and to love forever.

He drew back and studied her with a look of uncertainty. "Are you well enough to travel?"

"Why?" she asked. Brushing the hair from his face, she threaded her fingers through the soft strands.

"We must go into hiding in Wales. I don't know for how long."

As she gazed at him, her eyes reflected her patience and trust. She would follow him anywhere.

"The queen still wishes me dead?"

"Aye, soon she will ride against us," he said worriedly. "We must leave England for a while, but we will return someday. I cannot promise when that will be."

Putting her arms around his neck, she drew him back down to her. "I am ready to run with the wolf." She gently laughed against his ear. "In the wilds of Wales I may become a savage."

She felt his breath hot and moist on her neck.

"I believe 'tis already in your nature to be savage." He chuckled and nipped her earlobe.

"Can we proclaim ourselves husband and wife in Wales without fear of retribution?"

He kissed along the side of her neck, and her skin felt like velvet beneath his lips. "We will be living in the wilds of the blue mountains. 'Tis of little importance to the wolves and squirrels what we proclaim ourselves. We may crown ourselves king and queen for all they care."

He kissed the top of her head, breathing in the scent of

her hair. "We will be safe in Wales," he assured her. "I will not allow harm to come to you."

"Nor I you," she said.

Holding on to him in the half-shadows of the room, Riley felt invincible. Surely no one could harm them as long as they were armored in this love that they shared for each other.

Chapter Twenty-one

L ord David has married Riley Snowden," Daggot muttered to himself as he plodded into the stable. He could not believe what he had overheard the chaplain discussing with the steward. He had thought Lynchburg and Riley were enemies, but now they were married. What of the Lady D'Aubere who lived in seclusion above the chapel? Wasn't she the earl's rightful wife? He sighed as he picked up a thick bristled brush. It was all so uncommon strange.

"At least Riley has a future for herself," he said to the slumbering horses. There was no future for him, not beyond these stalls, he thought dismally as his nose filled with the scent of fresh manure.

It tweaked his conscience that he had broken so quickly under the queen's torture. Her soldiers had terrified him. The first blow had driven out his courage before his first drop of blood could spill. He was no soldier, he moaned inwardly.

Stepping on a discarded crust of bread, he lifted his foot and glanced down at it, then kicked it aside.

"Is this to be my future?" he wondered aloud as he drifted into a stall. As if in agreement, the mare snorted and tossed her mane. "Am I always to be a groom, a landless man?" he asked her as he began to brush her brown coat. "Am I destined to be remembered as nothing more than a foolish boy who thought to pursue an unobtainable dream?"

A glitter caught his eye, and he looked toward the loft. A shining object was gleaming down through the planks. Tossing the brush aside, he mounted the ladder, each step creaking beneath his weight. At the top, he spied a furry bundle half-hidden in a pile of hay, a red stone glimmering at its tip. He approached it curiously, the straw silencing his steps. Kneeling next to the bundle, he carefully pulled it from the straw and unwrapped it. To his shock, he discovered that it concealed Lord David's sword.

"Holy Mary," he whispered.

He jumped as a shriek pierced his ears. The pile of hay was shifting, and a woman was struggling to emerge from behind it. She looked as if she had been asleep. Her hair fell in a rumpled braid, and her dress was wrinkled and covered with bits of straw.

"Put it down!" she cried. "That is my sword. Put it down!"

"Who are you?" he asked as he gazed at her, astounded. "How did you come by my master's sword?"

"He gave it to me," she replied, her chest heaving. Her eyes, still puffy from sleep, were locked on his.

Daggot grasped the hilt and unsheathed the weapon. It was in good condition, no harm having been done. "'Tis intact," he observed. Angling the blade, he carefully inspected it. "Because you have not abused it, your life may be spared." Sheathing the weapon, he gripped the scabbard firmly in his hand.

"That sword was given to me by Lord David," she insisted. Reaching into the straw, she pulled out her satchel and slung it over her shoulder. "If you do not hand it over to me right now, I will . . ."

"You will what?" he asked, his brows raised in question.

She lunged for the sword, but he swung it beyond her grasp, causing her to stumble.

"What else are you stealing?" Grabbing her satchel, he

tried to wrestle it from her grip, but she held firmly to it. With one yank he ripped the bag in half, and the engraved box spilled out onto the straw. A sick fear gripped his stomach as he knelt and opened it. Inside an array of coins gleamed against a red velvet bed, each one signaling her doom.

"Did Lord David give you these coins as well?" he asked.

"Aye," she said, tossing her head back defiantly, "to give to the poor."

Daggot almost laughed at her brazenness. "My master did not give you this money," he said incredulously. His eyes skimmed up her body to her face as the revelation swept through him with the swiftness of a lightning strike. "This is the chaplain's treasury! You are the one who stole it."

She dived toward him, but he deftly scuttled out of her way, causing her to land face first in the straw. As she skidded to a halt, she left a spray of straw in her wake.

"You had best follow me," he ordered. "I am taking you to Lord David."

"I am not lying to you about the sword," she explained, clamoring to her feet. "He did give it to me."

His eyes lingered on her fair hair and lean form. She had the beautiful dark eyes of a fawn, and her hair was the golden color of the straw. "I hope my master deals mercifully with you. It would be a shame to see such a lovely woman put to death for greed. Your beauty far exceeds the worth of the master's sword or of any of those coins."

Her eyes once murky now lightened with hope. "You find me comely?" Walking toward him, she ran her palms suggestively across her breasts and fanned out her fingers along the flat of her stomach. "Have you ever lain with a woman?" she asked huskily.

Daggot swallowed hard, saying nothing. His hands begin to dampen with sweat. "No." He wanted to turn away but remembered Lord David's warning that to turn away was to show weakness. Still, it was difficult to face her. She was so lovely that she made him feel simple-minded and weak. "Nor do I wish to lay with a thief," he said, matter-of-factly, displaying much more resolve than he felt.

"I am not a thief," she laughed lightly. "If I were a thief, would I be living in the lord's stable? No, I would have run away."

"But you could not get away," he reminded her. "The gates are sealed."

She burst into tears, and for several moments, all he could do was watch her helplessly. As he stepped toward her to comfort her, her body slammed against his, knocking the breath from his lungs. His feet went out from under him, and he grabbed her hair, pulling her down with him.

"You slippery fox!" he cried, rolling over and pinning her beneath him. "I'll tree you if you run."

Looking into his face, she saw youthful eyes, pure and innocent, framed by a mop of soft curls. He did not look like a cruel man and yet he would hand her over for judgment.

"You will tree me anyway!" she cried. "Fasten me to an oaken beam and set me on fire for witchery."

"What?" he asked, befuddled. "What are you talking about?" He rolled off of her and stood up, pulling her to her feet. "Lord David will show mercy, I know it. Will you come with me? Or must I wrestle you every step of the way?"

"Do I tax your strength?" she asked, sharply.

"Aye," he confessed, pausing to catch his breath, "but only because the sight of your beauty has already weakened me greatly."

Her hair was coming loose from its braid and stray strands were tickling her nose. "You have a honeyed tongue." Twitching her nose, she blew the hair from her face. "I envy the girls in your life who often hear such fond words."

"There are no girls," he confessed. "Only horses to hear my fond words."

"Would you not rather have a woman than a horse?" she quipped.

His eyes roved down her shapely form. "Depends on who the woman is," he commented with a small shrug. "Even a wild and unbroken mare would be easier to handle than the likes of you."

"Bah." She clucked her tongue at him. "In the hands of the right man, I would be a kitten." Reaching out, she caressed his upper arm, causing him to stiffen with suspicion. "'Tis a pity you are not married. You are a handsome man. And very strong."

Pity, he thought angrily. That was the last word he needed to hear. "'Tis you who are to be pitied, not me." He shrugged off her hand. "Now follow me."

With a sigh of defeat, she fell to her knees. *Was every man within this castle chaste?* she wondered. "If I am to be pitied, then take pity on me. Set me free." Her braid hung in loose tendrils as she leaned over, her breasts swaying beneath her bodice.

The thought of cupping her naked breasts in his hands caused a flush of excitement to bloom on his cheeks. Did she really find him handsome and strong, he wondered, or were her kind words meant to throw him off his guard? If only he had some knowledge of women, he would know better how to deal with this one, but he was as ignorant of women as he was of all else in life.

"'Tis not up to me to set you free. But I will speak to Lord David on your behalf." She looked at him, her eyes hopeful and her lips parted in a smile of surprise. They were lovely lips, he noted, red and moist.

As she rose to her feet, she gripped her skirt, revealing her shapely calves. He eyed the slender curve of her ankle, and his mouth watered for want of kissing that sweet flesh.

"'Tis all you can do," she said. Heaving her shoulders in a shrug of exaggerated woe, she raised her skirt a notch higher.

Daggot felt his mouth go dry and his hands grow weak until he feared that he would drop the sword of David

D'Aubere. Not even Riley had ever had such a disabling effect on him. *Riley,* he thought, the woman who had once consumed his thoughts, but who, at the moment, seemed to be nothing more than a distant memory.

While Lynchburg collected their food supplies from the kitchen, Riley headed for the stables to ask Daggot to prepare their mount. She was still weak from her illness but eager to leave with her husband as soon as possible. Dressed in a shift and gown of coarse wool, she was determined to take nothing from the castle more valuable than what she had brought with her.

As she pushed open the stable door, she saw Daggot climbing down from the loft with Lynchburg's sword in his hand. A woman was trailing him, clutching her skirt as if she were frightened.

"What's this about?" she called to Daggot.

He looked down at her, surprised that she would question him. "'Tis a matter that I must take before your husband," he answered.

"Husband," Elda gasped. "She is not wife to Lord David. She is a maid."

Daggot hopped down from the ladder, then assisted her from the last rung, setting her on her feet.

"I am both," Riley countered, relieved to finally be able to proclaim the truth about herself. "The lord has no time to discuss any matters with you, Daggot. I need you to prepare his mount."

"For who?" he asked.

She looked at him in exasperation, her arms akimbo. "For Lord David and myself."

"I cannot prepare a mount unless the lord orders it."

"The lord is ordering it," Lynchburg said quietly. He stepped through the stable door, carrying two bags of supplies. "Prepare my missodor at once as Her Ladyship asked."

Daggot was surprised to see him dressed in common attire instead of clothes befitting a lord. Why, he was wearing nothing more than a green woolen tunic over a brown doublet and hose.

"My lord," Daggot greeted him and pushed Elda forward. "This woman was caught stealing."

Lynchburg cut his eyes at her, remembering the bitter draught that had rendered him unconscious. As Elda withered beneath his cold glare, he set the bags on the floor.

"That woman is a healer," he said, placing one arm protectively around Riley's shoulders. "I gave her my sword in payment for saving Riley's life. If 'tis my sword that you accuse her of stealing, then you accuse her wrongly. She came by it honestly."

"She is the healer?" Riley commented, her eyes wide with curiosity. The woman was very fair and seemed fragile and distraught. "I thank you, Mistress Elda, for your service to me."

Lynchburg raised his hand, gesturing for her silence.

"Did you give her these coins as well?" Daggot asked, holding up the box.

"No," Lynchburg said, strangely calm. "Fetch the chaplain so that he can identify the box."

Elda shrank in fear, and Riley felt a shudder of sympathy for her. She had a vivid memory of what Cornwich's dungeon was like and did not wish such a fate on anyone. Why would Elda have stolen the coins anyway? she wondered. The sword was worth more than she could have ever spent. It made no sense. Besides, Riley was certain that she'd never seen a more innocent face in her life. The woman practically glowed with goodness.

As Daggot shuffled off to follow his master's orders, Elda crumpled to her knees. Without his arm supporting her, she was too weak to stand.

"I pray thee, sir," she pleaded, "do not send me to the dungeon."

His eyes grew heavy with disappointment as he watched her. "Why did you steal the coins?"

"I did not steal for myself," she explained, frantically.

"I had to get rid of the money in order to save Lady Jeanette."

"You are a liar," the chaplain blared as he charged through the stable entrance, startling its occupants. He halted, his eyes blazing and his head thrown back like a reined-in horse.

"That woman is not only a thief but a witch!" he snorted in outrage.

Daggot trotted up behind him, cradling the box under his arm.

"He will harm the Lady Jeanette!" Elda cried, her voice bordering on hysteria. "I can prove it. There is a note in the box to the bishop, asking for an exorcist." Her eyes swung wildly over the faces of the group, hoping to see some sign of understanding. Exorcism was one of the churches most gruesome and useless practices. Were they enlightened enough to realize that? she wondered.

"Open the box," Lynchburg ordered. "I never gave permission for an exorcism."

Daggot obeyed and brought out a small parchment, which he handed to the earl. Lynchburg read it and turned his eyes menacingly on the chaplain.

"'Tis for the best, sir," the man explained, holding out his arms as if he could not fathom their inability to understand. "The girl will be healed."

"What is for the best," Lynchburg said deadly, "is for the Lady Jeanette to be removed from your care."

"That woman is a heathen!" he shouted, thrusting his finger at Elda. "She clubbed me, and she will pay for it. She will be excommunicated, totally alienated from all Christian contact."

"But how do you know 'twas she who clubbed you when you have no memory of the event?" Lynchburg reminded him. "And no witnesses."

"The nuns," he said, his eyes liquid with rage. "They will attest that she was near the chapel causing trouble. Besides, how else could she have come by the money?"

Lynchburg gave him a slow, contemplative look. "If

that is true, then what were you doing alone in your private chamber with this young woman?" He held out his hand to her, inviting the chaplain to look at her. "She is beautiful and fragile, not strong like you. How could she have rendered you unconscious? Perhaps she found the money and was going to return it. The bishop surely will have . . . questions."

He most definitely will have questions, the chaplain thought desperately. *The castle is racked with scandal, and now the earl wishes to create speculation that I am as corrupt as he. The bishop will discharge me from my duties without haste for allowing the castle to fall into moral ruin.*

With a huff of frustration he lowered his eyes to the straw-covered ground, speechless. Why would the earl not side with him? Did the man not fear for his soul?

"Wait," Riley implored them. "With your permission, my lord, we may resolve this matter now."

He looked at her in annoyance. "What do you suggest?" he asked, a challenge in his dark tone. She could tell that he would not tolerate her interference, but she would not retreat.

"This young woman has saved my life. And she has saved Lady Jeanette from a painful ordeal. Elda, do you wish to continue to help her?"

"Aye," she said weakly, her body still trembling with fear. "I can help her. I know I can."

"Then you must remain at Glenwood Castle as a healer. You will live in an apartment over the chapel. And you will minister daily to Jeanette, who needs your healing touch."

Elda shook her head as she glimpsed the chaplain. "I cannot live here where everyone will think of me as a thief. The chaplain will make sure that my reputation is one of disgrace."

"You will not be disgraced," Riley assured her. "The coins you attempted to steal will be given by Lord David to the widows and orphans of the village. The money will be given in honor of your healing powers. The steward will distribute it and record the donation in his account books. Your shame will be turned into glory among the people."

"You offer is kind and generous, my lady," she said softly. Her lashes fluttered down over eyes that were dark with fear. "I would gladly accept your offer, but I would never feel safe within these walls with that man." Her eyes flitted coolly to the chaplain. "I would rather return to Gersham, where I feel safe. The vicar there is a kind man. I have never felt any threat from him."

"I will protect you!" Daggot offered eagerly. Stepping forward, he seemed to plead for redemption. "I am sorry I thought you a thief. If you stay, I vow no harm will come to you. I will guard you myself."

Riley and Lynchburg looked on him in surprise, and Riley could not help but smile at what his offer implied. The boy was taken with her.

"The chaplain will be no threat to you," Lynchburg stated, rolling his eyes at the man. "He will not be on the premises much longer. He is going on a pilgrimage."

The chaplain looked at him with soulless eyes. "I have no plans to go on a pilgrimage, sir." He spoke as if he were grinding the words between his teeth.

"Ah, but you do," Lynchburg corrected him. "You will write to the bishop tonight and tell him that you are leaving for a pilgrimage. A long pilgrimage," he said, drawing out the words. "And you will ask him to appoint the vicar of Gersham as your replacement here. You will do it before the sun sets on this day. And I will see that 'tis safely delivered."

The chaplain looked at the earl, angry and arrogant, a smirk pulling at his lips.

The earl stepped toward him as swiftly and smoothly as a wolf moves through the grass, silent but with deadly intent. He stopped before him, his breath hot and panting with anger. "If you recant and attempt to return here, then I will return here as well. I will seek you out, and I will strike you dead."

The chaplain felt chilled as if he had been stripped of his robes and was standing naked in the cold of the stable.

"If that results in my excommunication," Lynchburg continued, "then so be it." He stepped nearer until he could smell the fear on the man. "I do not fear alienation from all Christian company."

The chaplain glanced around at the faces of the others, none of whom appeared sympathetic. "Aye, my lord," he acquiesced. "It will be as you command. But no good will come of this. You have turned this castle over to the forces of hell."

Lynchburg looked at Elda, her braid shining like a ribbon of light, and Daggot's eyes filled with boyish infatuation.

"No," he said with a sigh of relief. "I think that now all will be well within these walls."

At dusk Riley sent a messenger to the village to announce that the plague was over and to implore the servants to return to Glenwood Castle. To hasten their return, she ordered a hog butchered for a celebration feast. As preparation for the festivities began, she and Lynchburg slipped into the stables where their horse and supplies were waiting. Her only desire was to ride with her husband beyond the gates of Glenwood Castle and simply disappear.

As they were about to mount the missodor, the steward rushed in, breathless from fear and exhaustion.

"My lord! My lord! I have been searching everywhere for you," he cried. Although the air was chilly, a bead of perspiration rolled down the side of his face. "You must come at once. There is an army approaching."

Lynchburg felt an icy fear sweep through him. Margaret had moved quickly against him. Rushing from the stable, he headed for the gates and swiftly climbed up to the parapets. The wind was cool on his face, milder than in days past, and the snows were melting. The sky was filled with the orange glow of sunset, but he could see clearly across the fields to the approaching army. As he waited, he watched, his eyes sharply tuned to the banner carrier.

Although she was still very weak, Riley clamored up to the parapets to stand beside him. "Who attacks us?" she asked, leaning against him, her arm clutching his waist.

Locking her in a protective embrace, he looked out across the field. A banner came into view bearing the image of three suns merging into one.

"The boy who would be king," he growled. " 'Tis Edward. Edward, Earl of March."

Chapter Twenty-two

Lynchburg strode across the bailey, shouting orders as he headed for the stable.

"Steward," his voice rang through the cold air. "Call out every man of the castle guard. Tell them to prepare the crossbows and mount the battlements. Put a man on every garderobe chute and cover the well."

"Daggot!" he cried as he entered the darkening stable. "Ready my mount."

He gripped his side where his sword once hung and grimaced at the reality of his disarmament. "Never mind." He sighed as he heard footsteps scurrying into the stable behind him. "I'll ready my own mount. Just find me a weapon."

"I have a weapon, sir."

He turned to see Elda in the half-shadows of the stable door, her arms cradling his sword, its ruby hilt shining like the first star at dusk.

"Elda," he said, surprised. "You wish to loan me the sword I gave you?"

"No, milord." She smiled at him and marveled at the thickness of his arms, his chest. The sword was an extension of his warrior's strength and belonged at his side.

As the sunlight slanted through the doorway, it fell

across his face, brightening his hair to a lighter shade of brown and reflecting back at her through azure eyes.

"I am returning your sword to you."

He furrowed his brows in puzzlement as his eyes slid along the cold length of the blade. "Are you? Why?"

"What good is it to me if I am dead amid the ruins of a sacked castle?" She held it out to him and watched with satisfaction as he lifted it from her grip. He reminded her of a woman who embraces a child once thought to be dying who is now well. "It would serve me better in your hands, sir. I know not how to wield it."

He looked at her with a depth of tenderness that touched the essence of her soul.

"I must reward you for your generosity," he said.

She lowered her eyes, her lashes fluttering like the gray wings of a dove. "I am already rewarded by being allowed to remain here. 'Tis what I have wanted for years. And if you wield the sword to win the war, I will be rewarded further still. When this war is over, Lord Philip will return, and my loneliness will be at an end."

He held the sword in silence, wondering if he would ever get used to the emotional speeches of women. "I thank you for taking care of it," he said, simply. "'Tis as clean as I've ever seen it."

"Aye, I cleaned it well for you. And rubbed it with juniper. That will protect you from disease and evil."

A small laugh escaped him, and he held up the sword, a teasing glint in his eye. "Then I shall be fearless, Mistress Elda."

She leaped forward, surprising him by clasping her arms around his neck and hanging from him like a long, flowing streamer of yellow silk and green wool. "I wish you victory, my lord. I will do all in my power to help you."

Peeling her from him, he gave her a hearty smile and took her elbow in his hand turning her gently toward the door. "You already have given me power, Elda. By saving Riley's life, you have given purpose to my own." With a gentle nudge he propelled her from the stable. "Now get thee to the east tower and anticipate Cornwich's return."

As she hurried across the bailey, he held up the sword. The dying light of the sun lined its edges in a silver glow.

"I pray her juniper works," he murmured under his breath. "For soon this sword will be all that stands between me and the army of York."

The drawbridge lowered, and Lynchburg, mounted on his missodor, rode out slowly to meet the usurper. The land was soggy, the melting snows having turned the fields to marsh, and the mud sucked at his missodor's hooves.

Edward sat astride his warhorse, his dark form silhouetted against the red blaze of twilight. His brown hair fell to his shoulders, and his eyes, the color of midnight, were fixed on the approaching rider.

As Lynchburg drew nearer, he recognized Edward as a strong opponent, one who would bear the swiftness and fearlessness of youth.

In Lynchburg, Edward saw a man who had weathered many battles, an experienced soldier, an excellent swordsman. His reputation was so concise that when men spoke of him it was with few words and simply put. He never lost.

As Lynchburg reined his mount to a halt, his cold, searching eyes locked onto the youthful, challenging ones of Edward. "What do you want here, Edward of March?" he asked.

Edward straightened his back, suppressing a smile as he spoke. "My proper title is King Edward IV of England and France, and Lord of Ireland."

Lynchburg felt his heart turn to lead. All that he had fought for was lost. The kingship was gone, stolen by this boy. "So 'tis true. You have usurped your king and placed yourself on the throne."

"Come now, Lynchburg." He laughed as he glanced out across the snow-mottled field. The wind thundered across the land and whipped his hair about his face. "You know as well as I that my father had a weightier claim to the throne than Henry."

"You did not come here to give me this news," Lynchburg stated harshly. "What is the purpose of your visit?"

"I wish to enter Glenwood Castle," he replied innocently. "Without weapons or men. My intentions are honorable."

"What are your intentions?" Lynchburg demanded, eyeing the line of horsemen on the horizon.

"I am here at the request of Lady Riley Snowden's kinsman." Edward half-laughed at the recollection of events. "I was on the training ground of Smithfield when suddenly Gertrude Snowden appeared out of nowhere. She started bleating about how you had imprisoned the Lady Riley and had made her your whore."

He paused to check Lynchburg's reaction but saw only a stony glare as hard as the edge of winter.

Wrinkling his brow in mock seriousness, he continued. "Before she could say another word, Lord Geoffrey Seward appeared. He began spewing apologies and grabbed his sister in a dreadful pinch. It was a rather raucous scene. I had to bring it to an abrupt halt and demand that Lord Geoffrey unhand her." He shook his head, sighing heavily. "He then told me that Lady Riley had freed him from a Lancastrian prison. Had saved his life, he said." Peering past Lynchburg's shoulder, he eyed the high walls and rising towers of the fortress. "He beseeched me to rescue Riley from her most grievous plight as your prisoner. Then Gertrude began screeching that Riley is your very willing prisoner. That is until Geoffrey boxed her ears and gave mine a blessed rest. As he dragged his sister from the field, I promised him that I would rescue Lady Riley." He gazed at him, his eyes alight with boyish charm. "Indeed, stealing your mistress seemed like a rather sporting thing to do."

"You will not have her!" he shouted and grasped the hilt of his sword.

Edward threw up his hand in a calming gesture. "Stay

your hand, David. I am willing to negotiate a ransom for her."

"There will be no ransom," he snapped. "I wish nothing from you. And will give nothing to you."

Edward steadied his mount as it began to stamp restlessly and paw the ground. "If you will not part with her, then I shall make a bargain with you. If you agree to my terms, then you may have the girl." He held out his hand in offering. "I will give her to you."

"I would never agree to any terms of yours, March." His face hardened with disgust. "Besides, the woman is not yours to give."

"Oh, but she is," he said, the fading sunlight flashing in his eyes. "I am her king, and I can give her to whomever I wish."

The man's arrogance was enough to turn his stomach. "She is not a cow, or a flask of wine, or one of your whores for you to take and give. She is my wife."

"Your wife!" Edward roared, his face registering his shock. "She is a Yorkist. Does this union mean that you have mended your feud with the Yorkists?"

"It means that I am married. That is all."

Edward rolled his eyes heavenward to the darkening sky and inhaled deeply the scent of a snow-soaked earth. "My spies tell me that you have withdrawn your allegiance to Henry."

"Aye, but that does not mean that I have placed it elsewhere."

Edward gave a half-grunt of amusement. "Margaret is waiting for you at York. She thinks you will return to her. The Earl of Cornwich has convinced her of it."

"Nay." He shook his head rigidly in denial. "'Tis not to be."

"David, I did not really come here for the girl," Edward admitted, his gaze drizzling down the face of his enemy. "That was my pretense in coming. To be truthful, I came here for you."

He waited for a response but saw only Lynchburg's unflinching gaze.

"I wish to have your allegiance. You know that I will fight for England until my dying breath. I lead my men; I do not hide in dark corners like the coward, Henry. What must I do to win your loyalty?" He swept his hand toward the four towers of Glenwood Castle. "Is it the estate you want? I will confiscate it from Cornwich and give it to you."

"I will not give you my allegiance, Edward," he said, stubbornly. "I will not fight against the king whom I vowed to defend. I wish only to leave this country with my wife."

Edward looked bemused as he considered the hopelessness of Lynchburg's predicament. "Love does soften a man's mind. 'Tis a pity. If you will not swear your allegiance to me, then you leave me no choice but to take the girl."

Lynchburg glowered at him, his brows knitting into a black frown.

"Then you may leave the country," Edward continued, "under my protection, of course. I will arrange for a ship to transport you safely to France. But Riley will remain in London, with me." A slow smile spread across his youthful face. "In time you will be willing to pay the price for that which you hold so dear. You will return to your beloved country and serve your lawful king, if you truly want the lady back."

"I will never let her go with you, March."

"'Tis not your decision," he chimed. "'Tis mine. I will tell her to come with me, and she will obey."

"She will not go with you," Lynchburg said. The sun sank deeper into the horizon, turning his eyes to an icy black.

"Of course she will," Edward stated merrily. "I am her king, and I command it. She has no choice."

One brow winged upward sternly. "The lawful king is

Henry. And when he is dead, the crown will be placed upon the head of his son, the Prince of Wales."

Edward whistled long and low at that remark. "Ah, yes, the little Prince of Wales. I do admire that boy. He's a bloodthirsty little cub. A real fighter. 'Tis a pity that I shall have to kill him someday." The laughter faded from his eyes as he fixed his gaze on his opponent. "I leave on the morrow, David. I expect you and the Lady Riley to be prepared. My men will come at dawn to collect you."

Turning back in the direction of his army, he galloped across the soggy fields, leaving Lynchburg alone in the deepening shadows of the walls.

Riley paced the floor of the solar as the fire blazed in the fireplace. She had poured herself a goblet of wine but could not drink it. Her stomach was too knotted with fear.

Had Edward decided to lay siege to Glenwood Castle? she wondered. *And why had Lynchburg ridden out alone to meet with him? It could be a trap.*

When she heard footsteps on the stairs, her heart pounded so fiercely that she felt as if she could not breathe. The door opened, and she let out her breath in a cry of relief when Lynchburg appeared at the threshold.

"Where have you been?" she demanded, wanting to beat her fists against his chest. "What has taken you so long to return to me with news?"

He took her in his arms and held her against him, feeling the soft warmth of her body.

Wriggling from his grip, she stepped back and glared at him anxiously. "Will you please tell me what is happening?"

He walked to a chair by the fire and sank into it, splaying his legs in tired repose. "Edward has been proclaimed king in London. He wants my loyalty, but I have denied him that which he came to claim."

"What will he do now?" she asked fearfully.

"He has offered me safe passage on a ship to France." He rubbed his hand across his forehead. "'Tis a trap. Next he will tell me that I must board this ship unarmed and alone. As soon as I set foot on deck, his executioners will carry out my death sentence. And pitch my body into the sea."

She gasped and pressed a clenched fist to her mouth. "You mean he has offered you his protection so that he can kill you? I cannot believe it of Edward."

He leaned his head back against the cushioned chair and stared at her through hooded eyes. "Of course not. You do not know the ways of a man who wants to be a king."

She looked at him bewildered. "Why would he want you dead?"

"Because there is a Lancastrian who is far more dangerous than I. The young Prince of Wales. Even in exile I could form an alliance with him."

"But the prince is a child!" she exclaimed. With shaking hands, she poured him a goblet of wine and brought it to him. "He is a boy of no more than five."

As he took the wine, he held her fingers in his own, the power of his touch calming her trembling hands. Bringing the goblet to his lips, he felt the raw burn of the wine on his tongue. "Edward knows that in a few years the prince will emerge as usurper. He will ask me to lead his army, and he will fight like a lion for the crown once worn by his father." He ran his tongue slowly along his lower lip, tasting the lingering flavor of the grape. "If I am dead, then he will be less likely to succeed."

She knelt before him, clinging to his hand. "We must escape tonight into Wales," she pleaded.

He lifted her palm to his mouth, kissing it gingerly. "The outside walls are heavily watched. And Edward is determined to take you with him in the morning when he returns to London."

"Me? Why?"

He entwined her fingers in his own and caressed them gently.

"He claims he wants to use you to barter for my loyalty.

But in truth, I believe he wants to arrange a marriage for you."

"A marriage?" she cried, indignantly.

"Aye, when the war is won, you will become a Yorkist heiress. Edward will return your father's estates to you as he should. That will gain him the trust of all Yorkists. You will be a wealthy widow with properties in several counties. There are many noblemen to whom he owes his favor. He will offer you as a wife to one of them."

"I will not go to him," she hissed. She stood up abruptly and began to pace the floor. Her shoes padded softly against the tiles, and her hair swung gently against her back.

"We will escape," she stated firmly as she paced back toward him.

"'Tis not possible, sweeting." He held out his arms to her, but she turned away in frustration. "His army surrounds us. If we try to leave, we will be caught. I would rather face Edward on the field like a soldier than be caught sneaking out into the night like a coward. Tomorrow this will all be behind us. I will battle Edward and claim you as my bride once and for all. We will leave England in peace, and we will leave together."

"How?" she asked. "How will you battle Edward and win? His army stands poised to destroy you."

He scratched the stubble on his chin and wondered how he could explain to her what he knew she would never understand. "On the morrow I will issue a challenge to Edward."

"What?" She faced him, her eyes wide with disbelief. "You would put your life at risk?"

That remark piqued his ire, and he gave her a dark look of reproof. "I have put my life at risk each day for years. Need I remind you that I am a soldier? I have fought far more experienced opponents than that boy."

"What if he does not agree to your challenge?" she asked, propping one hand on her hip and flagging the other at the window. "He has an army out there. All he need do is command them to kill you, and it will be done. Why would he fight you over me?"

Lifting his goblet, he took another sip of wine and swallowed thickly. "He wouldn't. That's why I plan to tell him that it was I who executed his father at Wakefield."

"No, you mustn't." She stepped back, feeling cornered. There was nowhere for them to run. And all she wanted to do was run. Take his hand and flee as far away as possible.

"I must because I love you." His eyes slid down her silky mane of hair to the gentle slope of her hip. "Challenging Edward is my only chance to have you."

His words of love seemed smothered by the threat of loss. How could he act so unaffected at a time like this? she wondered. One would think that challenging the King of England was ordinary to him.

"You are a fool gone mad," she cried, "to challenge Edward with a Yorkist army ready to conquer you. We must escape tonight."

"That is enough," he said, throwing up his hand. "My nerves are frayed from this day."

"Well, then, go and find yourself a quieter chamber, for I will be weeping throughout the night for you. You will have no peace in my bed."

He felt the breeze of her passing as she walked to the portal and pulled open the door.

Lynchburg sprang from his chair, tossing his goblet aside. "You dare to drive me from my own bedchamber?"

She stood stubbornly beside the open door, meeting his glare with equal determination. "I do, for if you do not leave this room, then I will. And the servants will wonder at the great Lord David D'Aubere, who makes his wife sleep in the kitchen among the hounds."

Raising his hands in surrender, he stormed from the room, his booted feet pounding the stairs as he descended like a demon hurdling back into hell.

She knew what she must do. If she were going to save him, she must go to Edward herself and offer him an agreement. He was her cousin. He would listen to her. He must.

When she returned to the castle, she would have gained her and her husband's freedom.

Quickly she removed her gown of coarse wool and donned the green velvet dress over the yellow chemise. Bundling her hair up on top of her head, she hastily pinned it into place with ivory pins, then pulled a heavy cloak around her shoulders. Cracking the door, she peeked out, making sure that Lynchburg was gone from the tower. Noiselessly she flew down the winding steps and out into the night.

Chapter Twenty-three

The moon shone white like a sphere of ice casting a silver glow across the castle. The night wind blew through the bailey, the only sound that penetrated the sealed realm. The men on the parapets stood armed, waiting, their eyes trained on the velvet darkness beyond the horizon.

They did not see the shadow emerging from the south tower and flitting across the bailey, weaving in and out of the undulating shadows until it vanished into the stable. Riley saddled a mare and pulled her hood down over her face then calmly walked the animal to the gatehouse.

"Who goes there?" a guard shouted as she approached the gates.

She stopped, her head bowed lower. "I am the healer," she replied. "I am needed at a nearby farm. There is a rumor among the villagers that the plague has befallen a family there. The earl bid me go."

The guard backed away from her and clumsily pried the bar from the gate.

"Go then," he said. "God speed you on your journey."

Keeping her head down, she led her horse through the gate and over the drawbridge.

Beneath the moonlight, she mounted the mare and rode out at full gallop across the open fields. Her hood was blown back by the wind as she crossed the expanse of land to the dark outline of tents.

As she rode into Edward's camp, several soldiers rushed toward her, their bows drawn. She felt herself being pulled roughly from her mount and shoved to the ground. Her cloak fell from her shoulders and was trampled underfoot as many hands reached for her.

"Release her!" a voice commanded.

A silence fell over the men, and they dropped back. Stepping away, they opened up a path before her, and she saw Edward slouching toward her. She noted that he was a man of great height, and that his face had the stern air of authority. His features, framed by thick locks of chestnut brown hair, were youthful but bore an edge of hardness.

As she scrambled to her feet, her hair came undone and cascaded over her shoulders, creating a bewitching effect in the moonlight. His dark eyes brightened in recognition, then roved boldly down her body, lingering on every curve.

"Sire." She curtsied. "I am Riley Snowden, your cousin. I have come in peace."

"You need not introduce yourself to me." He lifted a silken tress and held it delicately in his palm, then replaced it gently against her shoulder. "I would know that red hair anywhere. When we were little, I used to tease you about it."

"So you did." She remembered playing with him as a child, but now he was so much bigger, matching Lynchburg in size and strength. She felt awkward in his presence. And small.

The wind blew coldly through the camp, and she shuddered without her cloak. Seeing her discomfort, he quickly removed his coat and draped it over her shoulders, pulling it tightly around her.

"Why, my sweet coz, do you come to me?" he asked.

She looked at him, pleadingly. "I must speak with you in private."

"Of course," he agreed with a nod of consent.

"Sire, she must be searched for weapons," a guard warned, but Edward waved him away.

"I know all about the weapons of women," he commented with a dry laugh and gently took her hand. "I daresay my cousin is too young to have acquired most of them."

Linking her arm through his, he walked her past the crowd of men to his tent. When she entered the inner chamber, she felt the welcoming warmth from a brazier and longed to sit down. Tired and weak as she was, she knew that she could not sit before the king. The chamber's only chair looked large and soft, and was invitingly stacked with red and gold velvet cushions.

"I am disappointed in you," he said sullenly as he pulled the curtain of the portal closed. "How could you have married an enemy of your king?"

She turned to him, her face beautiful in the muted light. "I was his prisoner." Taking a slow, deep breath, she clasped her hands firmly against her throbbing chest. "He wanted a babe as my ransom and took my virginity. When he offered to marry me, I agreed. 'Twas the honorable thing to do. As his wife and your cousin, 'tis my duty to mediate this argument between you."

He smiled, a playful gleam rising in his eyes. "Lynchburg is not a man to send a woman to plead for him. I would wager that he does not even know that you are here."

"Aye, Sire, he does," she said, her voice winded from nerves. "I come to you with the terms of our peace agreement."

He stared at her for so long without speaking that what little courage she had began to falter. His eyes bored through her, and she wondered if he were reading the truth in her heart.

"I have come to plead with you to release us," she continued quickly. "We will go into Wales and never return to England again. As your blood kin, I swear to you that we will never bear arms against you. And in exchange for our freedom, I will forfeit all property that was once my father's and relinquish it to the Crown." Finishing her speech, she lowered her head in exhaustion.

He walked up to her with steps as swift and tender as an approaching lover's. "Why do you lie to me, little cousin?" Tucking his fingers beneath her chin, he gently lifted her face to his and gave her a slow patient smile. "Did I become a king through idiocy? I think not. The Earl of Lynchburg is a powerful opponent. Am I to believe that he will live just across the border and never be a threat to me?"

"Perhaps," she whispered. Her heart was beating so wildly that she feared he might see the throbbing pulse at her neck.

"Perhaps," he mocked her mildly. He strolled to his chair and sat down, crossing his legs. "*Perhaps* I will let you keep your father's lands and your husband, too."

Her lips parted in a half-gasp of surprise.

"On one condition." He lifted his forefinger in caution. "If you can gain Lynchburg's loyalty for me."

Her mind reeled at the thought of such an impossible task. "I cannot," she said. "He is a man of honor. He swore his allegiance to Henry and will not give it to another."

Stretching out his legs, he crossed his ankles and folded his hands across his lap. "How is it that you became his prisoner?" he asked.

She squinted her eyes at him like a child being forced to confess her role in some mischief. "I infiltrated Glenwood Castle hoping to kill Cornwich. When Lynchburg returned as the new master, I thought to gain Lancastrian secrets from him."

He rolled his eyes in dismay and sighed, frustrated. "Winning his allegiance to me should have been your strategy all along. A warrior of his caliber is far more valuable to me than any secrets his army may be harboring. The magnates of England respect him. They follow his lead. With him on my side, I will be unstoppable."

"I cannot sway him," she said, her voice strained.

"You must." As he looked at her, his eyes grew hard with determination. "If you love your country, then you must give me Lynchburg."

"But how?" she asked, causing him to laugh out loud at her naïveté.

"Look to your Bible, madam. 'Twas a woman who brought about the downfall of all mankind with her seductive power. And I thank her proudly for it. For if not for her tempting fruit, then man would never have known the sweetest fruit of all." He gripped his crotch. "That which ripens between a woman's thighs."

She took a step back, shocked by the crudeness of his gesture.

"Your power over Lynchburg as his wife is far superior to mine as his king. Use it and glorify our cause. Win me his allegiance, Riley. Your husband's life will be spared, and all of England will be saved."

As if I could save all of England, she thought.

He stood up and walked toward her until she smelled the scent of the night air on his clothes. "Beguile him in your bed. Tell him he must serve me. If he loves you, if he wants you, he will succumb to your wiles." He gripped her arms, startling her. "Think about it, coz. The two of you will have a high place of honor in my court. Land. Wealth. England will be strong again. And the bloodshed will stop."

The bloodshed will stop. The words trickled down deep into her soul. How badly she wanted for the war to end, but she could not control Lynchburg, not even through sex.

"Sire, you are my king, not my whoremaster. I cannot use sex to manipulate my husband."

His grip tightened, becoming almost unpleasant. "I am your king, madam, so why will you not obey me?"

"I am sorry, Sire." Wrapping her cool fingers around his wrists, she looked at him imploringly. "If only you will accept the terms of our agreement, then my husband and I will gladly go into exile."

He looked down at her, his face breaking into a sly grin.

"Oh, no, Cousin Riley. I cannot return you to Lynchburg. He is a traitor. I must place you under my protection and take you back to London with me."

"What?" she cried. "No, you cannot do that."

He sighed as if he were growing bored with the conversation. The boyish sparkle in his eyes was beginning to dull. "How kind of you to turn yourself over to me just as I was wondering what clever strategy I should use to tweak him. When Lynchburg rides out at daybreak, he will find us all gone and his mistress abducted." He laughed gruffly, but the sound quickly faded into a low snarl. "If he wants you back, then he will have to come to London to claim you. And he will have to pledge his loyalty to me."

"You are abducting me?" she asked, feeling tears of outrage moistening her eyes.

He gave her a stiff smile, his eyes hooded with growing impatience. "Aye, 'tis not the first time I have abducted a lady. I find the practice rather thrilling."

All hope drained out of her as she sank to her knees, exhausted by her fear and her failure. Lynchburg would come for her, and when he did, he would have to fight Edward, surrounded not only by Edward's small army but by a fortified city full of Yorkists. *We are undone,* she thought bitterly, her mind growing dark and despondent. In her attempt to save her husband, she had put his life at even greater risk.

If he had faced Edward at daybreak, he might have had a chance, but now there was none. She buried her face in her hands, feeling as if she had delivered the final fatal blow to him herself.

In the predawn hours they departed for London, and by late morning they were nearing the small monasteries and hostelries, kennels and fencing schools that surrounded the city. Edward sat tall and fearless in the saddle, a godlike man of impressive stature. His cloak of royal purple flowed down his back and draped over the rump of his missodor. People rushed from their homes and businesses to greet their king, and Edward waved to the crowds, at times dismounting to give children loaves of bread and cheese.

Before them the Roman walls of the city rose up, enclosing graveled streets and shops and houses of wood and plaster. High above the city loomed their destination, the foreboding walls of the Tower, a massive fortress of twenty towers covering eighteen acres on the River Thames.

Accompanied by heralds and drummers, they rode through the gates of London, the sun in splendor banner held high. The people welcomed Edward with a reverence that Riley would have thought impossible. He was after all only mortal, but the Londoners approached him worshipfully.

As the entourage passed the booths and stalls of the merchants, the women and men waved and called out to him, hoping to gain a glimmer of his attention. At times he would dismount and walk among his subjects, allowing them to grasp his hands. The deeper they journeyed into the city, the greater the swell of the crowd and the slower the procession moved.

The wind was still brisk with winter, but when it subsided, they felt the sun and a mild hint of spring. The turn of the season had always given Riley a sense of hope, but today there was none. She felt barely alive as she sat astride her horse.

When they arrived at White Tower, Edward did not dismount but rode the grounds for several minutes greeting his people, knights and fishmongers alike. The grounds smelled of manure from the animal pens and of fish from the vendors who hawked their wares on the lawn. Riley wrinkled her nose at the strong odors and fell in beside her king as he rode toward the great hall.

"Do not fear, coz," he spoke to her in a tone beguilingly fond. "I will give you a safe haven. Your kinsmen Lord Geoffrey and his dear sister, Gertie, are here at court. How delighted they will be to see you."

Gertie. The word swept over her like fire. The last person she ever wanted to see again was Gertie. *Could my life get any more dismal?* she wondered.

They reined in their mounts before the great hall, and Edward leaped from his horse as if the long journey had refreshed him.

"Although you've married a traitor, 'tis to your credit that you saved Bellville's life," he commented. His strong hands encircled her waist, and he lifted her from her horse.

She thought it strange that he would assist her himself rather than have a servant do it, but everything about this king was different.

"I did what I felt I had to do," she said numbly.

"Come now, pretty coz, you need not be humble with me. I do not care for that trait." He set her on her feet and smiled down at her. "You rescued a nobleman, and you shall be rewarded for your valor. I will give you a place of honor at my table tonight. While Lynchburg rides to collect you, you will be dining like a queen at the table of his enemy."

Her heart sank deeper as they climbed the steps to the great hall. It had been hours since she had last seen Lynchburg, and she hungered to feel his arms around her, to see his eyes like blue fires fixed only on her, and to feel safe once again in his arms. The pain of her loss was growing so heavy that it felt as if it were pressing the breath from her lungs.

The great hall was teeming with members of the garrison crushing in around her. As Edward strode across the massive chamber, he left her in his wake of chamberlains, constables, keepers, and marshals. Separated from him by his entourage, she slowed to a stop, unwilling to keep up. She had never felt more alone in her life.

"Begging your pardon, Lady Riley."

She looked up to see a girl of no more than twelve or thirteen years old. Her hair was hidden in a gray linen veil, and she wore a dress of brown homespun.

"The king wishes me to show you to your chambers."

Riley nodded and followed her across the great hall, then up winding stairs to the apartments above. They entered a room that smelled of newly polished brass and wood. On a trestle table long candlesticks burned brightly, illuminating the colorful tapestries on the walls. Several trundle beds had been set up throughout the room, and she realized that this chamber must be reserved for unmarried ladies of the court.

There was no one present when they entered, and she was thankful for the seclusion. In this castle filled with strangers, she desperately needed time to release the grief in her heart and weep for the husband she might never see again.

"You are so beautiful, milady," the maid commented as she removed her cloak. "'Tis no wonder the king is smitten with you."

She felt her heart skip with fear. "What do you mean?" she asked curiously.

The maid blushed as she hung Riley's cloak on a peg. "I heard the king tell his chamberlain that before this day is done he will have a private audience with you. Is that not exciting?"

No! she wanted to shout but bit her lower lip to hold her tongue at bay. The last thing she needed was for this young girl to relay a message to the king that she didn't want his company. She couldn't risk challenging Edward's pride. There was still a chance that he might listen to her. She could not abandon the situation as hopeless. To do so would be to abandon her husband forever, and her heart and mind could not survive the magnitude of that loss. If Lynchburg should die, she would become like a dead person, too.

Feigning a stomachache, she dismissed the maid and laid down on one of the cots. The life seemed to be flowing out of her, leaving her numb, her heart beating a slow and hollow rhythm. When the maid returned, bringing her wine for her stomach, she would not drink it. Nor would she eat the bread that the girl brought up later. By late afternoon she had descended into a pit of moping so deep that the maid could barely rouse her from it.

"You must rally," the girl urged. "'Tis near time for your audience with the king."

Riley's eyes rolled beneath closed lids. "Prepare a bath," she murmured, *anything to delay my audience with him.*

When the tub was full, she climbed into it, sinking up to her chin in the steamy water. Not until the water had grown cold and an hour had passed did she budge, shivering, from the tub.

Reluctantly she donned a gown of scarlet damask, which the maid had brought from the wardrobe tower. As she poured herself a cup of wine, she could hear the growing revelry of the men in the great hall.

"Who is present below?" she asked. With hands slightly shaking, she brought the cup to her lips.

"The king and his assembly," the maid replied. "Most of the ladies ate earlier in the evening. They are in one of the apartments engaged in games."

Riley had often heard that the men of court gathered late in the evening for drunkenness and whoring. She would rather starve than eat with them.

"May I dress your hair?" the girl asked.

"Aye," she droned absently. She hated being dressed up like a pretty package to set before the king, but she knew she must endure it.

With gentle strokes the girl began to brush out her long hair. She wove it into a braid and wound it into a tight coil at the crown of her head. When she had finished pinning her hair in place, she brought out a headdress. It was a rich scarlet fabric with a gold band along its border.

"Can my audience with the king not wait until morning?" Riley asked hopefully.

"Nay, milady," the maid mumbled, puzzled by her reluctance. She lowered the headdress over her hair. "'Tis the king's command that you join him tonight."

And what else will he command of me? she thought as

she rose from her stool. Straightening her headdress, she made her way down toward the great hall.

As she entered the chamber, she saw Edward seated on the dais with two other men. He was clean shaven, and his hair had been trimmed to chin length, showing off his square jaw and handsome features. The light of a thousand candles cast a golden aura over the gathering.

Upon seeing her enter, he beamed proudly and motioned for her to join him on the dais. She didn't want to be displayed before his male guests, but she knew that she had no choice.

As she mounted the dais, she glanced out over the long tables, and her breath caught. Seated below her at a trestle table were Lord Geoffrey and Gertie. She barely heard the king introduce her to his chaplain and his Lord High Steward.

Edward hammered the table with his fist for silence, and a ghostly quiet fell over the room. Standing up, he held out his hand to Riley, and she coolly placed her slender fingers in his.

"Allow me to introduce the Lady Riley Snowden," he announced to the crowd. "She is the daughter of Lord Robert Snowden, Earl of Ewesbury."

The men nodded in acknowledgment, and she forced a smile in return. She knew that Gertie was glowering at her, and she avoided her eyes, unable to look into those depths that were so filled with hate.

The king's table had been set with silver plates, silver spoons, and cups of crystal laid upon white cloth. Sitting down next to him, Riley held out her hands over empty bowls, allowing the servants to pour warm water over them. As she dried her hands on the tablecloth, she watched the servers entering with dishes of peacock baked in pastry shells, trays of roasted pheasant, swan, and pigeon. She prayed that this would be over soon so that she could retreat to her quarters, away from Gertie's cold stare.

With great care Edward lifted a morsel of peacock from

his plate and offered it to her. She picked up her spoon to accept it even though she was not hungry.

"A beautiful bird for a beautiful woman," he stated matter-of-factly. Leaning to her ear, he whispered, "I shall give you all on my plate and appease your appetite if you will in turn appease mine."

"I do not know what you mean," Riley said with feigned innocence.

"Do not be coy with me, Lady. I am well schooled in the games of men and women."

She remained silent, hoping that he would find her stupid and pursue other more interesting conquests. For a time he seemed interested in the Lady Elizabeth Lucy, the only other woman present besides Riley and Gertie. Sending her passionate looks, Edward brought a sensuous smile to her lips. She was a pretty lady, Riley noted, with a cherubic face and soft eyes. By the end of the meal some three hours later, he had grown bored with this flirtation and had returned his attention to Riley.

"I am going for a walk along the battlements," he announced. "It will be good to feel the cold, fresh air after so long a meal. My body aches for exercise."

Carnal exercise, she thought.

"Would you like to join me?" he asked in a low, seductive tone.

She lifted the edge of the tablecloth and dabbed primly at her mouth. "I am very tired from our journey, Sire. With your permission, I shall retire for the night."

He smiled blandly. "Of course. I hope your quarters are to your satisfaction." He glanced out over the crowd to meet Lord Geoffrey's tense gaze. "Lord Geoffrey wishes for you to return with him tonight. But I cannot allow that. You are after all a heroine for saving his life. I must honor you with a place at my court." He chucked her gently beneath her chin. "That's only the beginning, Riley. When you gain Lynchburg's loyalty for me, there will be far greater rewards."

"Aye, Your Grace, I understand," she said appreciatively. The last place she wanted to be tonight was under the same roof as Gertie, whose murderous looks throughout supper had wilted what little appetite she'd had.

As the knights and administrators filed out of the hall, she followed them into the corridor. Mounting the stairwell alone, she climbed to the upper floors, her footsteps sounding hollow on the stone stairs. When she reached the third floor, she saw the long passageway before her, a lonely tunnel lit by only one torch. The dark timbered walls were framed with shadows and hazy with smoke. She silently cursed herself, realizing that she had left Glenwood Castle without so much as a small dirk to protect herself.

As she walked softly, she heard no sound other than her own faint footsteps. Shivering in the drafty air, she walked faster, never seeing the quick movement to her right or the hand that came down over her mouth.

Her screams were muffled as the hand clamped tightly over her lips. She flailed her arms until another hand grasped both of her wrists in one iron grip, paralyzing her. This was an enemy whose strength far outmatched her own, she realized, or even that of most men. As she struggled, she was dragged down the stairwell and out into the night. The cold air struck her, and she smelled the pungent odor of the Thames.

The hand of her attacker was fastened so tightly around her face that it felt bruising. When his grip finally loosened, she whirled to face him and was not surprised to see Edward leering back at her.

"Welcome to my garden, Eve," he whispered.

She spun in a circle, her eyes searching the darkness. Through the moonlight she saw tall hedges forming a rectangular-shaped garden.

'Tis a private garden, she thought, *possibly the king's private garden, which means that no one will dare enter without his permission—even if they hear a woman screaming.*

"How do you like my love garden?" he asked.

Her eyes darted from corner to corner, seeking an avenue of escape, but she saw no gateway. Near the center of the garden was an oak tree with a stone bench beneath it. There were no rocks, nothing that she could use as a weapon to protect herself against him.

"The oak represents the Biblical Tree of Knowledge," he explained, his eyes trailing her gaze. "The stone bench is where lovers sit and soon fall from grace."

Leaning down, he attempted to kiss her neck, but she scooted away from him.

"Surely, Your Grace, you do not intend to dishonor me," she said with measured authority. Hastily she adjusted her headdress and straightened her skirt. "I am married."

"That is of no consequence to me." He clasped her face in his hands and brought his lips to hers in a crushing kiss.

"Please, Your Grace," she pleaded, trying to push him away.

"Do not fight me, little cat." He snatched her tightly against him, knocking the headdress from her head. Her hair fell free in a long braid, causing his passion to rise to dizzying heights. "I will take you willing or not."

He kissed her again, thrusting his tongue into her mouth until she latched on to it, biting down hard. Shoving her away, he brought his hand to his mouth where a bubble of blood had appeared at the corner of his lips. To her fright, he drew his dagger and advanced toward her. As she turned to flee, he grabbed her hair and forced her to the ground. Sprawling on top of her, he pressed the knife to the back of her throat.

"Do not deny me, Lady."

"I will deny you," she said. "Kill me now in this garden of evil. I will not be taken against my will by any man. Not even a king."

With his free hand, he gathered up her long skirts and hoisted them to her waist. "I will not kill you, and you will be glad of it. For after I take you, you will thank me. And you will burn to be taken by me again and again." His knee thrust between her legs, forcing her thighs apart, and she felt a scream rising to her lips.

The sound of footsteps took him by surprise, and he looked up to see who dared to trespass in his private garden.

It was Gertie, her face gray with shock as she stepped through the shrubbery. "Your Grace, I—I am sorry." She curtseyed clumsily. "I followed you, hoping to warn you of treachery in your court . . ." Her voice trailed off as she spotted Riley beneath him. "I see you have already sampled our family's wanton."

"I was about to," he said, rolling off of her.

Riley felt the blood rush through her limbs and her lungs fill with air. She had never been so glad to see Gertie. But her joy was quickly shattered.

"Your Majesty, this girl is a menace to the House of York," she proclaimed loudly, her eyes narrowing into reptilian slits. "I wish to speak to you at once if it pleases you, Sire. To warn you of her."

Riley sat up, pushing down her dress. "Do not listen to her, Your Grace. She does not speak out of love for you but out of hatred for me."

"She is Lynchburg's whore!" Gertie shouted.

"I know," Edward droned. "What of it?"

"I wish I were not the one to tell you this, but I must." Gertie forged ahead. "'Tis my duty as your loyal subject."

"Gertrude!" Geoffrey roared, his shadow looming at the periphery of the garden. With much sputtering, he made his way through the shrubbery. "Forgive her, Sire. I fear she is much distracted. I will take her away now." He grabbed her elbow, but she snatched free of his grip.

"I will have my say!" Gertie cried. "And you will not stop me."

"What in the devil is this about?" Edward demanded, clamoring to his feet. "Stand back, Geoffrey, and let the woman speak."

"Lynchburg killed your father," Gertie blurted. As the cadence of her voice died, the silence grew thick around them. "'Twas Lynchburg who killed your dear father on the battleground of Wakefield! And this wench has gladly filled the executioner's bed. We have forsaken her. She is no longer our kin. I beg you, Sire, do not hold her crime against us."

Geoffrey lowered his head in shame and defeat, unable to face the woman who had risked her life to save him, a woman who was now beyond his help.

"Lynchburg killed my father?" He looked at Riley fearfully. "Is this true?"

Standing up, she wiped stray strands of hair from her face with trembling fingers. "I do not know, Sire," she said, tucking her hair behind her ears. "I was not there."

"Did Lynchburg confess it to you?" he cried.

She swallowed hard, saying nothing.

"Answer him, harlot," Gertie raged. "Answer him or you doom your family to ruin."

"'Twas war, Your Majesty," she said softly. "He did what he had to do. Your father had been captured and the battle lost."

"Enough!" he cried, his voice bitter with emotion. "Why did you not tell me this before?"

"Because David is my husband," she said, lowering her head in anguish. "I did not want him harmed."

His face reddened, and he sliced the air with his dagger. "I will slay him for this. And you will be a widow all the days that you live." He jabbed at the air, causing her to retreat several steps. "I will not ask Parliament to reverse your family's attaintment. You will never regain your father's property. I will banish you, and all your kindred from this land."

Gertie gave a shriek of anguish and buried her face in her hands.

"Please, Your Grace," Riley begged him. "Geoffrey and Gertrude are loyal to York. I will stand trial and die a traitor's death if I must, but please, I beg you, do not punish my kinsmen. They are innocent."

His eyes shifted to Gertie, then to Geoffrey, the glow of the moon causing a silver light to reflect in those black depths. "Get thee from my sight if you value your lives."

Geoffrey immediately retreated, striding through the break in the shrubbery. Gertie hesitated for only a moment before she broke free from Edward's gaze and followed her brother.

"The bastard, Lynchburg, shall not live," Edward said spitefully. "I will avenge my father by spilling his blood. And you will watch him die."

He eyed her contemptuously as his large hand closed around her throat, raising her up onto the tips of her toes. "How do you draw out a rat, coz?"

"With cheese, Your Grace?" she asked, her voice squeaking past her constricted throat.

"Aye, with cheese." He released her neck and slid his hand up to her chin. Grabbing it in a painful pinch, he forced her to look up at him. "And you shall be that tasty bait. I will hold a week-long tournament for all the unmarried knights. The winner of the tournament will be challenged by me, and if he bests me, then he shall be rewarded." He smiled wickedly and rubbed his thumb roughly along her chin. "I shall give him an estate in London. Not just any estate, but Tinsley Manor in Essex. The one that once belonged to Charles D'Aubere—your lover's father."

With Riley's chin still locked in his hand, Edward turned her face from side to side, examining her beauty. "And I will offer you to the victor as his bride. That will draw Lynchburg out."

She winced as his grip burned her skin. "What if he will not come?" she asked. "What if he is done with me?"

"I have no doubt that he has already come, my lady," he sneered. "Once I have the tournament announced from St. Paul's Cathedral, then I need only wait for him to surface. He will easily defeat all opponents in the tournament. Then he will face his greatest foe of all, his king. For I will slay him." He released her and slid his hand down over her breast, gripping it painfully. "With his blood still dripping from my hands, I will take you to my bed. And you will be mine for as long as it pleases me."

She wanted to vomit. *Never,* she thought. *You will have to kill me first.*

"Guards!" he called, and within seconds two guards bumbled through the break in the shrubbery. "Seize this woman," he ordered. "She has committed treason."

Riley felt the blood rush from her face as the guards grasped each of her arms, nearly lifting her from the ground. Her legs had gone completely weak and could no longer bear her weight. "I will meet my fate with the courage of the Snowdens!" she cried. But she was more than a Snowden now, she knew. She was the wife of David D'Aubere, a man who had sworn never to give her up to any fate.

Chapter Twenty-four

Riley stood on the battlements, a fine mist blowing against her face as she watched the first flush of sunrise pinken the sky. Muffled in her fur-lined cloak, she looked down over the River Thames and watched the water flow darkly to the sea. For days she had been confined in a private apartment with an occasional morning stroll being the only taste of freedom allowed her.

She had not seen Edward or received any word of his plans to hold the tournament. The servants were mute around her, and she knew that it was useless to try to gain information from them. They feared Edward and, under his orders, would tell her nothing. She wondered if Edward was right about Lynchburg, if he was lurking about the city, seeking an opportunity to rescue her.

Why would he want me, she thought in agony, *when I ran from him right into Edward's arms.* She had done it to save him, but she knew that he would see it as a final act of faithlessness on her part.

"Lady Snowden!"

She startled slightly at the sound of her name. It had been days since another human being had spoken to her.

The Lady Elizabeth Lucy was running toward her, her skirts raised above her dainty ankles and the veil of her headdress flying out behind her.

"Do not address me as Lady Snowden," she stated as the girl approached her. "I am the Lady D'Aubere."

"Lady D'Aubere then," she said, pausing to catch her breath. "The king wishes you to go to the inner ward. A horse and cart await to carry you to Smithfield."

She felt as if her every nerve had been startled like a flock of birds. Her insides were fluttering wildly. "Lady Elizabeth, my fate is upon me. Tell me, I beg you, what awaits me at Smithfield."

The woman's eyes turned away in shame as she spoke. "A tournament has been held all week. The king will now challenge the winner, and the prize will be you."

Riley felt her heart skip and her knees go weak. "Who is the winner thus far?"

Lady Elizabeth shook her head and peeped up at her from beneath worried brows. "I wish I could tell you, but I do not know. No one knows. He hides his face behind his helmet. But he is strong and fierce, my lady. He fights as if his very life depends upon it."

A sense of hope filled her as she nervously clenched her hands at her sides.

"Is this fighter your husband?" Lady Elizabeth asked.

"I do not know," she said truthfully and drew a calming breath deep into her lungs. "I suppose I must go and find out."

As she started back toward her chamber, the Lady Elizabeth touched her shoulder, stopping her.

"There is more," she explained, and Riley noticed the hesitancy in her voice.

"The king says that you are to . . . to wear only your shift. And that your hair is to be loose and free."

"What?" she gasped.

Her eyelids fluttered in embarrassment. "He wishes you to be carried in a cart, nearly naked before all of London."

So that was Edward's plan, she realized sickly, to put her shamefully on display. "He means to humiliate me."

"'Tis his order, Lady D'Aubere. But the sky grows

fair," she added with a note of encouragement. "In an hour's time it will not be so very cold."

"Thank you for that reassurance," Riley said sarcastically. With a snatch of her skirts, she headed back to her apartment.

When she entered the chamber, she flung her cloak aside. The Lady Elizabeth hurried in behind her, hoping to comfort and assist her.

"The king is a good man," she declared with heartfelt sincerity. "'Tis better to be disgraced than executed. You are guilty of treason. Your fate could have been far worse than humiliation."

"Could it?" she asked hotly. "You talk like a woman who has no honor. I would rather be dead than to be Edward's . . ." She stopped, unable to say the word that might become her destiny.

As Riley pulled off her headdress, her long braid uncoiled from its perch and fell down her back. Lady Elizabeth carefully unbound it, pulling the strands free and scattering them across her back. The copper tresses streamed down over her shoulders, covering her to her waist.

"What were you going to say?" she asked, her voice soft with fear. "What are the king's plans for you?"

Looking at the Lady Elizabeth, Riley felt a stab of pity. "You love him, don't you?"

Lady Elizabeth looked away to hide the flush that bloomed across her cheeks. "The king has spoken of marriage. He has promised that we shall soon be betrothed."

"I see," Riley said, uninterested. "Well, then, I hope that someday he becomes worthy of you."

The lady's eyes widened in surprise. "'Tis I who hope to be worthy of him."

Riley wanted to weep for her. How little she knew about the man she loved. How blind she was to him. "Will you help me remove my dress?" she asked and wondered how this kind woman could love any man who would treat a woman so shamefully.

With Lady Elizabeth's help, she stripped down to her shift. It was not a sheer garment, but she knew that the wind would mold it to her body, making her feel exposed.

"'Tis time to go," Lady Elizabeth urged, arranging her hair so that it covered her front and back. "Your hair covers you nicely, Lady Riley. 'Tis prettier than any garment."

"Thank you," Riley said, feeling somewhat encouraged by Elizabeth's words. She hesitated for a moment, then took the lady's hand in friendship. To hold on to a supportive arm even for a brief spell was calming. "Your kindness has been a comfort to me."

Lady Elizabeth smiled back and gripped her hand encouragingly.

The floor was cold beneath her bare feet as she left the chamber and walked down the corridor. When she stepped out into the courtyard, she began to shiver and wondered if it was the cool weather or her own fear that iced her flesh.

The hour was still early, and the grass was dappled with dew. The lawn felt wet and cold beneath her feet as she walked to the horse-drawn cart. A guard attempted to assist her, but she pushed his hand away. Climbing into the cart, she pulled her sleeves up past her elbows to ensure that her shift would not slid off of one shoulder. She'd not give Edward or any of his subjects one titillating glimpse of her naked flesh. With a nod, she gestured to the guard that she was ready for her journey to begin.

As the cart started off, she struggled to maintain her balance. Gripping the sides of the cart as it swayed to and fro, she jolted across the grounds of the Tower. It wasn't until she arrived at Smithfield that she realized the full import of Edward's tournament.

Stands had been erected, and it seemed as if every seat was filled. The people swept across the landscape in a blur of color, men and women clothed in scarlet, greens, yellows, and blues, all roaring for their king, their champion.

The guard led the horse once around the wide field, and Riley understood the king's ploy. He wanted the citizens of London to cast their derision on her as a traitor, to throw onions at her and call her names. *How must I look to them?* she wondered as her cart rolled past the stands. Her slender form was draped in white linen, and her hair cascaded over her breasts in waves of copper and gold. Clenching her jaw, she was determined to withstand the verbal insults of the crowd, but to her surprise she heard nothing. As she passed, the voices of the crowd fell silent, and many people turned their heads, refusing to look on her shame.

At the far end of the field, Edward sat astride his missodor, scowling at the uncooperative assembly. His purpose was to disgrace Riley Snowden before all of London, but to his deepening disappointment, the people seemed to be filled with admiration for the woman.

His chamberlain watched grimly from his mount beside the king. "Forgive these people, Your Grace. But I fear that they do not understand her punishment." His eyes flitted nervously to his king. "Word has spread of her rescue of Lord Geoffrey Seward. You did after all proclaim her a heroine."

"I then proclaimed her a traitor," he rasped, "a Lancastrian spy. What's wrong with these people that they treat her with respect?"

"Sire," he began cautiously. "You have accused her of treason, but you have not announced the details of her crimes. The people do not understand your sudden vengeance against her." He swallowed hard, knowing that this next part would be difficult. "I have heard it whispered that her only crime is that she rejected you as a lover."

"Be damned," Edward growled. "Bellville is responsible for this disaffection. He has been about the city all week bragging of her exploits. But these people will not hold the Snowden woman in their hearts for long. I swear it." He glanced toward the stands, his eyes searing the crowd. "On this day, London will see the power of their king, and they will never again question my decisions."

The cart came to a halt before a dais, and Riley stepped down, her bare feet sinking into the wet grass. Alone, she climbed the many steps of the dais where she was to stand

and watch the proceedings. When she reached the top, she was surprised to see Lord Geoffrey and Gertie seated there. Keeping her eyes down, she tried to avoid their gazes and quickly turned her back to them, facing the field. Gertie reached out and grabbed a handful of the thin fabric of her shift, knotting it in her fist.

"'Tis a pleasure to see your shame," she smirked. "You, who could have been a queen, brought down like a common whore. The bastard Lynchburg will not win against Edward."

She felt her heart bump painfully in her chest. "Lynchburg is here?"

"He is, Riley." Gertie laughed hoarsely. "There is only one man left who has won against every opponent. He is large and very strong. He is Lynchburg, though he hides his face behind his black armor."

Lord Geoffrey smacked Gertie's hand away.

"Dear girl, you must be strong," he told Riley soothingly. "Your shame will melt in the fires of your strength. The people here have already seen your courage and your grace. It has foiled any humiliation Edward wished on you."

"Do not encourage her," Gertie spewed, rubbing her wounded hand. "Her shame is evident aplenty. She stands naked before all of London. And more's the pity that we must bear this humiliation as well. We must sit here and watch her being held up as some wanton prize."

Riley turned her head, giving Gertie an apologetic glance. "Did the king punish you as well? I did not wish for that to happen."

"No," Geoffrey assured her. "He did not. We have been absolved, and there will be no retribution against us. I asked the king's permission for us to be placed on the dais with you. I would not have you go through this alone."

"What?" Gertie cried. "I knew nothing of this. Do you wish to make fools of us all? I think Edward needs no help with that."

"Be silent," he ordered. "Or I will strike you before all of these people."

"You would not dare."

"Would you dare tempt me?" he asked, drawing back his hand.

Seeing the surety in his eyes, she slunk back against her seat and said no more.

The sun glimmered across the wet grass as Edward took the field. The crowd cheered him, and many women waved colorful kerchiefs at him while chanting his name.

Sitting tall astride his mount, he looked magnificent in his glory of gilt armor, holding his jeweled helmet under his arm. Next to him rode his chamberlain, wearing scarlet robes trimmed in gold braid.

"How do you know the winner of the tournament is Lynchburg?" the chamberlain asked.

"Who else could win repeatedly against the finest knights in my kingdom?" Edward replied as he held up one hand, acknowledging the crowd. "I know the fighting strength of every warrior in this realm. I know their weaknesses, too." He nodded briefly toward Riley. "There stands his. What a vision she is in her white shift, eh?"

The chamberlain smirked as he gazed at her. "Lynchburg will be so incensed when he sees her shamefully displayed that you shall get a good fight out of him today."

A missodor galloped onto the field, snorting and raising up on its hind legs, pawing the air. The warrior shrouded in black Dutch plate held his shield in one hand, his lance in the other. With the sun streaming down across the field, Edward could easily detect the rubies encrusted in his opponent's sword. He turned a sidelong gaze on his chamberlain, his eyes glowing in anticipation.

"He's here."

As Edward lowered his helmet over his head, his chamberlain rode to the center of the field, waving the green flag. When he dropped it, the joust would begin. As the flag fluttered to the ground, the chamberlain rode hard from the field amid the crowd's screaming cheers.

Riley gasped when she saw the sunlight glint across the ruby hilt. Could there be another sword like that of Lynchburg's? she wondered painfully. Could this really be him, charging onto the field, fighting a king to claim her?

Her heart felt heavy with love and fear. Closing her eyes, she did not want to see this battle, but a firm pinch from Gertie jolted her eyes open and forced her to watch.

The two men charged toward each other, their missodors sweating, hooves kicking up a spray of dirt. As Edward passed, Lynchburg raised his shield, deflecting a blow from his lance. Thrusting his weight into him, he hoped to unseat the king. A lesser opponent would have been sent sprawling from his horse. But this was no lesser opponent, Lynchburg realized. This was a warrior who at nineteen years of age had usurped a king. He swung his mount around and waited for Edward to charge again.

Raising his lance, Edward galloped forward, his aim deadly accurate. The lance struck Lynchburg's shield, breaking it in half and sending the pieces spiraling to the ground. Now he was without protection from Edward's weapons. Riley felt her heart stop. She wanted to run to him, to protect him. Behind her, she heard Gertie's low cackle.

Edward slowly turned his horse and faced his enemy. Dismounting, he dropped his lance and pulled off his helmet, tossing it to the ground. Lynchburg quickly followed suit. Leaping from his missodor, he removed his helmet and faced the youth. His eyes blazed with the passion of the fight, and his blood coursed through his veins, flooding him with a mad desire for victory.

Edward unsheathed his sword, and the blade flashed brightly in the sun. Lynchburg's hand closed around the ruby hilt of his sword, and he squeezed it tightly, seeking the strength of his father. Pulling it free, he sliced the air with it.

Edward was an excellent swordsman, sharp of mind and swift of foot. But the earl was older, stronger, and more experienced. As the two men advanced toward each other, they moved in a wide circle, the sun reflecting off of polished armor and steel.

Edward wielded the first blow, which barely missed the earl. The young king stumbled and cursed beneath his breath. Rallying quickly, his sword clashed against Lynchburg's. Steel clanged against steel, and the sound filtered down through the nearby streets and along the waters of the Thames. Riley watched, her heart pounding in her ears. How long would this go on? she wondered.

The crowd was on their feet, screaming and straining forward to better see the fight.

Lynchburg lunged at Edward so swiftly that when the king raised his sword to deflect the thrust, he received a deafening blow to his chest. Thrown off balance, he toppled to the ground and struggled to regain his stance.

Before he could rise, Lynchburg pressed the tip of his sword against his throat.

"Do you ask for quarter?" he seethed.

"No," the king replied. "Nor do I give quarter."

The crowd was growing still now as they watched the scene unfolding.

"Have you harmed Riley? For if you have, I will drive this blade through your neck."

"The lady has not shared my bed," he half-snorted, "if that is what you mean."

To the king's bewilderment, Lynchburg drew back and sheathed his weapon.

"Then I do not want your life."

Edward clamored to his feet, waving away Lynchburg's extended hand.

"We will meet again," he promised, a boyish petulance in his eyes.

"No," Lynchburg replied. "We will not. I am done with this war. I wish only for Riley." He looked toward the platform on which she stood, her hair blowing in the breeze, and her white shift caressing every curve of her body.

"Take her," Edward sulked. "She is yours. And the

Essex estate is yours. You have won the tournament." Angrily he sheathed his weapon.

"I wish to live in peace," Lynchburg stated with a note of warning. "Now and forever."

Edward looked at him glumly. There were few men who shared his height and could look him directly in the eyes. Only one who could best him in battle.

"Is that not what we all want?" Edward asked, tossing his head toward the platform. "Take her, but you'll find no peace with a wench such as that."

Lynchburg gazed at the woman whose eyes shone in the sunlight beneath an abundance of red hair, a woman who stood out above all others. "May she never lose her thorns." He smiled. "My wild rose of York."

As he strode toward the dais, he saw a flush brightening her cheeks. The sight of him excited her, and she felt overwhelmed with relief. As she was about to run to him, Gertie's words stopped her.

"Aye, the bastard gallops toward you like a frothing goat. But 'tis not your body he wants, my lady. Look into the beast's eyes and see the fury there. You will pay now for your sins, for you have yoked yourself to a violent cur."

Riley shivered. In his stride was a malice that chilled her. As he drew closer, she could see the bright fires of anger in his eyes. He had warned her never to run from him again, and she had run from him straight into the Yorkist camp.

As he reached the dais, she fled down the steps hurdling toward him, her shift falling loosely about her shoulders.

Would he ever forgive her, she wondered, this man who had abandoned a queen to save her and had fought a king to claim her? She would suffer his anger in whatever form it took, but she would let him know how much she loved him. As she reached him, she threw her arms around his neck and buried her face against his ear. "I beg your forgiveness," she plead softly. "I went to Edward only to try to bargain with him. I offered him all that was my father's in exchange for our freedom." She felt the hard plates of his armor and the cold chain mail that encased his neck. Sliding down the steel length of him, she came to rest on her knees. "I know you are angry at me, for I see it in your eyes."

He reached down and gently lifted her to her feet. "Look at me," he commanded. The sound of his voice was like an angel's touch, soothing her fears. She glanced up at him and saw his eyes turning a grayish blue, their anger spent. "If my eyes burned with anger, 'twas at Edward for so mistreating you." He smiled and stroked her cheek with the tips of his knuckles. "You will never run from me again. For I intend to fill your belly with a child and stop these flighty ways of yours."

She laughed and placed one hand against her belly, wondering if his child already grew within her. Cupping her chin in his hand, he lifted her face to his and kissed her deeply, stirring a froth of excitement within her. A warm spring breeze ruffled across the grass and touched them with the scent of bluebells. Snuggling against his hard frame, she felt his cold armor on her cheek and the strength and security of his arms, more protective than any fortress.

For several moments, they were unaware that the crowd had erupted into cheers. As the couple drew apart, they glanced around, realizing that they were providing a fine spectacle for the people of London.

"I thought they would boo us in favor of their king," Lynchburg commented as he hooked one arm around her shoulders. "I suppose they like a happy ending."

"'Tis a wonder they see it that way," she said, resting her head against his chest. "I am a traitor, and you are a Lancastrian wolf."

"Nay." He hugged her to him, and she could feel the love and strength flowing through his limbs. "I am a husband who is in love with his wife. If I was a wolf, I have long gone tame. I am," he sighed, relieved, "domesticated."

Scooping her into his arms he carried her past the cheering stands and away from the sunlit field. When he reached a great oak along the river bank, he set her down in the grass.

She looked at her shift that had slipped from one shoulder, partially revealing her breast. "I am ready to go to our new home in Essex," she said, simply. "But I suppose I should dress first."

He smiled as he eyed her attire and ran his finger along the rim of her loose neckline. "I think that would be wise else we will not go far before I take you to bed."

She laughed and thumped her fist against his armored chest. "You are a rogue, sir."

He kissed her again, deeply this time, until he felt her soul ignite and fuse into one with his own.

"I will never run from you again," she promised, her arms locked about his neck. "There is nowhere left to run. All the boundaries that separated us have been conquered."

"Aye, and the victory was sweet." His smile struck her as a burst of sunlight fell through the limbs of the tree. Wrapping his arms around her, he lifted her feet from the ground, kissing her heatedly as the day turned warmer. Somewhere nearby a bird warbled, its tune penetrating the quiet of their sanctuary.

With their arms encircling each other, they spun in a slow dance, their laughter rich with joy and their faces uplifted into the sunshine of spring.

Epilogue

Riley lay against bloody sheets, her body soaked in sweat and weak with exhaustion.

"The babe, is it well?" She felt terror overwhelming her as she lay waiting, almost too frightened to speak. "I hear no sound from it."

Elda laid the tiny bundle of limp flesh on the bed and pressed her mouth against the blue lips of the infant. With little sucking breaths, she freed its throat to breathe, then spit out the yellow mucus onto the bed.

A tiny squall touched Riley's ear, and she began to weep in relief.

Wiping the baby's face with a clean linen towel, Elda stared into the blinking eyes, blue eyes like her father's.

"You have a fine girl," she announced. Swaddling her in clean linen, she laid the infant in her mother's arms.

"Take away these bloodied sheets," she ordered a maid as she slipped the sheets from beneath Riley's prostrate body.

Riley looked up at her midwife with eyes swollen from fatigue and emotion. The ordeal of childbirth was always long and arduous, but she was fortunate. The end result had always been a blessing for her. She had her son, a five-year-old whose strength would someday match his father's. And now her daughter.

"She is beautiful, Elda," she said softly. "Thank you for coming to Tinsley Manor. I trusted no one but you to deliver my child."

Elda looked at her in bemusement. "As if I would say no to the Earl of Lynchburg," she scoffed. "When he says 'come,' I come."

"Where is my husband?" she asked.

"Banished," she replied darkly. "I will not allow any man in a house where a birth is occurring. He paces beyond the barn, upsetting the hens until they will not roost. He is like a bull, thrashing about, terrorizing the livestock. I will not fetch him until you've had a few more moments to rest."

Riley snuggled the baby against her and felt her wet warmth. "How does your family fare, Elda?"

"Very well." She sighed, easing down on the bed beside her. She placed her thumb against the baby's forehead and gently stroked. "Philip returned to me for a while, but the war took him away again. He was killed at Towton."

"I heard," Riley stated sadly, for she knew that Elda had shared a special bond with him. "Is the new lord fair to you and Daggot?"

"Oh, aye, he is," she said with a smile. "He allowed us to stay on after the castle was confiscated. I told him I could care for Jeanette, and he let her come and live with me. She does many things for herself these days," she added brightly. "She even helps me with my herbal garden. She loves to crush the leaves."

Riley smiled at the thought of Jeanette happy and useful.

"And Daggot, does he prosper?"

"Aye, Daggot saved his wages and purchased his own land. He would not marry me until he felt himself worthy."

Riley cuddled her baby closer to her. "I never doubted that he would prove himself someday."

"He is a fine husband. And he is good at business, too. His sheep farm prospers mightily." She raised her brows at

Riley as if amused. "He discovered a better way than battle to obtain status—wool production."

"I shall pray for his continued good fortune," Riley said
gently. Kissing her baby's cheek, she giggled as the baby
turned suddenly in an attempt to suck. "I must nurse her
soon." She studied her daughter's features, the blue-black
eyes and impish nose.

"My children prosper as well," Elda continued. "They
follow Daggot about, and he says he will teach them many
things, even how to read. They will need many skills to
help him in his business. He wishes to establish a weaving
center."

Riley's mouth opened in a small gasp of surprise.
"What a wealthy man he will be someday."

"He is wealthy already, and he knows it." She rose from
the bed and dipped her hands into a bowl of water. "Rich
in love and contentment." Drying her hands on a towel, she
flung Riley a look of resignation. "And now I must go herd
the bull back into the pen to see his fine daughter. The
grounds are not safe with him unleashed."

Riley watched her daughter blinking sleepily and her
tiny mouth puckering. "Tell him she is beautiful," she murmured.

"I shall," Elda assured her as she watched her patient,
bloodied and battered. She had fought a battle harder than
any Lynchburg could have ever imagined. *Women are the
real warriors,* she realized, *with the courage of the saints.
And the patience.*

"She is destined to be many things," Elda whispered
dreamily. "Beautiful and smart, for that is in her blood. But
her character, her heart, she will learn from her mother."
She smiled, giving mother and child a knowing look, an in-
tuitive glance that passes between women who have experienced the depth of life. *She will have her mother's heart.
And that is the heart of a warrior.*